IRISH
MAGIC II

Morgan Llywelyn
Barbara Samuel
Susan Wiggs
Roberta Gellis

IRISH MAGIC II

*Four Unforgettable
Novellas of Love and
Enchantment*

𝑘

KENSINGTON BOOKS
http://www.kensingtonbooks.com

KENSINGTON BOOKS are published by

Kensington Publishing Corp.
850 Third Avenue
New York, NY 10022

Library of Congress Card Catalog Number: 96-077838
ISBN 1-57566-140-3

First Printing: March, 1997
10 9 8 7 6 5 4 3 2 1

Printed in the United States of America

Contents

EARLY IRELAND

ULSTER

Emain Macha

MEATH • Dagda's Sidhe

CONNAUGHT

Cruach •

Brugh na Boinne

Leenane • •An Fhairche

Brí Léith •

Boyne

• Uaman

• Tara

• Sraith Salach

• Galway

Galway Bay

LEINSTER

MUNSTER

• Dingle

0   50 miles

0   50 km

Welcome!

Imagine a world where wishes have wings and all your dreams come true. A world of emerald green fields and ancient legends and enchanted love.

We invite you to explore magic Ireland with us, to immerse yourself in this world where the faery still wander, where music has immortal power; a world of changelings and enchanted springs and elusive beings; a world where even the most forbidden and impossible of loves has a chance for happiness.

Roberta Gillis

Barbara Samuel

Morgan Llywelyn

Susan Wiggs

THE
CHANGELING

Susan Wiggs

For Jim Wiggs, who loves Ireland

ACKNOWLEDGMENTS

Thanks to the book fairies:
Barb, Betty, Christina,
Joyce, Debbie, and Denise

May the ones who we love, love us.
For those who do not love us, may God turn their hearts.
If God cannot turn their hearts, may he turn their ankles
So we may know them by their limping.

—Irish saying

Chapter 1

"A TRUE man honors his promises, boyo."

Hank Farrell scratched his head, turned, and searched the crowded immigration lobby of Shannon Airport. He could have sworn he'd heard his grandmother's voice. But that was impossible. Throughout her ninety-five years, Margaret Molloy Farrell had always had plenty to say, but Hank hadn't expected to hear from her again.

It was fatigue, pure and simple, he reasoned. Jet lag. He was hearing things.

And no wonder, he thought with weary exasperation. He had arrived in Ireland with three unwanted burdens—an impossible quest, a lonely heart, and his grandmother's ashes. Of all the tomfool, harebrained missions he had undertaken on Granny Molloy's behalf, this one was the most outrageous.

A true man honors his promises, boyo.

Now, what the hell did that mean? What promise? And why did the words echo in his head as if Granny herself had hissed them in his ear?

Sleep-starved, he ambled through the airport, his patience taxed to its limit by the long lines at Customs and Immigration. A customs agent had eyed Hank's suitcase, but mercifully decided against opening it and waved him on through.

Hank had tried not to look too relieved. After an all-nighter that had begun at the Dallas/Fort Worth airport, he had not been eager to explain the urn of ashes cushioned by hastily packed Levi's, socks, and sweaters.

In the international lobby, a female voice, laden with a heavy brogue, made an announcement on the PA system, then repeated it in Gaelic. The sounds of the foreign tongue teased at Hank, reminding him of Granny, who used to sing songs in the language of the Ancient Ones, as she called them. Granny and her fairy stories, Hank thought with a mixture of affection and irritation. She had believed in magic with the absolute faith of a child. She'd wanted Hank to believe, too, but one by one, life had mown down each legend and tale with the sharp scythe of reality.

Hank yawned to relieve the pressure in his ears, then spied a bank of hotel phones near the exit. The display featured backlit photographs of each hotel, with blaring offers to provide a bed for weary travelers "in a thoroughly modern environment."

" 'Weary travelers,' " Hank said to the bank of phones. "I'm your man." He reached for the phone and started to punch in the number for the Longview Inn, which looked in its photo like a postwar cell block with a painfully cute leprechaun mural. It was the picture that made him hesitate. Granny Molloy would wince at the cartoony artwork.

"Rubbish!" said a voice. "Makes a body do worse than wince."

Hank froze. Then his hand, poised above the receiver, started to tremble. Almost furtively, he glanced around. Inside the lobby, members of a huge family hugged each other and jabbered greetings. An American tour company guide shouted into a bullhorn, trying to corral everyone. Hank stood alone with the hotel phones.

"I'm losing it," he said between his teeth. "Hearing things. Next thing you know, I'll be seeing ghosts." The lighted photographs on the phone bank blurred and swam in his vision. The first one to come into focus was Carrygerry House, an eighteenth-century manor with a horse pasture in the background.

Almost without thinking, Hank dialed the exchange. A pleasant male voice answered.

"Do y'all have a room for the night?" Hank's Texas drawl sounded conspicuous. Hell, he *looked* conspicuous, at six foot four towering over most of the people on the walkway outside—mothers pushing strollers overloaded by toddlers with runny noses, spry men with rosy cheeks and flat wool caps, surly teenagers with pierced body parts and improbably colored hair.

" 'Tis certain we do, sir," the man on the phone answered. "Will that be for one, then?"

"Yes. Only one." Even now, it still hurt to say it. To admit he was alone, and likely to stay that way for a while.

"I've a ground floor room with a private bath suite, if you'll be wanting that, sir."

"Oh. Yeah. That would be fine."

"Lovely. It's out to the kerb with you, then, and I'll be around shortly to collect you."

"Fine, I'll—"

A rude series of blips ensued; the man had rung off.

Heaving a sigh, Hank reached for his suitcase. He stopped, eyeing the plain black bag with suspicion and then feeling foolish for doing so. He gave a self-derisive snort, shouldered his carry-on bag, and picked up the case. "Carrygerry House it is, then," he said to no one in particular.

"A grand choice, boyo," said his suitcase.

Hank dropped it. His ears must be clogged. He thought he had heard— "Jesus Christ," he muttered.

"I've not yet met Him, and won't either," said Granny Molloy's voice, "unless you do as you promised."

He blinked, his eyes burning from the artificial air and close quarters of the endless trans-Atlantic flight. Hallucination. That was it. Hallucination induced by jet lag. Suitcases didn't talk. Especially not in the brogue of his late grandmother.

He picked up the case again and held it to his ear. A passing porter frowned at him, and Hank flushed. People might think he was listening for a bomb. Feeling more foolish than ever, he went to the exit. With an electronic sigh, the glass doors whispered open, and he stepped outside. The damp air of an Irish July slapped him in the face. The reek of jet fuel swirled around him. Odd, round-fendered trucks and battered cars and taxis crawled past in a line.

Dang, these crazy Irish drove on the right side, so that it appeared no one was driving.

"Welcome to Ireland," he grumbled. "Land of ghosts and fairies."

He stood at the kerb, wondering how the driver from Carrygerry

House would recognize him, and thinking about Margaret Molloy Farrell, his grandmother. He glanced furtively at the suitcase.

She had been at the center of his life for all of his twenty-six years. Soon after Hank's birth, his mother had up and left for a life of glamour in the big city. His father, as solid and silent as the wide Texas plains surrounding the Farrell Ranch, had given Hank over to Granny Molloy. After Hank's father had bled to death when his arm was mangled in a baler, Hank and Granny had been left to manage things, barely surviving some years.

Surrounded by a subtle fey air that had clung to her all her life, Margaret Molloy had emigrated as a girl of seventeen to Texas. There, she had become the bride of Henry Vincent Farrell, a successful cattle rancher. An only child, Hank had been raised on her stories, told in a lilting Irish brogue. At Granny's knee, he'd learned the tales that had been with the Molloy clan since time out of mind.

To hear Granny talk, you'd think every rock, every tree, every stream, and every hillock was a haven for little knowing souls only a lucky few could discover.

Granny claimed she could see them as clearly as the mesquite trees on the horizon. Though common sense told Hank her flights of fancy were just that, a hidden part of him wished he could believe in her magical worlds and predestined events. When he met Kay-Lynn Johnson, former Watermelon Thump Queen of Luling, Texas, he tried to tell himself their love affair had been ordained by a higher power.

A few months later, Kay-Lynn had put to rest any lingering notions he'd had of magic and destiny. She helped herself to a wad of cash from the ranch office and took off for California. After Granny's death, Hank had put the ranch up for sale. The place had nothing to offer him but hard work and heartache. He didn't mind the work, but the loneliness got to him, piercing as a coyote's midnight howl.

The trouble was, the property had been listed for months and he hadn't even had a nibble. Impatience nagged at him. He wanted to get away from the sere, unforgiving land and find a place that was lush and green, like the Ireland of Granny's stories.

Now that he was seeing the real Ireland, though, Hank was having second thoughts. So far, he had seen only concrete and asphalt and low, boxy modern buildings. He felt awkward, out of place. He was starting to wonder if he'd inherited his grandmother's gift for grand pretenses.

All of his dreams and desires seemed too big and impossible to fit into an ordinary life.

A dull red Range Rover rumbled to a halt in front of him. The driver leaned over, cranked down the window, and asked, "Is it Carrygerry House you're after, then?"

"That's me." Hank slung his bags into the back and climbed in the passenger seat, noting the array of dashboard virgins and St. Christophers, the brimming ashtray and a horsehair blanket covering the seat. "How did you know?"

The driver, ruddy and cheerful in a coat with patched elbows, ground the truck into gear. "And who else would I be looking for but a long-legged fellow from Texas?"

Hank gave him a weary grin. "I guess you have me pegged. Hank Farrell, of Muleshoe, Texas."

Tapping the horn, the driver pulled out into the lane of moving traffic. It was all Hank could do to keep from lurching for the dashboard. It felt totally wrong to be sitting on this side of a car and not be driving.

"Gerry Finn, proprietor of Carrygerry House," the man said. "And it's a welcome before you. Tourist, are you?"

"Not exactly," Hank said.

"Have you family here, then?"

"Sort of." Hank glanced back at his suitcase. "I don't mean to sound vague, Mr. Finn. I'm bringing my grandmother's ashes home."

"Ah." Finn frowned ahead at the road. "Cremated, was she?"

They left the airport behind and wound along an impossibly narrow road lined with hedgerows so tall and ancient they almost formed a tunnel.

"Yep." Hank suspected a bit of disapproval in his host. A devout Catholic, Granny herself had worried about being cremated.

Finn's disapproval lightened. "I suppose it's the only proper way to bring her home, then."

"That's what she figured."

Only a few kilometers from the airport, the landscape turned green and luxuriant, fields and villages couched in the soft slumber of a place time had passed by. Rock-strewn meadows with placid sheep grazing here and there rose on either side of the road. The car passed a wrought-iron gate, and Carrygerry House came into view.

The photograph had not done it justice. Like a jewel on a cushion, the manor lay within the green velvet folds of a hill. Mellow ochre walls and rustic dark timbers formed the outer structure. High windows over-looked a courtyard paved with cobblestones rounded by the tread of un-counted centuries. A fence of unmortared stone enclosed the horse pasture. Two mares—one of them pregnant—grazed there. A hand-some yearling trotted back and forth across the high meadows.

"Good-looking horses," Hank commented.

"My daughter looks after them. Fat lot of trouble they are, too. I ought to sell them off." Gerry Finn hefted Hank's suitcase and led him across the courtyard. A sign with the slogan "Guinness is Good For You" hung outside the small, cozy-looking taproom. Situated across the courtyard, Hank's room was furnished with an antique armoire and a railed chair by the window.

"I'll just take your passport, then," Gerry said pleasantly, "and see to the paperwork."

It never occurred to Hank to protest handing over his passport to a virtual stranger. Weariness buzzed around him like a swarm of bees, and it was all he could do to nod pleasantly at Finn and close the door of his room. He opened his suitcase and took out the urn, setting it care-fully on the mantel. Then, half stumbling from fatigue, he peeled off his clothes and collapsed on the bed.

Granny Molloy used to say Ireland forced every mind to dream. As Hank slipped deeper and deeper asleep, he put up no resistance. Im-ages spun across the path of his mind in a relentless colorful pinwheel: Kay-Lynn in her Thump Queen sequins, turning into a bird and flying away. Granny closing Hank's hand around a piece of carved black bog oak, her voice whispering, "Take it with you to Ireland, lad, if it's magic you're wanting." The little carven figure burst out of the pocket of Hank's faded jeans to metamorphose into a dazzling Celtic god and dis-appear on a wisp of flame. The center of the flame, blue-white and cold as ice, became a stranger's eyes—beautiful eyes, they were, with secrets in their depths, jewels dwelling at the bottom of a crystal well. Haunted eyes that saw deep and clear through a soul; eyes filled with a sadness that brought an ache to the chest. And then this image shattered like breaking glass and Hank saw himself running, hard and fast, past a bog he had never seen, where a turf cutter paused in his labor to push back his hat and stab his narrow turf shovel into the ground.

Hank awakened to a raging thirst and a gnawing hunger. Squinting, he stared at the dull glow of his watch. Four thirty-five. Was that A.M. or P.M.? Texas time or Ireland time?

He levered himself out of the bed, shivering a little in the dark chill as he made his way to the bathroom. The face that greeted him in the mirror would scare a banshee. Hair sticking out in spikes. A two-day growth of beard bristling down his long face. The veins in his eyes a stinging red map of his trans-Atlantic route.

He drank three glasses of icy-sweet tapwater, brushed his teeth, shoved his hands through his hair. He pulled on jeans and a flannel shirt, then opened the window to look outside. Cool air, redolent of loamy earth, rushed in at him. He felt like an alien on another planet. Looking over his shoulder, he glared at the sealed urn on the mantel.

"A fine mess you've laid on me, old girl." He grimaced. Talking to Granny only compounded his sense that he was losing his marbles. What sort of idiot would come traipsing halfway around the world to Ireland to fulfill the deathbed request of a ninety-five-year-old lady?

"An honorable idiot."

Granny's voice again. This time, Hank refused to admit he'd heard it. He tugged open the armoire to pull a sweatshirt out of his bag. While his back was turned, he heard a grating sound followed by a dull crash. The urn of ashes had fallen to the floor.

Shock held him immobile for a moment. He'd put the urn securely on the mantel, hadn't he? He hadn't touched it, had he? A sense of horror burned through the shock as he surveyed the damage. The pewter urn hadn't broken, but ashes and small bits of something he didn't want to see spilled across the ancient clay tiles.

"Je—oh, damn it," he said, catching himself. Then, between clenched teeth: "*Damn*." A few more choice words sat on his tongue, but it seemed irreverent and vaguely ghoulish to utter them. His first impulse was to clean up the mess as quickly as possible. He grabbed some stationery from the desk and tried to scoop up the ashes, but the flimsy paper only made everything worse. "I don't believe this," he muttered. He left the room quickly in search of a broom and dustpan.

He hoped the Finns and their guests were sound sleepers. He didn't relish having to explain why he needed the broom.

He stepped out into the middle of the open air courtyard and took a deep breath. Dark Ireland closed around him like a black, silken cloak. Watery starlight cast a glow over the house and grounds, the quiet pastures, the hills sloping toward the mouth of the river Shannon. The crystal clarity of the night made his eyes ache. The air sped down into his lungs and then raced through his veins until he felt the tingle of its icy energy. The sensation felt new, exhilarating, confusing. Ireland, he decided, was as strange and fey as Granny Molloy.

When his eyes adjusted to the darkness, he crossed the courtyard to a door marked "Staff Only." Pushing it slightly ajar, he could see the silhouettes of pots hanging from hooks overhead and smell the faint odors of lard and scouring powder. He let himself in, moving carefully past long steel counters and sinks. He went through another door, entering the kitchen proper, lit by a single yellow bulb suspended above a sideboard. There, another fragrance wafted over him. The smell of baking bread. At that particular moment, it was more appealing than sex.

Hank closed his eyes, inhaling deeply.

He opened them and found himself staring at a woman.

She lifted a rolling pin high in one hand and parted her lips, preparing to scream the house down.

Chapter 2

"Please!" Hank hissed. "Don't scream!"

"And why not, I ask you that?" she retorted, her slim arm still upraised.

He spread his hands, palms out. "I just came looking for a broom and dustpan."

Suspicion flashed in her eyes. They were large eyes, wide set; in the predawn shadows he could not discern the color. She had dark eyebrows and a thin face pinched with distrust. A kerchief covered her hair.

"Honest, ma'am," he assured her. "I didn't mean to scare you."

"You'd be the Yank, then." She lowered the rolling pin.

"Texan," he said automatically.

"We call all Americans Yanks. Now. Why would you be needing a broom at the crack of dawn?"

Hank swallowed. He tried to grin but only managed a sick half-smile. "I spilled . . . something."

"Faith, you're making less sense than the gombeen man." She set down the rolling pin and turned to the counter, pouring steaming tea from a pot into a thick china mug. Wordlessly she added cream and sugar and handed it to him.

Hank couldn't remember the last time he'd drunk hot tea, but obediently he took a sip. "My name's Hank Farrell," he said.

"I know." With quick, efficient movements, she went to a closet and removed a broom and metal dustpan with fluted edges. "I'm Aislinn Finn."

She left the kitchen, and Hank trailed along behind. "Ma'am," he said, "you can just give me the broom and I'll take care of—"

"Sure and that's no way for me to treat a guest," she said briskly, using one hand to fasten the top button of her sweater.

He followed her across the courtyard. When they reached the door to his room, Hank put out a hand to block her.

She stopped and glared at his arm, which crossed her field of vision. There was a peculiar clarity in her profile, the clean lines edged by faint predawn light. "Mr. Farrell—"

"Hank."

"Hank. I work here. Tidying up after the guests is my job. You needn't worry about a little spill."

"All the same, ma'am—"

"Aislinn." She pronounced it sort of like Ash-lee, but with more of a hush.

"Aislinn," he repeated, liking the taste of it. "This is sort of . . . awkward. It would just be better for me to do it."

Before she could answer, he heard the sound of a car door slamming. Great. More witnesses. Another door slammed, and then the sputtering engine noise faded as the car drove away.

"That'll be the milkman," said Aislinn. She stared pointedly at his arm. "I have things to do."

Hank wondered why she was being so stubborn. He wondered a lot of things about her. She was an unusual woman, small and compact, sharp-featured and forthright in the way she spoke to him. She interested him, but not in the way an ordinary woman interested him. He found himself wondering what sort of thoughts and dreams lurked behind her large, deep eyes, her wide-lipped, somber mouth.

But now was not the time to speculate about strange Irish girls he'd never see again after today. "Look, just let me take care of it."

She took a deep breath and regarded him steadily. The soft colors of dawn had started to gleam at the edge of darkness, and a faint pink tinge highlighted her cheeks. "Mr. Farrell. Hank. Just what is it you spilled in your room that's got you in such a dither?"

He swallowed hard past a sandpapery throat. "My grandmother."

"Your grandmother."

He nodded, feeling a sense of unreality. "Her name was Margaret Molloy."

"Did you say Molloy?" she asked.

"Yes. Do you know the family?"

She shook her head. " 'Tis a common Irish name, is all."

Hank cleared his throat. "I—uh—I brought her ashes to Ireland. It was her last wish."

"And you spilled her."

"Uh-huh."

"On the floor in your room."

"Yes."

Just for a moment, a flicker of time, the blink of an eye, something shone in her face. It came and went so swiftly that he thought he might have imagined it—imagined the swift, fragile beauty that softened her bony features and sweetened her unsmiling mouth.

"So you brought your gran's ashes to Ireland, and spilled her in your room."

Though her words were matter-of-fact, a feeling of ease spread through him. "Yeah," he said, glad, somehow, that she'd made him tell her.

With a gentle push, she put his arm aside and went into the room. Her movements were light and economical, reminding him of a hummingbird that was never completely still. She bent over the mess, and all Hank could see was her narrow back with apron strings trailing down. She was finished in a trice.

Thank you, he thought. Thank you for not making me do it.

And that was the moment he knew—he'd been afraid. Afraid to touch the powder and grit of Granny's mortal remains. Afraid to remember that she had been his granny, his mother, his mentor. A person he had loved beyond ordinary love. A person who held his devotion even now, months after she had passed away.

Aislinn Finn set the pewter urn on the mantel and turned. He wasn't certain how he knew it, but he could tell she was shaken.

"Thanks," he said. "Listen, I know you've got work to do, but I wonder if you'd like to get yourself a cup of tea and watch the sunrise with me."

She froze as if she'd turned to stone. Her eyes were cast down. He still hadn't figured out what color they were. "What do you say, Aislinn?" he urged her.

She nodded gravely. "I should like that very much, Hank."

Chapter 3

A ISLINN fetched another cup of tea and led the way out of the court-yard through the old-fashioned carriage gate. Gray shadows and wisps of fog hung in the hills around the manor. The green smell of damp grass and the fecund odor of turf filled Hank's nostrils. They walked up a slope to a railed fence, and Aislinn whistled softly.

Their footfalls softened by the fine grass, three horses shambled over to the fence. Aislinn murmured to them softly in a strange, musical tongue, and they responded with throaty grumbles of contentment.

"That's the Gaelic," Hank said, surprised.

"Mm. Some of us still speak it. Out in the Gaeltac region west of here, there's a movement to revive the language, teach it in schools. Did your gran have the Gaelic, then?"

"Yes. Her name for me was *a storin.*"

" 'My treasure.' It's lovely." One of the mares sidled close.

He watched Aislinn for a moment, her silhouette drawn sharply, outlined by the coming dawn. "Thank you," he said. "For . . . you know."

"You needn't thank me." She rubbed her hand along the mare's neck.

He stuffed his hands in his pockets. "One way or another, I've been cleaning up after Granny Molloy all my life. She was a fine lady, but not what you'd call low maintenance."

Aislinn turned to him and smiled. The smile transformed her face.

Suddenly her features were not pinched and plain, but alight with humor and warmth. "Some are like that."

He found himself smiling back. "Are you?"

She moved into a stream of new light and looked up at him. In that instant, he saw her eyes clearly for the first time, and what he saw shocked him. They were the stranger's eyes from his dream. The haunted eyes, deep as wells, blue as flame, with pale ice shards flaring outward from the centers.

"Go on with you," she said. "Here I am up before the sun to fix breakfast for a houseful of tourists."

Her hands, gently patting the horses' necks, were small, with short, neatly manicured nails. He suspected her palms would be dry and callused to the touch. She flinched a little, as if Hank's intent stare had touched her physically. "Is something the matter?"

"You have beautiful eyes. I didn't mean to gawk."

"Then don't," she said.

Hank had the distinct impression that she wasn't accustomed to being gawked at. He let the pregnant mare sniff him around the head and shoulders.

"You're easy about the beasts," Aislinn remarked, clearly more comfortable speaking of horses than of herself.

"I live on a ranch in Texas. We use quarter horses." These were Thoroughbreds with high arched necks, noble skulls, deep chests, and dainty feet. They could run like the wind, but probably wouldn't cotton to cutting calves out of a herd.

"Do you like it?" she asked. "Living on a ranch?"

"It's all I've ever known. Gets wearying, sometimes, putting your heart and soul into raising livestock that end up in the slaughterhouse." Though the woman was a virtual stranger, Hank found himself admitting, "I'd rather raise horses. After Granny died, I put the ranch up for sale. No takers yet."

"I can certainly understand your wanting to raise horses. This one," she said, rubbing the nose of the other mare, "was sired by a steeplechase champion. She's skittish for everyone but me." Aislinn set aside her mug, climbed the fence, and mounted the horse.

Just like that. No saddle, no reins. Only her own graceful way with the horse. Hank had never seen anything quite like it.

When she nodded in the direction of the pregnant mare, he hesitated, then followed suit. The horse tolerated him well enough. The beasts seemed to obey Aislinn's will, as if she held them under an enchantment. This day, he decided, had definitely taken a turn for the better.

They walked the horses to the top of the slope. Either Aislinn had a great internal clock, or they were incredibly lucky, for they reached the summit the same moment the sun did. It was a clash of light and darkness so dramatic that Hank blinked with the wonder of it.

One moment the cool shadows cloaked them; the next, the sun bombarded them in long pink bars of brilliant light from the east.

"Next parish, America," Aislinn said, shading her eyes.

"What?"

"I said, 'Next parish, America.' Ireland is the last bit of Europe the rising sun touches before it goes across the Atlantic to wake the people there."

"My grandmother told me she said those same words as she was leaving Ireland as a girl." It sounded eerie, the expression being echoed by this stranger.

" 'Tis a common saying in these parts, you'll find. Even more common in the west, in County Kerry."

Aislinn gave him that smile again, and it was doubly intriguing in the coming light. A few tendrils of dark hair had escaped the kerchief. How old was she? he wondered. Her skin was as soft and unblemished as a young girl's, but her eyes held a fathomless, ancient, and unusual beauty. In a way he couldn't put his finger on, she seemed as wise and fey as Granny Molloy.

"I often think of keeping horses at a place of my own someday," Aislinn said. "I suppose I'm like you in that."

For no particular reason, a chill tiptoed up Hank's spine and prickled across his scalp. Since the moment he'd laid eyes on Aislinn Finn, he'd felt a sense of exhilaration and inevitability. His hand brushed the pocket of his jeans, where he always carried the small bog oak carving. His luck charm, though it had never brought him any good fortune to speak of. Yet he caught himself wondering if his luck was about to change.

"Maybe you will," he said noncommittally. He surveyed their surroundings—the greening hills sloping down to the sparkling mouth of the rivers Shannon and Fergus—and added, "I doubt you'd find a place nicer than this."

"Then you've not seen much of Ireland."

"Nope," he admitted, then surprised himself by adding, "but I'd like to."

She squeezed her mare's sides with her knees and turned her toward a barn with a low sheeted roof. "You're riding my ticket away," she said.

"The foal?"

"Aye. It'll fetch a good price if its sire does well in the racing season. And my parents have promised it to me. There's a piece of property out beyond Dingle that—" She broke off and flushed as if she'd said something she shouldn't.

"Tell me about it," he said, keeping his voice gentle. Damn, the woman was as skittish as the Thoroughbreds. And in a way he couldn't put his finger on, as different. A different breed. He had no idea why he thought that, but it occurred to him and he couldn't shake the crazy notion.

" 'Tis no more than a dream," she said, "and will probably stay that way."

"My grandmother always spoke of dreams as if they were real."

Aislinn sent him a wistful smile. She started off, leading the way down the hill. In the barn, they fed sweetened oats and flakes of alfalfa to the horses.

Tacked to the wall was a page from a glossy catalog. The headline read, "Shamrock Ltd. Estate Agents." Hank peered at the photograph. It showed an old-fashioned farmhouse situated on the green brow of a hill. Beneath a curl of clouds, high meadows overlooked the sea. In the distance beyond the house rose a perfectly rounded knoll crowned by a single tall stone. Hank felt a jolt of something he could not name— recognition, yearning, exultation?

Jet lag, he told himself. Hallucination.

"Nice place," he said in the understatement of the year.

"It's called *Ard-na-sidhe*. It's been for sale forever," Aislinn said.

"*Ard-na-sidhe*," Hank echoed, stumbling over the Gaelic words. "What does that mean?"

"Rise of the fairies." A flush stained her cheeks. "I don't know why I keep the photograph. Just a foolish dream, I suppose."

"Why does the world think all dreamers are fools?" Hank asked.

A seemingly harmless rhetorical question, yet she had the most extraordinary reaction. Her cheeks drained of color. Backing toward the door, she pressed the palms of her hands to her apron as if to wipe them clean. She hastened outside and practically fled down the walkway toward the house.

Puzzled by the swift change of her mood, he followed her. "Aislinn, what—"

"I'm certain I don't know, Mr. Farrell," she said grimly. "I'm off to serve breakfast, then."

"I'll give you a hand."

"Never that! You're to wait in the parlor until the meal is served." With a bossy twitch of her full skirts, she returned to the house.

Aislinn stopped in the kitchen scullery and leaned against the scrubbed pine table, her eyes closed and her chest filled with the most peculiar sensation. She could hear Peig, the daily girl, clattering about with pots and dishes and pitchers of orange juice, but for the moment Aislinn could not bestir herself to help.

Something had happened to her this morning.

Something that changed the color of the world.

Instead of facing the dawn and seeing nothing but shades of gray, she had looked out across the hills and seen all the hues of the rainbow.

She did not—dared not—ask herself why. But the questions came anyway, sliding like smooth music through her mind. Why him? Why now? What did it mean?

And how in heaven's name would he ever understand her? How would he know that she was not what she appeared to be, that the blood running through her veins made her more than human, but less than a woman?

All her life, she'd hidden behind the shield of dull devotion and duty, hoping to protect herself from the curse that had plagued her family since time out of mind.

What a fool she'd been, to think she could escape her destiny. For destiny—in the unlikely form of a Texas cowboy—had pursued her right to her very home. With his pointed questions and his unknowing candor, he had cast aside her shield as if it were no more than a wisp of samite.

"Are you ill, then, girl?" asked a sharp voice.

Aislinn dragged herself out of her reverie, straightening her shoulders and brushing absently at her apron. She would be horrified if some of the poor old lady's ashes clung to her. "Morning, Mum," she said to her mother. "I feel fine. I'll just be after getting breakfast."

"Aye, do that." Julia Finn was a solid woman, broad of face and shoulder, light of eye and hair, with ruddy skin and hard hands that weren't afraid of hard work, nor hesitant to deliver a cuff now and then if the situation warranted it. "There's something different about you," she said, her voice edged with suspicion. "You've not been dabbling in . . . you know."

Mum never actually said the words that made Aislinn so different from her brothers and sisters, who had left home long ago for careers in London and Dublin.

She felt the warmth of a flush in her neck and cheeks. "Sure I don't know what you mean, Mum."

Julia drew back her hand. Aislinn braced herself, but her mother merely touched her cheek with strong, work-worn fingers. "You're a strange one, that you are, Aislinn. Always dreaming. Best you remember what Father Tracy says about pagan things. 'Tis for you to deny them, no matter how seductive they seem."

"Yes, Mum." Ducking her head, Aislinn went to the parlor where the guests gathered before breakfast to decide what they wanted. The retired couple from Canada asked for their eggs fried and their rashers crisp. The Scandinavian cyclists requested muesli with cream, and the loud golfers from North Carolina ordered the full breakfast. The whole time she was taking orders, Aislinn was conscious of him—of Hank. She watched him out of the corner of her eye, aware that he was seated in the overstuffed chair by the hearth, leafing through one of the large books of photographs left out for the tourists.

When she finished with the other guests and they filed into the dining room, she turned to Hank. Ah, what a picture he made in his faded Levi's and scuffed cowboy boots, his russet hair tousled by the morning wind. Healthily tanned, with lines of good humor fanning out from his blue eyes, his was the face of a Hollywood movie star. Yet it was the character indelibly stamped on that face that captivated her. Part of her couldn't believe a man of such strong male appeal sat here in her parlor.

"And what would you like?" she asked softly.

His eyes answered the question without words. She tried not to know his thoughts, but in her mind she heard them as clearly as if he had spoken aloud. I want to know you, he seemed to be saying. I want to know your dreams and desires.

She cleared her throat, chiding herself for the flight of fancy. Surely a man like Hank Farrell had more interesting things on his mind than a plain Irish girl in a dusty apron.

"I'll have the biggest breakfast you can serve," he said with a grin so comely she felt it all the way to her toes. "I'm starved."

"Lovely," she said, and started to turn away.

"Aislinn." His voice was quiet, tentative.

She turned back. That was when she saw what he held in his hands. The book was chillingly familiar to her—an ancient tome of black pages bound between wooden covers. Corner tabs anchored the old amber-toned photos—some of them tintypes—in place.

"Where did you find that?" she asked urgently.

"Right here on this shelf. I'm not sure why I picked it up. But when I did, I felt—I don't know. Fascinated. Like these people should be familiar to me. This picture in particular."

He indicated a photo she knew well; she didn't have to look at it to recognize the plump, pretty girl standing beside the proud, dark-haired young man, dapper from his boiled collar to his spats. The laughing woman had a soft, round-faced prettiness and a look of hopefulness in her eyes. Hank traced a finger across their eternally still faces. "Strange, huh?"

Strange indeed, she thought. He should not know the people in the old book, stiffly posed and staring out at eternity, but she could see the truth in his face as he gazed down at the fading sepia photos. The images were tugging at something deep inside him.

" 'Tis a family album, and no business of your own, Mr. Farrell," she said, sounding terse and brisk, as if they had not just spent an hour together this morning. As if her life had not just changed because of it.

As if she had not just swept up the ashes of the very girl in the photograph.

"This way, please," she said.

"Look, I'm sorry," he said, getting up. "I didn't mean to pry."

"You weren't prying. Someone left the book out for all the world to see. I have no idea why. The family certainly isn't some monument like the Rock of Cashel."

"Hurry up there, girl," Julia said as they entered the dining room. It was Aislinn's favorite room, with a glass roof and plants growing abundantly in hanging baskets. Old Celtic airs played softly on the stereo. The fragrance of coffee and fresh rolls and rashers filled the air.

"Coming, Mum." The whole time Aislinn served the guests, she felt Hank's eyes following her. Look away, she wanted to tell him, to beg him. There's naught but trouble for you with a creature like me.

Yet he kept staring, and each time he caught her eye, he smiled.

As if he knew her.

As if he knew the truth about her.

As if he didn't care about the curse that bound her.

"Aislinn!" Her mother's voice cut into the seductive dream that was drawing her closer and closer to the stranger from Texas.

She snapped to attention, turning away from Hank to clear the bicyclists' table. From the corner of her eye, she saw her mother wink conspiratorially at Hank. "Never was one to keep her mind on her work," she said.

"Can't say I blame her. Doesn't take much of a mind to do work like that," Hank said. His tone was pleasant, his drawl fascinating, yet Aislinn saw Julia recoil as if he had struck her. Most guests were quick to agree that the strange darkling girl was suited only to menial tasks. Hank was the first to suggest otherwise.

"Gerry says you've brought your gran's ashes home to Ireland," Julia said, clearly eager to turn the subject.

"That's right." He added a dollop of cream to his second cup of coffee.

"And where would that be?" Julia asked.

Hank leaned back in his chair, his legs far too long for the table. "I'm not rightly sure. Granny talked in riddles sometimes. Said she wanted me to take her back to where she'd left her heart." His smile was small, sad. "Problem is, she didn't say exactly where that was, so I've got some detective work to do. All I know is that she left her first love behind, back in 1917. Man named Ronan MacNab of Dingle."

Aislinn felt every hair on the back of her neck stand up. Julia's hold on the coffee pot slipped, and she caught it just before she dropped it. Her face drained to white. "Mr. Farrell, I'm certain your gran was a lovely old soul, but I'd advise you to deposit her in the local cemetery and hasten back to Texas where you belong."

Chapter 4

WHILE Hank went to the airport to hire a car, Aislinn wondered if he would take her mother's advice. Surely it would satisfy his sense of duty to simply take the pewter urn to the local church. He could do that today and leave on a night flight for Atlanta.

It was exactly what he should do, she decided as she busied herself washing up after breakfast. So why did she feel this ache in her chest, this sense that opportunity had held out its hand to her, and she hadn't seized it?

She took care to avoid her mother. Hank's mention of Ronan Mac-Nab had given Julia quite an unexpected turn.

And no wonder.

The name of Ronan MacNab was a curse in the family, and had been for generations. The youngest son of the best family in Dingle, he'd been marked for the Church. But Ronan, inexplicably dark in a family of fair-haired MacNabs, had ideas of his own. The day before he was to go off to the seminary, he'd told his family he had fallen in love with a turf-cutter's daughter and wanted to be married.

What happened after that was an oft-told tale in the family of Julia MacNab Finn. The cautionary story was brought out to prove the folly of wanting something too much, of dreaming rather than doing one's duty. Even now, Aislinn felt a chill just thinking of the family history.

The sputtering sound of a motor drew her to the kitchen window.

Driving with the typical hesitancy of foreigners disoriented by steering on the right side of the car, Hank maneuvered a teal Nissan Sunny into the car park. Unfolding his long form limb by limb, he got out, then stood staring at the compact car and shaking his head.

The very sight of him made Aislinn's heart smile. She ached to know Hank Farrell, to hear more about his life and his world. But after today, he would be gone, never to return.

"He's bound to get lost on the little byways of the Dingle peninsula," Peig remarked, reaching up to hang a skillet over the sink.

"He'll be fine," Julia said, coming into the scullery with a stack of tablecloths to be laundered. " 'Tis none of our affair."

Aislinn gripped the windowsill. "He's going to do it, then? He'll try to find the place to leave his gran?"

"Aye, the young fool," Julia muttered. "I tried to tell him to just leave her and be done with it, but he wouldn't listen."

Morning sunshine flooded down on Hank as he bent over the hood of the car, studying the map spread out there. He had a look of concentration on his face, and his thick hair shone with ruby highlights.

Aislinn took a deep breath for courage. "We should tell him," she said softly.

Julia dismissed Peig with a look, and the daily girl hurried out to start cleaning the guest rooms.

"There's not a blessed thing to tell him," Julia insisted.

"Ah, Mum." Aislinn turned from the window and eyed her mother with mingling affection and exasperation. "Something brought him here, all the way from Texas."

"Chance brought him here. Pure, blind chance. How many Americans land at Shannon Airport, I ask you? How many come to Carrygerry House to stay? Let him have done with his business and be on his way."

Aislinn heard the tension in her mother's voice. The fear and the superstition. She'd lived with it all her life. "Telling him about Ronan Mac-Nab doesn't mean you have to tell him about me."

"We'll tell him nothing, do you understand?" Julia stuffed soiled tablecloths into a large withy laundry basket. "Nothing at all. Now, go and help Peig and don't be daydreaming about the Yank."

She's afraid, Aislinn thought, watching her mother's quick, jerky movements. She's afraid of losing me.

Though she wanted to reassure her mother, she found that she could not. Something—a force made of dark and light and voices she heard in her heart—drew her to Hank Farrell. Almost against her will, she fetched the old photo from the album in the parlor, then went to her room and took out a set of clothes she'd found in the attic but had never worn. After she'd dressed, she grabbed her handbag. Her heart pounded with the boldness of what she was about to do. For her. For Hank. She had known her life would change the moment she laid eyes on him.

Now she knew she had to take the first step.

"You're forgetting something, boyo."

Hank froze, his hand on the hatchback door and his guts tying themselves into knots. That voice. *She* was talking to him again. Granny Molloy. In the crisp air of the midsummer morning, her gentle brogue lingered in the silence.

Gingerly, he let go of the hatchback and stepped back, eyeing his suitcase as if it were a wild animal. Just like at the airport, the voice came from the suitcase.

Only now he was rested. His ears were clear. There was no wind to speak of.

He glanced left and right; then, feeling like the fool of the world, whispered, "Granny?"

No response. Was he really such an idiot that he expected one? "Come on, old girl," he said between his teeth. "The sooner I get you to your final rest, the better."

Glancing back at the manor house, he wished Aislinn would come out and tell him good-bye. Another foolish notion. They had shared an extraordinary morning, nothing more. It was over.

He put the suitcase in the back. The hatchback door slammed down on his fingers. "Shit! Shit! Shit!" he said, using his other hand to fumble for the keys and free himself. His fingers felt bruised to the bone. Grating out "shit, shit, shit," like a mantra, he ducked into the washroom of the pub and ran cold water on his hand. Nothing seemed to be broken, but his fingers throbbed.

Common sense told him to take Julia Finn's advice—give Granny's ashes to the local cemetery and get home where he belonged.

Except that he had never fit in at the ranch. That had been his grandfather's dream, and then his father's. Never Hank's.

Flexing his hand, he walked back toward the car. When he was halfway across the courtyard, a beautiful woman stopped him. She was small and trim in dark leggings and a linen blouse that looked as if it had come from a vintage clothing shop. Her sleek black hair was caught back in an antique silver clasp.

Hank stared for a moment as the shock of recognition engulfed him. "Aislinn."

She smiled. "Faith, I don't spend all my time looking like a scullery maid," she said.

His gaze swept her from head to toe. "I guess not. Sorry. I didn't mean to stare."

She held out a curling piece of thermal fax paper. "This came—it's to your attention."

He had called from the airport to let his ranch foreman know how to get in touch with him. Glancing down, he felt a grin start in the very center of him, radiating outward until he forgot the pain in his hand. "I'll be damned."

"Good news, is it?" she asked, tilting her head to one side.

"I've got a buyer for the ranch." He folded the message and tucked it in his pocket. He felt a distinct lightening of his heart. This was right. It felt exactly right. It was time, past time, to leave the ranch and figure out what his own life was about. The only question was, where should he begin?

He glanced down at Aislinn. In different ways, they had both put their dreams on hold. "What would you do," he asked impulsively, "if you could suddenly do anything you wished?"

Her breath caught. For a moment, she looked flustered, her teeth pressing into her lower lip and her blue eyes widening. "Sure, and that's a silly question. My lot is to stay here, help out with the family."

"Why?"

"Because . . . it's expected of me. Because I owe it to them."

The estate agent's picture of the farm flashed in his mind. He turned on his heel and started toward the car. "Let's go."

"Go?"

"You're coming with me."

"But I—"

"Do you want to?"

"Yes," she blurted. "But—"

"You're a grown woman, Aislinn Finn. And don't tell me you dress like this to change bed sheets."

A blush suffused her cheeks, confirming his suspicion that she had wanted to come all along. He took her by the elbow and steered her to the car, opening the door to the passenger side for her. Before she could protest, he helped her in. When he seated himself behind the wheel and started the engine, he sent her a sideways look. "Okay?"

"I can't believe I'm doing this."

"I'm harmless. Trust me. You'll be back tonight." He jerked the Sunny into gear and moved out into the narrow roadway. "I need a guide, anyway. Can you do that for me, Aislinn? Can you guide me?"

"I suppose so," she said. "You'll be wanting the T11 past Limerick."

As he acclimated himself to the driving, he remembered the eerie voice he'd heard earlier: *You're forgetting something, boyo.*

But now, with Aislinn beside him, he didn't feel he was forgetting anything at all.

Chapter 5

IRELAND greeted Hank with open arms. It was a much warmer greeting than he'd gotten at the airport. The road ambled down through sunny vales and between ancient hedgerows. Little villages, as sleepy as the distant past, marked their progress southwestward.

Between the towns lay emerald meadows studded with grazing sheep. A dreamlike quality hung in the air; the day was fine and bright, the blue sky topped by clouds swept into high crests by a wind from the sea.

"Ireland suffers from an excess of splendor," Hank remarked.

"Perhaps because we have little else."

"In the States we'd call that a defeatist attitude." He drummed his fingers on the steering wheel as the Sunny crept around a switchback curve. "You're a bundle of contradictions. You've got three of the finest horses I've ever seen, yet you feel bound to work at your family's B&B. You keep a photo of *Ard-na-sidhe* tacked on your wall, but you say it's only a dream."

She sent him a smile that failed to banish the melancholy from her eyes. "True, it's wishful thinking. I should know better." Before he could challenge her, she neatly turned the subject, asking him about Texas.

Aislinn Finn was an easy woman to talk to. One look into her wise, dark blue eyes, and Hank found himself confessing his own dreams and goals, his hope to see what the rest of the world had to offer a cowboy who didn't seem to fit in anywhere.

"Sorry," he said, catching a sidewise glare from Aislinn. "I don't guess you need to hear about my achy breaky heart." He studied a curious, battered road sign warning of "Loose Chippings" followed by a fall of broken rocks along the shoulder.

He thought some more about the photograph tacked to the wall of Aislinn's barn. The memory stirred a curious sadness in Hank, a wistfulness. And a sense of recognition. "I stayed on the ranch for Granny," he admitted. "Now that she's gone, I'm free to go." He looked down at his long, bony hands gripping the wheel. "Sometimes I get the feeling that I waited too long. It's too late."

"Staying where you're needed is not such a bad thing," she said.

Time and distance slipped by unnoticed as they talked. Out from under the press of duties at the manor house, Aislinn was a fluent talker, a natural storyteller. There was not a well nor crumbling fort nor ruined abbey she did not know. She was like Granny Molloy in that—the stories were tucked away inside her like family heirlooms in a box, and all she had to do was take them out and share them.

As they turned west along the T68 to Dingle, she pointed out beehive huts and stone circles, Celtic crosses and monuments standing in the midst of sheep meadows. The road narrowed and roughened as the Sunny climbed to the heights of the Brandon Mountains toward Conor Pass.

Herds of sheep, their dirty white coats splashed at the rump with bright colored paint to mark them, scuttled across the road now and then, stopping traffic. They encountered the occasional "van"—a horse-drawn covered wagon for traveling Gypsy-style.

Then, through a shroud of fog that hung in the vales, the pass came into view, majestic as a throne of the gods.

Sharp crags scraped the sky, and in places disappeared into a thick mist. Aislinn fell silent. Hank sneaked a glance at her. She was suddenly tense, her face pale, her hand clutching the door handle.

"Are you all right?" he asked.

"Stop the car, Hank."

Alarmed, he pulled over at a car park at the summit, where people could stop for a view of the pass. Aislinn let herself out and hurried to the edge, her arms wrapped protectively around her middle. Summer had not reached the heights, and the air held a penetrating chill. Hank paused long enough to grab a hooded sweatshirt out of his bag, then went to her side.

"Put this on," he said, settling it around her shoulders.

She accepted the garment with a grateful nod. Her face was still pale, the skin almost translucent at the temples. She looked like an ice princess, more beautiful than he ever could have imagined. How had he missed that fragile sweetness this morning? How could he ever have thought her plain?

"What's the matter?" he asked gently.

She didn't look at him, but continued staring out at the pass, across high lakes and meadows that gave way to the empty valley toward the town of Dingle. "I thought I could do this," she explained. "I thought I could come here with you, that it would do no harm."

"Of course it does no harm."

"You're wrong." A cold wind skirled down from the heights, blowing the lace on her antique blouse, and she pulled the sweatshirt more snugly around her. "There are things about me you don't know, Hank, things I can't explain."

She started to tremble. An irresistible instinct to shield and protect took hold of Hank. Such a need had been the driving force in his life, keeping him on the ranch to care for Granny long after he wished to be gone.

He had no idea why, but the feeling now applied to Aislinn. He drew her close, settling his arms around her and pressing her cheek to his chest. He barely knew this woman, but in his arms she felt as familiar and beloved as someone he had known all his life. Her lack of resistance pleased him, yet he still felt tension in her shoulders as he held her.

"Try me," he said. "You'd be surprised at the things I can understand."

"I'd be surprised if you understood me," she whispered. "I should never have come with you."

He took her hand and led her over to a bench at the edge of the car park. "Let's start at the beginning. Before I dropped my poor granny all over the floor this morning, you didn't even know me. Now you've decided you can't be with me?"

She looked vulnerable, with the cold wind plucking at her hair, stealing thin black tendrils from the silver clasp. "I don't suppose there's any way I can get you to believe this," she began, "but my fate was decided hundreds of years ago, Hank. Perhaps thousands of years ago."

Chapter 6

THOUGH its population numbered less than a few thousand souls, the town of Dingle boasted more than fifty pubs. Each one of them looked inviting, from the Guinness signs on the plaster exterior walls to the tourist menus scrawled on chalkboards in the doorways. Hank parked the Sunny in front of one of them. The engine died with a sick-sounding cough.

Once they were seated in the dim interior and had ordered pints of stout and sandwiches, Hank eyed Aislinn across the table. She was wise and fey and timid, she spoke in riddles, and he wanted to understand her. "I think we'd better talk."

She reached into her handbag and drew out a picture. It was the one from the photograph album Hank had leafed through that morning. The one he had stared at for a long time, wondering why the amber-toned figures seemed so familiar to him.

"I shouldn't have snapped at you when I saw that you'd found this," she said, her voice soft, slightly tremulous. "But I was frightened. You were getting . . . too close."

Hank frowned. "Too close to what?"

"To the truth. Turn the picture over, Hank."

He did so. On the back, in a small script in fading brown ink, were the words:

Ronan and Margaret

Dingle, 1917

He felt a tingling sensation on the back of his neck as he flipped the picture over and stared intently at the woman. "Margaret," he said. "Margaret Molloy." Despite some similarities to his grandmother—the shape of the face and mouth, the set of the shoulders—the person in the photo was a stranger. This girl had a dazzling smile and a face so full of hope that it made him ache just to look upon it.

His grandmother had never appeared that way. Kindness and contentment had characterized her. But never the wild joy he sensed in the laughing girl.

"She was supposed to marry him," Hank said. "I never knew until the end of her life, when she started talking about the past. She said she was going to marry her true love, but had to go to Texas instead."

"Is that all she told you, then?"

"Yeah." Eyes narrowed, he sipped his stout, savoring the cool mellow taste of it and gazing across the rim at Aislinn. "How is it that you've got a picture of my granny in your family album?"

She touched the photograph on the table. "Ronan MacNab was *my* great-grandmother's brother."

"Jesus." Hank ran a hand through his hair as a stark chill rushed over him. "This is weird. Weirdest coincidence I ever heard of." He stared at Aislinn. She looked incredible with her wind-tossed hair spilling over the shoulders of the antique lace blouse.

Their forebears had been lovers. What were the odds of them meeting?

"Could Granny have known?" he wondered aloud.

"She knew enough to send you to Ireland."

Hank nodded. He wouldn't have come, save for Granny's last wish. But the phone bank at the airport. Of all the places he could have chosen to stay, he had picked the home of Ronan's great grandniece. Why? *Why?*

Aislinn lifted her glass off the cardboard coaster on the table. The design on the coaster was a Celtic knot, the lines weaving in and out without beginning or end.

He took a bite of his sandwich, made with local sharp cheese, brown bread, and grainy mustard, and chewed thoughtfully. "Granny left unfinished business in Ireland. This Uncle Ronan. Is he still alive?"

"Oh, heavens, no. Mum never said what became of him. Only that he was to become a priest. No one speaks of him—it's almost as if he's a forbidden subject. The love affair was a bit of a scandal, but it was over soon enough. I assume he went back to the priesthood."

"But you don't know that for certain."

"No."

"Why were you so afraid to come here with me, Aislinn?"

She took a sip from her glass, her eyes wide and filled with apprehension. "I'm afraid of what we might find out. About your grandmother. About Ronan." She knotted her hands in her lap. "About us."

Hank thought for a moment. "We're not related, if that's what you're worried about. Granny's son wasn't born until she'd been a married lady in Texas for four years."

"I wasn't worried about that."

They finished their lunch and left the tavern. Despite Aislinn's hesitancy, they decided to inquire at the local church.

In the rectory Aislinn spoke in fluent Gaelic to an elderly woman called Maeve Morrigan.

"There now, I'm not so old and daft I don't know my English," Mrs. Morrigan declared. "What is it you're after, then?"

"We want to find out whatever became of Ronan MacNab," Hank explained.

The ancient woman's wizened face crinkled even tighter. "Is that so? And why would you be wanting to know that?"

"It's a long story, ma'am," Hank said as politely as he could. "Someone who was close to me knew him long ago."

"Didn't we all?" she said cryptically, then with light, almost birdlike steps led them to a storeroom lit by a naked bulb and by sunlight coming through a dirt-streaked skylight. The musty smells of old paper and ink filled the air. "You can inquire with Father Carne by leaving a message in his box," she said, then glanced from Aislinn to Hank. "You were right to come here."

"I'm not sure what you mean, ma'am."

"Sometimes when one soul starts a journey, another one must complete it." She left the room quickly.

The records were in surprisingly decent order. Most were written in Gaelic—births, deaths, marriages. During famine years, the death rate was heartbreakingly high. "Gone to America" was listed as the fate of a number of people.

The year 1917 had been a busy one. They scanned the page, but saw no mention of Ronan MacNab. "Look at that," Hank remarked. "Maeve Adare married to Sean Morrigan, 18 June 1917. The woman's probably older than Granny. Maybe they even knew each other."

"We could inquire on our way out."

Hank's gaze was drawn to the fading ink at the bottom of a curling, brown-stained page. "What's this?"

The entry read "*Ronán Mac-an-Aba.*"

"That's him," Aislinn said, excitement in her voice. "That is his name in Gaelic." She frowned at the rest of the entry. Then, with a gasp, she slammed the tome shut and backed away from it.

Hank jumped, startled. "What the hell—what's wrong?" he demanded.

"We should go. This was stupid. What does it matter to us what happened to people so long ago?"

Hank advanced on her, backing her into a corner of the storeroom and gripping her shoulders. "Listen," he said, "I came here looking for answers. But every time we get close, more questions are raised. What did you see in that book, Aislinn? What is it that made your face go pale, put that panicky look in your eyes?"

"Ronan MacNab never did become a priest," she said.

"Just tell me. Aislinn, I need to know."

She glanced over his shoulder. "According to the records, he died on July 21, 1917."

A heavy sadness settled over Hank. Long ago, Granny had told him that she had embarked for America on that very date. Midsummer's night it was; she'd been very clear on that.

He went slowly to the table and put all the registries back. "Damn," he said. "I wonder if Granny ever knew. Did she leave Ireland because her fiancé died? Or did Ronan die because she left?"

Aislinn took his hand. "Let's go. She said she wanted you to take her ashes back to where she left her heart."

Hank swallowed past an uncomfortable thickness in his throat. "I guess I know where that is now. We just have to figure out where he's buried."

They left a note in Father Carne's box, then went to find Mrs. Morrigan in the registry. But when they got there, the small, cluttered office was deserted. Mrs. Morrigan had vanished without a trace.

Chapter 7

"I'M sorry, Mr. Farrell," said the mechanic at the garage. "The car needs a part from the shop in Tralee. We don't get a delivery from them until tomorrow."

Hank and Aislinn exchanged a glance. She should have felt horror at the idea of being stranded with a stranger, but instead, a quiet, almost defiant exultation rose up inside her. She would have to call Carrygerry House and explain the delay. She'd need to stop at one of the shops along the waterfront and buy a few toiletries for the night. They would have to find a place to stay.

"The rental car company doesn't have an office in Dingle?" Hank asked. The Sunny had died outside the church, and they had walked several blocks to the garage.

The mechanic smiled mischievously. "Sure and what would a town of this size be wanting with a service like that?"

"I suppose," Hank said, "there are worse things than being stranded in a town with fifty pubs."

Aislinn agreed with him. Though the horror and despair of learning Ronan MacNab's fate still haunted her, she felt her mood lift as she found a B&B in a well-thumbed local directory. "Mickle House, west of the town," she told Hank. "Furnished in antiques, views of the strand, long walks, private baths."

Aislinn rang up the B&B, reserving rooms for the night. The mechanic gamely lent them a two-seater bicycle. "You'll see more of the countryside that way," he said cheerfully. "And such a day it is for it."

She looked at Hank and felt the darkness within her part, making way for light bubbles of laughter. "I'm certain you hadn't counted on a bicycle tour, Mr. Farrell."

"It'll be something to tell my grandchildren."

She refused to let the reference to family dim her mood. Instead, she took the front seat of the bike and headed for the shops. Within an hour, she had everything she needed—more than she needed. A beautiful mohair cardigan the color of the sky. A serviceable nightgown, ankle length. A small bag of toiletries. All the purchases, along with Hank's smaller bag and the urn of ashes, fit in the large wicker basket of the bike.

"It stays light forever this far north," he said, swinging his leg over the bike as if it were one of his quarter horses. "Let's play tourist."

Aislinn knew her mood was wavering between despair and joy, and she wasn't certain why. All she knew was that it felt right to be with him.

"Let's," she said. How liberating it was to be far from home, in the company of a handsome cowboy. She could not remember the last time she had felt so contented or carefree.

She warned herself not to enjoy her freedom too much. Hank was here for a brief time; soon he would go back to Texas and she'd never see him again. She would return to Carrygerry House, watching the tourists pass through her life, growing old and strange and quiet as a spinster.

She wasn't like other women. Couldn't want what other women wanted. Hadn't her mother always told her so?

They left the town behind, taking a country road westward. Hank insisted on stopping to inspect Dunbeg Fort, built in the Iron Age, and then the Gallarus Oratory, masterpiece of the early Christians.

"Come inside with me," Hank said.

Aislinn hung back, suddenly ill at ease. It would do no good to explain to Hank that these ancient treasures had an unpleasant effect on her. They seemed to pull at some vital part of her being, filling her with images or memories of other times, other lives.

"I'll stay with our belongings," she said with forced cheerfulness.

He shrugged, ducking his head to fit through the low doorway of the oratory. Unique in all the world, the place was made of unmortared stone fitted flawlessly together to make the structure water tight. The window facing east was the Eye of the Needle. All souls must pass through it in order to be saved.

The oratory was known to have interesting acoustics—or ghosts, depending upon whom one asked. Hank put his hand through the window and gestured at her. On a hasty burst of courage, Aislinn followed him in, and was immediately sorry.

Whispers rushed through the damp, dark air inside. She heard the voices of the ancients, hissing curses and jabbering in tongues as old as time. The unseen forces here were worse here than at Conor Pass. She had to fight to keep from clapping her hands over her ears. She looked at Hank, but he busied himself with studying the Alphabet Pillar carved with ogham and Roman characters. He seemed oblivious to the babble and roar of sound that battered at Aislinn. Only she could hear them. Only she knew what they meant.

She was getting too close, daring too much. Forces far stronger than herself were rising up and preparing to hurl her back. Shaken, she stepped outside the stone building and waited for Hank to join her. When he emerged from the oratory, she hastened him along so he wouldn't notice her shakiness and pallor.

The late afternoon was soft and bright, a perfect July day. They continued along the country road, marveling at the scenery, until the far western tip of the peninsula swung into view. Hank pulled the tandem off to the side.

"Wow," he said, staring at Slea Head.

Aislinn stared, too, feeling a deep wrench of yearning and exultation as she regarded the high, rounded landscape, the dramatic cliffs with the waves leaping up. In the shimmering blue-green distance lay the Blasket Isles, a tiny archipelago of wild islands that stretched out into the deep Atlantic.

"The Blaskets were inhabited until the fifties," she told Hank. "Then the families there had to abandon their farms. They were just too poor. Couldn't make a living. The children kept growing up and leaving. But the isles were the home of the greatest Gaelic storytellers of this century."

Hank nodded. "Granny told me about the Blaskets. Told me some stories from the islands."

Aislinn took a deep breath. "Did she tell you a lot of the stories?"

"Endlessly. Filled my head with them. My father used to ask her to tone down the spooky parts, but she never did."

"What sort of stories?" She had to know. Perhaps, if she could get him to believe, then she could get him to understand.

"I imagine you've heard them all, being Irish. Legends about giants and heroes. Cattle raids and kings. Fairy stories."

Aislinn kept her face expressionless, her voice flat. "The fairy stories. There are dozens of those."

Hank grinned fondly and glanced at the basket containing the urn. "She never praised me when I was little. Never said I was a handsome boy, or smart or helpful." He laughed. "Not that I was, but one day she told me why she'd never say those things aloud."

"And why is that?" Aislinn knew the answer, but she wanted to hear him say it.

"She swore that fairies were always listening in on mortals. If they spotted a particularly fine specimen of a human child, they'd take him, and then replace him with one of their own. The changeling would grow up as a member of the mortal family, but he was usually treated like a stepchild." Hank chuckled and got back on the bike. "Crazy, huh? I always wondered why she worried about such a thing in Texas."

"Because maybe it's worth worrying about," Aislinn whispered. But the wind snatched her faint words, and Hank never heard.

They pedaled on. After a few kilometers, he leaned forward. "Did you say something?"

She felt a prickle of nervousness at the base of her neck. "Just now?"

"Uh-huh."

"No. Did you hear something?"

"I thought you said we should turn right here."

"I didn't say a word." She saw him looking over her shoulder, frowning intently at the wicker basket. His gran, it seemed, was very much on Hank's mind. Impulsively, Aislinn added, "Let's do."

The lane was rutted and littered with rocks. Tufts of grass grew high on the center strip. The track curved round the side of a hill and climbed gently. Then, abruptly, the hedgerows gave way to a vast meadow. It would have made perfect grazing land, but there was no sign of a herd or flock.

On the hillside was a house. *The* house. Aislinn knew it in her heart even before her eyes recognized the sight.

"What do you know?" Hank said. "It's your farm, honey. The one in the picture hanging on your barn wall."

It was deserted, though well kept. A small sign from Shamrock Limited Estate Agents announced that the property was for sale. Farmhouse, barn, and outbuildings. Sea views and a panorama of Slea Head.

" 'Interesting archaeological ruins on grounds,' " Hank read from the fading sales sheet posted with the sign.

Aislinn's heart pounded until her chest hurt. "We'd best go," she said.

"We've barely looked around. Let's see if we can find the ruins."

She remembered the voices. The ominous whispers at Conor Pass, the gateway she had dared to breach. And then the roar of protest that had flooded her at Gallarus Oratory. Who was she to think she could challenge her own destiny?

"No, Hank. Please—"

"What are you afraid of, Aislinn?" He leaned the bike against the stone fence and turned to face her. Prodding. Daring. Demanding.

"Us," she whispered brokenly. "I'm afraid of us."

 # Chapter 8

H ANK took her hand between both of his. "Us?"

She nodded gravely, her blue eyes haunted.

He was going to deny that there was any such thing as "us," but he couldn't. From the moment he'd laid eyes on her, seen her standing in the kitchen with a rolling pin held high above her head, some bond had formed between them.

I could love this woman.

The thought tiptoed like a night visitor into his mind. It stunned him; he had never been one to plunge into a relationship. Had never trusted himself to share his life, and had given up all expectation of doing so.

Yet here, on the other side of the world, he found a woman who tugged at his heart, who held him with the gentle yet inexorable force of the moon on the tides.

"Let's go find the ruins," he said, wondering if she felt even the slightest inkling of the thoughts that swirled through his mind.

"I know where they are," she said, leading the way up a slope behind the house. The hill was a perfect circle, as if it had been made by man.

"You've been here before?" he asked.

"No. Never. At least, not in person," she added cryptically.

He shaded his eyes against the orange burn of the lowering sun. "What is it, like Stonehenge or something?"

"Or something."

He grinned at her. "Could you be a little more specific?"

"You might hear it called a fairy ring or mound." She hung back as if loath to move closer to the top of the hill.

Baffled by her reticence, Hank took her hand, overriding her protests to lead her to the summit. He stopped and stared at the stone monument at the top. "I'll be damned," he said.

"What is it?" she asked fearfully.

Hank dug in his pocket, drew out the piece of bog oak, and held it in the palm of his hand. The carved figure matched the stone monument.

Aislinn took a harsh breath. "It is Lusmore—you can tell by the hump on his back and the fairy cap he wears."

"This charm belonged to my grandmother." The feeling of awareness that had plagued Hank ever since he'd set foot in Ireland intensified. Granny had known he would come here. But how? Why? He remembered the voice, telling him to turn right. Aislinn hadn't heard it. Surely it was all an uncanny coincidence.

Aislinn had walked back down the hill. Hank joined her by an overgrown hedge that was covered with berries. She subjected him to a long, probing stare. Her eyes were troubled. She, too, seemed discomfited by all the strange synchronicities.

"Hank, I have to tell you something."

He leaned against a low, broken wall of fieldstone. "Shoot."

"You'll think I've run mad."

He winked. "You and me both, darlin'."

"Remember the tales of the changelings?"

"A fairy left in place of a mortal child," he supplied. Granny used to recite a poem about it—

> Come away, O human child!
> To the waters and the wild
> With a faery, hand in hand—

"—For the world's more full of weeping than you can understand," Aislinn finished for him. "Yeats, isn't it?"

Hank nodded. "But he was a poet. He made this stuff up. Didn't he?"

She took a deep breath, then spoke quietly, almost reluctantly. "In the MacNab branch of the family, each member is fair in coloring, like my mum. Light eyes and hair—all my brothers and sisters have it. But every once in a great while, there is a dark child, one who doesn't seem to fit in with the rest of the family."

He studied her small, angular face. Audrey Hepburn, he thought. Dark and lovely. Large eyes with mystery in their depths. "Like you."

"And like Ronan MacNab."

He recalled the young man in the photo. Yes, there was a resemblance, a distant and shadowy spiritual quality.

"What are you getting at, Aislinn?" He gave a disbelieving laugh. "Are you saying Ronan was a changeling? That you are?"

"I knew you'd think I'd run mad."

"It's genetics, Aislinn. Not magic."

"It's a curse."

"Now *that's* ridiculous. A curse?"

"Ronan McNab died the day he was to have married your grandmother," she said coldly. "It's forbidden for someone like me to love and be loved. Each time a dark one tries to defy fate, a tragedy occurs."

"Says who? What Ronan MacNab did in 1917 has nothing to do with you," Hank said, irritated. "It was a bizarre chance. A terrible accident, or perhaps he was sick."

"His grandmother before him came to a bad end. She was a darkling, too. 'Tis said she was murdered. For as long as anyone can remember in the family, tragedy has befallen those who try to break the curse."

"You're cra—" He stopped himself. It was exactly what she had told him he'd say. "Aislinn, you're a grown woman. You've got a mind of your own. Don't tell me you believe in this stuff."

"Then explain how you came to choose Carrygerry House. And then this." She encompassed the property with a sweep of her arm, pointing at the carved stone. "Coincidence doesn't cover it, Hank."

He blew out his breath in exasperation and started up the hill.

"Where are you going?" she called.

He strode to the middle of the hill and turned to face her. "See? It's nothing but grass and rock. What did you expect? For goblins to jump out at me? Snatch me down to the underworld?"

She stumbled back, clutching blindly at the fence behind her. "Don't make sport of it, Hank. Don't pretend the curse doesn't exist."

He stretched his arms toward her. "Come here, Aislinn. Do it for me."

Her eyes were wide, filled with distress. He took a step toward her. At the same moment, a creaking sounded. Hank looked to the side to see the huge, ancient stone toppling toward him.

The next happened as if filmed in slow motion. Aislinn called out a Gaelic command in a voice he had never heard before, someone else's voice. She raised her arms skyward. A force that felt like the wind swept Hank out of the way, swept him as if he were weightless, of no more substance than his grandmother's ashes. He fell to his knees at the base of the hill with no idea how he'd gotten there.

He turned back just in time to see the tall stone slam to the ground. "Jesus!" The exclamation burst from him. The monolith lay like a felled tree, precisely on the spot where he had just been standing only seconds earlier.

"You could have been killed," Aislinn called. She looked drained, sagging against the rock wall. "Come away, Hank. Please."

He struggled for composure. "Come and rescue me," he said. "Come on, Aislinn."

She spat a string of Gaelic words, probably cursing his immortal soul, but she started up the hill. He grabbed her outstretched hand and pulled her against him.

"One thing puzzles me," he murmured into her hair. It smelled like flowers. "What the hell did you shout to make me get out of the way?"

She pushed away from him. "I've been trying to explain myself to you, Hank. I'm not like . . . ordinary women. There are things I can do that—" She broke off and waved her hand in frustration. "It's useless. You're too much the skeptic."

"And you're too superstitious." He sat on the fallen stone, pulling her into his lap. She gasped and struggled, but he held her fast. "See, honey?" he asked, thoroughly enjoying the feel of her pressed against him. "Nothing to fear."

"You were nearly killed by a stone that's been standing upright for two thousand years. Another coincidence, Hank?"

"Of course." He touched her beneath the chin, brought his mouth close to hers. "Kiss me, Aislinn."

"No." But she didn't move.

He could feel the warmth of her breath, the tension in her shoulders. "Kiss me."

"No," she said again.

"Now I know for sure you're no fairy. Just an all-fired, stubborn woman."

"But—"

"Shut up, Aislinn." He insured that she would by covering her mouth with his.

Kissing her was like eating warm butterscotch. Sweet, delicious. Addictive.

He held her tighter and plunged his tongue deep, probing rhythmically. She crushed her fists into the fabric of his shirt, but she didn't push him away.

He kissed her again, unapologetic and demanding, but she didn't seem intimidated at all. Instead she clutched harder at him, clinging, her ardor rising, as urgent as his. He found the hem of her blouse and started to slide his hand up under it, to see if she felt as soft as he imagined.

God, he wanted her. He felt as if someone had set fire to him. As if he'd go up in smoke if he couldn't have her. "I changed my mind," he mumbled against her lips, brushing his mouth back and forth across hers. "You're magic. You've put a spell on me."

She jumped up. "I can't put a spell on you. Weaving a love spell is not one of my gifts."

At that moment, three black crows swooped overhead, cawing madly. Aislinn stared at the sky, leaving Hank sitting on the stone.

"We must go," she said. "Now."

Damn. The woman had left him as hard as the stone he sat on. And all her weird superstitions were starting to feel spooky. "You're a cruel woman, Aislinn Finn," he muttered, levering himself up. "A damned cruel woman."

As she sat in the parlor at Mickle House with her hand on the telephone, the old stories swirled through Aislinn's mind, licking at her like flames. She held the legends inside her like long-buried secrets. It was said that if a changeling ventured too close to a sacred place, the *sidhe* could snatch her back amongst them. If she dared to love a mortal, it would mean certain doom—wasn't the tragedy of Ronan MacNab and Margaret Molloy proof of that?

Aislinn shuddered, remembering the power of the ancient hill pulling at her, mocking her, daring her to challenge her own destiny. In Hank's arms, she had been tempted, had even thought of defying the stars, but the appearance of the crows could not be ignored.

They were an unmistakable sign. A warning.

She squeezed her eyes shut and tried to pretend she felt no yearning. But it wouldn't go away. How she wanted all the things she could never have. Hank, with his open grin and gentle strength. The farm called *Ard-na-sidhe*, a place that had fed her dreams since time out of mind.

She drew in a harsh, shuddering breath and rang the exchange for Carrygerry House. Come on, Da, she silently urged. Pick up. Her father was far more agreeable than her mother when it came to unexpected changes of plan.

"Carrygerry House." It was her mother.

Aislinn gripped the receiver tighter. "Mum. It's me—"

"Aislinn! Where the devil have you gotten yourself to?"

"Still in Dingle, Mum." She explained about the car.

"Then you should take the coach back."

"It's too late in the day. We decided to tour the area a little."

"Tour the area!" Julia's irritation snapped like a whip. "And us with a houseful of guests. What'll we do in the morning, I ask you that—"

"Mum—"

"Have you no thought for your family? You've a duty to—"

The receiver was snatched out of Aislinn's hand. She looked up in surprise to see Hank putting it to his ear. "Howdy, Mrs. Finn. Just wanted to let you know that Aislinn is fine, ma'am." A slow grin spread across his face. "And you know, I'll just bet the world won't come to an end if she's not there to wait on the guests for a day or so. In fact, I'm sure of it. Y'all have a good night now, ma'am."

He clapped down the phone.

Aislinn stared at him, trying to decide whether she should be outraged or amused. "You had no right," she said. "My mother—"

"Is a pain in the butt."

She couldn't help herself then. She gave in to the smile that kept threatening to appear. "Yes, but she depends on me."

"There's a limit to what we owe our parents, Aislinn."

"You're one to talk."

"What's that supposed to mean?"

"How long did you stay on your family's ranch, simply because it was expected of you?"

"Too long," he admitted. "But it's over now. I have a buyer." He took her hand and drew her to her feet. "So you see, darlin', I've got something to celebrate. Let's go dancing tonight."

"No one's ever taken me dancing before," she said, feeling a dark, forbidden thrill.

"You don't know how?"

That made her laugh. "I never said that, Hank Farrell. I was born knowing how to dance."

"Fine. Then you can teach me."

" 'Twould be a miracle if I could teach you a blessed thing."

Before she could stop him, he bent and kissed her lips. "You'd be surprised, Aislinn. Very surprised."

Chapter 9

THEY rode to the outskirts of the tiny village of Ventry, stopping at a pottery shop with an adjacent restaurant. Murals depicting Celtic myths adorned the walls in a riot of colorful whorls and shooting stars. A Ceili band played hard and fast, and Aislinn taught Hank to dance. Though he felt impossibly clumsy beside her, the rhythm, clapped out by spectators, seemed to fill him up completely.

It was nearing midsummer night, the longest day of the year, and the sun didn't disappear until nearly ten. Hank felt exhilarated and full of wonder. "It's been some day," he remarked to Aislinn, quenching his thirst with a pint of Guinness.

"Aye," she said softly, then turned away with a secretive smile teasing her lips. "That it has."

They lost their way getting back. The low beam of the bike's lamp wavered on the narrow track. They laughed at themselves when they reached Ventry proper, a few miles west of Dingle. Hank felt an inevitable tug, as if some force outside himself were drawing him along the road.

He watched Aislinn's narrow back as she steered the tandem. Each moment they were together seemed to shimmer with unspoken awareness.

A part of him was starting to open up—the part that had been aloof and patronizing when Granny had told her stories. "The greatest powers on earth and elsewhere be those ye cannot see," she used to tell him.

She told him again now, whispering in his ear with the voice of the wind.

"Stop here," he said to Aislinn.

Two long, narrow stones lay tumbled askew at the roadside. "The Gates of Glory," she said, getting off the bike. "They were built to honor Finn MacCool's victory."

"Over Daire Doon, the King of the World."

She looked at him over her shoulder and smiled. "You've been studying the guides."

Finn MacCool. Finn. Aislinn Finn. In the moonlight, the round-topped hills glistened with a peculiar iridescence. As if dusted with—

He stopped the thought. "That's right," he said. "I wonder if any of it really happened."

She gazed pointedly at the huge stones. "And why else would someone put up a monument such as this?"

A sense of inevitability closed around Hank. He took Aislinn by the shoulders, gazed at her shining eyes for a moment, and then kissed each one so that they were closed. The wind from the sea stirred his blood, and the ache of loneliness that had been part of Hank for so long grew suddenly sharp and needy.

He brushed his mouth over hers and then kissed her hungrily. She returned his embrace with wild abandon, clinging to him and pressing her body close.

Hank lifted his mouth from hers. "I know this will sound nuts, since we've only known each other for a day, but I have to say this."

"Then say it. You're the skeptic, not I."

"I want to make love to you, Aislinn."

"I know." Her eyes told him what her lips refused to admit. *I want it, too.*

"But you won't let me."

She turned away with a little cry of despair. "I can't."

"Damn it, Aislinn, how can you know that? I don't blame you if you want to wait—"

"It's not a matter of waiting." She held her back stiffly as if a high wind were blowing her. "There are things about me that you refuse to see, Hank. Things you can't possibly understand."

He walked to the edge of the cliff and looked out to sea. Again he felt the pull, the inevitability, tugging at him. It was deepest night, and out here in the coastal wilds, there was no light save the moon and stars, yet he saw the ocean clearly, the horizon a silver thread far off in the distance.

"Try me," he said without looking at her.

"Try what?"

"Tell me what it is you're afraid of. Me?"

"No."

"Men in general? Intimacy?"

"No, nothing like that. Hank—"

"Tell me, for Christ's sake, Aislinn." He spun around and glared at her in frustration. "Tell me before it's too late."

"Too late for what?"

"I don't know. I have no idea what I meant by that." He drew her next to him and settled his arm protectively around her shoulders. "We both know we're attracted to each other," he said. "Can you deny that?"

"No," she said simply.

"We're adults. We should be able to deal with this. Why are you so skittish? Why are you so convinced we shouldn't be together?"

"I tried to explain earlier. Weren't you listening?"

She couldn't be serious.

"You're saying you're a—a—" He felt silly even speaking it aloud, so he broke off.

She was silent, gazing out to sea.

Hank felt a queasy twist in his gut. This was beyond crazy. There was no such thing as changelings. Or magic. Or destiny.

But a small voice in his mind reminded him about the words he'd heard from Granny's ashes. The way he'd seemed fated to visit Carrygerry House. The car breaking down. The farm with the carved stone. There were too many strange things happening to be explained away as coincidence. Too damned many.

"Every darkling child in my family comes to a bad end, Hank. What else should I think?"

"You should think that you've got a mind of your own, damn it, and a heart of your own. There's no such thing as a curse. My grandmother used to tell me stories about changelings, but that's all they were. Stories."

"Then why did she make you bring her here?"

"Because she was Irish," he burst out. "You Irish are all crazy!"

She tossed her head and glared at the night water. "Believe what you will, but let me believe what *I* will. Do you think I don't have a heart? Do you think I don't want to be held and loved?"

"Then why—"

"Because it's forbidden. I can't love you, Hank. I can't love anyone."

He touched her beneath the chin and took a risk. "I think you already do, Aislinn. I think you already love me. And I already love you."

With a sharp cry, she wrenched herself away from him. "Don't you dare say that."

"Why not? It's true." And he knew it with such solid conviction that his heart took wing.

"We can't let it be true. It's a danger to us both. Ronan MacNab died the day Margaret Molloy left him. That's where love led him."

"No," said Hank with assurance. "She didn't leave him of her own accord." He saw it all as if it were a story unfolding before his eyes. Granny must have told him long ago. He didn't remember her telling him, but he could picture it. "They planned to run away together. To elope."

"She went to Texas and married a rancher. What, did she take a wrong turn somewhere?"

"Hell, I don't know." Hank felt angry for the long-dead Ronan and frustrated by the gaps in the story. "They weren't kept apart by some supernatural force. Maybe that old story about the curse scared them, just like it's scaring you. Maybe the MacNabs didn't want to lose Ronan the same way the Finns don't want to lose you—because you do all the work. So they filled your head with nonsense."

She caught her lip in her teeth. "What if they're right?"

"They can't be."

She faced him steadily. "Hank, you have to believe in the magic, or you'll never believe in me."

He almost scoffed at her, but stopped himself. She was deadly serious, almost vehement. Her eyes were silver mirrors of the moon. To Hank's eternal surprise, he *did* believe. He remembered the strange voice he'd heard on the hill earlier, remembered the feeling of being swept out of harm's way when the rock would have crushed him.

There was a power that dwelt in the depths of Aislinn's eyes, and he couldn't deny it.

But that power was jealously guarded by Aislinn herself. She was skittish; long ago she had talked herself out of doing anything more than dreaming.

"You have to take a risk," he said with a certainty that sprang from a strange, new place inside him.

"What sort of risk?" she asked.

"Come on." He helped her to her feet. "I'll show you."

"What if I don't want—"

"I'll show you anyway, Aislinn." He walked her to the bicycle. He got on the front so he could steer.

She seemed to know what he intended the moment they set out. "No," she said. "Hank, we can't—"

"We can. And if that damns both our souls to hell, then at least we'll burn together."

Chapter 10

THE high, butter-colored moon lit their way. He took her up the hill to the abandoned farm, the house and outbuildings dark hulks against the sky. As he approached the fallen stone monument, he could feel Aislinn's fear. It was palpable, like a rush of breath on his neck.

Anger rose in him—not at Aislinn, but at the people who had made her fearful, filled her head with nonsense about a family curse. He knew then that he could never let her go back to the life she endured at the bed & breakfast, where the wildness in her was reined and buckled by propriety. They were blind to her needs and her gifts. They tried to keep her blind as well.

He got off the bike and took her hand, leading her toward the hill.

She balked, digging in her heels. "Hank, don't do this." Her eyes were enormous in her small face; in the moonlight they glistened brightly with fear.

"Honey," he said with all the patience he could muster, "you told me I should believe in magic. Now I'm asking you to believe in me."

He could see her resistance melting. It started in her eyes; they softened as if they had filled with tears. She swayed toward him, fitting her body close to his and allowing him to lead her into the center of the hillock.

The moonlight surrounded them in a sparkling ring, keeping them safe and separate from the rest of the world, as if they were alone on an island for all eternity.

"Kiss me, Hank," Aislinn whispered, trembling against him.

He lowered his mouth to hers, brushing lightly, moving his head from side to side. She shivered against him and pressed upward, deepening the contact. A thrill shot through Hank; he had held women in his arms before, but it was never like this. He had never before had the feeling that his destiny hung upon a single kiss.

He opened his lips over hers, hungry, wanting to devour her fears and her sweetness and her promise all at once. His tongue explored her, pushing past the fullness of her lips and into her mouth in a deep, sliding motion that made her whimper in the back of her throat. He felt her hands glide along his back and across his shoulders; then her fingers delved into his hair and she held him there, close. He sensed no fear in her now, but hunger and surrender and a need that burned as high as his own.

"God, Aislinn," he murmured against her mouth. "Let me . . . please . . ." His voice trailed off, but his hands finished the work, parting her cardigan, moving it aside and slipping up under her blouse to find the warm, silken flesh beneath. Her full breasts filled his palms, and he bent to put his mouth there, reveling in the taste and texture of her. She threw back her head and cried out a Gaelic word, echoing the glory and wonder that surged through him. As he sank to his knees, he brought her with him so that they faced one another, the grass soft beneath them and the stars seeming to spin in the sky.

The shivery midsummer air passed over his skin as he tore off his shirt and spread it beneath them. Feeling pagan, almost savage, he disrobed her inch by inch, revealing her pale, smooth limbs and torso, kissing long, tender paths across her body, his mouth following the breeze on her skin.

Aislinn felt the cool wind and his warm mouth all at once, and she knew a power that was unlike any gift from the Otherworld. It was stronger, more enduring.

She was swept up in a wave of sensual abandonment. Never, not even in her most forbidden dreams, had she imagined feeling this way, as if she were part of the wind and the sea, governed by nature and impulse, free from all constraints.

Hank was gentle but insistent, yet he needn't be. Not anymore. She had left her resistance somewhere outside the charmed circle of moon-light. Now she was ready to give herself up to him, to the need that consumed her, to the inevitability of their love.

Low, ancient voices sang with the breeze as it glided in from the shore, tangling in her hair. Hank pressed her back upon the bed of soft summer grass. She closed her mind to the voices, for she knew what they were—the voices of a force too strong to be denied.

Except when she was in Hank's arms. Safe in his embrace, she could see only the beauty of possibility.

She clung to him; then in a frenzy of movement she helped him as he cast off his boots and his jeans. It all happened quickly, with a sense of urgency. She did not want to lose one precious instant together after all the long barren years she had endured before this moment.

"Take me," she heard herself say. "I want you—need you— to take me."

"Yes." The admission rasped from him as he stretched out beside her, pressing close, his hands sweeping sensually over her. "God, Aislinn, I want you so much it hurts. I want it to be good for you."

"Then hurry," she whispered. "Please . . ."

Here. Now. Her heart cried out to him in silence, and in silence he seemed to understand, for he parted her thighs and joined with her swiftly. There was no hesitation, no second thoughts, no regrets, no promises beyond the moment. She cried out with the sharp beauty of the sensation, and she wrapped herself around him, her entire being awash in pure love.

Aye, love it was, love such as she had only dreamed of before this day. She knew that what they were sharing was extraordinary, forbidden, inevitable. He brought her higher and higher, though she never left the ground; the earth was solid beneath her and the sky split apart with shooting stars as she climbed and then shattered like the great celestial mirror overhead, shattered and sprayed like diamonds flung against an endless field of black velvet, shattered and was made whole again, until she lay quiet and close to him.

Nothing moved and neither of them spoke for long, uncounted moments. Finally it was Hank, shifting slightly so that his shoulder couched her head and his lips touched her temple. "That was . . . the first time for you."

"It was the first time I ever had the courage of my desires," she said, still incredulous at what she had dared, what she had risked.

And what the rewards had been. "It was the first time I thought it worth the risk."

"Aislinn," he said, his voice a deep rumble in his chest. "I don't know what to say. I'm so sorry. What you've given me—"

"No!" She turned in his arms and pressed her fingers over his lips. " 'Tis what you have given me, Hank Farrell, and I'll not be taking credit for anything that happened tonight."

A grin played about his lips; she felt the movement beneath her fingers. He put aside her hand, chuckling. "Have it your way, then. But something happened and it wasn't all my doing."

She laughed with him, and mingling with their laughter was something else, a glittery sound that wasn't human, seeming to radiate from the hill itself. There was no threat in the sound, though, not as there had been in the oratory.

Aislinn felt brave and easy as she never had before. She and Hank put on their clothes, interrupting each other now and then with kisses. A shadow darkened the moon, and she pretended not to notice. Pretended not to care. It was not until they returned late to the B&B, letting themselves in with the key the owner had given them, that she finally allowed herself to look to the sky.

The moon rode low now, and as she watched, an ugly cloud shadow, like an ink stain, streaked across the orb of light. She clutched at the window frame, wanting to shield her eyes yet unable to look away.

"Ah, God," she whispered, "what have I done?"

Chapter 11

A T breakfast, Aislinn worked hard to discard her fears and accept that Hank had been right. They needn't deny their love. This didn't seem difficult at all for Hank. He ate with great gusto. Eggs and rashers, stacks of toasted bread, and sautéed mushrooms and tomatoes disappeared with remarkable speed. Even the owner of Mickle House was impressed, and hastened to keep Hank's coffee cup refilled.

He was such a typical man in this way that, for a moment, Aislinn truly believed they could love as other couples loved—in safety, with no doubts or shadows to creep over them.

But love itself was filled with doubts and shadows. Sometimes it was constructed of darkness entirely. Didn't she know that? And more, could she live with that?

He covered her hand with his. "You're awfully quiet, darlin'."

"I've a lot on my mind."

He set down his fork and regarded her steadily. "Regrets?"

"No." *Not yet.* She refused to admit that something lingered and festered at the back of her mind—something black and frightening. A reckoning was coming; of that she was sure.

"Come outside with me, Aislinn. I need to ask you a question."

They thanked Mrs. Mickle and walked down the front path of the house. The gentle rise of a hillock gave them a view of the distant road snaking around to Slea Head. It was a perfect summer morning, scented with wild flowers and the tang of the sea, the breeze rippling across the tall soft grasses like an invisible hand stroking its lover's hair.

In spite of the warmth of the sun, Aislinn shivered. "What is it?" she asked.

He took her by the shoulders and turned her so that they were facing one another. In the little tarn at the side of the yard she could see their reflections. He towered over her, so big and strapping and *American* that she felt small and utterly foreign beside him.

He caught her chin with a finger and held her gaze to his. "I've decided something."

"What?" She felt a need to brace herself, but there was nothing to lean on, nothing but him.

"I'm going to buy the farm. I'm going to buy *Ard-na-sidhe.*"

Her heart soared. True, the farm was her dream, but so was Hank. If she could never live there, at least she would know Hank was there.

"I want you to be with me. I want you to be part of it."

"I don't understand."

"You haven't let yourself do anything about your dreams. Neither have I until I came to this country. And it's time, Aislinn. It's past time."

"Hank, what are you saying?"

He took both her hands in his and lifted them, brushing his lips across the backs of them. "I'm saying I love you with all my heart, Aislinn. I'm asking you to marry me."

Her world exploded with sudden vivid color. It was like spring covering the ravages of winter all in a rush, in the blink of an eye, the grays turning to greens and blues so bright it made the eyes smart. She looked up into Hank's rugged face, and her heart took wing. It was all too much. Too much to think that overnight, her world could change.

She felt tears coursing down her cheeks but made no move to brush them aside. "Ah, Hank. Hank, I don't know what to say."

"A simple 'yes' will do."

"But there's so much to talk about, so much to consider, and we're still waiting to discover what—"

"Mr. Farrell!" Mrs. Mickle called from the stoop in front of the house.

Aislinn flushed with embarrassment and brushed surreptitiously at her cheeks.

"Of all the lousy timing," Hank muttered under his breath.

"It's the phone," Mrs. Mickle explained. "You can take it in the parlor."

Aislinn watched him go into the house. A bank of clouds closed like a plague of locusts over the morning sun, and the brilliant day was plunged into murky shadow.

Hank's tread was heavy as he left the house and stepped out to the front where Aislinn was waiting. Even with the sun tucked behind the clouds, she looked beautiful against the backdrop of green hills and rock fences with the long blue smile of the sea in the distance behind her.

She turned to him and waited.

In that moment he could believe she was magic. Her hair glistened with the blue-black sheen of a seal's fur. Her body was as slim and supple as the boughs of the willow tree growing at the verge of a pond. The sculpted beauty of her face was softened by the depths in her eyes, eyes that looked at him and shone with a love he felt like an arrow to his heart.

She would have consented to marry him just moments ago, but what he had learned from the parish priest was going to change everything. Hank knew this with a sick dread that dragged at each of his footsteps as he approached her.

He tried to think of a way to avoid telling her the truth. But he could no more lie to Aislinn than he could to himself. She had to be told. She had to know that all she had anticipated, all she had foretold, all she feared, turned out to be true.

"That was Father Carne," he said.

She jerked her gaze to his, and all traces of a smile disappeared from her pale face. "Did he find out anything about Ronan MacNab?"

"He did."

"And?"

"Aislinn, I want you to answer my question. I want you to say you'll marry me."

Her mouth drew taut and bitter. "That's not fair."

"If I have to cheat to have you, I will," he said starkly. "I don't think you understand what I mean when I say that I love you. I'm saying I want you now, forever, to be with me. I want you to share my life and my world for the rest of our days. And if you're going to let something an old man on the phone told me about a dead guy change that, then we have a serious problem here."

"Hank."

"What?"

"We have a serious problem here. I have to know."

He took a deep breath. He had to have faith that no matter what had happened in the past, their love would hold fast. They wouldn't let their future together be governed by something that had happened to a man years gone and an old lady's last wish.

"All right," he said. "According to Father Carne, we won't be able to bury Granny in the churchyard next to Ronan."

"Why not? Couldn't he find the marker?"

"Ronan is not buried there."

He watched her shoulders stiffen as if she were bracing herself for a blow. He longed to soothe her and reassure her, but he didn't dare touch her. She was like a bird that would take flight at the first alarm.

"Then where is he?" she asked.

Hank swallowed hard. His throat felt raw and dry with the unspoken news. "He's . . . his body was never recovered."

She turned her head sharply to the side as if he had struck her. "Tell me. A murder, then?"

"He took his own life." A sick feeling roared through Hank, a sensation of horror and despair and dizziness. Simply thinking about what Ronan had done gave Hank a taste of the hopelessness the young man had felt. "He took a dory out at Slea Head and climbed the tall rock called Croghan. And then he jumped into the sea."

Hank watched a tremble ripple through her. She made a terrible, soft sound in her throat and turned away from him. "Don't tell me the stories are all nonsense now, Hank Farrell," she said quietly. "I should have known better. Last night . . . was a mis—"

"Don't say it!" He grabbed her and spun her around, pressing her against him. "Don't say we made a mistake last night. It was meant to be, Aislinn. We were meant to be."

"No." She wrenched herself away from him. "I'll just go up and get my things. The car should be ready today."

Hank winced as a twist of pain snaked through him. He was losing her. Just when he had found her, he was losing her. "Aislinn—"

"What?" She stopped and turned, the breeze teasing wisps of inky hair around her face.

"You never answered my question."

An immeasurable sadness bathed her large eyes in unshed tears. "Aye, Hank, I did. You know I did."

He watched her walk into the house. At his side, his hand clenched into a fist. He had come to believe that he was in Ireland for a reason. And, damn it, it wasn't to get his heart broken.

Chapter 12

As it turned out, the car wouldn't be ready until afternoon. Aislinn and Hank spent the day together, yet avoiding each other. She could not seem to shake off the feeling that the discovery about Ronan MacNab was bound up in her own destiny. As she stood on the walkway beside Hank's suitcase while he spoke with the mechanic, she looked at the town through a blur of tears.

Had Margaret Molloy stood just here, watching women at their shopping and workmen ambling down to the docks? Had she felt the summer breeze on her face and tasted the tang of the sea on her tongue? Had she looked upon the man she loved with all her heart and felt such a wave of futility that she wanted to sink to her knees and scream at the sky?

Aislinn could believe it. The feelings that roiled through her like a fever had the feel of an ancient curse. Surely she was not the first to suffer it. To come so close to loving . . . and then to have the dream snatched away . . .

If she was strong enough, perhaps she could stand the pain when he left. Perhaps eventually she would forget this magical time with him, forget that she had come close to touching the very face of happiness.

Ah, her foolish thoughts. Of course she would never forget. For the rest of her days, she would take Hank's image with her wherever she went. He would be enshrined in her heart, her brash American lover, the one man who could force her mind to dream. To hope.

She shook back her hair and dusted the tears from her cheeks before any of the passers-by noticed. Hank came out of the garage, a quizzical and slightly suspicious expression on his face. "Did you say something?"

"No. Nothing." She didn't trust herself to speak. All the way from the B&B he had told her the things she had known he would say—that it was foolish to let her life be directed by an unconnected event in the past. That they could be happy together if only she would let go of her fears. That her insistence on staying with her family was cheating them both out of a future. That last night, they had made magic—real magic, not the kind told of in legends and fairy stories.

"You didn't say something just now," he said.

"No, Hank. I've been standing here, saying nothing. What is there to say?"

He did a curious thing then. He looked down at his suitcase. He bent and shook it a little. "Damn. I heard it again."

"Heard what?"

His ears reddened. "Nothing. I've got Granny on my mind."

She suspected he wasn't telling her everything, but she forced herself not to care. It hurt too much to care.

"We need to pay a visit to Maeve Morrigan," Hank said.

"Mrs. Morrigan from the registry?"

"Yep."

"Why, Hank?"

He was behaving so oddly. It was hard not to wonder what he was about.

"Old Maeve, is it?" asked the mechanic, wiping his greasy hands on a rag and calling through the open door of the garage. "Sure, and she still lives in the house with the blue door in Bay Street. Lived there for as long as anyone alive can remember. She must be a century old by some reckonings." He poured tea from a thermos into a tin cup. "She'd welcome company."

Maeve Morrigan came to the door herself. Her home was a tiny bungalow with limewashed walls and a bright tiled roof, flowers rioting in a long box beneath the front window and the smell of baking wafting from the kitchen.

Hank stood on the stoop, feeling awkward. He reached back to take Aislinn's hand, but she held herself away from him. Damn. He *was* losing her—to a past he couldn't control or even understand.

Yet here he stood facing a little old lady because his suitcase had sent him.

"Mrs. Morrigan?" he asked.

She cocked her head with a birdlike delicacy. "Why, 'tis the young folk from the registry. I thought you might come to see me." She poked her head out the door and peered at Aislinn.

"How do you do?" Aislinn said politely.

"Ma'am, I'm sorry to disturb you, but I was wondering." Damn. Where to start? And where the hell was he going with this? "I came to Ireland because of my late grandmother, Margaret Molloy."

Maeve's smile wavered. She looked from Hank to Aislinn and then back again. "You'd better come in and sit down," she said.

Despite the warmth of the summer day, she had a bit of peat burning in the grate. The sharp, coffeelike aroma tinged the air. Hank and Aislinn sat on a sofa with fading, flowered upholstery. "You knew her, then?" he asked.

"Oh, aye." Maeve sat down slowly and carefully. "It was all such a long time ago. Margaret and I were school friends."

"And Ronan MacNab. You remember him?"

A wistful sadness suffused her face. "Aye, Ronan as well."

Hank explained why he had come, and Maeve listened thoughtfully. "We just learned this morning that Ronan isn't buried in consecrated ground. He committed suicide."

"It's true, he did. Cursed, he was, and no mistake."

Beside him, Hank felt Aislinn stiffen. It had been a bad idea to come here. This old crone would only reinforce the nonsense about the curse.

"Why do you say he was cursed?" he made himself ask.

"Well, not in the sense you would think. There was some foolishness about him being a darkling child, different from the rest of the family and one of the *sidhe*."

"Foolishness?" Hank felt a little better now.

"Aye, for though that might have been true, it was no curse. The great curse on his life was his meddlesome family."

Aislinn leaned forward. "His family? But what about Margaret? Didn't she abandon him for the chance to marry a Texas rancher? Didn't she break his heart?"

"Ah." Maeve's voice snapped loudly in annoyance. "That is what was put about, but it's a lie. Margaret did nothing of the sort."

Realization came to Hank in a blaze of light and hope. "It was his family, wasn't it? They kept them apart and convinced Ronan that Margaret had left him?"

"That's right. It was all done quite neatly, with the cooperation of the seminary school. They told Ronan"—her voice broke, and she took off her spectacles to wipe her eyes—"that he couldn't father children."

A foul word came to mind, but Hank clenched his jaw to keep from uttering it.

"Aye, they reminded him of his recent case of mumps and said the fever had affected him. And so he refused to see Margaret, leaving word that he would enter the priesthood after all."

Aislinn touched Hank for the first time since their quarrel. She took his hand and squeezed hard.

"Margaret took ship for America. I remember well the day—Midsummer's Day, 1917. Eighty years ago to this date, it was."

"And Ronan?"

"That same night, he went out to Slea Head and cast himself into the sea." A sad smile touched Maeve's lips. "Good it is to see that Margaret made a life for herself in America. Alas, it was more than poor Ronan ever had." Maeve walked them to the door. Her last words were directed at Aislinn. "So you see, it was no dark magic that cursed the lovers, but human ambition and meddling. One would hope future generations would rise above such stuff and nonsense."

They went back to the garage to find that the car was ready. Hank gripped the steering wheel and stared straight ahead. "She's right, Aislinn, and you know it."

"She's an old lady. How do we know—"

He pounded the steering wheel with the heel of his hand. The violence of the gesture made her flinch.

"Because we know, damn it!" he snapped.

She fell silent, and he gunned the engine. The Sunny rattled over Dingle's ancient main street as an afternoon rain pelted the windshield and roof. Aislinn stared straight ahead, watching the road shrug off the town like a worn shawl. Meadows rose up, green pillows on either side of them, and to their left lay the rocky shore. The sea, kicked into a frenzy by the coming storm, exploded against the cliffs.

Hank drove fast, and Aislinn knew he was urged on by anger. Anger at her. Because he thought she refused to see reason.

The problem was, she understood too well what would happen if she gave in to her heart's desire.

She thought of Ronan MacNab, of his large dark eyes and solemn face in the yellowed photograph. Finally she dragged in a breath. "You're going to Slea Head, aren't you?"

"No reason to wait now that the car is working," he said.

"The weather's terrible. Maybe you should—"

"Maybe I should do what I came to do and then get the hell out of here."

Aislinn pressed her lips together. She had asked for this. Had asked for it to be over between them, quickly. She had no business taking offense now.

He pulled the car off the road to a car park strewn with loose gravel. The rain came down in slanting sheets, and the great Atlantic reared like a herd of wild horses. Waves leaped skyward and then impaled themselves on the jagged rock edges of the cliffs. In the distance, the emerald string of the Blasket Islands lay ghostlike, in a shroud of mist.

Hank got out of the car, lifted the hatchback, and fetched the urn from his case. A lump rose in Aislinn's throat. Ronan and Margaret had been torn apart in the cruelest of fashions. She had grown old still dreaming of him, right up to the end of her life, her yearning so strong that she had sent Hank on this quest.

Hank headed toward a row of light boats which lay like black beetles, upside down on the grass. This area was so remote and unpopulated that no one bothered to secure his boat. If someone borrowed a dory or curragh now and again, no one minded.

Grasping his purpose, Aislinn shot out of the car. "Hank," she called over the howling wind. "You can't go out in this."

He said nothing; he merely glanced at her over his shoulder and

shoved one of the curraghs down a slanting ramp toward the sea. Aislinn stood in the rain and watched in helpless desperation. He was furious now. He didn't seem to care about the danger. Didn't care that this
very spot was the most treacherous in the world.

She ran down the path after him. He had one foot in the boat, the
oars in his hand. "I'm coming with you," she called.

The wind snatched his response away so that she couldn't hear it, but
she knew from the set of his shoulders that he didn't want her to come.
Defiantly she stepped into the boiling surf, soaking her feet before she
was able to clamber into the curragh.

She watched his mouth form her name. Bracing her arms against a
rock, she pushed off. It was too late now. If he wanted her out of the
boat, he would have to start over entirely.

He was still shouting, and she caught a wisp of sound: ". . . danged
stubborn woman . . ."

In spite of herself, she smiled. He looked incredibly appealing as he
rowed with all his might, the waves rising at his back and snarling toward him, his hair plastered to his brow and small rivers running down
his face and arms. In that moment she knew he was touched by magic,
not the sort she was familiar with but something different, something
human yet just as powerful as the sorcery of any immortal. Hank Farrell possessed a strength of heart and a depth of commitment such as
she had never seen in a man.

He would move heaven and earth to grant his grandmother's last request. And she knew he was that way in all things—he protected the
ones he loved, no matter the cost to himself.

"I love you," she called to him in a sudden shout of joy. "I love you,
Hank Farrell!"

Without ceasing the rowing motion, he lifted his shoulders in a shrug
that told her he had not heard. She pressed a wet hand to her mouth
and blew him a kiss.

For the first time since the phone call that morning, Hank smiled at
her. Her hopes rose on a surge of gladness. This could work. They could
be together. Curse or no curse, their love was strong enough to prevail.

It had to be. She knew it with a certainty that took her breath away.

A small, traitorous voice in the back of her mind hinted that Ronan,
too, had once felt that same certainty.

She pushed aside the doubts and held the sides of the boat as it bucked over the churning waves toward the rock called Croghan. The storm had worsened. Whirlpools drilled the surface of the water. Founts of salty spume shot up like geysers. It was the height of foolishness to be out on the water, yet here they were, and she felt no fear. She trusted Hank's quiet strength implicitly.

The light boat labored up one side of a swell only to plunge with sickening speed down the other. Horror warred with exhilaration in Aislinn's chest, and by the time the bow of the curragh nudged the rocks at the base of Croghan, she was ready for a respite.

Hank moored the boat to a rock, using a length of stout rope. He gestured at Aislinn to stay put, and this time she had no thought of defying him. She was only too happy to stay in the boat while he strewed the ashes around the base of the rock.

But Hank, it seemed, had other ideas. He draped the bag with the urn over his shoulder and across his torso, and started to climb.

"No!" Aislinn screamed, watching him scale the sheer rock face.

But he didn't hear, or if he did, he ignored her.

With her heart in her throat, she forced herself to watch him. The wind blew the rain in great, slanting sheets, plucking cruelly at Hank as he climbed the slick black face of the huge rock. He reached with one hand and then the other, and each time he gained a purchase, she held her breath a little longer, a little tighter.

When he was perhaps twenty feet from the summit, he slipped.

Aislinn shot to her feet, setting the boat to rocking drunkenly. An unholy scream issued from her. Hank dangled, holding on with his hands while his feet scrambled. She wanted to look away. She didn't want to see him fall to the rocks below. But she made herself watch.

Temptation stabbed at her. She could use her powers to help him, just as she had when the Stone of Lusmore would have crushed him. It had nearly drained her to save him, but she would do it again. She would risk anything for Hank. Doing so would mean giving up who and what she was. But she didn't care. All that mattered was Hank—his safety, his well-being.

She spread her arms wide and prepared to hurl the nameless force inside her to the heavens.

Before the first sound was out of her mouth, Hank's foot caught, and he was climbing again.

Shuddering with relief, she sat down again and tilted her face skyward to watch. Rain pelted her, but she didn't care. This was a sacred moment for Hank. He was about to release his grandmother's spirit to the place it had longed to be for eighty years. She knew that in a way, Hank's own spirit was bound up in this act, in this moment.

He set down the urn and pried off the lid.

At the same moment, a furious gust of wind whipped toward the summit of Croghan.

Aislinn saw the wind in the distance, and it seemed possessed of a dark energy, like the banshees roiling in to snatch a wayward soul. She was possessed of something, too, possessed of a pure, shining love that was worth any risk.

But as she watched the terrible wind bearing down on Hank, she had never felt so helpless in her life.

Exhausted from his climb, Hank felt his hands shake as he pried off the lid of the urn. "I hope," he said, panting, "you're satisfied."

Though the words were spoken wryly, he let his heart fill up with love and grief. He made himself look down at the gritty powder of her mortal remains. "I love you, Gran," he said, his throat raw. He knew he had to let go, yet he hugged the urn to his chest. "God, I miss you so much."

It was time. She had waited long enough to join with her Ronan. And if it couldn't happen in this world, he would make it happen in the next. He had to believe that by doing this, he would let them be together for all eternity. If this didn't work, then nothing made sense.

Instinctively, he recognized a change in the atmosphere. The sky grew darker. The wind howled with an ominous rhythm like a steam engine. But he shut it out and applied himself to the task at hand.

" 'Bye, Gran," he whispered, lifting the urn high, tipping it to shake out the ashes, the soul of her, the essence of the love and spirit that had once been Margaret Molloy. Somewhere, out there, Ronan was waiting with open arms. Waiting to take her hand and lead her into a golden eternity.

A wind whisper swirled around him, forming words that seared themselves to his heart forever.

Thank you.

A man's voice, not his grandmother's.

Hank knew in that instant that he had done the right thing. And he also knew that Aislinn had known the truth after all. There were forces of magic at work here, things he could not even pretend to understand. And now that he accepted the magic, he could accept who and what Aislinn was. He couldn't wait to tell her.

Just then the wind gust caught him. The urn was snatched from his grip. In the next instant, Hank was falling. Falling toward the black and jagged rock base of Croghan.

Aislinn released every shred of power she possessed, but it wasn't enough. He fell like a helpless ragdoll, plunging toward the lethal rocks.

The ancient magic slammed through her, and it hurt more than she could have imagined, as if she had been hit by a lorry.

And then she felt the change. Something inside her lightened. She could feel the power leave her like a bird freed from a cave, flying ever upward. As she watched in speechless wonder, the puff of ashes Hank had released from the urn formed a cloud of sparkling dust.

The flashing cloud swirled in the furious wind, gusting beneath Hank's free-falling body and wrapping like a translucent net around him, bearing him gently downward.

Aislinn knew in her heart that this wasn't sea smoke whipped up by the wild wind, but the spirit of Margaret Molloy answering Aislinn's plea. The old woman's soul, joyful in a shining new world, had joined with a young woman's. Margaret's spirit had risen up to perform a last act of love for the grandson who had shown her such care and faith.

He settled safely on the ground, with only the slightest of jolts, and the sparkling dust dispersed on the wind and the rain. He stood for a moment, swaying and looking dazed. Then he was running forward, stumbling over the uneven rocks. Aislinn leaped out of the boat to join him. She sobbed, clinging to him in thankful relief. He covered her face with kisses.

"What happened," he said, "God . . . I'll never understand. But all I could think about was that you were right about the magic. You were right all along, and I should have believed. I love you, Aislinn."

"I love you, Hank. Ah, I do." He tasted of the sea and the salt of her own tears as she spoke from the heart. "There is no life for me without you."

"Then I think," he said, moving his warm mouth over his, "that it's high time you answered the question I asked you this morning."

"I have an answer for you now," she said. "It's yes. Yes, yes, and a hundred thousand yeses."

Their hearts beat as one. They both felt it. Both knew the rightness of it. With a whoop of gladness he picked her up and swirled her around. The wind howled louder still, but deep within the torrents of sound the lovers heard something else, something they sensed with their hearts rather than their ears—the ringing joy of a woman's laughter.

Afterword

As far as anyone knows, the real Carrygerry House at Newmarket on-Fergus is not inhabited by fairies or changelings. In fact, it's the loveliest place to stay in the vicinity of Shannon Airport, and is as charming as it appears in this story. If you go there, you'll learn what every visitor to Ireland is bound to discover—magic is what you make it.

EARTHLY
MAGIC

Barbara Samuel

 Chapter 1

THE CALL

Is there no help at all for me,
But only ceaseless sigh and tear:
Why did not he who left me here,
With stolen hope steal memory?

I'll go away to Sleamish hill,
I'll pluck the fairy hawthorn-tree,
And let the spirits work their will;
I care not for good or ill,
So they but lay the memory
Which all my heart is haunting still!

—Samuel Ferguson
The Fairy Well of Lagnany

A MISERY of alternating sleet and drizzle fell from the predawn sky. Laith of Inishmoor, wandering bard, cursed the darkness and the wet. All night he'd walked through the forest, fearing if he stopped for even a moment, he'd freeze.

Now his worn cloak was sodden, and the rain had made of the ground a cold muddy muck that seeped through the seams of his shoes. He comforted himself by imagining hot soup and spiced cider in a kindly village or rath.

The forest seemed to whisper about him. Laith remembered there was fairy hill nearby, where once the sidh had made their homes. A clasp of gooseflesh crawled on his back, and he smiled at his own foolishness.

A new god had come to Eire, washing away the magic and rituals that had been upon the land for as long as any could remember. Memories of the Other-world and the old ways grew dim, and all forgot the respect a bard of his standing would once have commanded.

In the old times, Laith of Inishmoor would have been revered and feasted, and he would have wandered the land on a horse with ribbons braided into its mane and bells hung round its neck. Upon its back like a prince would Laith have ridden, his cloak a splendor of seven colors, a torque of red-gold around his neck.

But the new god had swept magic from the land, putting in its place empty rituals, and Laith of Inishmoor, descended of the great bards of Eire, was only a poor wandering minstrel with a thin cloak and worn shoes and an empty belly.

The forest thinned and he came to a wide grove cut through by a slim silver stream. Pausing on the edge of the field, he peered across, hoping for some sign of the village he knew to be nearby, or even a woodcutter's cottage where he might be allowed to warm his feet for an hour or a day.

Only the faintest lightening of the heavy clouds hinted that dawn soon would end this long night's misery. His toes were blessedly numb, but the muscles of his limbs felt stiff with the cold. And he was hungry. In his pouch he carried half a loaf of a kindly goodwife's bread, but a little butter might not go amiss.

But no smoke scented the air, no friendly cow grazed. No hut perched cheerily at the other side of the clearing. Wearily, he sighed. Surely he could not be far now. Clutching his cloak more tightly around him, he lowered his head against the drizzle and moved forward.

So deep was his misery that it took long moments for him to realize his feet followed a track of freshly flattened grass. He raised his head. The tracks ran in an arch toward a small rise topped by trees.

Enlivened by the promise of shelter, he hurried along the tracks, eager to find the soul afoot this gloomy morn.

He saw the cloak first—a blaze of scarlet nearly painfully bright against dim gray, then a spill of loose dark hair. A woman. He slowed, afraid he might frighten her away if he called out to her. 'Twas a time of battles and rogue soldiers, and a woman alone would be rightfully wary.

She stood unmoving in the stillness. At her feet, a spring bubbled up between the roots of an ancient hawthorn tree. Laith moved closer, struck by her slim brightness against the dark day.

There was an air of defeat about the set of her shoulders, a weariness Laith knew only too well. With his bard's mind, he pondered what had led her to this cold place before dawn, what grief she carried. Perhaps her lover had spurned her, and once they had been happy in this place. Even as he thought it, she reached out with one white hand and touched the bark of the tree—but out of memory or a need for strength, he could not tell.

Feeling an intruder, he half hid himself behind a tree. As he watched through a crotch of branches, the woman straightened suddenly. With a swift gesture, she unfastened the heavy brooch at her shoulder and flung aside her scarlet cloak. Beneath she wore only a thin kirtle that lay lightly upon a gracefully curved collarbone, and Laith saw her shiver in the cold. Protectively, she pulled her knee-length hair around her.

Then—oh, then!—she reached for the ties at the neck of her shift, and tugged them free. The kirtle fell from her shoulders and caught at her waist, leaving her torso bare to the cold drizzle, and to Laith's astonished and grateful eyes. She had very beautiful breasts, high and white and crowned with deep rose.

A hundred times, a thousand, Laith had sung of speared hearts. Until this moment, he had not known the truth of the words. She looked like a pagan or a priestess with her sober white cheeks, the sorrow around her lips. It near wounded him to look upon her. He could not even find the breath to call out to her.

She knelt at the small pool at the base of the tree and dipped her cupped hands into the water, then washed her breasts, letting the water cascade over the smooth white flesh. In the stillness, he heard her gasp. Slowly, she repeated the ritual.

Without breath or heartbeat, Laith watched her, afraid to make even the smallest sound lest she cease her bewitching ceremony. Had he known anything of beauty till this moment? It was etched in the angle of her dark eyes, the small chin, in the fine bones of her shoulders and slim arms.

Nor had he known desire. The sword in his heart was joined by a sword of an entirely different sort as he watched the path of her hands, dipping first into the water, across the small open space, over the bare and glistening flesh.

The ritual tugged his memory—three times washing her breasts. He frowned, thinking. In a rush it came to him: 'twas said to be a way to open the door to the world of the faerie, who might then be coaxed to grant some wish.

A bittersweet pang twisted in Laith. He wished that so fair a creature could bring forth one of the lost folk.

But no more did fairies dwell in the deep forests of this land. The priests had chased them out of reach, where they had withered from lack of faith. Plainly, the woman at the well believed.

Laith resolved that *he* would grant her wish when the fairies did not come. Perhaps she would even mistake him for one of their number.

When she had anointed her breasts three times, she rose, tugging her kirtle to her shoulders once more. Fabric stuck to her damp skin, and her hair moved around her as if it had a life of its own. Once around the well she went, disappearing into the shadows behind the tree, emerging on the other side.

As she completed her circle, Laith thought he saw a shimmer at the edge of the well, a shifting of light. He stared at the place, remembering the hill deep in the forest that was said to house the sidh. A taut excitement grew in his belly.

But as she began to circle a second time, a quiver of unease mixed with the wonder, and he found himself moving cautiously from his hiding place, his intent gaze upon the changing light that was now undeniable. From the gloom emerged a silvery shape that grew brighter as the woman disappeared behind the tree. As she emerged again from the shadows, Laith saw the light take on shape and form.

Another man, confronted with so magical a sight, might have been stricken to frozen wonder. Pure instinct, primed by a dozen generations of bards in his blood, drove Laith forward before he knew he would even move.

"No!" he cried, his voice a violence against the quiet. "My lady, no!"

He rushed toward her, his heart slamming against his ribs in terror as the silver coalesced nearby the well, taking the firm solid form of a man.

The woman did not hear him. With a cry, Laith leapt across the spring, grasped her by the waist with no gentleness, and flung her to the ground before the third circle was complete.

She cried out as she struck the earth. Laith landed atop her and heard the air rush from her lungs. His elbow stuck a rock and he, too, grunted in pain.

But those sounds were blotted out by an unholy roar of frustration. Laith clapped his hands over his ears, terrified.

It did not shut out the voice. "Bard!" it said, a voice within Laith's mind, or without, he could not tell. It made his blood cold. Beneath him, the woman beat at him with her fists, sobbing. For one brief moment, he stared down at her face, and was moved once more. He put his hands on her smooth cheeks. "My lady, the danger was mortal, I vow it."

Eyes the color of the forest floor, green and brown and gold, filled with misery. "You do not understand."

He wished to linger, to put his thumb against the swell of that wine red mouth and smooth away the sadness. A tear fell over her cheek. He wiped it away.

"Laith of Inishmoor, I vow you'll rue this day!"

Laith bolted up at the fearsome sound of that voice, and he whirled to face the being on the other side of the spring.

And being it was, for he could never be mistaken for anything mortal—though it was a man in form, as tall and broad and sturdy as any warrior. A cloak woven of silver and gold hung from wide shoulders, and a girdle of precious stones belted a tunic of some shimmering fabric.

Laith almost could not look upon the creature. He raised a hand, blinking. Palest gold hair fell around a face of unholy beauty, and the eyes were the color of moonlight.

Purest wonder filled him for a moment. Wonder that such marvels still walked this land, that Laith should be so blessed as to see him with his own eyes.

But the wonder was submerged by the fury in the Other's eye. Laith inclined his head and raised a brow. "How is it that you know my name, Prince, and I have none to call you?"

An ironic smile graced the prince's face. "Call me Finn, for surely you know no mortal can speak a fairy's name."

Finn, for fair. "Ah," Laith returned as ironically. "So 'tis true."

"Aye, that and more."

"Well, it seems, my prince, that I have won here today. You'll have to seek another beauty to carry away to your unholy world."

The silvery eyes glittered with cold. "You have robbed me, Laith of Inishmoor. I've awaited Ciarann of Connaught since her birth."

Behind Laith, Ciarann made a sound—halfway between wonder and terror. She would have pushed by him, but Laith caught her arm in a fierce grip. "Wait, my lady. I beg you! You do not understand all."

She shoved at him, her enormous eyes fixed with desperation upon the fairy. " 'Tis you, minstrel, who do not understand."

The prince made to reach for her, but he could not penetrate the veil between the realms. He clenched his fists, then stepped back and lifted his chin. "You have won today, bard," he said. "But in the end, I will have her. With one kiss, she will be mine."

"No!" Laith pushed her behind him. She struck his ear, and the blow stung against his cold flesh. "You'll not take her, for I have what you do not—mortal power to walk the earth at my will, to stand with her here while you are trapped there."

"Ah, beware, my friend. On the fires of Sahmain, and Beltane, and Midsummer, I am free to wander your world. Beware, for I will claim my kiss, and my lady." His voice rang with terrifying beauty into the cold dawn. "And today, for what you have done, I curse you."

A brittle smile turned his mouth. Laith held the woman firm, but fear struck through him. Now he would pay the price of his lust and impulsiveness.

"Without your voice, you cannot sing, and without your songs, you are nothing," the prince said. "I curse you to a year and a day without your voice, Laith of Inishmoor."

And he was gone. Once more the glade was still with a gray drizzle, and very cold, and Laith's feet were wet in his shoes. He turned to the woman, whom he saw now was barely more than a girl.

She stared at him, her eyes pools of welling sorrow. "What have you done?" she whispered.

He opened his mouth to explain, but nothing emerged. He tried to whisper but his tongue seemed to have forgot the shape of words.

"Oh, God!" she cried. " 'Tis true! He cursed you!"

Chapter 2

CIARANN stared at the man in horror, then covered her own mouth as if in sympathy. "What have I done?" she breathed.

The bard seemed not to understand yet. His mouth opened again and no sound came, not a gasp or whisper, or faint sound of protest. Something terrible blazed over the vivid blue of his eyes then, and he clamped his mouth closed.

He yanked away from her and sank to a rock by the pool, bending his head to his hands. He was only a poor minstrel, his cloak worn and thin, his feet bound in rags. She sank next to him and put a hand on his knee. "You were trying to protect me?"

He lifted his head and she saw misery there. His face was narrow and comely, with a cleanness of features she expected women liked very much. His mouth was wide cut with deeply colored lips, and Ciarann found her gaze lingering, caught by the promise in such a mouth. Women liked that, too, no doubt.

In answer to her question, he nodded, looking toward the well helplessly.

Ciarann bowed her head. "I did not know 'twould really call the sidh." She stood, her hands clutched before her. "I looked only to cure my grief."

He raised his brows.

The darkness of her sorrow rolled back into her breast, all the more searing for the respite she'd had. "I was to be married at Christmastide, but my love died in battle two weeks past." An image of Colin's face—bold and bright and laughing—pushed into her vision, and she gasped at the fresh wound, putting her hands over her eyes. "A peasant told me the ritual at the well would cure my grief."

The bard rose and Ciarann felt his urgency as he took her arms in his hands and gripped them tightly. He shook his head fiercely, frowning.

"You think he is dangerous?"

He nodded, and took a breath, opening his mouth as if to speak, then closing it again. Casting his eyes heavenward in an expression of frustration, he sighed hard. Then he did a most extraordinary thing: he touched her face with his long, graceful fingers, tracing a line from temple to jaw.

And closed his eyes. His lashes were black as his hair, and fell childlike over his cheekbones. Ciarann was suddenly dizzy, thinking how beautiful the pair of them—fairy and bard—had been, standing face to face in the falling snow. One gilded, shining, as golden as morning, the other dark and fierce as a moonless sky.

The bard looked at her slowly, at her eyes, then her lips for a long time, and lower still, to her breasts. His hands moved on her arms, softly. He pulled his lower lip against his teeth, then let it go.

Ciarann felt a strange warmth move through her. She thought of herself bared to the still forest. "Did you see me bathing?"

There was sultriness in his slow smile, in the glitter that bloomed in his eyes—and Ciarann saw the well-practiced knowledge of a man who had his way with women.

She scowled and shoved him away. "Knave!"

One dark brow lifted unapologetically. With a smooth gesture, he retrieved her cloak from the ground and held it out to her.

Ciarann realized her shift was yet damp and the thin covering hid little. She tossed the red wool around her, flushing. The brooch was gone and she kicked at the ground, looking for it.

The bard found it first, and held it out to her. She snatched it and pinned her cloak. "Laith of Inishmoor, is it?"

He bowed mockingly.

"A bard with no voice will starve. Come." Imperiously, she whirled and began to make her way back toward her father's house. She'd gone several yards when she realized she heard no sound behind her, and turned to see where he was.

He had not moved. Patches of color burned on his cheeks, making his eyes seem made of sapphire. The rich mouth was set in a thin line, and she saw by the cock of his chin that his pride was ill-pleased.

"Oh, come!" she cried with annoyance. "Do not make me beg and plead. 'Twas my act that saw you cursed. Will you not let me see you fed for your trouble?"

He turned his face away and did not move. Wind lifted his glossy hair, and an edge of the thin mantle, and she thought of his hands on either side of her face. Taking her skirts in her hands, she walked back to him.

She took his big hand in her own. "Please, my lord bard, will you come to my humble house and stay until my father returns from his business?"

His mouth quirked into a half-smile, and his fingers tightened around her own. Ciarann led him from the grove.

As night fell, Laith found himself settled in a fine corner of a very fine rath, with a boy to run his errands, and a brazier full of coals to warm him, and a stomach so full of bread and hearty stew he could scarce take a breath. Half drunk with warmth and relief, not to mention the honey-eyed ale he'd consumed by the tankard, he fell on his pallet. Through the heavy woven curtain that separated his alcove from the hall, he heard the clumsy plucking of a harper, and a reedy, wavering voice. He closed his eyes. The soldiers were so drunk none would care how harsh the music was.

When Laith and Ciarann returned to the rath this morning, they'd slipped in amidst a victorious band of soldiers who'd trounced the king's enemy to the south. It was only then Laith had understood Ciarann's father was king here, and engaged in a vicious battle with another petty king. He'd sent these warriors home to rest a night or two.

A king's daughter! In his pallet, listening to the warriors take up a bawdy song in boisterous voices, Laith shivered, and allowed the first fingers of despair to seep through him.

Ciarann was blithely unaware of the consequences of her act this day. She thought the prince beautiful, an immortal man who would never die and leave her grieving, a man who could grant her a world of eternal and unchanging beauty. She did not understand what Laith knew to be true: from this day forward, he and the fairy were locked in a fearsome battle for Ciarann's very soul.

One kiss, the fairy said. Finn had only to kiss Ciarann in order to steal her away to his world.

One kiss.

A swell of need rose in Laith's limbs. For one kiss of that mouth, he would gladly forego comfort the rest of his life. For the pleasure of kissing her beautiful breasts, he'd trade the use of his voice forever more.

Groaning, he covered his face. Smitten on sight with a king's daughter! What a fool he was.

Without his voice, he could not win her. For all that he came from the noblest bards in all of Ireland he was only a poor wandering minstrel without a single coin to offer her. The fairy had struck cleanly to the truth of all Laith was—without pretty words and his voice, he had nothing.

"Master," said the boy he'd been given, "would ye like a candle lit?"

Laith touched the boy's shoulder and nodded his thanks.

The lad scurried from his place in the corner. The tallow spluttered, then burned in fair enough light. The boy poured a cup of ale from a pitcher and put it in Laith's hand.

Laith drank deeply, hoping to halt the spinning chatter of his thoughts. The fairy prince could take Ciarann with one kiss. How could Laith forestall such a simple act?

If the prince could win with a kiss, what then would give Laith victory? There was always a fairness to these things, at least according to the tales he sung. If victory were possible for the fairy, it was possible for Laith as well.

Could it be so simple as winning a kiss himself? He frowned at the spluttering candle. It seemed too simple a task, since Laith had the advantage of daily contact with her.

But perhaps he should begin there. In two weeks would the fires of Sahmain burn and the fairy reappear. Laith thought surely he could win so simple a thing as a willing kiss in two weeks, even without his voice. Women liked him. Surely even the highborn Ciarann would not be totally immune to his persuasions.

Chapter 3

"You needn't be so ill-tempered," Ciarann said. " 'Tis many months till the curse is finished."

Laith glared at her, resenting her cheerfulness this gloomy Sahmain Eve. It was not called Sahmain any longer, of course, but the people were slow to give up their ancient feasts, and Laith knew in all but name it was still Sahmain.

In the cold gray morning, Ciarann wore a kirtle of green, woven at the edges with gold and silver thread. The color snagged emerald hues in her forest-colored eyes. A flush high on her cheeks belied the excitement she tried to hide.

Tonight the prince would come for her.

Laith shifted sullenly, all too aware of his dull tunic. He'd made no progress on so much as stealing a kiss, much less gaining one willingly offered. She did not begrudge his presence, and unlike many of the others of the household, did not treat him as if his lack of speech made him a simpleton. As if to make up for her part in his silence, she spent some time each day with him, playing games of chance.

But all the while, she was annoyingly oblivious to his most practiced smiles, his most wicked glances. She seemed not to notice him as a man at all.

So much for the kiss. If Laith possessed the wits of a sparrow, he thought darkly, he'd let the sidh plant his kiss, and be done with the mess. If the fairy won his mortal bride, surely the curse on Laith would also end. He was most heartily weary of muteness.

Plucking his harp restlessly, Laith glared at Ciarann, laughing now with her woman, Megan, their heads bent together in some shared secret. He did not know why he'd thought her such a prize to begin with. Beautiful she was, but he'd known many more beautiful women, and they'd not patronized him like an invalid uncle.

His fingers plucked a harsh discord. Ciarann and her woman looked up in surprise from the tender little sweets they were making of honey and nuts for tonight's feast.

Abruptly, he stood and patted angrily at his clothes. He wanted a fine tunic and a mantle. If she saw him as he truly was, a man who'd pleased more than his share of willing women, he'd wager she'd not so disdain him.

In her face he saw her chagrin. "You wish to have clothes for the feast." It was not a question. "I should have thought . . . I'm sorry." She put aside the nuts. "Come."

Next to her, Megan gave Laith a strange, measuring look. She halted her mistress with a hand to her elbow. "Let me, my lady."

"But I need to look—"

"Nay. I'll find the handsome lad something befitting his noble form." She winked, eyeing him boldly from head to toe.

Laith gave the plump matron his best smile. At least some female could see past his poor cloak and silence. He cut his glance to Ciarann, but she only gave him the vague, benevolent smile of a queen to her minions. Laith knew he was forgotten before they ever left the room.

In the passage, Megan took his arm. "Don't mind milady, young bard."

He scowled.

"Oh, I know. I see well enough, though she don't say, what she's dreaming of." She led him to a small chamber behind the hearth. "Sit."

She pawed through a trunk full of clothes that smelled of sweet herbs. One after the other, she held up tunics and mantles, examined them and tossed them aside. "You know what ails her as well as I do— she's fairy cursed. It has been many years since I witnessed it, but ye don't forget the look of it."

Grimly, Laith nodded. Megan pulled out a finely woven linen tunic of deepest blue, and he held out his hand.

"Ah, you like tha' one?" She held it up to his chest. "Not quite. There was one in particular I was thinking of here." She disappeared into the bowels of the trunk. "Here 'tis!"

She drew out a woolen tunic woven of the same scarlet wool as made Ciarann's mantle. A deep embroidered border edged the hem and sleeves. "See what you think of that. 'Twas made by Ciarann's own mother, for her brother."

Laith fingered the fine cloth. Soft as down it was, and he could not help rubbing his palm over it. To please Megan, he held it up to his chest and lifted a brow.

She clapped her hands before her ample bosom. "Aye, that's the one." From the pile on the floor, she took a striped mantle and leather boots, and from the trunk brought out a girdle woven of copper and yellow and white golds.

"She'll not overlook you tonight, I warrant." Megan winked. "I'll send water for you to be bathed, and oiled—methinks there's a girl or two hereabouts who won't mind *that* chore."

Impulsively, he grabbed her in a quick, fierce hug and planted a kiss to her ruddy, aging cheek. She sobered and patted his cheek. "The girl's been my charge for more years than I have teeth. Save her, boy, for me."

He put his hand on his heart in solemn promise. All he could do was try.

Ciarann could not sit for even a moment, nor eat even a morsel of the feast spread over the tables in the hall. The noise of merrymakers and music and dancing seemed overly loud as she prowled the hall and the yard, looking, looking. She felt fevered and overwrought.

All week, her dreams had been filled with visions of the world beyond the silvery veil at the fairy well, and she knew they were not dreams at all, but true glimpses of that place where none ever grew old or infirm, or died.

The morning when she had gone to perform the ritual at the spring, she had only wanted respite from her grief. She had not dreamed there were still living beings in the Other-world, that it would be a shimmering, golden being who could cure her sorrow. One glimpse of his beauty had been enough to bring her senses back to life, and she longed to see him again.

In her dreams of the Other-world, he had been frustratingly elusive. She sensed him, almost as if he were part of the mist or the air or the leaves moving on the breeze, but each time she thought he would be beyond the next tree, or the bend in the water, there was no one there.

But tonight, with the fires of Sahmain lit against the night, he would come. And when he did, she would willingly kiss him, and he would take her to his gilded world.

That world where there was no sorrow.

She'd had her fill of sorrows these past years. Her father and his rival had between them slain a hundred warriors, disfigured dozens more. Like young Owen, who hid in the deepest shadows even on this feast day. He'd taken a sword cut to the face and the wound had festered, and now small children ran in terror from his twisted, monstrous visage. Seeing him alone in the shadows, Ciarann paused at the banquet tables and poured him a tankard of honeyed ale. "Drink up," she said with a wink.

Gratefully, he bowed his head, taking care to keep his hair over the marred half of his face. It pained her—and she touched his smooth cheek impulsively. "You needn't be anyone but yourself with me, good Owen."

"Would the world were so kindly, milady."

"Come dance," she said, tugging his hand.

He shrank closer into the shadows, and Ciarann let him be. For some of the wounded and widowed and fatherless, she could do nothing, but surely there was some woman who'd be glad of a strong virile man in her bed. She'd think on it.

She stepped out to the yard, and as had happened so often, her sleeping grief awakened like a kicked dog, snarling and biting, tearing at her soul.

Colin!

The festive scene melted away, and a sharp clear picture of him rose in her memory. Colin, with his big red head and bluff laughter and warm, strong arms, had been her sweetheart since earliest childhood. And like so many others, he'd been lost in another of the endless battles.

A messenger had brought the news, and hearing it, Ciarann had crumpled where she stood. For weeks, she'd been unable to lift her head for grief. Thinking of all her years stretching, bleak and dull before her, without the sound of Colin's laughter, she had not wished to live.

And her father, knowing how wounded she would be, and how angry with him, had still not returned home to face her.

It had been a village girl who crept into Ciarann's chamber and whispered the promise of forgetfulness the ritual at the well promised. Ciarann had not believed it would call the prince.

Or had she? When she saw him at the well, his face had been elusively familiar. She thought now she must have glimpsed him at the odd feast or fair.

Even the thought of him now eased a little of her grief, and she paced the yard and hall in her green and silver and gold, hoping it would please him.

At last—at last!—came the sound of a distant horn, and through the open gates rode a party of great splendor. Ciarann stared, and looked to see if the others gaped as she did. But no one seemed to take notice. For a faint, worrisome moment, she felt uneasy that they were enchanted—magic was afoot here!

But then she looked back at the troop of fairies, and wonder seized her. They rode white horses with braided manes, horses of uncommon grace and light-footedness. Their saddles were made of gold and silver. Jeweled collars flashed sparks of color into the dimness.

And the people! Silvery and young and gloriously beautiful they were. A lady in a silken tunic the color of a twilight sky, with golden hair to her feet, rode at the front. Her face was cool and beautiful. There were others, all women who would make the strongest man fall to temptation, but the lady was obviously their queen.

The men were their equals, as splendid as sunrise, and amid them, Ciarann at last spied her prince. Tonight he wore a silk tunic the color of moss. His silver-blond hair spilled over his broad shoulders, and his cloak was cast back, fluttering behind him as he rode nobly into the yard. He had not seen her, and she took a moment to absorb the stunning, vivid reality of him.

At the wonder of it, she laughed.

He dismounted and gave the reins of his steed to a boy waiting nearby. Ciarann folded her hands, her eyes fixed hungrily upon him.

But between them came another figure, tall and lean and graceful as the prince, and even more vividly colored. 'Twas Laith, dressed in a scarlet tunic with a mantle of seven colors, as befitted a bard of old. A girdle of braided gold and jewels circled his waist, the stones glowing as if with some inner light. His black hair shone in thick glossy falls over his shoulders, down his back, and for one traitorous moment, Ciarann wished to put her hands in the thick, lustrous mass.

He was beautiful.

His face was sober as he halted before her. Ciarann forgot the prince and stared at Laith, seeing him as if for the first time. His eyes were extraordinarily blue against the red tunic, and she noticed again the sensual promise of his mouth, so wide and full.

How had she gazed upon him these weeks without seeing him at all? How had she played dice and sung him songs and listened to his harping without seeing the pure male power that radiated from him now?

He reached for her hand and pulled her close to him, drawing her into a dance. At the first touch of their bodies, a bolt of something moved in Ciarann, a quickening and a pain, mixed together. Her breasts touched his chest, her legs brushed his thighs, and Ciarann let herself dance.

His unbroken gaze never left her face, and Ciarann found it impossible to look away. It was an intent and deeply serious look, and Ciarann pressed closer, feeling a spell over her senses. The blue of his irises seemed to grow and deepen, and suddenly, she heard a soft voice in her mind:

Beautiful Ciarann.

Was that *his* voice? That low, resonant bass? She'd heard him speak at the fairy well, but the moment had been so confused and frightening, she could not now remember what he'd sounded like.

I want to kiss you.

The words that were not words rolled down her spine like a slow, exotic caress, making gooseflesh rise on her arms. A bard would own a beautiful voice—'twas the singular mark of such men.

Her breath shortened, and as if he knew it, his expression shifted to something darker and more sensual. Ciarann grew aware of the strong play of muscles in his body, so close to hers, and smelled the sweetness of his breath.

Caught in the blaze of his eyes, she saw a vision of herself at the well.

She saw her kirtle fall from her body, and her breasts bared to the dark, wet dawn.

It puzzled her at first, and then she realized she was seeing herself through Laith's eyes, in a memory come from his own mind. Through his eyes, she was far more beautiful than she knew herself to be in reality, her shoulders an elegance of pure lines, her breasts uplifted and rose-tipped, her hair thick and glossy. Her fingers tightened convulsively on his arms.

At her touch, his nostrils flared, and his hands moved against her back, his fingers sliding lightly over her nape, fluttering over her neck.

I want you.

"I can hear you," she whispered. "I can see your thoughts, and hear your voice."

He startled, his hands clutching her suddenly. His gaze slipped to her mouth and he moved closer, as if to plant a kiss upon her lips.

But the instant his gaze broke from hers, the spell shattered. Over his shoulder, Ciarann glimpsed the splendid party of horses, and her heart went cold.

"No!" she cried, pushing him away, grabbing her skirts out of contact with him.

He caught her sleeve, but Ciarann turned angrily. "Leave me!" She dared not look in his face for fear of the spell overcoming her senses again. He dropped his hand.

Heartsick, Ciarann looked wildly around the yard for the prince. The sidh seemed to have blended into the crowd, though she would not have thought it possible. It was like her dreams of nearly catching sight of the prince, only to have him dissolve into a tree or a brook or the wind.

But unlike her dream, Finn suddenly appeared before her, made all of gold and silver and gilded light. "My lady," he said, holding out an elegant hand. "How I have waited for this night."

For a fleeting instant, she thought him pale in contrast to the resplendent brilliance of Laith's jeweled colors, but the thought was quickly swept away as the prince tugged her close.

His clasp was light and he moved like the very wind. Dancing in his embrace was like whirling through clouds—her feet scarce touched the ground. A sense of pure light moved in her, chasing away despair and grief and the disturbing, earthy feel of Laith.

"In my world," Finn said, "you will ever feel thus. No more to worry or sorrow or weep, Your only dish will be joy, only light, only pure content. And there will I make you a queen, beautiful Ciarann. There will you live as immortal as I."

Oh, yes, Ciarann thought. No more battles, with bloodied men screaming in agony while she looked on unable to help. No more plagues stealing toddlers, or mothers dying in pure, unholy agony while a babe tore her apart. No more priests piously waving censers over rotting limbs and pronouncing it God's will.

"Take me," she said.

He smiled. She saw both triumph and anticipation in the expression. "Gladly do I seal this bargain." He lowered his head—

Into the air rang an ungodly racket, a displeasing discord of tortured harp and misused flute. The villagers cried out in annoyance, and Ciarann winced.

But the prince made a terrible cry, and covered his ears, backing away. In the crowd, the fairies who'd seemed invisible only moments before now stood out like children in a king's war room. To a one, they had their hands pressed over their ears. The horses reared and whinnied, their bells and saddles clattering.

"Laith of Inishmoor!" Finn roared. "I will have my revenge!"

Running, half-stumbling, crying out in pain, the fairies ran for their mounts. Ciarann saw Laith standing on a wooden platform nearby the guard towers, the pipe in his mouth, his harp in his hands. It seemed impossible that one such man could make so much discordant noise. He did not cease until they had disappeared, swallowed by the night like phantoms.

Which, Ciarann supposed, they were.

Across the wide expanse of the yard, Laith lowered his harp and gazed at Ciarann. Unafraid at such a distance to meet his eyes, she looked back. His chin lifted unapologetically. In answer a wild anger swelled in her chest.

I hate you! she cried in her mind, hoping he did hear, that the spell worked both ways.

It did. *I know.* In Ciarann's mind, the words were low and deep and thick with regret.

She whirled and ran to her chamber. Never again, she vowed, would she look Laith of Inishmoor in the eye.

 # Chapter 4

THE FIRES OF BELTANE

Where the wave of moonlight glosses
The dim grey sands with light,
Far off by the farthest Rosses
We foot it all the night,
Weaving olden dances,
Mingling hands, and mingling glances,
Till the moon has taken flight;

To and fro we leap,
And chase the frothy bubbles
While the world is full of troubles
And is anxious in its sleep.
Come away! O, human child!
To the woods and waters wild,
With a fairy hand in hand,
For the world's more full of weeping than you can understand.

—William Butler Yeats
"The Stolen Child"

THROUGHOUT the long winter, Laith lived in a misery of silence. Ciarann deserted him. Left to his own devices, he found small work to occupy his hands—and it took him places he'd never gone in all his years. Manly or noble pursuits, he cared not for such distinctions. He only wished the comfort of humans around him in his silent, lonely world.

In the kitchen he discovered the honor to be had in kneading bread, and the rhythmic pleasure of chopping vegetables. He discovered he liked the faint scent of women mixed with the aromas of simmering onions and the heady, yeasty note of bread on the rise. He liked the light in the kitchen, too, the leaping orange fire from the hearth mingling with the cool, rain-grayed light from the window. Sometimes he played his harp for the kitchen maids, something he'd never thought to do, and found himself hungry for their gratitude.

In the yard, he tended chickens and collected eggs. In the mews, he watched the master teach his birds. At the blacksmith's hut, he sat for long hours, finding in the clang of the hammer and the ruddy power of the blacksmith a compelling, somehow exciting power.

Orphaned at ten and left to his own wits to survive, Laith had always thought himself an outsider, a loner. He'd taken a certain arrogant pride in the solitary path his life required, clinging to the memory of his father's great booming voice telling him of his noble bard's blood. He'd told himself 'twas the way of such men to be alone.

But until now, he had not understood true isolation. How simple it was for all to overlook him! How hungry he grew for even a kind glance, a gentle touch, the focus of a man who took time to make a joke to him.

The kitchens and mews and simple peasants made bright images in his head. When once again he had his voice, he would have wondrous new songs to sing. In the quiet of his chamber, with only the boy— Sean—to hear, Laith plucked melodies on his harp and sang the words inside his head.

And ached for a chance to sing them to Ciarann. Only she could hear him. The trouble was, she had to look at him, or touch him, and steadfastly and stubbornly refused to do either.

Not once since that terrible moment in the yard had she looked into his face. Not once. And more—she avoided him, as if afraid to be in his presence and know for a single moment what lay in his heart. It grieved him to know that she hated him.

For he had never been truly in love in all his life, and he knew the sorrow of it now. From hidden corners in the hall and shadowed hollows in the garden, he watched her with such hunger he thought it would be simpler to endure a hanging.

'Twas not simply her beauty, though her willowy form never failed to kindle the same desire he'd known upon first sight of her. 'Twas her kindness as she knelt to put her face on the level of a child's and laughed at some small joke the child made. 'Twas the sweetness with which she listened to the battle tales of grayed warriors deep in their cups, never seeming to mind that the same tale had been told a hundred times. Her hounds followed her when she moved from room to room, for she spoiled them with treats and chatter. In the kitchens, she worked hard, and never asked any to perform a task she would not do herself.

As winter rains moved toward warming spring, he fretted about the impending return of the prince at Beltane. The meadows bloomed with the first yellow and rose kisses, and a wide range of birds began to nest in the greening trees, and Laith walked the fields restlessly, trying to come to some answer of how to stymie Finn this round.

In the days of old, there had been a powerful form of sorcery given to the bards, a magic greater than any in the realm of even wizards and fairies. Laith knew of it, but had never given it true attention. It had three prongs—the music of laughter, the music of sorrow, and the music of sleep. His father had shown him the spells with a glint of humor in his eye, and Laith learned them in the same spirit of good humor.

Wryly he plucked a spray of tiny blue flowers. In truth, he had not believed in fairies and magic, nor the magic of his harp. It had seemed nothing more than a quaint story of the heroic days.

Now he knew otherwise, and the spells might be his only hope at thwarting the prince. The trouble was, the magical music required both words and harp, and Laith had much time to serve on his sentence of silence.

And he thought the fairies would be prepared for the half-remembered discords he had played at Sahmain. Weren't there other magics, other ways? It seemed to him there were. Herbs, perhaps. Frowning, he tried to remember, and could not. Megan would know. How could he convey to her his wish?

The answer was so sudden and plain, he grinned, and hurried back the way he had come. Ordinarily, he skirted the forest glade where lay the fairy well, out of a sense of powerful revulsion. Today, the sky was blue and clear, and the sun gilded the woods with a soft gold light that made all seem safe and clean. It was quicker to detour through the glade.

At the edge of the clearing, he halted, as he had once that snowy morn before Sahmain. And as before, he spied Ciarann. In the soft moss and layers of sweetly scented leaves at the edge of the pool, she slept.

His heart squeezed. Had she come here to call the prince? He wondered why she had not done it before now, since it was plain she wished only to be united with her unholy lover at all costs.

It made him vaguely angry. He thought of the way her hounds would howl for her when she crossed into the faerie realm, thought of the old warriors who would have no one to tell their stories to. Did she not know how much she was loved? How lost they would be without her?

A bar of sunlight plucked at the gold in her hair and honeyed the edges of her cheek. A treacherous thought crossed his mind: 'twould be so simple to steal a kiss from her sleeping mouth. If she dreamed of her fairy lover, she might even sleepily return the kiss, and thereby the spell might be broken.

He moved and knelt at her side, silent as a deer. A strange, sharp pain clutched his heart as he gazed at her sleeping face. Rarely had he seen her so peaceful. Always the hint of sorrow clung to her eyes and made her mouth hard. Now the lips were soft as two petals, dewed and gilded by sunlight. He bent toward her.

A nudge of conscience made him hesitate. What right had he to disturb her gentle sleep? What right had he to end whatever dream gave her so sweet a rest?

But if he did not, soon or late the prince would win. And not only Laith, but her hounds and her women and the villagers and old soldiers would mourn. For them, and for Ciarann herself, he must end the enthrallment. One day, when she was old and knew the truth of life, when she understood the ebb and flow contained both joy and sorrow, she would thank him.

Slowly, braced on one hand, he bent over her. Her sweet breath brushed his chin, and he had to close his eyes to the ripeness of that mouth for a moment, willing himself to brush only the gentlest of kisses over her lips.

Their arms touched. In a sudden wash of wavery vision, Laith saw himself across the reddish light behind his lids. Himself as he had been the night of the Sahmain fires, his red tunic and freshly washed hair. In his loins, he felt a rolling heat, and fierce hunger—and he knew it did not belong to him, but to Ciarann.

The realization struck him fiercely, trebling his desire. She did not dream of the prince at all, but of Laith himself!

He kissed her. A vivid force bolted through him, back through to her. He felt it, bright and hot and strong, binding them as one being.

In her dream, and now in the world, she kissed him with rare passion, her arms winding round his neck to hold him close, pull him down next to her on the fragrant ground. Laith gave himself over to it, astonished and grateful. He slid his hands along her slim arms, and into her weight of silky hair, and at last over the inviting rounds of her breasts that had been so beautiful to his eyes and were no less pleasing to hands that had fair ached for this touch.

She lifted her head to look at him. In the golden light, her irises seemed to reflect the bottom of the well, where leaves had fallen for generations and lay in brown and gold and water-greened layers. He gazed back at her, moving his hand over the tip of her breast.

Ciarann!

The voice did not come from Laith, but some other source, a loud, peremptory command that echoed through them both. Laith forgot himself and looked over her shoulder.

And the moment was lost.

Ciarann shoved Laith rudely, and only a quick scramble saved him from muddying himself in the pool. "Curse you, Laith of Inishmoor!" she moaned.

A flicker of something very like terror showed on her face as she stood in the glade by the pool, her eyes darting toward the trees. Laith wondered what had happened to put that fear in her, when before she'd been so eager. If she feared the gilded one, why then had she come to sleep by the pool?

Ciarann!

There was no doubting her terror as the voice sounded again, not a true voice, but carried on the wind, into their minds, unmistakably the voice of the fairy prince. Ciarann grabbed up her skirts and fled the grove.

Even after so many months, Laith opened his mouth to call after her. When no sound came, he wasted no time mourning, but instead ran after her, afraid she would be hurt in her headlong flight.

Chapter 5

CIARANN ran until her breath came in tearing gasps, until her legs were watery, until she was sure she was far beyond the reach of the door to the world of faerie. She did not hear Laith behind her until she stopped, and he caught her arm, fierce enough she did not even try to escape.

Leaning against a tree, she bent over and struggled for breath.

His voice, so rich and resonant, so unlike the terrifying voice of the gilded one, wove through her mind: *Why?*

It frightened her. She pulled from his grasp, stumbling away from him. What had she unleashed that autumn morning? What had she done that now not one, but two men could come into the privacy of her mind this way?

As much as she wished to run all the way to the rath, her weary legs would carry her no farther. In defeat she sank to the ground. At least the bard only wished to bed her.

Of the fairy, she was less sure.

Laith settled beside her on the ground, folding his long legs comfortably. For a moment, he made no move, only lifted his head, as if listening to the forest. Ciarann listened too, and heard the small song of birds hidden in the branches, and a soft wind making a quiet moan in the treetops.

Since Sahmain, she had not dared look at his face. There was no avoiding it now. The dark hair had been tied back this morning, revealing the narrow jaw and angled bones that made his face so uncommon. She had forgotten the vivid blue of his dark-lashed eyes, and the unbearable fullness of those lips.

She had forgotten, too, how fierce and self-contained he was. As if he needed no one.

"I should be angry with you," she said at last.

He took her hand. And raised his brows in question.

" 'Twas not very noble of you to steal a kiss when I was sleeping."

He clutched her fingers, and a picture of herself asleep by the pool floated over her vision.

She looked away from the bewitching eyes. His hands were pale and long and elegant, and she focused upon them. "I dislike that you can come into my mind so easily." Heat rose in her cheeks as she remembered her dream. " 'Tis unfair."

With gentle fingers, he touched her chin, and lifted her face so she would look at him. He frowned and faintly she heard, *You have the same power over me, dear lady.*

"Is it difficult, putting the words in my mind that way?"

He nodded.

With a faint smile, she said, "You see me as far more beautiful than I am, Laith of Inishmoor."

Laith shook his head, soberly, and Ciarann thought of the way his mouth had tasted. She wanted to kiss him again, wanted to lie with him now in this quiet grove, amid the wildflowers. Then she thought of the harsh voice of the prince, and her blood ran cold.

Why are you afraid?

Ciarann closed her eyes. In that moment by the pool, with Laith's kiss upon her mouth, and his hands upon her breasts, she had felt a curious harmony, a feeling of peace so wide it was almost frightening.

"The battles have been bloody and fierce," she said quietly. "When Colin was killed, all light left the world. I could not bear it, and I thought to run to the world of the faerie, where I would no more have to grieve, not for anyone, not for anything."

Urgently, he squeezed her hand, but Ciarann did not look at him. She would not have him know her thoughts just now. "When he spoke my name back there, it was the first time I thought to wonder what he

stands to gain from my crossing. What could such a being need of me?"
She raised her eyes to meet his gaze. "I wondered, too, why a stranger
would try to save me from such a glorious fate . . . and a bard, who would
know the stories of the other land far better than any other."

Now he was silent, when she would have heard his thoughts. "His
voice was very angry. I feared—" she halted, but the words formed in
her mind and might as well have been spoken, *I feared that he would
kill you.*

Laith grinned, a swift and mischievous expression. He lifted her hand
to his mouth for a kiss. His lips pressed lightly to each of her fingers,
and a quiver moved along Ciarann's spine. The long black lashes shadowed his eyes, and he seemed wholly intent upon his task.

It roused her madly, and the heady, dizzying desire she'd felt by the
pool now moved through her again. "Laith," she said softly.

He lifted his lashes, and Ciarann glimpsed mischief in his face, a
lightness she had not seen before. Deliberately, he took the tip of her
index finger into his mouth. It shocked her to feel the wet and heat of
his inner lips. Ripe excitement flared in her breasts, and spread along
her thighs.

As if he knew it, she saw triumph and laughter in his eyes. Embar-
rassed, she yanked her hand away.

The knave only grinned more broadly. She thought it was the first
time he had ever smiled in her presence, and with a distant sort of wonder, saw that he had beautiful white teeth, unmarred with gaps or marks
of decay.

Without attempting to touch her again, he stood and shook his
cloak, then gestured toward the rath. Feeling unsettled and annoyed,
she refused to move. "Make your own way back, you insect."

He reached for her hand and tugged her to her feet, and Ciarann wondered how he kept his thoughts to himself when she could not. In equal
measures she wanted to hurt him and to kiss him.

With a glare, she shoved him and moved away, holding her head up
as arrogantly as the queen she would one day be. As he followed behind,
she swore she heard a laugh.

It was only later, as she sat spinning with Megan, that Ciarann realized a terrible truth: that sense of peace she'd felt in Laith's arms was
as close to love as she'd ever come in her life. With Colin, she had felt

many things—laughter and protectiveness and the comfort their long friendship had lent.

But any desire she'd felt was mild. She'd not known true desire until that cold gloomy morn, she had known two waves of purest hunger, one for the mortal bard, the other for the gilded prince.

She must have made some small noise. Megan said, "Are you all right, milady?"

Ciarann ceased her spinning, dropping her hands to her lap. "I do not know. I think I have just learned I have a wanton heart."

Megan gave her rusty, bawdy laugh. "Oh, nay, milady. Many a wanton have I known in my days. Is it young Laith who rouses you so?" She cackled. "Were I a younger woman, he'd not slip free of me, I tell you!"

Ciarann rolled her eyes. "You ever lust for boys!"

"Aye," she admitted unapologetically. "And men, too."

"So how can a woman trust your judgment of a wanton?"

"Listen to me, child. There's a wealth of joy in what a man and woman give each other in the dark of a night. Your heart was broken before you found that pleasure—so you haven't known till now how it feels."

Ciarann plucked at the wool in her lap. She wanted to ask what a woman was to do when it was two men, not just one, who kindled passion in her. "I am afraid," she whispered. "I am afraid of what I have unleashed. I fear the prince will kill Laith—or that I am meant for the prince, and Laith will chase him away forever."

"Ah." The word was layered with knowledge. " 'Tis a quandary."

"Aye. They both . . . there is so much . . . they are so different."

Megan took her hand gently. "You must have faith, lass."

"Faith!" Ciarann spat the word. "Faith in what? The lost gods, or the new one? In magic or priests?"

The old woman's hand moved, dry and calm over the back of Ciarann's fingers. "The answers are in your heart, milady."

She dreaded sleep that night. As Beltane approached, the dreams of the Other-world had come every night, but there was more, too. Now sometimes the prince appeared to her, and in those dreams his hands and lips moved on her body in ways she would not have admitted aloud to another soul.

Tonight, she was afraid of him. A warm wind blew through the window of her small chamber, but she closed the shutters against it, and left a candle burning. It was no help. When she slept, she dreamed. Dreamed of the Other-world, where none were old or sick or even ugly, and music poured like sunlight through the air. It wrought a sense of calm joy in her to be there, a sense of belonging.

And neither did she have to seek the prince. He came to her across a meadow, clad in silk the color of emeralds, his gilt hair tumbling over the manly shoulders. His flesh seemed made of light.

She had forgotten how her heart soared at the sight of him. He moved close, smiling gently, and took her hand. Ciarann went eagerly into his embrace, and when he bent his head to kiss her, she gave him her mouth with abandon.

And then, oh, then, he undressed her, and gazed at her with rapt attention. Ciarann felt sunlight tumbling warm over her breasts and belly, and then she felt his hands and his mouth, all over her. He discarded his own silk coverings, and Ciarann could do naught but stare at the astonishment of his form, the shoulders and ribs and muscles and flesh all meshing in exquisite perfection. She reached for him, for that light-infused skin and elegance of form—

She woke up in her scented pallet, with the candle burned to a nub. Alone.

But heat still burned in her body, an arousal so intense and wild and yearning she did not know how she could bear to live this way. How could he cheat her like this?

It was only then she remembered Laith and the startling arousal his mouth, sucking lightly on her finger, had given. She moaned.

Light or dark? Mortal or fairy?

Ease or struggle?

Life or death?

She would have to choose. And she did not know how she could.

Chapter 6

THE day before the eve of Beltane, Laith sought out Megan. Finding her in the kitchen, he took her hand and drew her outside to sit on a small bench by the herb gardens.

"What's this, my boy?" she said with a twinkle in her eye. "You've come to steal my heart with your beautiful harp, I suppose."

He grinned at her and wiggled his eyebrows wickedly.

"I knew it. The poor lad's besotted." She smoothed her hair in a mocking imitation of a young vain girl. "Play, lad. I can at least give you my ear, since I fear you are far too young to appreciate anything else I'd give."

For days, Laith had been sorting through the songs of faerie, and at last had found one he hoped she'd know by its melody. He plucked it now, a lively warning of the Queen of Faerie who sought a mortal lover. The mortal's wife was not quick to give up her husband, and secretly thwarted the fairy at every turn. It spoke of herbs and simples, but without specifics.

It was the specifics Laith needed.

At first, Megan only listened, her round ruddy face alight with pleasure. "Ah, lad, you play so sweet. 'Tis plain you've the blood of the old ones in you."

Laith nodded, impatient for her to understand his meaning. He began again, but she still did not seem to understand he wished her to sing the words, so he touched his lips, then hers.

After a moment, she understood, and picked up the ballad, forgetting words here and there, laughing as she stumbled through them. When she got to the verse about the simples, Laith stopped playing and pointed to the garden.

She frowned, not taking his meaning. Frustrated, he sighed and bowed his head, trying to think of another way to communicate his needs. By the goddess, he was weary of this wretched curse. It made him feel a simpleton to gesture and point and wiggle about. Even grunts and laughter were denied him.

But there was naught to be gained by giving in to his frustration. He played the song again, and pointed. Megan peered at him, and sang slowly, then looked at the garden. "Herbs and simples did Sweet Mary employ/To thwart the Queen and all her glory . . ."

Comprehension dawned. "Ah, lad, I'm sorry to be so dense. You want herbs to keep the prince away."

He gave her his most dazzling smile, and planted a kiss upon her rosy cheek.

" 'Tis rue you'll be needing, then." She hauled herself to her feet and knelt in the garden, plucking a whole plant and presenting it to him.

Laith bowed his thanks.

She patted his cheek. "Save her. I vow I'd miss her most sorely."

Getting the herb into Ciarann's clothing proved the biggest challenge. Laith bound the simple into small bundles tied with string and tucked them into his girdle when he dressed for the feast. Again he wore the red tunic and jeweled belt. The cloak of seven colors he left in his small curtained chamber. Until he could again claim the title of bard, he would not wear it.

Anticipation made him restless as they waited for dark to fall and the feast to begin. He wandered the yards and into the village, a hound companionably trailing him. The villagers, who'd grown used to him, waved and called out, their spirits high at the break in their routines.

May Day, they called it now, the old Beltane. Twilight had set upon the old Celtic ways, and Laith eyed the waiting pyres with mixed emotions. Each time the bonfires were lit without remembrance, a little more of Erin's magic slipped away.

The thought was an old one, and gave him pause now. Always had he dreamed of the noble past, and sung of the great deeds of yore. Had he ever believed in it before the prince came to the well?

Now he had to admit he had not, had not believed in magic at all until that enchanted morning. And in his heart, was there not just a little catch of joy at the discovery that it was not all some old dream, some legend—but real?

There was. The anticipation he felt tonight was as much a hunger to see the fairies on their grand steeds as it was to thwart the prince. For a time this morning, Laith had thought the easiest way to prevent the prince from winning a kiss from Ciarann was to sprinkle the rue across the openings the gates made.

But he had not wished to keep them out completely. He wanted to know again the wonder of seeing them ride into the gathering, splendid and beautiful as nothing mortal ever was. He wanted their enchanting number to wind through the villagers, so their lives, too, were touched with magic.

Instead, he had to secrete the herb upon Ciarann's clothing. And now, before it grew dark.

He found her in the hall, adorned in a rich tunic of brightest gold. For a moment, he allowed himself a moment of full pleasure at the look of her—the glorious fall of hair and the thrust of young breasts and her graceful simplicity of movement.

Then he crept up beside her and took her hand, careful to school his thoughts. She startled, and when she looked up, made to pull away. Laith closed his fingers tightly around hers.

One dance.

"Nay!" she said fiercely. "This will end now. Tonight, I will go with the prince."

But she did not look away, and he saw in the depths of the leaf-colored eyes her ambivalence. His thoughts rose in a tangle, a wordless mix of hungers and pleas and argument, and none clear enough.

He lowered his head, tightening his fingers so she would not flee. In his sleeve was the bundle of rue and he did not know how to put it on her without her knowledge.

"Let me go!" she said.

A plan blossomed in his mind. He raised his eyes and looked at her with his whole heart. *One kiss.*

Before she could protest, he swept her slim form into his arms, the rue in his hand. He kissed her passionately, his arms tight around her. For an instant, he forgot he had a task, forgot all in the mead-sweet taste of her lips and the smell of lavender in her hair. He clasped her close so she would feel the urgent need he had of her, and he felt her response, a softening of her body against his for a fleeting instant, before she pushed at him again.

Holding her against her will, he tucked the rue into the back of her girdle, into a fold of cloth where she would not feel it.

Then he let her go, smiling at the fury in her face. She wiped a hand over her mouth. "I do it for you, you fool."

Laith allowed himself one moment of sobriety, and very slowly shook his head in denial. Then quickly, before she could see the triumph in his eyes, he gave her his most courtly bow and turned away.

He let himself indulge then, indulge in the gaiety of the feast, and the free-flowing wine and mead and ale. He ate of every succulent dish on the table, and when he could eat no more, took a place with the other minstrels to play his harp, play all the old songs with a pleasure he had not known in many months.

And when the moon rose high, he carried a great tankard of honeyed ale outside the gates with him, and leaned on the wall, and waited.

They came from the forest, only a faint glow at first. The glow grew and gained shape, first the horses, high-stepping and bejeweled, with only wraith-like shapes upon them. And then, at last, could Laith see the fairies themselves, not the tiny beings of legend at all, but as large as humans, and a thousand times more beautiful. Their flesh and hair outshone their silken finery as if they were spilled from the moon itself.

Among them Laith saw the prince—noble and proud and easily the most beautiful of all. There was determination on his arrogant brow, and a certain eager leaning.

Laith waited until the prince spied him, and lifted his cup in greeting, without bothering to hide his slightly tipsy grin of triumph. The fairy's eyes flickered over him as if he were a troublesome insect, and that only added to Laith's enjoyment. If he could have, he would have laughed aloud.

Chapter 7

FROM her post on the steps to the great hall, Ciarann also watched the troop of fairies come through the gates. On Sahmain, she'd been too anxious to give thought to the whys and wherefores of the appearance of the moon-colored beings, but tonight she found herself amazed that none of the villagers seemed to notice the strange beauty of the creatures. They rode in and took their places among the villagers as if it were their right.

Had it been so all of her life?

It seemed to her all at once that it must have been so. She watched as the glorious queen dismounted and wove her way through the dance, laughing and making sport with the men. No woman looked after her with wild envy; no child cowered in fear of her dazzlement.

Nearby her, a hound whined softly and turned tail to creep into the shadows of the hall. And now Ciarann noted that all the hounds had made themselves scarce. Only the beasts could resist the enchantment.

A chill moved over her limbs at the thought of them coming every feast night this way, all of her life, and her with no memory of it except those shreds of dreams that had stirred her to go to the fairy well in the first place.

She crossed her arms, shivering in the warm night. Now across the yard came the prince. Firelight cast a red shine over his pale hair and across his noble face. He moved with sultry intent, a grace that was near to seduction itself. It was the same movement that had kindled such hunger in her when he came to her dreams, and his mouth was turned in the smile she knew so well.

But as she stood there on the steps, watching him approach, Ciarann felt nothing, only the faint chill of fear. His smile was not kind so much as cold and sure. There was no passion in the cool gray eyes, only intent, and once again, she had to wonder what such a being had to gain by taking her as his lover.

As if he sensed the change in her, he paused at the foot of the steps and propped one foot on the lowest stair. "Fair Ciarann, what troubles you this night?"

Oh, yes, he was beautiful in his silken robes, with his elegant limbs and fine face and long shining hair. "I have only lately come to wonder why you should want a mortal lover, my lord. I fear there is some trick here."

A faint flicker of something showed in his face—annoyance?—before he schooled it away. "No trick," he said. And now there was soberness about his mouth. "Only a wish to protect you from your sorrows, and from the cruelties of old age. Ever have I watched you, Ciarann."

"Have you always come to the feasts this way? Is that how I knew you?"

He smiled. "Aye." He gestured toward the merry crowd gathered about the fires. "And do we not add a bright note to this good feast?"

Ciarann looked toward the yard, seeing the gilded number like poppies in the grass. "But why do you come? What can you gain from mortal folk?"

"I will tell you," he said. "If you will but come and dance with me, so I might hold you in my arms as I've longed to do these many months."

From the corner of her eye, Ciarann caught a flash of red. She looked up to see Laith leaning negligently against the well, a tankard in his hand. There was about him a vastly amused air.

And for the smallest space of in-drawn breath, she felt a start of excitement at the sight of him. The red made his hair blacker than ever, and his eyes seemed to dance in his dark face. A warmth moved in her limbs, and a faint, fond smile came to her mouth as she wondered what he was about.

The prince glanced over his shoulder and his eyes narrowed. "Is it the seduction of some minstrel that stays your heart, my lady?"

"No!"

"So you say." His eyes were cold as he looked back to her. "Think now, how this will end. He is only a wandering bard, with a string of ladies from north to south, all pining in his wake. When he has his voice, he'll be on his way, and you'll be here alone again, and I will not come back."

"If it is his tongue that keeps him here, why then did you choose that curse, my lord?"

He drew himself up and lifted one shoulder. " 'Twas a poor choice, I admit. He made me angry."

The simple confession stirred her. She smiled. "So you are not perfect in all things, then?"

A genuine laugh came from his throat, and the sound was rich and deep and musical. "Nay. I have a quick and foolish temper." Now did Ciarann hear the elusive and musical notes of his words, too. "And I've taken no small ribbing among my own folk for my foolish love of a mortal maid who bewitched me when she was but four years old."

"Four?"

He leaned on the rail. "You brought me ale on Midsummer Night, and I picked up you in my arms to dance. You laughed and laughed, and put your hands in my hair."

Ciarann cried, "I remember!" and laughed as the memory flooded back. "I thought you the most beautiful creature I had ever seen."

"And do you still, my lady?" His voice came quiet and sober to her.

Well she remembered the feel of his silky hair against her hands, the wonder she had felt staring into his pale eyes. And now her dream of them naked in the grove came back to her, rousing once more the heat that had left her so restless. It seemed all at once that she could barely breathe for her need to put her body against his. "Why did you not stay, the night I dreamed of you? Why did you leave me so hungry?" she whispered.

And now she did see true desire in his face, in the softening of his mouth and the heat in his eyes. "So we might be united in truth, not dream. True, not false, and binding."

"That binding you speak of frightens me."

" 'Tis binding for us both, as a vow or a promise. Please," he said. "I ache for you."

She hesitated, but her mind filled with the glory of his kiss, the remembered feel of his mouth against her body.

"Come." He held out his hand.

Eagerly, Ciarann rushed down the steps, reaching for him.

Abruptly, he backed away. "Lady, what foul thing have you done?"

"What? Nothing."

The prince whirled in fury. "You!" he roared, pointing an accusatory finger at Laith.

The bard lifted his tankard with a slightly off-kilter salute, his mouth turned up in a crooked and triumphant grin. The prince moved toward him, and Ciarann cried out at the violence reeking from him. "Do not harm him!"

Finn halted, his shoulders rigid. " 'Tis only her pleas that save you, Laith of Inishmoor. But know that you'll have no peace as long as you thwart me." He stalked away.

Ciarann looked at Laith. His face showed no remorse, and her tangled emotions rose in a rush. "You're a fool. He'll outwit you soon or late, and who then will be the loser?"

The irritating man only lifted one dark brow and gave her a crooked, drunken smile.

Chapter 8

MIDSUMMER'S EVE

It was by yonder thorn I saw the fairy host
(O low night wind, O wind of the west!)
My love rode by, there was gold upon his brow,
And since that day I can neither eat nor rest.

They tell me I am cursed and I will lose my soul,
(O red wind shrieking o'er the thorn-grown dun!)
But he is my love and I go to him tonight,
Who rides when the thorn glistens white beneath the moon.

—Moireen Fox
"The Fairy Lover"

SPRING ripened, and life came back to the land. Ciarann went about her tasks with a strange sense of impending doom. 'Twas only seven weeks between May Day and Midsummer, and as if both knew it, her suitors seemed engaged in a mad competition for her heart.

By night, the prince came to her in her dreams, and tormented her with heated visions, visions she only half-remembered, visions of her body naked, and his hands gliding over her, touching her and teasing her until she thought she would go mad.

Each morning she awoke aching and empty, her breasts and thighs heavy with yearning. The very brush of her linen coverings irritated her. She could not bear it. Nor could she speak of it. Not even to Megan. How could she tell anyone the things she had been feeling?

By day, Laith seemed to be everywhere. He played his harp for her, and wandered with her whenever she left the high walls of the rath. No matter how annoyed she was with him, he would not stay behind. She worried for his safety more than for her own, but she had to admit sometimes his presence was a comfort.

And more. His eyes danced with mischief, and glowed with wonder at things she had long taken for granted. In ways, he was like a child, taking pleasure in small beauties, like the butterflies that lit upon new flowers in the herb gardens, and the blaze of sunset across an evening sky.

Over and over she tried to speak to him of the curse the prince had leveled on May Eve. "Do you not fear what punishments he has in mind for you?" she would ask.

Always, Laith only gave her his rakish, crooked smile and shook his head. Ciarann thought darkly he had the foolish bravado of a boy, too.

Finally weary of his steadfast refusal to acknowledge the danger he was in, Ciarann said, "I am in love with him, you know."

They sat in the shade of a rowan tree alongside the brook. Ciarann idly carded fresh black wool, but she looked directly at Laith as she spoke, waiting for his reaction.

He was far more skillful than she at letting by only what he wished to communicate, so she did not even know if he would respond.

The reaction she received was unexpected. He winced, as if the words cut him to the quick, then looked away and shrugged.

An answering cry lit in her breast. "You do not care?"

He shook his head stubbornly. A wash of light glossed the black tresses, hanging loose and thick on his shoulders.

She frowned and tried to goad him. "The prince comes to me at night, in my dreams. He touches me."

Laith only stared at the water, his jaw hard.

"Look at me!" she cried.

He moved suddenly and grabbed her arms. On his face was a fierceness she had not seen. His bright blue eyes filled her entire vision.

What do you want of me? His voice was anguished and angry.

And then, somehow, his hands were on either side of her face, and he was kissing her. There was no gentleness in the touch, no magic or charm or seduction. He kissed her with the fierce inelegance of urgent need, his teeth digging into her lip with a tiny pain.

Something in Ciarann broke free, and she clasped him close, pulling him down with her to grass, so his big long body was over hers, pressing her with reassuring weight to the true and cradling earth. Under her palms, she felt the rough linen of his tunic over the fluid warmth of muscle in his back. She felt his thighs lace between hers, and his hair on her face, and most of all, his deep, hungry kiss.

Here was no wraith who would be gone if she moved or looked away—or suddenly awakened. Here was the whole, corporeal, solid mass of man against her. With a little sob of relief, she put her hands in the thickness of his hair, and gave back to him his kiss. Tears rolled over her face.

Real.

His kiss gentled, and his hands skimmed with curious tenderness over her cheeks and neck and arms. Ciarann grasped him more closely, afraid to let him go, afraid he would end this kiss when she needed to keep feeling his solidness around her.

He moved his mouth to her cheek and kissed her tears, then her eyes and chin. She dug her fists into the cloth over his warm back when she felt him raise his head. "Do not let me go!" she whispered.

With his fingers, he brushed away her tears. He shook his head soberly. *I must,* he said very clearly in her mind. *You must find your way on your own, Ciarann.*

His kiss had awakened all the aching, yearning places on her body, and she liked the feel of his big body against her. Liked his lean thighs against hers, his chest lightly touching her breasts, and there—his manhood, ready for the opening of her thighs.

Her breath caught a little in her throat. "If you make love to me, perhaps he will leave me alone."

Ciarann watched his eyes carefully, so she saw the liquid heat that darkened his vivid blue eyes. She saw the faint flare of his nostrils. His mouth, so full and rich, hovered close to her own.

He closed his eyes, as if against temptation, and Ciarann wanted to weep at the sight of his long glossy eyelashes lying on his cheekbones.

With a single fingertip, she brushed the edges. His hands tightened around her ribs, and she thought, now, now he would lift that elegant hand and touch her breast and she would—

But instead, he pushed himself away without speaking, and walked to the edge of the brook. With a violent movement, he dropped to his knees on the bank and put his whole head under the running water, then raised it, took a huge breath and plunged his face under again.

Ciarann, stung by embarrassment, sat up and straightened her skirts, and her hair, taking leaves and little sticks out of the long tangled strands.

At last Laith looked at her, his eyes burning and fierce in his face. *I'll not quench a fire he's lit.* The narrow, beautiful jaw lifted with pride.

"Go, then!" Ciarann cried. "I have no need of thee."

Oddly, he smiled at that, his lips quirking up into a genuine smile. *Do you not?*

With a cry of frustration, Ciarann grabbed a harmless bit of stick and threw it at him. "Go!"

She swore she heard him laugh again, before he did exactly that. Left alone in the shadowed meadow, Ciarann bent her head into her arms. Her body was afire and her heart in a tumult and even her quick, clear-thinking brain seemed to have deserted her.

She did not like the woman she had become. Never had it been her way to be petty or mean-spirited or sharp, though she had to admit she could give a tongue-lashing when one was required. But she didn't get mulish.

'Twas only Laith who made her feel so. He brought out the worst of her, all those nasty bits of her character she tried to hide. He roused her anger and her whining and made her see herself as selfish.

Why would she even want to spend time with such a creature?

Brushing her skirts off, she gathered her wool into a linen pouch. She did *not* want to spend time with him. It was that simple. Not for anything. If he would not assuage her lust, then she had no use for him.

The thought, so unexpected, brought her up short and cold. When had she become a woman who could think such things? When had she ceased to consider each life as its own precious collection of moments, sacred and whole, and begun to see those moments as belonging to her?

Her hands began to shake.

The morning she called the prince was when this small, dark change in her had begun. No more did she take pleasure in singing with the other women in the kitchen. The notion of kneading bread annoyed her. It seemed a petty task. The same was true of other things, as well—as if she'd become a great queen, who had no use for such menial duties.

Was this the price she would pay if she left the mortal realm? Would she pay with her own humanity?

Winded, she put a hand to her throat and stared at the fence posts of the rath on the hill. It seemed so plain. What other price could there be? To join her gilded lover, she would have to accept him in his world, as one of them.

Troubled, she began to walk back. Was that not exactly what she had been wishing that cold, autumn morning when she circled the well? To leave the mortal coil behind?

A vision of the prince, with his long beautiful limbs unclothed, came to her mind—and with it that powerful lust he stirred. And shame filled her, for she thought it might be worth the price of her humanity to lie with him in his light-drenched world and dwell there forever more, never to worry again.

Perhaps in the end, she was too much a coward for this world.

Chapter 9

In the dead of the night, Laith crept into Ciarann's curtained chamber, his heart pounding with anticipation and terror. No one stirred but the guards murmuring quietly between themselves at the gates, and he had learned over many years of sometimes dangerous affairs to move silently.

Her hounds slept near her feet—a good sign. If the fairy invaded her dreams this night, the beasts would flee. Instead, one lifted a head incuriously, thumped its tail once against the floor, and closed its eyes.

In every corner of the room, Laith placed bundles of rue, hidden among the rushes. Ciarann slept below the single window, and he reached over her to put a bundle on the sill.

She slept deeply, one hand flung from below the light covering. Her shoulders were bare, and faint moonlight gave the delicate bones a misty halo. For a moment, he paused, thinking of the kiss they had shared this afternoon, and the sweet taste of her mouth, and her request to make love.

He wanted to lie down next to her, and press his face into her breasts, and put his hands to her flesh. He wanted to feel her bared length next to his own naked limbs and torso and sex. He wanted to taste the whimpers of pleasure upon her lips and draw low dark groans from her smooth white throat.

But he could not. Setting his jaw against temptation, he tucked the other bundles of rue into the straw mattress, reaching over her once again to put one between the wall and the bed itself. He felt her warmth along his belly, and he could smell the freshness of her skin, and for a moment he held himself rigidly still, praying for strength.

If he touched her, he would see her dreams, and might influence them. This ritual was meant to free her to make her own choice. He could not interfere.

Clutching his hands into tight fists, he straightened and stood by her bed. She seemed not to know why the prince wanted her, what he stood to gain by taking her from this mortal realm, but Laith knew. Finn wanted her for her uncommon beauty, a beauty that would be long preserved in the land of faerie. He wanted her mortal blood in his fairy children, and her mortal laughter in the land.

And as he watched her, Laith, too, found her beauty enchanting and arousing, but there was so much more to her. Qualities he saw fading as the months of her enchantment grew. Perhaps she had always been selfish, in her heart where it did not show, but he didn't think so. Her sorrow had been deep and real that first day at the well.

A wave of despair closed over him. Even if she chose him, there was little he could offer her, a king's beautiful daughter. He had only his harp and his songs.

And his noble blood.

The thought edged into his mind sideways, surprising and unexpected. He came from the noblest bards in all of Erin's fine history, bards to whom kings had come to make the music of laughter and the music of love and the one of the highest of all—the music of satire.

His heart quickened. If he could keep Ciarann safe from the prince until his voice was restored to him, perhaps Laith could engage Finn in a contest of magic and win Ciarann fairly.

It frightened him to think of it. The prince had never disbelieved the power of magic, while Laith had never had faith in it at all until now. His grandfather had given him the tools, but could he remember them well enough to best the prince?

Ciarann stirred restlessly, and turned toward the wall. Her hair and the light woven blanket slipped down, showing her long, slim back, almost pearlescent in the night, her spine a curved shadow. He took a step backward to avoid the temptation of touching her.

And yet, he did not go. Not yet. There was bittersweet pleasure in watching her this way, in knowing the rue protected her from the prince. He'd never known the sweet pleasure of conversation would seem so dear, but he ached to have long ambling talks with her, and sing her songs, and have her laugh aloud at his jests. He'd not known until he lost such things, how much a part of him they were.

In secret, he would practice the songs his grandfather had taught him. He would purify his thoughts and his body, and like the old bards, he would fast before the battle.

Quiet pride rose in him at the resolution, the pride of the birthright that had been lost to him, and now was reclaimed

As the weeks hurtled toward Midsummer's Eve, Ciarann recovered small bits of herself. No longer did she awaken with the restless hungers burning low in her belly, with a graininess in her eyes and a sharpness to her tongue. If the fairy came to her dreams, she did not remember it.

It was a relief. Her step once again grew light, and she found herself laughing at the silly jokes of the children in the village, and glad to knead bread in the kitchen. It was as if she had again become the self she lost the cold morning at the well—no, even before that—the day the news of her lover's death had come. That day had all joy died for her.

Perhaps, she told herself, she had only needed to examine her life to put it back to rights. She'd had to face a reckoning that day with Laith at the stream, and it had made her realize what was important. Not some Other-world where things were always the same, safe and calm, but this very messy place with all its ups and downs and mortal calamities. By clearing her conscience, she was able to sleep, and her temper improved.

Simple.

Her resolve was tested a little when the miller's wife screamed all one night with a babe that would not come, and died before dawn in puddles of her own blood. Both babe and mother were lost, and the miller heartstricken. Ciarann took him fresh bread and hearty soup the day after the burial, and sat with him while he cried. She was prepared to do it for as many days as he needed it, but after the second day, he gathered himself, squared his shoulders, and got back to work.

That day, Ciarann looked for Laith. He'd kept himself scarce since the day they kissed by the stream, and she found she missed his steady companionship. There were things in her heart she wanted to express, and it was to his ear she wanted to pour her thoughts.

She found him at last in a secluded corner of the open yard within the gates. He sat comfortably cross-legged on the ground in a simple blue tunic, his head bent over his harp with deep concentration. Sunlight put glossy white arcs in his black hair.

The sight of him was unexpectedly welcome, and Ciarann hurried forward. "There you are!" she cried. "I've been looking everywhere for you this morning."

He lifted his head, and Ciarann felt a strange, heated tingle rush through her limbs at the startling blaze of his bright blue eyes. How had she not noticed how unusually blue his eyes were?

No smile bloomed on his face, and she did not hear his voice in her mind. She'd finally realized it was not an easy thing to communicate with her, and he did not always choose to put forth the effort.

She halted a foot or two away. "Am I disturbing you?"

He put his harp aside in the grass and motioned for her to sit with him. She settled stiffly nearby him, vividly aware of his long limbs and the fall of his hair and the beauty of his gentle, rich mouth.

Shyness made her mute. Her thoughts, which had seemed so urgent while she looked for him, now fled, and she could not remember what it was she had wanted to tell him. With restless hands, she plucked at the grass.

As if he sensed her mood, he captured a purple wildflower and held it out to her. A fall of sunlight made the petals transparent, and she could see blue veins within the fragile structure. His thumb was very long, his hand traced with elegant bones. It was a very large hand, which she had not particularly noticed before, and his nails grew in neat, clean ovals.

He held the blossom patiently, and finally Ciarann took it with a smile. She lifted her eyes. "Thank you."

Again the vividness of his eyes startled her, and the tingling in her limbs grew more insistent. To her astonishment, she felt the tips of her breasts lift eagerly, as making themselves ready for his touch or kiss or—

His smile, so gentle a moment before, now quirked up at one corner in mischievous acknowledgement. Ciarann made a noise and bowed her head. " 'Tis vexing this way you have of seeing my thoughts!" She covered her face with her hands.

Laith took her wrist and pulled her hands from her face. He held her hand and looked at her closely, and she knew that made it easier for him to "talk" so she did not pull away. Still, it was a kind of torture to feel those long fingers folded loosely around her own.

Why did you seek me out today, my lady?

She took a breath, and at last she did remember. "I was with the miller this morning. His wife died three days ago, and he went back to work."

Laith let her go, but he nodded his encouragement.

"He has other children, and they must be fed and tended. He cannot simply stop because life has given him this blow. And in truth, though I know he loved her—'twas a true love match—there seemed to be some pleasure in him at the wheel. It was bittersweet to watch him with his children, and watch him try to make them smile, to forget their loss, though I know his heart is heavy."

Soberly, Laith listened, his eyes fixed upon her face. Ciarann swallowed. "I found myself glad for him, and thinking his wife would be glad, too."

He took her hand and folded it over his own, and gave her fingers a light quick kiss. *Yes.* He seemed to hesitate, and Ciarann waited, sensing he wanted to add more.

"Take as long you need," she said. "I am patient."

He smiled wistfully and shook his head. *It is too hard.*

A sudden commotion at the gates made them both look up. A party of warriors came through, horns bleating out in celebration of their arrival. Villagers and servants ran toward them, and Ciarann jumped up with a glad shout. "It is my father!"

Chapter 10

CIARANN was swept into the activity that followed her father's return, and Laith did not see her again until night, when a rich feast was laid out for the king and his warriors. Then she sat with her father, a gray-bearded man of no small stature, and chattered eagerly with him.

As the meal wound down, an old harper began to play, and Laith joined him nearby the hearth, even if he could not sing. The old man was a master, and Laith was well pleased to be able to join him, to play as he had not been wont to do these past months. As if the old bard had opened some door that had been tightly closed through the long winter, Laith found himself seduced by his harp, by the sounds it made and the way his fingers flew.

All the small things he'd learned to hear while the silence was on him now came to bear, and Laith felt magic in what his hands did. He and the old bard found rare accord, and in each thing Laith uncovered, so the bard echoed it. Then for a time the bard would lead and Laith follow, embroidering and weaving magic through the sounds. The magic of a blacksmith's hammer and women's laughter in the kitchens and the cry of hawks in the mews.

While the music was on him, he forgot Ciarann and his silent tongue. He forgot his quest and the world and became the music of his harp.

The old bard smiled at him and took a swig of ale, passed the tankard to Laith, and when he was finished, the harper fixed his rheumy eyes on Laith and began to play.

Laith joined him, and together they wove music of singular beauty, the harper using his fine voice to add deeper notes. From somewhere came the high, light circling of pipe to Laith's ear.

Dimly, he heard the hush that fell over the hall, and distantly he saw the tears flowing down the faces of listeners. But he did not cease, only followed the master bard through this song and into the next. It seemed to Laith he heard more pipes, and singing of unholy loveliness, but it did not matter.

He played.

And joy welled in him, deep and full, and it welled in the throats of their listeners, too. Laughter rang into the room, and boisterous singing, and clapping.

And still they played, Laith and the old harper, played a lullaby as sweet and seductive as the softness of an evening breeze, blowing out the light of day before it. In the hall, heads drooped, and snores rang out, and the faint high voices faded away, as did the pipes, until all that was left were the whispering voices of the two harps.

Laith met the eyes of the old bard, and they smiled together. The bard put his harp aside and inclined his head. "I knew your father and your grandfather before him. They'd be proud to claim you."

A thick lump came into Laith's throat, and even had he had the use of his voice, he could not have spoken.

"I am Indiu," the bard said. "And 'tis plain you are fairy-cursed and fairy-blessed all at once." A rueful smile cut his wizened visage. "It has been many years since I heard the fairy queen sing."

As the meaning of his words penetrated, Laith gaped. Those sweet high, unworldly voices! Fairies. Unexpectedly, fierce emotion filled him, and he bowed his head to hide his reaction. To have lived all these years without magic, or even the promise of it. He did not know how he'd borne it.

Just then, Ciarann let go a cry of terror and protest. Laith bolted toward her, remembering too late that there was no rue hidden in the rushes of the hall, and he'd unknowingly thinned the veil between the Other-world and this one by playing his music with the bard.

He reached her before anyone else, for the rest of the company was yet in enchanted slumber and would not wake till morning coaxed their eyes open. Would Ciarann wake, or was she trapped in the clutches of the prince? She sobbed softly, and he took her shoulders, wishing for his voice so he could coax her awake.

But she did not wake, and Laith pulled her limp form into his arms, putting as much of himself against her as he could. Gathering all his strength, he emptied his mind and carried her to her chamber.

A scream tore from her as they crossed the threshold, and she rose up so fast in his arms that her chin crashed into his lip. Laith struggled to hold her thrashing form, even as he tasted blood, and managed to get her to her bed.

There she quieted a little. Keeping his mind blank, he sat beside her and stroked her hair for a long time.

The day before Midsummer's Eve dawned clear and dry, but Ciarann met it with dread. Her dream clung to her like an odor, undercutting every act.

The prince was angry. So angry! In her dream, he had shown her terrible things, prophecies or promises of what he would do if she did not come to him. She had seen death and destruction and starvation. Did he have that power? Could he curse the whole village over the rejection of one mortal woman?

Her head ached as she helped cook the evening meal. It seemed she could not free a single clear thought—they chased each other like squirrels, round and round and round.

What had she done?

And how could it be undone?

In her distraction, she put her hand against a searing hearthstone when she tried to take a pot from the fire, then dropped the pot to the earthen floor, spilling the boiling contents in a splattering pool. The kitchen women cried out, and Ciarann burst into tears, putting her burned hand to her mouth.

"Milady!" cried Megan, bustling forward. "You've burned yourself. Quick, plunge it in this water so 'twon't blister." She tsked. "That's a nasty one."

Ciarann only stood there, tears streaming down her cheeks like a small girl. She stared at the mark, blistering in spite of the water, and it seemed to her an omen of evil to come. It made her dizzy. "Megan, I feel quite ill. Help me to the garden."

Megan clapped her hands at the girls staring in mute discomfort at their mistress. "Get on with it now! Mop up that spill and put another pot on. I'll be back."

Ciarann clutched Megan's arm for steadiness and they went out the side door to a stone bench nearby the herb gardens. Shakily, Ciarann breathed the redolent scents of sun-warmed herbs. Bees, heavy with nectar, made bumping, low flights between plants, buzzing in drowsy contentment.

The scents seemed to end the spell, and her head cleared as she sat there. "Thank you, Megan."

"Are ye all right, milady? You're terribly pale."

She took the old woman's hand. "I had a brutal dream. I fear an ill wind will blow here tomorrow night, and it will be my fault it comes to pass." She looked into Megan's eyes. "What have I done?"

Megan bowed her head. It gave Ciarann another stone of guilt to add weight to those already collected. "The gentry are a fearsome lot," she said quietly. "And ne'er have I seen so fierce a one as your prince."

"How do I thwart him now? Or do I simply go with him, to spare the rest of you the punishment he promises?"

"I know not, milady. Mayhap you should ask our young bard, there playing his harp in the corner."

Ciarann lifted her head. She had not seen Laith when they came out, but there he was in the dappled shadows cast by an apple tree. He looked at her with a sober expression. Her heart leapt in her breast. "Yes. I will ask him."

Laith stood as she approached, and Ciarann hurried toward him. He lifted a hand as she got close, and Ciarann did not hesitate—she flowed into his embrace, putting her face against his chest. He smelled of sunlight and apples, and as his arms circled her, holding her close, she felt her panic and despair flow away. "Help me," she whispered.

He stroked her head and her back, holding her until her trembling ceased. A kiss might have lit upon her crown, but it was so quick and light, she could not have said for sure.

His face was grave. *You must face him and deny him.*

"But he casts a glamour I do not know how to resist!"

Laith nodded. From his girdle he drew a bundle of herbs, braided and woven in a particular way. He put it in her hand. *Keep it upon you.*

Ciarann closed her fingers over it. "Thank you, my friend." She did not look at him as she got to her feet.

 # Chapter 11

CIARANN'S sense of dread did not abate as the evening wore on, but only grew more intense. She seemed alone in her misgivings. Her father drank heartily with his men, telling tales of bravado in battle. The old harper and Laith sat off by themselves, playing one challenge and then another, oblivious to the presence of anyone but themselves. Ciarann wandered restlessly, longing for the days before all this sorrow and magic had fallen upon her. Once she had enjoyed these quiet suppers, with all content and calm.

She climbed to the battlements and looked out over the dark landscape, lit only by the clear crystal points of stars. Tonight, no troop of light-washed fairies came from the forest. No fairy pipes or harps or voice lent merriment to the songs.

Faintly she heard something on the wind, and it struck fear through her heart. Had she wished them to appear? The noise grew louder, and all at once came a herd of horses and warriors, spilling down over a rise in grim silence, their harnesses and horsefalls the only sound. Not a torch broke the darkness, and only the sheen of drawn swords showed where they were.

Ciarann turned and cried out. "Shut the gates! Soldiers are come!"

But it was too late. Before anyone could act on her warning, the warriors rode into the yard, and the peace of the night was shattered in a torrent of shouts and cries and grunts and screams, buried by the thunder of horses and their high whinnies.

Ciarann was swept from her post by one of her father's men. He clamped a hand over her mouth. "Forgive me, my lady. You must be hid, or the ransom will be dear."

She knew this to be true, and let him lead her to a tiny hidden room behind the kitchen, built for just this purpose. She hated to be so hid, instead of fighting with the others to defend the rath, but who knew what such blackguards would do to the daughter of their enemy? Perhaps ransom would be only the smallest misery.

Her wait was long and tense. From her dark hiding place, she could hear only thin screams and cries, sounds that seemed to go far too long. When all was silent at last, she crept out and made her way to the hall, pausing to peer from behind a curtain to be sure it was safe before she emerged.

A moan escaped her lips, but it went unnoticed in the chaotic scene. Tables had been shoved aside to make way for the wounded, and it seemed at first the entire village had been run down. A child screamed in a rhythmic, searing cry, and there were low groans and gentle weeping, and below these sounds, nothing, only the pure, dead silence of shock.

"Dear saints, will this never end!" she breathed, clutching trembling fingers into fists.

She saw Laith, wiping away the tears of a child, then turning to touch the head of her mother, who nursed a babe and wept. Laith's clothes were torn and dirty, and she saw blood on his face, as if he'd been in the thick of the battle. A wave of sickness spread in her belly at the thought, and she turned away quickly, breathing slowly to keep the nausea down.

When she was calmer, she moved into the crowd, and began to tend them as well as she was able, ordering hot wine with herbs to be made, and hearty bread and butter to be passed around, and rags to be torn for bandages. In all, it was not so terrible as it seemed at first glance— only one man had been killed, and none of the women raped. The injuries had come when the terrified number trampled and fell over each other in their haste to escape the invading soldiers. Scrapes and bruises, a broken bone or two, a lost tooth and a bloodied nose.

They had been lucky.

When all had been soothed and some had even gone to sleep, Ciarann spied her father, coming in with a bandage around his head, and one on his arm. His face was pinched and gray, and she recognized well the mulish fury in it. He would have his revenge.

The world for that instant narrowed upon him, upon his face that she had loved as the sun when she was a child, a face she still held dear, but now saw clearly. His pride and his arrogance would kill them all.

She found herself striding forward, alight with anger. He saw her coming at him and lifted his chin. When she raised her hand and slapped him soundly, there came a hush of pure, terrified shock through the room.

"Damn you for your pride," she said in a quiet and ringing voice. "Look at this misery your foolish war has caused."

With a roar, he retaliated. "Not even my own daughter can speak thus to me!"

Ciarann did not wince away from the blow he gave her. She stood straight and strong and stared him down, though she could not control the shaking of her arms or the tears that spilled out. "That does not change what is all around us, Papa. There is still misery and suffering, and you have not the wit to see you can stop it."

He trembled with rage, but before he could strike her again, Laith was there, putting himself between the pair, Ciarann behind him. He could not speak, but held up a hand to the king.

"Get her away from me before her impertinent tongue is cut out for her," the king growled.

Laith turned and shoved Ciarann before him, not gently. She flung off his arms, but moved away. A pulse pounded in the place below her eye where her father had struck her. Her hand stung from the force of her slap.

Laith took her arm firmly and half dragged her from the hall. In the yard beyond, all was silent. A fire burned low, and hounds wandered close by it, snuffling for scraps in the dirt. The gates had been closed, too late.

Ciarann took a long breath of the cool air. She felt stretched taut as a hide ready for scraping, and her hands still trembled fiercely. "I felt dread all day, and it was not the fairies at all I had to fear, but Man himself."

His hand fell on her shoulder, warm and heavy, but Ciarann did not turn. "Have you a charm against marauders?"

He grabbed her chin and turned her to look at him. *Nay.*

Ciarann saw with dismay that the blood on his face came from a cut over his eye, not deep. His eyes were shadowed, and she suspected the mark on his jaw would by morning be a purple bruise. "That eye needs tending."

Slowly, firmly, he shook his head. And then he put his hands on her face, one on each side, and tilted his head, and kissed her.

His mouth was hot and wet and demanding. It was the wild kiss of a man held too long at bay, a man who had fierce and insistent need. His long elegant hands cupped her face, and his mouth moved, and Ciarann felt all the yearning and restless, nameless hungers in her body ignite at once, flaming in her lips and tongue, and along her cheekbones where his hands touched her, and in places that did not touch him at all.

With a cry, she pressed into him, and put her arms around his neck to pull him closer, and a small, low noise rolled from her throat as he braced her hard against the wall and pressed his body against hers. And there was no need of words then. Ciarann plunged her hands into the night-dark depths of his hair, and found it cool and thick. His mouth was narcotic, as rich to taste and explore as it was to look upon. His body was lean and strong and hungry, and she pressed her whole self into him, yearning and aching.

His breath tore from him in ragged gasps as he moved that hot and pleasing mouth from her lips down her throat. Ciarann gripped him closer, and touched his high round buttocks and the backs of his thighs and arched against the earthy thrust of his full-blooded organ.

She wanted to please him. She wanted to kiss his throat, and see the whole expanse of his uncovered flesh in the moonlight. She wanted his hands—those elegant, dark, bard's hands—upon her breasts.

But once before, she had ached for him thus, and he had rejected her, and she did not want to be spurned again. When his hands slid between them and clasped her breasts, she twined her fingers in his hair and made him look at her. In a voice deep and breathy and not at all her own, she said, "Laith of Inishmoor, 'tis you I want this night. No other."

He stared at her, then gripped her head in a fierce hold, and kissed her with such open, agonized need that she knew he would not leave her tonight.

Trembling with hunger, Ciarann let him take her hand, and together they ran down the steps and in through a side door that led back to her chamber. And there, with stuttering breath and open-mouthed kisses, they disrobed each other without grace or care, until they stood at last, naked flesh to naked flesh. Ciarann's heart caught, and she stared at him for one fleeting second, then she was in his arms, reveling in the sinuous slide of his skin against her own, his hands upon her body and in her hair, his mouth on her neck and then on her breasts, his hair skimming her shoulders.

In a pool of milk-white moonlight that fell on her bed, they stopped, looking into one another's eyes without speaking or thinking. Ciarann ached at the beauty of him, at the narrow line of his jaw and the breadth of his shoulders and the long length of his limbs. Against the white light, he was dark as the earth itself, and he smelled of that earth, of work and sunlight and even blood.

And then they were joined, and Ciarann cried out at the sharp, deep pleasure of it, at the harsh grate of his breath and the way he threw back his head as if he could not bear it. There was faint surprise in her, and wild pleasure and something so holy and deep she could not name it.

So she spoke his name, softly and with fierce recognition, and held him close as her body at last met its need, holding him deep and close as he, too, found release.

His head fell on her shoulder, big and heavy and sated. She closed her eyes and smelled rue in his hair. "I love you," she whispered, and knew, at last, that it was true.

Laith buried his face against her neck when they were finished, and Ciarann felt his hands and arms trembling with the power of the thing that had passed between them. Her heart ached with a wild, pounding pain, and for a long moment, she feared she might weep with the fullness of him. He clutched her closer yet, and pressed his broad brow against her neck, and Ciarann thought she could die in this moment and never miss the rest of life. She kept her eyes closed, willing the moment to last forever.

"I cannot breathe for the fullness of my heart," he said.

Gladness spilled through her at his admission. "Nor I."

"That morning, when I saw you standing by the well, I told myself I had not known desire, or beauty until that instant."

Her eyes flew open, and she saw that he was speaking, not thinking. His voice was deeper than it was in her mind, and infinitely richer, a sound as beautiful as his harp. "Laith," she whispered, her fingers clutching his shoulders.

He shook his head. "You think you are not beautiful, my love, but—"

The import of hearing his own voice stopped him.

Ciarann stared up at him. "The curse is broken!"

He laughed, and the sound rolled out into the room, deep and loud and beautiful. "So it is!" And his voice, too, was a wondrous thing to hear. "There have been so many things I wanted to say. So many things. . . ." he trailed off. "And now I can only stare at you in stricken love, for my heart has been stolen away this night."

" 'Tis well you could not speak before now, for I have ever been skeptical of men with glib tongues."

"You dislike a glib tongue? There are things glib tongues can do that have nothing to do with words."

Her body was languid and boneless as water, but at the low dark promise of those words in his voice, she felt a rolling awareness begin anew in her body. "Is that so?"

"Aye," he breathed and bent his head to show her.

And it was then, as he illustrated by putting his agile tongue to the crown of her breast, that three soldiers burst into the room. Ciarann cried out, and Laith hastily shoved her behind him. Terrified, she peeked around his arm.

Her father stood flanked by his warriors, a grim expression on his mouth. "So my daughter turned whore while I left."

"No!" Laith protested. "She is no whore, my lord. We are in love."

"Are ye now?" the king said with deceptive congeniality. "We'll see how long it lasts once you've been banished."

Ciarann cried out. "No, Papa! You do not understand! He saved my life at risk of his own. You cannot mean to punish him for that."

The king acted as if she had not spoken. "Bard, I hereby banish you from this place. If you are caught within seven miles, I will have you hanged."

Chapter 12

So it was that even as Laith regained his voice, he lost all else. Again he found himself wandering through a dark night, without friend or companion save his harp. It seemed uncommonly cruel that he'd regained his voice, so he might at last talk the way he'd longed to do, and laugh with her, and give her the tales he'd saved these long months, and now she was lost to him.

And to be cast out again was cruelest of all. To his surprise, he'd found a home at the rath. He liked his little bed, and the mews and the kitchen. He would miss Megan's bawdy jests, and the agreeable hounds who trailed him about, and he had looked forward to playing again with Indiu, the master bard who had known his father.

These were his thoughts as he tried to sleep in his worn cloak beneath a shelter of yew. Close to his chest, he cradled his harp, and wrapped around it the cloak of seven colors that befitted a bard.

In truth, petulance, which had been so much a part of an orphaned boy forced out to a cold and hungry world before he was ready, no longer suited him. And when he saw the faint brightness of impending dawn on the horizon, he remembered it was Midsummer's Eve, and Ciarann had no one but Laith himself to help her.

He washed his face in a cool-running stream and remembered how stricken she had looked, coming from wherever they'd hid her to the scene of wounded villagers in the hall. He had loved her before that. Had loved her from first sight.

But last night, he had at last understood her, understood her wish to flee the brutal pursuits of warriors and her father, and retreat to a place the violence could touch her no more. When she had strode through the hall, to slap her father the king, he had nearly laughed aloud. So proud and fierce she was! So bright and strong.

They needed her, her people.

So now as morning dawned on this most dangerous day, Laith sifted through the months of remembering the old ways, the old magic of a bard's harp and voice, and he made a plan. Having wandered these parts the past months, he knew well where to find what he sought: a hill with a hawthorn growing from its crown. There he took a thorn from the hawthorn, and from around a leather cord around his neck, a small perforated stone.

Already he had fasted. There were parts of the spell he would not be able to accomplish—by decree, there were to be seven bards, one from each school, and the hilltop should be at the meeting place of seven farms. This only had three, but three was a strong number. He would sing on his own the parts of seven bards.

And he would pray he had learned enough to cast an honorable satire upon Ciarann's father, so when the night fell, Laith could battle Finn without fear of death from her father.

It was his only hope, but even as he began he had grave doubts about his worthiness for the task.

All day he sat there, taking no water or food. As the sun sunk in the west, he stood, washed again in the stream, and donned his cloak of seven colors. He felt cleansed and pure—and filled with the magic and the nobility of his blood, but he fair ached with fear.

So many things could go wrong. To best the prince, Laith would need to be within the yard, and take the prince unaware. But if Ciarann's father found him before he could make the magic—or if his magic did not prove to be strong enough, not only would Laith die, but Ciarann would be forever lost. Her hounds would howl, and Megan would weep, and old soldiers would have no friendly ear into which to pour their stories.

The sidh could not need her more than the mortals in her realm.

He hid himself in a hedge. From his post, he could see the rath on the hill, and the villagers streaming round, building their fires and laughing. To his left, perhaps five yards distant, was the break in the trees through which the fairies had ridden on Beltane.

It seemed a thousand years or only minutes before the full darkness came, another thousand before Laith, cramped and cold in his hiding place, heard the unearthly pipes, and the musical jingle of the bells in the horses' collars.

Remember, he told himself, opening his eyes wide. Remember this.

First came a luminescent paleness that showed in shreds through the shadows of the trees. Then Laith saw their magnificent horses, those pale, high-stepping beasts, and then the fairies themselves in their gossamer draperies. Once more, he allowed himself to be dazzled by the pure shining beauty of the magical creatures, and prosaically wondered if they were so fond of green for the way it showed off their illuminated skin and light-struck hair. He watched them pass with held breath, admiring the long fine length of limbs made for nimble dancing and faces molded for the pleasure of mortals, and silk-draped breasts made to bewitch mortal hands.

When they rode through the gates, the aura of light seemed to be suddenly doused, and Laith could no more see the fairies at all.

Laith took his harp and moved toward the rath, breathing supplication to Dagda, Master of all harpers, for whatever help he could lend this night.

With a heavy heart, Ciarann dressed in her gold-trimmed green gown. Into her hair she wove cowslip and red campion and wild thyme. In the hall, she sat quietly with Owen whose face was so ruined. She visited the kitchens one last time, imprinting upon her memory the yeast and heat and woman smell of it. She lingered with Megan, and visited the miller one more time. Tonight his blue eyes were distant and misty as he beheld the fires, and she knew he thought of his wife.

What a foolish child Ciarann had been, wanting to escape this world, these people. Her dogs trailed after her anxiously, as if they scented some ill wind, and the eldest gave a faint whine every now and again, as if she were worried. Ciarann ached with the knowledge that they would pine for her. If it were possible, she would have taken them with her, but hounds held no love of the sidh.

And so, in her gown of green and gold, with fairy flowers in her hair, a grief-stricken Ciarann sat down on a bench to wait for the prince. Until last night, she had believed there might be a way to thwart him, that somehow, she could escape paying the price of her foolish call to the Other-world. But too clearly had she seen his wrath, and too frightening had been the soldiers' attack upon the village last night. To give them peace, Ciarann would go with the prince.

She knew nothing else to do, and with Laith banished, she had no one to help her.

Laith.

For one blinding moment, she felt him all around her, his arms and his kiss and his beautiful, unimaginably rich bard's voice, and her heart felt near to bursting with the grief of never seeing him again. But for him, too, did she act tonight. For her foolishness, he had paid enough—she would not ask him to pay with his life.

Through the darkness came the faint glow of light, and then the troop of fairies were through the gate, bringing with them a brightness and beauty unlike anything to be found on the mortal realm. In truth she was glad to know they still lived, that their beauty and magic still wove through the lives of her folk. It was not so much the fairies themselves that had brought this trouble as Ciarann's lack of faith. If she had believed they really lived, she would never have been so bold as to call them to her world, to offer herself to them.

She rose, clasping her hands before her. A king's daughter often married more for purpose than for love, and at least she would not be ill-treated.

But oh, Laith, Laith! Why could she not have seen sooner the truth of her feelings for him?

She saw Finn, long and gilded and graceful as the turn of an afternoon, and she saw when his gaze lit upon her in her green gown with red campion in her braided hair. Evenly, proudly she met his gaze.

He smiled, and bowed, almost ironically, as if he knew she came reluctantly. Without hurry, he moved toward her.

"At last," he said as he drew near. Extending one pale hand in invitation, he smiled. "You will not mind so much when these mortals have passed on, and it will seem like no time at all for you—or I. And the courts will sing of the fair Ciarann, who left her mortal coil to live with the sidh in their Realm."

She did not take his proffered hand. His smile grew the larger as he dropped his own to his side.

"Will they now?" she asked sharply. "I think they'll sing instead of Finn, who beglamoured the fair Ciarann, so she could not know her own mind until it was too late."

"Was it so unfair? What hope had I to win your heart when I may cross so rarely, and he could walk your world every day?"

"I beg you, Finn, give me back my life. I was a foolish girl, running from sorrow when I called you."

"But call you did, lass."

Ciarann bowed her head. "So I did."

"Will it be so terrible?" he asked. "I am no troll."

A king's daughter must first consider the folk in her realm, and so Ciarann put aside her shattering heart, and lifted her head proudly. "No, you are no troll, and I am honorable, so I go with you." She narrowed her eyes. "You may take my body, but you will never have my spirit or my heart, for both belong to that bard you would have silenced, and all my days in your eternal realm, you will know I am ever thinking of my Laith and his last words to me."

Vast amusement crossed the elegant face. "He is cursed—how came you to hear his pretty words?"

Ciarann smiled, very slowly. "The curse was broken last evening, when he lay with me." She raised a brow. "Did you not know?"

"I—"

Full-throated music, harp and a man's booming voice, interrupted him. Finn whirled, his eyes narrowed as he sought the source of the sound.

A trill of twined joy and dread moved through Ciarann, and she, too, looked for the music. There was Laith upon the ramparts, his harp in his hands, his cloak of seven colors and his hair blowing back as if from the force of the sound.

For there was great force, great power in the woven threads of his harp, which she had heard, and the glory of his voice, raised in song, which she had not. Every eye, every ear, turned in eager or doomed expectation.

And he played as he had the night in the hall with Indiu, her father's harper. The song of laughter first, booming and joyous and playful. Ciarann saw dancers leaping around the midsummer fires, and little children clapping as they laughed.

In the crowd, she saw the sidh dance, too. She saw the queen, that creature of the moon and the night, whirl with rare abandon, her green silk and ankle-length hair and pale white hands fluttering in the currents she created.

And she saw her father, coming out to stand on the steps to the hall, a tankard in his hands. His eyes caught on the bard who made such leaping music, and Ciarann went cold.

Laith had risked death by coming here. She knew well her father made no idle threats—he had promised Laith would be put to death, and he would make that promise true.

But even he seemed to fall under the spell of the music, and she saw him laughing as the music caught him, saw his eager lusty gaze light upon the gilded beauty of the queen he would not remember come morning.

Only Finn seemed uninfluenced. After his first rigid fury, he turned to Ciarann with a cold, cold smile. "He thinks he will bewitch me with his simple tunes—but I have no little magic of my own."

He strode away, and Ciarann watched in terror, unsure of what she should do. If she moved closer to Laith, it might draw her father's attention. If she did not halt Finn, he might kill Laith.

But she had no music in her, and no magic. She knew one who did, and sought him now, running through the crowd to find Indiu. She could not find him in the crowds, and wondered where he could have gone, when all at once, the music changed. Now from his high post, Laith played the infinitely wrenching music of sorrow, and Ciarann clapped her hands over ears so the sound would be blunted.

A whistle of pipe undercut the harp and voice, weaving through and changing the spell. Ciarann broke through a knot of villagers to see who played such piercing notes.

Finn. Nimble and bright and skilled, he played counterpoint to Laith's notes of sorrow, and around her, Ciarann heard the murmuring

gasps of the crowd. Indeed the air seemed to crackle, and she could almost see the music, see its long streamers that danced through them all
like bright and dark ribbons, wrapping them until they could not move.

And now there came an unholy voice, sweet and pure as a mountain
stream, fluting and embroidering Laith's chest-deep baritone, lending
poignance to the song of sorrow. Ciarann saw the queen, halting her
dancing to move through the still villagers to stand below the sidh and
the harper.

Ciarann clutched her hands to her breast, her eyes fixed upon the figure of her love, so tall and straight and dark, so noble in his cloak and
voice. 'Twas this the bards had been once, the keepers of the soul of Erin,
and Laith had brought it back again. Tonight, in the earth, the old soul
drank deeply of the nourishing song.

And in Ciarann, the song moved, too. It eased her weariness like a
cool hand upon a fevered brow. It stole away the last knot of sorrow she'd
felt over Colin, and eased the anger she felt toward her poor, misguided
father.

Oh, yes, tonight the soul of the land was risen and strong, and Laith
had made it so—not only because he was a bard of many generations,
but because he was himself made of the earth, made from the soul of
the land, and it needed him.

In a sudden rush, Ciarann bolted forward to kneel at the queen's feet.
"My lady," she cried, putting her hands around the queen's. "Help me!"

Not unkindly, the sidh looked down. "You must deny him," she said.
" 'Tis as simple as that. Tell him he does not exist, and he will not."

"That is all?"

"It is." She smiled. "You see how he grows stronger now, with your
faith and the bard, bringing him alive. Finn, more than any of us, depends upon the mortal faith to feed him, and he cannot bear to live
without it. These have been hard years for him, and I fear it will not
change."

Ciarann frowned, steeling herself against the wild music ringing
through her. "But will Finn die if I deny him? I do not wish for him to
die."

"He will not. 'Twill be centuries of unbelief yet before he withers from
lack of attention." The pale, luminescent hand moved over Ciarann's.
"But if you do not deny him now, you will be among our number be-

fore the night is through—and in truth, I think you unsuited to our ways."

"As do I."

"Claim your life, Ciarann, and have faith to see it through."

"Blessings to you, my lady. I will not forget."

The queen smiled. "I know you will not. Someday, we will meet again."

There was a faint break in the sound, and Ciarann turned, fearful Laith had been defeated. He had not, but there was on his brow a sheen of sweat, and his mouth was hard with concentration. The sidh's pipe seemed to swell just then.

"I deny you, Finn," she cried. Her voice, bold and proud, rang between the men. "I deny you!" She pulled the red campion from her hair, and the cowslip, and lifted her chin proudly as she let the wilting flowers fall to the earth.

Finn ceased his playing to look at her in horror. "No, Ciarann—you do not know what you do!"

"Do I not?" She smiled. "I deny you."

She had thought the race aloof and cold. For an instant, she read in his eyes passion and fury and regret—

Laith began to play, and Ciarann heard in the notes the sweet song of the mortal realm. She heard the earthy cry of babes and the ring of a blacksmith's hammer, and the sound of young girls laughing, and the howl of hounds, and love strong enough to weather death.

As if they could not bear it, the fairies were suddenly gone.

And then Ciarann heard her father cry out.

Laith heard the king's roar with a bolt of terror. At first he thought he'd been spotted, and the guards would seize him, and he would be put to death. Wildly, he looked over his shoulder—could he clear the ramparts?

No. They were too high, and he risked being impaled on the thorns that grew in a sticky hedge round the base of the walls.

Then he became aware that the roar was less a cry of anger than one of pain. The villagers and guards clustered around the king, as if they were afraid—and in the silence left by the vivid music, their voices reached him easily.

"My eyes!" cried the king. "I cannot see!"

Below, Ciarann turned to look at Laith, and he saw in her face her expectation that Laith had done this. Puzzled, he shook his head—and then he remembered the glam dicend, the musical spell he'd sung from the hill.

A blind king could not rule. And a bloodthirsty king should not rule. He smiled.

Ciarann smiled back at him. It was lit with the joy of a thousand love songs, the sensuality of a thousand joinings. In a rush, he bolted for the stairs, as Ciarann ran below, and they met at the foot of the steps in a wild embrace. He kissed her, full on the mouth, and spoke.

"Will you wed me, fair Ciarann?"

She tipped her head back and closed her eyes. "Ask again."

"Will you wed me?"

She lifted her shoulders and smiled. "You have the most beautiful voice I have ever heard."

He smiled. "Will you wed me, wench, or shall I go see if Megan will be more willing?"

Ciarann laughed, the full-throated laugh of an earthly woman. "Aye, that I will, good bard." Sobering, she put her hands on his jaw. "That I will."

As he kissed her, Laith thought he heard—ever so faintly—the lilting song of the fairy queen.

He took it as a blessing.

To Recapture the Light

Morgan Llywelyn

The Fairies, they say, are not immortal. They can live to a great age, but they too know death. And when one of their kind dies, the music of their mourning is the saddest, sweetest sound in all the world.

Chapter 1

As light as thistledown, as insubstantial as dreams, she floated. Sometimes she paused to exchange breath with a wild rose, or watch the patterns of light and shadow chase one another across the rolling hills as the clouds rippled overhead like liquid marble.

Sometimes she sighed.

Lasair was not unhappy, but she felt an emptiness that even the loveliness of the Irish countryside in summer could not fill. She had a profound sense of waiting, but could not have said what she was waiting for.

If she returned home in this mood, her kinfolk would laugh at her. "Come and dance and be merry," they would urge. "It is not like you to be melancholy."

They frequently criticized her, for she was unlike the rest of them in many ways. Yet they were never angry with her, for no one could be angry with Lasair.

She was too beautiful.

Drifting, dreaming, she paused to glance at her reflection in a fern-fringed pool. The dark water mirrored her face and then promptly filled with light, blotting out the image before she could catch more than the most fleeting glimpse. Tendrils of silken hair, huge eyes, a narrow chin, a mouth more sweetly curved than a rainbow . . .

. . . Gone. Swallowed by the light which now shone from the pool with an opalescent radiance.

Lasair was not surprised. Light always obscured her image, so that she must rely on others to tell her how she looked. "You are as gorgeous as whitethorn blooming," Greine was fond of saying, but because Greine desired her his opinion would never be objective.

They all desired her, with the passionless appetite of faerie.

How could it be otherwise? They—her kin, her people—were of the Tuatha Dé Danann, that mysterious race which had ruled Erin before the coming of the Gael. Rejecting the dangerous emotions of humankind, they utilized other energies to explore the spirit of nature and the nature of spirit.

Sorcery was their strength. By shaping thought with spells and rituals they could manipulate their environment, summoning storms or calming the most savage sea. The wind blew as they directed and the seasons rotated at their desire. Even time was bent to their will, its processes incredibly slowed. They made of Erin a paradise of beauty and serenity.

When the island was invaded by the Gael, a Celtic people from the European mainland, the Tuatha Dé Danann had confidently pitted their magic against the swords of the newcomers. But to their astonishment, sorcery failed against cold iron. Bitterly disappointed, they had fled from sight, retreating into earthen mounds or melting into the bark and bloom of thorn trees.

No matter where the Tuatha Dé Danann hid, however, the victorious Gael remained aware of them. By the prickling of their scalps they knew the magic was not dead, merely waiting. Incorporated into the land itself. Gaelic warriors were careful to tread lightly upon the earth, and looked often over their shoulders.

They ceased to speak of the vanished race as the Tuatha Dé Danann and called them simply the *Sídhe*, a name meant to encompass the inexplicable. As time passed the Gael enshrined their former enemies in folklore as supernatural beings and credited them with fabulous powers. In return for the compliment, a few of the female Sídhe appointed themselves as guardian spirits, watching over the destinies of certain Gaelic clans.

Together the two races shaped the soul of Erin, a land possessed in equal measure by a warrior aristocracy and a hidden, shimmering magic.

The centuries sped by, the rest of the world changed and changed again, but the island at the edge of the Atlantic slumbered on in a long dream. Christ was born, Rome fell, yet music from the realm of faerie continued to ring high and sweet through the forested glens of Erin. Gaelic wives set out bowls of milk to placate the ancient foe and Gaelic maidens decked thorn trees—"fairy trees"—with propitiatory gifts, while the great earthen mounds known as "fairy forts" were left strictly alone.

The forts echoed with laughter at the stories the humans told of the Sídhe. "They get such very peculiar notions," chortled Greine, holding his sides and howling with mirth at the latest tale in which the fairy folk were represented as wearing little green hats and pointed-toed shoes. "Can you imagine any of us refusing the kiss of the sun by wearing hats, or denying the earth beneath our feet by imprisoning them in shoes?"

Lasair had laughed with him. The very idea was preposterous. Any restriction was anathema to her; she could not even abide the burden of a jeweled girdle around her slender waist. She preferred to dress in spun cobwebs that had no weight and were pearled only by the dew. In such a gown she would dance for countless nights and days, twirling in starlight or pirouetting in sunlight with equal joy. She never seemed to tire.

The Gael claimed the Sídhe were immortal.

That, Lasair knew well enough, was not true. On days like today when a deep melancholy seized her, she felt every one of her many centuries.

Great changes had taken place in Erin during her lifetime. The warm green island had become known as Ireland, and its gold and timber drew other invaders. Vikings swooped out of the cold sea in longships with dragonheaded prows, bringing an era of blood and fire and rapine. The Sídhe had buried themselves ever more deeply in their hiding places, unable to accept a world in which such brutality reigned.

At last the Vikings had been subdued by a great Irish king and peace returned—for a moment. The Sídhe had crept from their hiding places and lit fires of celebration on the hilltops.

Then another king from across the sea had undertaken to conquer Ireland, slaughtering the descendants of the Gael to make room for his own subjects. Once more the Sídhe had gone underground. In their sanctuaries they waited, hoping the old Gaelic order would triumph again. They did not like the Saxons, who had no comprehension of Irish magic.

But it seemed as if the Saxons meant to stay.

Chapter 2

I N the language of the Sídhe, Lasair's name meant heat and light. Birds burst into song as she passed by. The most timid field mice crept out of the tall grass to cavort with abandon as long as she was near. Her caress could restore life to a frost-withered vine, and long-dormant flower seeds germinated in her footprints. She had only to look over her shoulder to see them blossoming in her wake.

Two thousand years ago, Lasair thought ruefully, her magic had brought forth larger flowers. More fragrant and more brightly colored.

If she could get a good look at her reflection, would she see faint lines beginning to trace like cobwebs around her eyes?

Even the Sídhe cannot live forever.

Perhaps that was what brought on this melancholy mood, she told herself. An awareness of time passing and nothing happening. But what did she want to happen? Perhaps it would be better to go back to the fort and . . .

She stopped in midstride like a startled deer, then retreated into a nearby clump of thorn trees. Their feathery foliage gladly enveloped her; their cruel thorns would not pierce her skin.

The air was shivering with a faint disturbance which to one of the Sídhe was unmistakable. Someone was approaching; someone human.

In recent times the Sídhe had grown less and less willing to encounter humankind. Lasair's father constantly warned against them. So she started to withdraw deeper into the shrubbery, intending to melt into the bark of a whitethorn for sanctuary. But at the last moment, an irresistible impulse bade her stay where she was.

He came down the footbeaten road with a bag slung over his shoulder and a broad, flat parcel tucked under his arm. He was walking slowly, scanning the surrounding terrain with a peculiar, restless movement of his head. Yet he did not move like a man fearing an attack. He was humming to himself as a man will do when no one is around and he longs for the comfort of a human voice.

There was something about him that called voicelessly to something within herself.

Trembling, yet unable to resist, Lasair stepped out onto the path.

At first he did not seem to see her. Then he gave a start and almost dropped his parcel. "I beg your pardon," he said in a deep, rich voice. "I thought I was alone here."

"You can see me?" she asked in surprise. Many humans these days—particularly the Saxon—lacked the ability. They had blind eyes; blind to beauty and magic and most especially blind to the Sídhe.

From his accent, however, this man was no Saxon. His crisp dark curls and rugged features were Irish, and he spoke in the tongue of the Gael as he responded, "I can see you, praise God, and it is a treat for the eyes you are. What is a lass like yourself doing alone in this wilderness?"

"Wilderness?" Lasair sounded puzzled. With a gesture of ineffable grace she indicated the thorn trees nearby, the green hills beyond, the hazy purple mountains in the distance. "But this is my home," she said.

Her voice reminded him of the chiming of the bells in the campanile in Ravenna. "No one lives here, surely," he replied. "I have seen neither castle nor cottage for many miles."

A shudder of distaste ran through Lasair's body. "Castles and cottages! I should not care to be entrapped by either."

"Where do you live, then? Not in the open surely, a maiden so tender as yourself."

She realized he was mistaking her for a human woman.

Dropping her eyes, she murmured, "No, not in the open. My home is . . . in the old style . . . not far from here."

"The old style? What does that mean?" While she hesitated he pressed on, "I am an artist and interested in everything in the Irish countryside. I do engraving work, you see, and am commissioned to prepare the illustrations for a travel book. So if there is an antiquarian residence of special interest in this region, I should be most grateful if you would show it to me so I may sketch it. Who knows, your home might become famous. People would travel great distances just to see it."

The very thought horrified Lasair. What would the others say if she drew such attention to them? Holding up her hand, she protested vehemently, "No, no, I implore you! Ours is only a poor dwelling of mud and stones roofed with grass, nothing that could possibly interest an artist."

For the sheer pleasure of looking at her, he sought to prolong their conversation. "I shan't be an artist for much longer, I fear. This will be my last commission, so it's very important that I do good work. If not your home, perhaps you know of some other site of scenic interest you could show me—a waterfall, perhaps, or a ruined bridge?"

Lasair took a step backward, wondering if she should flee. Would he pursue her? How could she escape without revealing her true nature?

Seeing her shrink from him he said hastily, "I apologize! Being so much alone has made me forget my manners. Of course a lady would not allow a gentleman to take such liberties when she had not even been introduced to him. There is no one here who can introduce us, however, so we must make do for ourselves. I humbly ask you to forgive me. My name is Cormac Casey and I am quite ordinary and respectable, I assure you, even if I am an artist."

Lasair fought the temptation to laugh aloud. Ordinary and respectable! How would he react if she said, I am one of the Sídhe and there is nothing either ordinary or respectable about any of us.

Although her eyes were sparkling with mischief, she solemnly replied, "I am called Lasair. From your name and language you are of the Gael, yet I hear something else in your voice, a faint distortion?"

"You have a good ear. I am Irish of course; before his death my father was a merchant in Cork City, and my mother's people came from Waterford. But I have spent a number of years abroad, principally in Italy, where I studied art. I must have picked up a trace of an accent there."

"Will you go abroad again?"

A shadow crossed his face. "I think not." He made an obvious effort to change the subject. "Lasair. How lovely—and unusual. Is that your Christian name or your surname?"

She had to bite back another laugh; the effort set dimples dancing in her cheeks. Christian name indeed! "I was called Lasair after an ancestress of mine. My father's name is Leary." She deliberately shaped the old Danann pronunciation into a form more accommodating to human speech.

Cormac's mouth was shaped for smiling, but the muscles were a little out of practice. "Well, Lasair Leary, now that we have been introduced, would you be willing to show me the local sights? Again I ask your forgiveness for acting with such impropriety, but you see, I haven't much time."

To her surprise she found herself walking beside him. The top of her head did not quite reach his shoulder, and she had to make an effort to keep up with his long legs. He noticed at once and considerately shortened his stride. Lasair rewarded him by saying, "There is a very fine glen on the other side of yonder hill, with some *ogham* stones. Is that the sort of thing you wish?"

"Ogham stones with runic carving? That's just what the publishers want. Are the hills high on either side of the glen? Will there be enough light for sketching?"

"As much as there is here," Lasair assured him. "You said you do something called engraving. I am not familiar with the term. What does it mean?"

"Engraving involves making prints from metal plates into which a design has been incised with special tools. Various gradations of tone can be produced so that one can replicate almost any original pattern, including quite complicated drawings. I studied the technique in Italy, following guidelines laid down by the old master Raimondi himself. First I sketch the scenes, then I transfer them onto the metal plates. Once they are printed into a book they are preserved so that generations of people may enjoy them."

"Do you mean that even if the trees were cut down, they could still be seen in your book?"

"I do."

She paused in the path. "And if you were to make a picture of me, could others see me?"

"They could of course. I would love to sketch you, Lasair, if you would give me permission. You would make a wonderful subject."

Anger flared in her. "I am no one's subject! We are free!"

"That is not what I meant," Cormac said hastily. "It is only an artist's term for the figure in a portrait." As he spoke, he slid the parcel from beneath his arm and began fumbling with the strings. "Please sit there on that rock and let me get out my sketching things. I shall do a quick drawing of you, just to give you some idea."

Once again she was moved by a powerful compulsion. Instinct told Lasair to flee, yet she seated herself daintily on the sun-warmed boulder beside the path and lifted her face so that he could study it as he set up a small portable easel and sketchbook.

With sticks of charcoal he made lines and curves on paper. Working swiftly, his head cocked to one side and his eyes narrowed, he seemed totally lost in his work, giving Lasair a chance to study him.

Cormac Casey's strongly modeled face had a hint of boyishness lingering about the mouth, although there were a few strands of grey in his dark hair. His eyes were also grey, with exceptionally large pupils. They seemed to bother him, for in spite of his intense concentration he blinked almost continually.

After a few minutes he threw off his traveling cape to free his arms for his work. His body in linen shirt and woolen trousers was well muscled, with broad shoulders and powerful thighs. Lasair admired the shape of his hands. As they deftly maneuvered his drawing sticks, his fingers appeared to dance.

"Do you like to dance?" she inquired.

He glanced up at her. "Dance? There has been little time in my life for dancing. It's hard enough to make a living without spending time on frivolity."

Yet he had that boyish mouth . . .

"Everyone needs some frivolity," announced Lasair.

"This is the Year of Our Lord 1860 and there is little frivolity left in the world," he replied. "Ireland has not really recovered from the Great Famine; perhaps it never will. Many of the sketches I have made so far are of tumble-down cabins whose inhabitants either starved or emigrated."

"If you find them unpleasant, why do you draw them?"

"Ruins, particularly those tainted with sadness, are considered picturesque."

"You should show happier scenes," said Lasair with conviction. "If you could see my people dancing . . ."

"Do they dance a lot, your family?"

A sudden smile wreathed her face with such beauty Cormac caught his breath. "We love to dance! When the moon is high we have the most wonderful festivals with pipers and harpers and everyone dressed in their finest. Ah, the music! And the laughter and the light-footed leaping!" In an ecstasy of remembering, she clasped tiny white hands to her breast.

His charcoal pencil dangled forgotten from his fingers. "I should love to see you dancing so."

She bit her lip. "Oh, but that is not possible. My people are . . . shy of strangers. Our festivities are very private."

"Like your home?" he guessed shrewdly.

Lasair was conscious of the intensity of his gaze. He was studying her as if he would memorize every aspect of her being; almost as if he could see through her delicate white skin to the burning spirit within. Stepping away from his easel, he came to sit beside her on the stone. When he spoke again, his deep voice was as irresistible as the sun beaming down upon them. "You are unlike anyone I ever met, Miss Leary. If I give my word not to trespass into any area where I am not wanted, will you tell me something of yourself and your people?"

The Sídhe never discussed themselves and never told the truth to any human. They were the most secretive of beings. Yet to her vast astonishment, Lasair heard herself say, "I might."

Chapter 3

CORMAC Casey was enchanted by Lasair. At first he had thought her a young girl, no more than fifteen at most, but now that he was sitting beside her he recognized a mature woman. Her eyes held ancient wisdoms. Yet her skin! Even when he was close enough to smell her fragrant breath he could detect no pores, no imperfections in that luminous complexion. Her bone structure was as fine as that of the classical beauties he had studied on the Continent but infinitely more fragile, as if a touch would shatter her.

Hers, he observed with an artist's eye, was not a Gaelic face.

"Where do your people come from?" he wanted to know. "You do not have the look of the Irish about you."

Her laughter rippled like a brook over stones. "We are more Irish than you, we have been here longer than your ancestors. We . . ." She stopped abruptly, as if she had said too much already.

But he wanted to know more; he wanted to know everything about her. His vision of the world, which had been progressively narrowing for the past year, had now narrowed even more until she filled it completely. Suddenly nothing else interested him.

She made a movement as if she would get up, and to restrain her he laid one hand on her sleeve. Through the gossamer fabric he felt an extraordinary heat rising from the arm beneath.

"Forgive my presumption," he said, hastily withdrawing his hand. Yet the memory of that heat continued to burn his palm.

He forced his eyes away from her face long enough to take a look at the clothing she wore, wondering why it did not burst into flame at her touch. Upon closer examination, Lasair appeared to be swathed in a combination of cobwebs and rainbows. Embroidery of an incredible delicacy ornamented neckline and wrist. Squinting, he discovered that what he first mistook for embroidery was actually living flowers.

And dewdrops, shimmering.

Cormac drew in his breath with a gasp. He raised his eyes to hers once more. A dreadful surmise was growing in him. "*What* are you?" he whispered hoarsely.

Sorrow sped across her face as a cloud darkens a bright meadow. "That is one question you should not ask."

"I must."

Her lips refused to form words that would define the gulf between them. Instead she raised one tiny white hand until it caught and held his eyes. Then, placing the hand palm down upon the stone beside her thigh, she stroked the bare boulder.

Once, twice, thrice.

When she lifted her hand, a soft green moss starred with tiny white flowers had begun to spread across the surface of the stone.

Icy prickles ran across Cormac's shoulders and down his spine. He knew then that he was in the presence of magic: the ancient magic which had once held all Ireland in thrall. "You are one of the Sídhe," he accused. "You are a banshee!"

While sketching the abandoned Gaelic fortress of Dunluce by moonlight earlier in the year, he had been startled by a spine-tingling ululation emanating from the roofless ruin. Never would he forget that sound of unearthly grief, nor the terror it aroused in him. Shaken, he had spoken of it afterwards at the inn where he was staying. "What you heard was the banshee of the O'Donnells," he had been informed. "A mortal man must fear for his immortal soul when the banshee wails."

But Lasair was shaking her head. "I am not what you think. A *beann sídhe* is a particular sort of fairy woman who acts as both guardian and harbinger of destruction for a Gaelic clan. Her scream of warning strikes terror in human hearts. I have no connection with any clan, however."

"Yet you are one of the magic people," he insisted.

She gave a small nod of affirmation. "I am what is called a *leannán sídhe*, or fairy sweetheart."

"Have you . . . a husband?"

Lasair replied simply, "We do not wed as you do."

Cormac was confused by his own feelings. He should be terrified, yet at the same time he was powerfully attracted to this woman. Since childhood he had been taught to fear the Sídhe, or as some called them, the Good People. The name was a deliberate attempt to mislead. They were not believed to be good, but selfish and spiteful and incredibly dangerous, lurking in the shadows awaiting their chance to do humans harm. "If you are naughty the fairies will steal you," his mother had warned him when he was no bigger than a potato dumpling. "They will wait until it's dark and spirit you away, leaving one of their changelings in your place."

It might have been better if they had, Cormac thought. Instead he had grown up in his parents' comfortable house, discovered a talent, come into a legacy and planned a future, only to have it all turn to ashes.

What could any fairy maiden do that was worse than what fate had already done to him?

He stopped being afraid.

"If you do not wed," he said, "does that mean you do not, er . . ."

She laughed at his human inhibitions. "Enjoy sex with one another? But of course we do. And children are born to us, though only very rarely."

Incredible her words might be, yet he believed her. He could not look at that face and think her deceitful. Such beauty must be built upon truth, or all faith was a lie.

She was gazing at him with huge eyes. He could count every curving eyelash. When he looked at her lips, they curved too, with a smile so sweet he ached to kiss them.

He did not have to be told it would be like no kiss he had ever experienced before.

A wave of thanksgiving poured over Cormac. He had thought his life ruined, and so it was, but as the bitter end approached, this wonderful gift had come to him, this flaring of magic. "They are true then?" he asked, hardly daring raise his voice. "The tales that old folk tell by the fireside?"

Lasair gave a less than ladylike snort. "If you mean the history of the Tuatha Dé Danann and the wars with the Gael, of course they are true."

"Many no longer believe them," he told her. "The Church condemns as superstition . . ."

"Whose Church? My people do not depend upon the belief of your priests for their existence. Do you only possess flesh and bone because we believe in you? Of course not! You are real and so am I. Does this not prove it?"

So saying, Lasair raised her two tiny hands and placed one on either side of his face. A flood of emotion unlike anything she had ever experienced surged through her.

Neither of them was prepared for what happened next.

At the touch of her palms on his cheekbones, a bolt of lightning shot through Cormac's skull. He was hurled from the boulder on which he sat and found himself flat on his back on the ground. All the wind was knocked out of him. His ears rang; red lights flashed behind his eyeballs.

Lasair sprang to her feet. She was very pale, her normally fair skin blanched of any trace of color. Holding her hands in front of her face, she stared at them in disbelief. Then she gave a strange, despairing cry, and fled.

By the time a dazed Cormac Casey got to his feet there was no sign of her anywhere. The ground might have opened and swallowed her.

Chapter 4

THE way which Lasair followed passed through a tangle of gorse and bramble, impenetrable to solid flesh. But as she sped toward the fairy fort she softened herself until she was no more substantial than mist.

There was always mist somewhere in Ireland.

Ahead rose the great green mound. It appeared no more than a hill to the uninitiated, but a hill of peculiarly rounded shape. No retreating glacier could have given such a symmetrical curve to the land.

At the entrance Lasair paused. There was no visible gateway, merely an expanse of grass. She felt curiously weak, uncertain of her powers as she gazed at the featureless hillside. But when she whispered the ancient words the grass disappeared and a tunnel opened before her. With a sigh of relief she entered the fort. Had she glanced back she would have seen the opening close up behind her.

Preoccupied, she followed the passageway to the heart of the mound.

Within the great hall a feast was being served. No one remarked upon the fact that Lasair arrived late for the banquet. She had a most independent turn of mind. She came and went as she chose and could not be relied upon for any specific occasion.

Nevertheless they were glad to see her. Whenever Lasair entered the mound a special light came with her, a radiance which put fairy candles to shame.

"There you are!" cried Greine, waving to her. "Come over and sit by me, share this delicious nectar made of apples and honey. Our friends the bees have overseen the fermentation once again and produced an exceptional brew this season."

Nereth jumped to his feet. "No, sit by me!" Half a dozen other voices chimed in with similar requests.

High, piping voices.

When Cormac Casey spoke, the words seemed to come from deep in his chest, Lasair recalled. Even his whisper was resonant.

Crossing the room, Lasair took her place at the table. A human would have seen nothing but darkness. But to the eyes of the Sídhe, the fort was richly appointed. The great hall had a vaulted ceiling from which brightly colored banners hung, while additional vivid hues were provided by tapestries upon the rounded walls. The long table that dominated the room was shaped of a single slab of crystal stolen from the heart of a mountain. A dozen or so of the fairy folk—one could never count them exactly—were seated around the table, drinking from cups hewed out of chunks of amethyst and eating from plates made of beaten gold. Such were the magically produced furnishings of Lasair's world.

Yet today she did not notice them. Her eyes were filled with the unfading image of a human man. She accepted a plate, let her cup be filled. Sat listlessly staring into space.

From the head of the table, Leary glanced toward his daughter and frowned. "You are picking at your food," he accused in a silvery voice. He was a silvery man, worn colorless by age.

"She is not eating at all, to be precise," interjected Nereth.

"I am not very hungry."

"Usually you have a fine appetite. What has affected you so?"

She would not meet her father's colorless eyes. "I had an encounter."

"An encounter?"

"With a human."

"Humans!" Plump and pearly Setach curled her upper lip with distaste. "They are so very *large*, aren't they? Gross, really. And hair grows inside their nostrils. No wonder you have lost your appetite." The fairy woman promptly reached across the table and helped herself to the choicest morsels from Lasair's plate.

Greine inquired eagerly, "Did you put a spell on him? Something to make him wretched?" His green eyes danced with malice.

"No."

"You should have done, they are terrible brutes. They destroyed all the forests in Erin," he added in an aggrieved tone.

"Not quite," Nereth corrected. "Three thousand and eighteen trees remain in the various places we were able to protect through our magic."

Lasair said, "It was the Saxons who destroyed the forests two centuries ago, to give the Irish chieftains no place to hide. The human I encountered was no Saxon but Irish himself, a descendant of the Gael."

Greine shook his head. "It makes no difference, they have all gone rotten. You should have withered him where he stood." He shook one fist in the air to make his point.

How small Greine was, thought Lasair. How slight. Strange that she had never noticed it before. She had a sudden mental image of Cormac Casey with his broad shoulders and his square, capable hands.

Human hands.

Human thighs, muscular and substantial.

Leary was watching her daughter intently. He knew her every mood, she was as transparent to him as springwater. "You did more than meet this human. You *liked* him," he said in an accusing tone.

Her shrug was noncommittal.

Leary felt a twinge of apprehension. "Allow yourself to feel nothing for a human, my child," he urged. "They are another race entirely, a degenerate race with coarse minds and dulled senses. It would be a grave mistake to form any sort of attachment to such inferior beings."

From her place at the foot of the table, Eevin the banshee spoke up. The skeletal woman with flaming red hair did not often dine with the others, preferring to stay on the windswept crag from which she watched over the fortunes of her chosen Irish clan. Everyone listened on the rare occasions when her voice was heard. "I have an attachment to certain humans," she pointed out. "I watch over the princes of clan O'Brien and warn them of impending doom."

"But you no longer allow them to see you, they can only hear you," said Nereth. "You stay safe on the heights, remote from them."

"What harm could a human possibly do us anyway?" Lasair wanted to know. "The Gael ceased waging war against us long ago."

His frown deepening, her father replied, "Their Christian religion wages war against us now. Their priests want to destroy every vestige of our race because our magic is too much competition for theirs. But for you there is a particular danger in human contact, Lasair. I have warned you before, though perhaps I have not been explicit enough. Now I repeat, you must avoid human men."

"Because like my mother, I am a leannán sídhe?"

"Just so." Rising to his feet, Leary beckoned to Lasair. "Come to my private chamber, daughter. We must talk."

The others looked disappointed at being excluded. "If any of you employ magic to overhear words meant for my daughter alone," Leary warned them, "you will have sand in your eyes and a hair on your tongue for the next century."

They returned their interest to their food.

"Your mother Rignach is no longer here to advise you," Leary reminded his daughter as they entered his chamber, "and I myself shall not be here much longer, so I must pass on my wisdom now."

"You are not leaving us!"

He laid a hand upon his daughter's head. "The seasons change, my child. When we are young and strong we change them; when we are old and weary they change us. How could it be otherwise? When our energy is spent we must return to The Source.

"Which brings me to the matter of which I must speak. Time and again humans have sought to capture us and extract favors from us, demanding that we provide them with unlimited wealth or long life or a spell to ignite love in an unresponsive heart. They know we have powers but have never understood the exact nature of those powers. We cannot explain our abilities to them, any more than a bird can tell a fish how it sings. But that does not stop them asking. They are very greedy, the humans, and the things they want from us drain our energies dangerously. So it is best if we avoid them altogether—except to take something from them."

"What could we possibly desire of theirs, Father?"

Leary gave her a faded smile. "Most of us want nothing from humankind. But for a leannán sídhe, a man can have a singular attraction. By making love to one, she can drain off his vitality for herself and thus add to her own lifespan. The undertaking is fraught with danger, however, which is why I have always discouraged you from having anything to do with men. I have never been specific about the reason because I found the subject painful to discuss. But now I see I must.

"If you lust after the energy this man contains, you can take it from him. Much as I might wish otherwise, I cannot prevent you. As my life span grows short, I can even understand the temptation you might feel to extend your own. Your mother . . ."

Leary paused. When he spoke again, his whispery voice was harsh. "But you must give nothing of yourself in return, Lasair. Never forget that the exchange can work the other way. If you allow him, he will siphon off that wondrous radiance of yours and drain you to a husk. The time left you then would be measured not in centuries, but in days. Do you hear me? In days!"

His voice vibrated with urgency. But Lasair was no longer listening. Avoiding his eyes, she gazed instead at the walls of the chamber as if she could see through them. "Have no fear for me, Father," she murmured. "I can take care of myself."

Our children always say such things, Leary thought. And they are never true. Clutching to a straw of hope, he raised his voice to draw her attention back to him. "This man you met, was he by any chance one of the last remaining practitioners of the Old Religion? A certain sympathy has always existed between ourselves and the Druids. There was a time when they listened and learned from us. While I would discourage you from any human, my child, I like to think a Druid would not harm you."

Lasair recalled Cormac Casey's sturdy form, and his windburned throat above the open collar of his shirt. "He is not a Druid," she told her father. "Around his neck he wears a chain with a small gold cross."

Leary's shoulders slumped. "A Christian, then, more's the pity. The Christians have undertaken to destroy the Old Religion as the Saxons have attempted to exterminate the Gael."

"Cormac doesn't want to destroy me," insisted Lasair. "How can you judge him when you've never even met him? It isn't fair; you don't know him. I tell you he is kind, and gentle." As she spoke her soft, sweet voice grew softer and sweeter still, and a mistiness came into her eyes.

Her father was dismayed. "Stay away from this man completely, I beg you! Humans are bent and full of darkness and he is no exception, whatever you may think. I am older than you and I know from experience.

"I see now that you are already feeling emotions which will make you vulnerable, allowing this human to steal your light and your life. You must avoid him as you would avoid cold iron, Lasair. *Listen to me.*" His voice was stern and his features commanding, but even as he gave the order Leary knew, with a sinking feeling, that Lasair would not obey him.

She was beautiful and independent and headstrong, his favorite daughter. Like her mother before her, she would do the very thing that was forbidden.

With a cry, he gathered her to his breast.

Chapter 5

THE evening was drawing in by the time Cormac Casey reached the nearest village. It consisted of a tumble of sod-and-stone cabins on either side of a rutted road, with one or two larger, whitewashed cottages suggesting a marginally more prosperous peasantry. The air was fragrant with the sweet, haunting smell of burning peat as cooking fires blazed on their hearths, and a woman's voice floated on the dusk, summoning her children home.

At first glance there appeared to be no public house where a man could take the edge off his thirst. The distilling and dispensing of alcoholic beverages was strictly forbidden to the Irish by their English overlords. But Cormac knew the Irish character. Numerous stills were surely hidden in the folded hills beyond the village.

He knocked on the first door he came to, rapping his knuckles gently against the wood to show that he was a friend who would ask and not an enemy who would demand.

Voices within suddenly ceased. After a moment the door creaked open. "Aye?" inquired a voice.

"I am a traveler seeking shelter for the night," said Cormac.

"Aye." There was a long silence. Then the door opened wider and a grizzled countryman thrust his head through the aperture. "Just across yon road, that's the Widow Hanratty's. She takes in the odd traveler from time to time. We would take ye ourselves but with a houseful of children there's no spare bed."

Cormac made his way to the indicated cottage and prepared to repeat his tentative knock. Before he could do so the door swung open, reminding him that in an Irish village everything was known at once.

"Mrs. Hanratty?" he asked the gaunt old woman who stood before him with her arms folded across her apron. She had him inside and shedding his cloak before he could catch his breath.

"God bless all here," he announced to the group he found seated before the fire. Two or three men who looked like farmers nodded in reply. A lanky, gawky boy just past puberty jumped to his feet to surrender his stool, and a careworn woman with an infant in her arms beamed a smile at the newcomer. "And yourself, sir," she replied.

In the strictest sense Hanratty's was no inn, merely a private dwelling whose owner had found a way to supplement the meagre income derived from the sale of vegetables and an occasional pig. The Widow Hanratty not only provided beds for wayfarers but also dispensed hospitality to local folk, such as those gathered around her fire this evening. Any visitor was welcome through her door—once she had ascertained that the guest was an Irish person and not one of "them English spies."

The Widow Hanratty had the most intensely blue eyes Cormac had ever seen. He longed to sketch her as she bent over the hearth, skillfully manipulating the iron crane. But to his regret there was not enough light for him to work. A turf fire and a few stubby candles could not furnish the illumination he needed.

Marvelous smells were wafting from the black pot simmering over the fire. Without asking if he was hungry, Mrs. Hanratty ladled out a brimming bowl of stew. "Eat all of this," she ordered. "Ye could be glad of it if the harvest goes against us." She then handed Cormac a cracked cup half full of colorless liquid. One sniff assured him it was not water. An aroma of peat smoke, herbs, and cold rain identified the best quality poitín. Distilled illicitly from potatoes, poitín was a fiery brew and obviously the widow's chief source of income.

After one long drink from the cup and an appreciative cough, Cormac took a mouthful of the stew. Chunks of mutton, potato, parsnip, onion, and cabbage swam in a barley broth seasoned with peppery watercress. Accompanied by half a loaf of brown bread slathered with sweet butter, the repast was, Cormac declared, "a meal fit for a king."

"Sure we've no kings here," his hostess said in a tone bordering on contempt.

"Unless ye count the king of the fairies," remarked the young lad under his breath.

The Widow Hanratty made a strangled noise at the back of her throat, and one of the men turned on his stool to glare at the boy. "Ye've no call to be mentioning the Good People and upsetting your Gran. And ye'd best pray to the Virgin that none of *them* heard ye."

A shiver of superstition ran through the cottage.

Cormac finished his meal in silence. But he kept one eye on the boy, Fergal, Mrs. Hanratty's grandson. When the others had gone to bed, Fergal stepped outside to answer a call of nature and Cormac followed him.

The summer night had grown chill. Glancing into the shadows, Cormac drew his traveling cape around his shoulders. "Fergal?"

"Over here."

"May I speak with you a moment?"

"Ye can surely." Fergal stepped into the dim oblong of light from the open doorway. He was a redheaded, jug-eared boy with a quick grin and his grandmother's blue eyes. "Want me to fetch more of Gran's poitín? A jug all for yourself, maybe?"

"I think not. Grand stuff it is, but I need to be keeping a clear head."

"Won't cost much. Tuppence, and ye keep the jug."

Cormac smiled at the boy's enterprise. "Thank you, no. It's information I'm needing, and I'm willing to pay for it."

The boy seemed to shrink inside his clothes. "Are ye an English spy?" he asked in a hoarse whisper.

Cormac hastened to reassure him, "Nothing like that, not at all! I am merely looking for local folklore. For a book. You mentioned the king of the fairies and I was wondering—are there any legends of the Sídhe in this area?"

The boy ground his toe into the dirt and studied it intently, then peered up from under his eyebrows. "Sure and aren't there legends of them everywhere in Ireland?"

"Indeed, but they vary from place to place," Cormac replied. "It is the local stories I want to hear. For example, do you know if there is a fairy fort nearby?"

When Fergal hesitated, Cormac thrust his hand into his pocket and jingled some coins. The boy's face brightened, then clouded over again. "I couldn't be taking money for talking about the Good People," he said firmly. "They would punish me something fierce."

"Tell me without pay, then," Cormac urged. "I am certain you know, a smart lad like yourself."

Fergal's grin flickered. "I know a thing or two."

"About a fairy fort?"

"There is one on the other side of the Ridge of the Butterflies," the boy confided. "A great big mound, so it is, with a ditch and a bank around it. It's at the top of Old Sullivan's farm, in what is called the high field. A fine field it would be too, if it were not for the fairy fort. Neither Old Sullivan nor his father before him would dare take a plough to that field for fear of a curse on his head, nor turn a cow into it for fear of her going dry. So there the land sits, no good to anybody."

"Does the king of the local fairies live there?"

"So they say."

"Have you ever seen him? Or any of them?"

The boy's face paled beneath its freckles and he sketched the sign of the Cross upon his chest. "Not me! All I know are the tales me father's father used to tell. Before he went away."

With a show of disappointment, Cormac murmured, "That doesn't seem much information for a shilling." He made as if to put his hand in his pocket again, then drew it out empty.

At once Fergal volunteered, "Tomorrow's a full moon night. If ye were to stop here for another day and listen sharp after sundown, ye just might hear a horn blowing in the distance."

"And if I did?"

"Then ye just might follow the trackway that leads to the fairy fort. Not all the way, mind; go only as far as the top of the ridge. But from there ye can see them leaving."

"Leaving?"

"On a full moon night the Good People have a procession. They ramble out over hill and meadow, circle past the village at a great distance, skirt the bog, then finally disappear into McNamara's hazel copse."

"Where do they come out again?"

The boy's eyes gleamed white like those of a spooked horse. "I wouldn't be knowing. I've never dared . . ."

"Did your father's father ever dare?" Cormac interrupted.

"Mayhap he did. Sometimes he got this look about him as if he was listening to something afar off, something that made his heart ache in his breast."

The artist replied with a faint, bemused smile, "Perhaps I know the feeling." Digging into his pocket he produced not one but two shillings, which he dropped into Fergal's astonished palm.

Next morning, fortified by one of Mrs. Hanratty's hearty breakfasts of stirabout and black pudding, Cormac Casey tucked his drawing things under his arm and set out. Aside from assuring his hostess he would be back long before dark, he said nothing to anyone. But the boy winked at him as he went out the door.

Brilliant sunshine greeted Cormac. After considerable searching, he came upon a muddy trackway that led him across fields and past an isolated farmhouse where two black-and-white sheepdogs ran out to challenge him. When he whistled to them and slapped his leg they recognized him as friendly and crouched down, waving their tails and grinning.

A scent of baking bread perfumed the air.

Beyond the farmhouse a small herd of milk cows stood in the muddy yard, their udders newly empty, and watched with warm, moist eyes as Cormac passed by. They too saw no harm in him. One calf even ambled up to the fence and thrust its head through so he could scratch between its ears. Tiny knobs of horn were just forming there, and they itched. When Cormac was certain no one would hear him, he murmured syllables of endearment to the little creature.

Some distance beyond the farmyard the ground began to rise, rolling upward like a great green wave to form a broad ridge that ran roughly east-west, offering an expansive view of the countryside. From the bottom the ridge did not seem very high, but he found himself breathing hard by the time he reached the top.

Slinging his cape over his shoulder, Cormac surveyed the scene.

To the south sprawled a badly neglected field enclosed by dense hedgerows of hawthorn and elder. Where the ridge sloped down to meet the field, an earthwork embankment was almost hidden beneath a riot of bramble. Within the protective circle of the earthwork was a large mound, equally overgrown.

Fairy fort.

In bright summer sunshine it was hard to imagine that dark forces might lurk within the mound. No scene could have appeared more tranquil. White clouds floated in an azure sky while birds poured out songs in the hedgerows. Myriads of the butterflies for which the ridge was named floated through the air like flying flowers. Such beauty would have captivated any artist.

Opening his sketchbook, Cormac began making a few preliminary drawings.

He tried to envision the scene with the overgrowth cleared away. For the grass-covered hillock he substituted a miniature castle modeled on one he had seen on the continent. The ditch encircling the embankment became a flooded moat. Towers and turrets grew under his skilful fingers. Instead of butterflies, multicoloured pennants waved in an imaginary breeze. Tiny guards in archaic armor stood outside the gates, spears at the ready, while other figures peered curiously from the arched windows.

"It isn't like that at all," said a voice in his ear.

Chapter 6

Cormac was so startled he dropped his charcoal pencil. But when he whirled around, there was no one behind him.

Shaken, he bent and picked up his pencil. Stooped over and with his back unprotected, he felt vulnerable. He straightened up again and gazed around defiantly.

Nothing. No one.

Yet he had heard the voice.

It had been as whispery as two sheets of dry paper rubbing together, like the speech of some very old man. But there was no mistaking the words. Someone had spoken to him; someone he could not see.

Cormac Casey felt a powerful desire to run.

But was this not the very thing he had sought, the promise of magic which had lured him?

Magic.

Lasair.

"Either I'm afraid or I'm not," he told himself aloud. "And I choose not to be."

There, he thought. If you heard that, whoever you are, you know my position.

He waited. The voice said nothing else.

After a time he began to feel foolish, standing atop the ridge with the sun on his head and birdsong trilling through the air. Perhaps it *was* his imagination. God knows, he had been through enough to make a man a little peculiar. In his travels he had learned something of the peculiar workings of the human mind. If he had begun hearing voices it might be some form of compensation, his mind retreating from a reality he could not bear.

Madness was commonplace in Ireland.

He gathered his drawing things and prepared to return to the Widow Hanratty's.

Just outside the cottage he encountered Fergal with a slender pole on his shoulder. "I'm off to do some fishing," the boy announced. "I can get another pole. Would ye care to go with me?"

Soon the two were sitting in companionable silence on the ferny bank of a swift-flowing river. The river was bordered on one side by an oak woodland, one of the few left intact in the country. Some trick of fate, thought Cormac, must have protected these trees when the English were busily destroying the rest of Ireland's forests. The oaks stood with their arms lifted to the sky in thanksgiving and their toes gripping the earth.

By the look of the river, it surely held fish. But nothing succumbed to the lure of the bait—tiny bits of hardened mutton fat from Mrs. Hanratty's larder. Fergal seemed unperturbed by their lack of success, however. "Fishing is about fishing," he told Cormac philosophically after an hour or so. "Catching fish is about eating them. I don't really like to eat them, but I like fishing enormously."

"Why don't you like to eat fish?"

"Because I get so very tired of them during Lent," the boy explained. Then his eyes sparkled with mischief. "On Easter Sunday after Mass the first thing we do is 'drown the herring.' We skewer a fish on the end of a long pole and march around the village with it, then bring it to the river and hold it under while everybody sings and claps."

Cormac was amused by the country pastime. "Is that your version of the fairy procession?"

Fergal sobered. Laying his pole on the bank, he said, "Ye should forget about them."

"I thought I might watch for their procession tonight."

"It was wrong of me to tell ye. I was born on Whit Sunday, and those born on Whit Sunday are fated to be responsible for someone else's death, everybody knows that. Me own da was thrown and killed by a horse that was foaled on Whit Sunday. If any harm comes to ye because of me . . ."

Cormac forced a laugh which was not quite as hearty as it sounded. "What harm could come to me?"

"Ye'll find out," the lad replied darkly, "if the Good People catch ye spying on them."

They have already caught me, thought Cormac. And no harm came to me. But he did not tell the boy.

After another of Mrs. Hanratty's substantial meals that evening, Cormac yawned and announced he was going to bed, "after I have a breath of air and stretch my legs."

He saw Fergal glance in his direction, but this time there was no wink.

It took an act of will for Cormac to leave the cottage and venture into the mysterious night. But a strange desire spurred him on.

The dirt track leading toward the ridge seemed narrower and more overgrown than he remembered. Even by the light of a full moon he could hardly see well enough to make his way, so that several times he stumbled.

When he passed the farmhouse the dogs barked but did not run out to him. The night seemed to be holding its breath.

At the foot of the ridge he paused and looked upward. Had it been that steep this morning? He turned and gazed back over his shoulder, imagining the golden firelight in the Widow Hanratty's cottage and the comfort of his bed with its thick straw mattress.

But he would have the rest of his life to sit by the fire or lie in bed. There was hardly any time left for adventures and he was hungry for just one more, he who had always been drawn to the far horizon. He desperately needed something to hold in his mind's eye forever.

Squaring his shoulders, Cormac Casey began to climb the ridge.

At that very moment he heard the call of a horn, faint and far away. Sonorous as a hunting horn, it was faintly menacing. He could not identify the material from which the instrument was made, however, except it did not sound like brass.

Cormac kept climbing.

A north wind sprang up, sending threads of dark cloud scudding across the brilliant face of the full moon. His cape began to billow around his body and cold drafts made their way beneath his clothing.

The horn sounded again. Nearer.

When he reached the top of the ridge he stood panting. He had a sudden impulse to abandon the whole project and go back the way he had come, admitting to himself that he was out of his depth and afraid.

Say farewell to adventures forever.

Even as the thought crossed his mind, however, the wind changed. It abruptly swung around to the south, blowing warm and sweetly perfumed. Amid a scent of flowers he had a crystal-clear vision of Lasair's face, with her huge eyes gazing into his. She flooded his senses so that he could see her, smell her, touch her. With her memory came a sensual heat that licked his body like flame.

Never had he felt such desire—or such tenderness.

"Lasair?" he said aloud.

Someone laughed.

The laughter was high and clear and merry and should have been reassuring. But never in his life had Cormac heard such a soulless, inhuman sound, not even in Donegal when the banshee screamed.

A flicker of movement drew his attention. Glancing down the far side of the ridge toward the mound, he saw tiny lights dancing like slivers of stars. More minute than the smallest candle flames, they nevertheless created pools of illumination which expanded as he watched until the scene below was as bright as day.

For the first time he observed a pale pathway extending from the mound. It appeared to be . . . he rubbed his eyes and looked again . . . it appeared to be not upon the earth, but floating slightly above it. Meanwhile a dark patch formed on the side of the mound next to the spectral pathway. The darkness grew, took shape, became a pair of gates that silently swung inward.

At the third sound of the horn, a troop emerged from the fairy fort. But such a troop! Cormac's mouth went dry at the sight of them and his heart leaped in his breast like a netted salmon.

They were led by a silvery man on a silvery horse, an animal as gaily caparisoned as any king could wish. The saddle was scarlet, the breastplate and crupper were tasseled with gold. No bridle restricted the horse's head, yet the animal moved in perfect obedience to the will of its rider. He sat with his hands folded on his mount's withers and its white mane flowed over them like milk as it pranced and curvetted.

Behind this kingly figure came a shimmering crowd attired in the brilliant hues of butterflies, crimson and azure and emerald, amber and violet and sulphur yellow. Some wore diaphanous gowns, others were dressed in garments resembling coats and fitted trousers. The costume did not always correspond to the apparent gender of the wearer. A few elegant creatures showed off female curves in clinging jackets and hose, while others who were obviously male preferred the freedom of loose robes. But they all had long hair which they either wore unbound, or twisted into elaborate swirls and decorated with flowers.

Then at some unseen command all the costumes were altered, all the colors changed. Through the glamour of faerie the Sídhe were able to reclothe themselves at will.

Their inhuman laughter ran on the night air, clearly audible to the man on the ridge.

They appeared to be a small-statured folk, though not abnormally so, and there was nothing disproportionate about them. Indeed, they were more handsomely made than any comparable group of humans. With airy grace they began to caper to a wild, strange music, following the beat of fairy drums. Pipers skirled and harpers strummed while the dancers of the Sídhe sang in a language long forgotten. Their voices recalled the murmur of the sea, the hiss of the rain, the lonely sobbing of the wind through dark forests. Then the music changed. In a heartbeat it became all the promise of spring, all the joy of summer. Vivid notes cascaded as if from the throats of a thousand songbirds.

Tears sprang to Cormac's eyes.

Still singing, the fairy host set off down the hovering pathway. If they were aware of the watcher on the ridge they gave no sign. Straining his eyes to their utmost, Cormac sought to pick out one particular form among them. She would be, he felt sure, the most graceful of all. But he could not find Lasair in that dancing throng, though he did catch a glimpse of a gaunt, red-haired woman who chilled the marrow in his bones.

A great number continued to pour out of the mound, more than it could ever have held, had its boundaries existed within Cormac's reality. He could not make an accurate count of them no matter how hard he tried. How he wished he had his pencils and drawing pads with him, so he could capture the procession of the fairy folk! But it would have been impossible. The light moved with the Sídhe, it did not extend to him and his surroundings. He would have been attempting to work in the dark.

Like a glowing, glittering river the parade of the Sídhe wound across the countryside. The spellbound human watching from the ridge felt an almost unbearable desire to follow them; better yet, to be one of them. Their music spoke of a life without obligation or regret. They were as wild and as innocent as the elements.

Cormac's straining eyes had begun to itch and burn. He did not want to lose sight of the fairy folk for a moment, but he must pause to rub them. He raised his hands to his face.

Then in the fraction of an instant before his knuckles obscured his vision, he saw her. She had been among the last to leave the fort, a slender figure attired in gossamer veils that floated around her as she danced after her kinfolk.

She turned to look back at him so unexpectedly that his hands completed their gesture before he could snatch them away. He only had the most fleeting glimpse, but that was enough. No one else could possibly look like Lasair. Her image was already engraved on Cormac's heart.

By the time he could lower his hands, she was gone.

Chapter 7

CORMAC gave a groan of anguish.

He wanted to run after her, but as the shimmering procession disappeared from sight behind a hill, the night closed over him like a clenched fist. The moon was still high in the sky yet gave no light, as if the Sídhe had taken it all with them.

"Lasair?" he called into the darkness.

No voice answered. The fairy music faded and was gone.

He realized he was shivering. The wind was out of the north again and colder than before.

When at last he turned to go back the way he had come, he was forced to feel his way with one tentative step after another, trusting his feet to do the work of his eyes. Stones slithered under his feet as he cautiously worked his way down the slope of the ridge. His heart leaped. If he fell . . . alone, in a strange place . . . in the dark . . .

Since earliest childhood, Cormac Casey had been terrified of the dark.

Hours passed before he finally found the way to the village. No sooner did he set foot on the road than a familiar figure came trotting toward him. "Is it yourself?" called Fergal's anxious voice.

Cormac hurried thankfully toward him. "It is myself. I was . . ."

"Lost. And I've been searching for ye. It was wicked of me to let ye go, I shall have to confess it to Father Duggan."

"You could not have stopped me," Cormac assured him.

"No one could stop me granda, either, but at least *ye've* come back." The lad took Cormac's arm, a kindness for which the older man was grateful. They walked in silence for a time until the smell of peat smoke welcomed them.

"Here we are now," said Fergal. "Best we not wake me gran. She's no other guests this night, but she wants her sleep. Come inside quietly and I'll fetch a drop of poitín, 'twill do ye a power o'good."

The interior of the cottage was dark, with the fire dying on the hearth providing only a faint glow. But still it was not so dark to Cormac as the haunted night outside. He accepted the cup Fergal poured out for him and drank it off in one long swallow that burned from his tongue to his toes. The two then sat talking in whispers so as not to awaken the widow, though by the way her snores reverberated through the cottage, there was little danger.

"You said before that your grandfather 'went away,' Fergal. Do you mean he went off with the fairies?" Cormac inquired.

"No one knows for certain."

"But you have your suspicions?"

"Me gran does."

"Would she talk to me about it?"

Fergal replied, " 'Twould be worth your life to ask her. Either that, or she'd throw her apron over her head and be keening for a week, and there'd be no food nor drink to be had. She went on something fierce when he left. The priest came but he could do nothing with her. For a while 'twas feared she would throw herself in the river."

"When was this?"

"When me mam was just a girl."

"Then how do you know so much about it?"

Fergal replied, "Was I not raised on the story along with bread and buttermilk?"

Cormac knew all too well that in Ireland family histories were passed down warm with living breath, so that to each generation they seemed to be recent events, the emotions still raw. Fergal had heard the stories so many times that he was as familiar with them as the actual participants, but the mystery of his grandfather's disappearance obviously continued to intrigue him.

Cormac was likewise intrigued. "Did your grandfather see the trooping of the fairies?" he asked the boy, certain now of the answer.

"He did, but that's not when he disappeared. He came back changed, though. He had been a big strong man, but after his return he was thin and weak. Wouldn't talk to me gran, or even look at her, hardly. She thought he was taken with a fever but he insisted he was all right. Told her not to fuss over him. Me gran can be like a broody hen with chicks," Fergal added as an aside.

"What happened to your grandfather?"

"He went into a decline and they all thought he would die. Then at the next full moon he crept off without anyone knowing, and when he came back there was color in his cheeks again and he was stronger. Me gran was delighted, while the priest said it was a miracle due to the intervention of the Virgin Mary.

"Everyone was happy but me granda himself. His grief was awful to see. But he wouldn't explain the reason for it. And then one night . . . he just went away. No one ever laid eyes on him again," Fergal finished, shaking his head.

Cormac stared at the embers on the hearth until dawn crept through the cottage window. When at last he fell asleep, it was to dream of a river of shimmering light and a strange, wild music.

And a small woman who radiated heat.

In the morning Mrs. Hanratty took one look at his face, then signed the Cross on her breast. "Mortal man," she breathed, "ye risk your immortal soul."

He pretended not to know what she was talking about. "I have done nothing wrong."

"Perhaps not yet, but the wanting is in your eyes. 'Tis a terrible sin to want what God never meant ye to have. With your leave I'll send for Father Duggan and he can pray the wickedness out of ye."

"No priest!" said Cormac, surprised at his own vehemence.

He considered gathering his things and moving on, but where would he go? He no longer felt any urgency about finishing the sketches for the illustrations. What would another book more or less matter? A book was a foredoomed attempt to capture life within unliving pages.

Life itself was out there someplace.

Someplace close by.

If he took to the road again he would only be moving away from Lasair, so he must stay here. But he would brook no interference.

"It's not a priest I'm needing," he told the Widow Hanratty. "I've seen enough priests to last a lifetime. My little sister, whom I loved dearly, fell ill two years ago. I was in Rome at the time and I must have visited every church in the city, beseeching heaven to save her. But nothing helped, neither the priests nor their religion."

The widow's face filled with compassion. "Och, ye poor man. Was she with ye?"

"She was not, she was back here in Ireland. Since our parents died, I was her only living relative. Our father had made enough as a merchant to leave us a small inheritance, sufficient to maintain her at home while allowing me to travel a bit, if I was frugal. I wanted to be an artist, you see, so I went to Italy to study drawing and engraving. For several years I labored in various studios during the day, living on bread and cheese, then returned to some rat-infested lodging house at night content in the knowledge that my beloved sister was safe and comfortable in Ireland.

"But when Elizabeth became ill I had to give up my formal studies and take whatever employment I could find in order to pay for her treatment. I would have come back to Ireland to be with her but the passage was too expensive; the money was needed for doctors and medicines. I continued to work at my art at night, however, struggling to build up some small reputation. I felt guilty about not being with my sister, but life is a matter of choices, always choices. Some are dictated by circumstances we don't think we can change.

"Then I received a commission to do the illustrations for a book. It meant recognition at last, and enough money to take proper care of my sister. But no sooner were the contracts signed than word came from Ireland that Elizabeth was failing.

"I hurried back at once, but arrived too late. And to make matters worse, I discovered . . ." He could not finish. He did not want her pity.

She gave it anyway, bustling about to offer him strong black tea, a breakfast of stirabout, a seat by the fire, advice on coping with bereavement. "Like a broody hen with chicks," Fergal had truthfully said of his grandmother.

To be polite, Cormac let her fuss over him. So many years had passed since anyone had mothered him that he found the situation mildly embarrassing. "I can take care of myself," he said several times but she did not listen.

And perhaps it was not even true. True now, but not for the future.

While he toyed with his breakfast his thoughts strayed to the events of the night before, and Lasair. He knew now that the fairy folk were more than mere legend. A woman of the Sídhe had touched both his head and his heart.

What to do about it?

"Ye are not eating," Mrs. Hanratty accused. "Ye'll fade away to nothing, so ye will. Or is my food no good?"

"Your food is grand," he assured her. "I just have other things on my mind."

Her disapproval was thick enough to cut with a knife, but the Widow Hanratty knew a stubborn man when she saw one. No amount of common sense would dissuade her guest from his foolishness, so she let him eat his meal in peace.

But she took young Fergal aside and gave him a low-voiced order. "Be going to Father Duggan and tell him about this. Tell him we need him here, and to come at the trot. When there's decent women in this parish in need of a husband, I'll not be losing this nice young man to the Good People!"

Chapter 8

"I WILL not," cried Leary, slamming his fist upon the table, "be losing my daughter as I lost her mother!"

The others stared at him in astonishment. Such an outburst was rare among the fairy folk, who were generally unconcerned about anything but pleasure.

Nereth said, "Lasair is not lost, she is merely outside, gazing at the sky."

"In her thoughts she is lost to us," Leary contradicted. "How could this have happened? Have we not cherished her, protected her, given her everything she ever wanted? No child of the Sídhe was ever more pampered, yet now she turns her face from us and dreams of some human man."

"The very thought makes me ill," murmured Setach.

Greine spoke up. "It makes me more than ill. It makes me want to find this man and do him terrible harm."

"And what would that be? Give him a hump, or make his cows go dry?" Nereth wanted to know. "What truly effective weapons have we against his kind?"

"We can make them miserable."

"That is not enough. Humans are used to being miserable. Most of them hardly notice a little more."

"Kill him outright, then!" cried Greine.

A shocked gasp greeted this demand.

"Unlike humans, we do no murder. We are the Sídhe," Leary reminded his people with dignity. "I forbid such talk, Greine."

"Since it is your daughter who is at risk, I should think you would be more amenable to my suggestion. If another of the leannán sídhe took so much of his strength that he died, you would not object."

"No, because his dying would be incidental, the result of some weakness in himself that could not withstand the loss, and her act would be in accordance with her nature. We do not condemn the fox for taking the hare."

Eevin said, "Perhaps this rare fondness for a human is also in accordance with nature—at least with the nature of some of us. More than once in my life I have felt a genuine warmth toward some Gaelic chieftain who was particularly fine and noble. Your prejudice toward the entire race is ill-considered, Leary."

"My prejudice, as you call it, is the result of centuries of observation," he snapped. "And humans are not getting better, but worse. They do horrific things to their own kind, even to their children! Should I willingly surrender my child to one of them?"

Nereth replied, "Willingly, no. But you cannot prevent her going to him if that is what she chooses."

"I can surround her with an enchantment that holds her fast, so she cannot go to him."

Nereth shook his head. "You just reminded us that we are the Sídhe. Never in our history have we held one of our own kind captive, any more than we have done wilful murder. Besides, Lasair has considerable powers herself. She just might be able to break your enchantment, and then you would lose her even more surely, because she would never forgive you for having tried to imprison her."

"Then what can I do?" the frustrated father asked, throwing out his hands in supplication.

They had no answer for him.

While the discussion about her raged below, Lasair rambled across the field beyond the fairy fort suffering from a mounting resentment. Leary was treating her like a child although she had been mature for centuries. Yet for the first time she was taking a hard look at her life. Surely there must be more to existence than frenetic gaiety.

Using the sorceries they had spent untold generations perfecting, the Sídhe had overcome fleshly limitations. They had conquered pain and illness and made the ageing process almost negligible. Without those worries they were able to devote themselves to pleasure. Until they returned to the Source, they were able to exist as fully integrated components of the natural world without any of the artificiality practised by humankind. But such an achievement had not come easily and had meant giving up much.

Until today, Lasair had never questioned the cost. Like the others, she had considered herself supremely fortunate.

Now she was asking questions.

If she never experienced pain, how could she truly know pleasure?

Pleasure was what she felt when Cormac Casey smiled at her.

No, she must be precise, like Nereth. Joy was what she felt when Cormac smiled. Intense physical pleasure was something she only imagined, a dream of being held in those strong human arms; being kissed with those tender human lips.

Greine would hold her and kiss her if he got the chance, he was always pursuing females. But Lasair had no desire for Greine's touch. The idea had lost any appeal it might once have had for her. His overconfident embrace was too predictable . . . and forgettable.

Yet Lasair could not forget Cormac Casey no matter how she tried to redirect her thoughts. There was no denying her sexual arousal. The Sídhe were far from sexless; the creative energy at the heart of life was a powerful inspiration for their magic. Under the summer stars they mated with abandon, then laughed and danced on to mate again with someone else. But to feel physical desire for a human . . . !

Without realizing it, Lasair drifted out of Old Sullivan's high field and flirted briefly with the butterflies on the ridge, then wandered on again.

Toward the village.

She needed no magic to find him, unless love itself was a kind of magic. Even before she could see the thatched rooftops she knew exactly where Cormac was, leaning one elbow on the wall enclosing the Widow Hanratty's vegetable patch. The widow had loaned him one of her favorite clay pipes, but he was not smoking. He stood holding the bowl and gazing down into it as if bemused.

His thoughts were on warmth and fire. On Lasair. She could hear them silently calling to her.

Her every instinct was to go to him, but then her father's voice commanded in her ear: "No, my daughter! I forbid it!"

That was all she needed to lend wings to her desire. With a glad cry she ran down the road toward the whitewashed cottage and the man with the unlit pipe in his hand. When he saw her coming he blinked, rubbed his eyes, blinked again. Started forward to meet her.

"How did you know I was calling you?" he asked.

"How did you know I would come?" she replied.

There was no need for any further talk. He opened his arms and she rushed toward them.

Remembering what had happened the last time they touched, they both hesitated at the last moment. But only for half a heartbeat. Then Cormac's arms folded around Lasair. There was no shock of lightning, only a flooding warmth that spread through them equally, dispelling every fear.

She felt his lips touch the top of her head.

He inhaled the scent of her hair, a fragrance composed of sunlight and summer breezes. Then he realized she was snuggling closer against his chest, and she discovered the exact rhythm of his pounding heart.

"My father forbade me to have anything to do with you," Lasair whispered.

"I've been warned myself. Perhaps we should not stand out here in the road where people can see us . . . ?"

With one accord, they turned and slipped hurriedly between the nearest cabins, then followed the path leading down to the river.

Although the day was bright, it was dark in the shade of the trees bordering the river. No prying eyes would locate them there, Cormac thought with relief.

Lasair knew there was no hiding from the magical sight of the Sídhe. If her father wished to find them, he would. But perhaps they could snatch a few golden moments. Beside that possibility, nothing else mattered.

How strange. Nothing else mattered! In one moment all the questions were answered and life had become very simple.

She laughed aloud. Hers was not the inhuman sound that had so disturbed Cormac, but a warm and merry laugh that made him feel young and full of optimism. He found himself laughing with her.

"I have a fairy sweetheart in my arms!" he exulted.

"And I am embraced by a human man," she replied. "Is it not wonderful?"

"Wonderful indeed." Slowly, gently, he lowered his lips toward her upturned face.

She held her breath, waiting.

At first their kiss was as light as the touch of butterfly wings. He still could not believe his good fortune and half expected her to reject him. Then two soft arms locked behind his neck and hungrily drew him closer.

True magic was in that kiss, a magic they shared equally. Magic with all its glamour and terror, stopping the heart. Afterward, Cormac would never know how long their lips clung together. He would only remember that time was frozen but he was not; his body burned with passion.

In the course of his travels he had kissed quite a few women, but never before one whose lips were threaded with flame.

Lasair let her body melt bonelessly against his as if she could never get close enough. But her flesh did not dissolve into mist. It remained solid, with every nerve tingling.

When at last Cormac lifted his head long enough to draw a breath, he said with a shaky laugh, "My hands are trembling."

"So are mine," Lasair admitted. She started to touch his face, then stopped herself. She could kiss him with impunity, that much was certain, but to lay her hands on his head was a different matter, unleashing powerful forces whose nature she did not fully understand and could not control.

Leary had warned her and she had defied him, so she could not go to him now and ask him the question uppermost in her mind. Was it possible that a leannán sídhe and a human man could come together without one damaging the other? The answer was shrouded in mystery. She and Cormac would have to find it for themselves.

# Chapter 9

THE silent trees shielded their lovemaking and kept their secrets. In their dark green shade Cormac could hardly see Lasair's face, but he explored every inch of her with his hands. "Am I hurting you?" he whispered. "You are so small, so fragile!"

Her laugh denied the charge. "I am the least fragile being you will ever meet. The only way you could hurt me would be to let me go."

His arms clamped even more tightly around her. "I'll never let you go!"

She opened herself to him without restraint. "Your emotions will make you vulnerable," Leary had warned, "allowing this human to steal your light and your life." But she wanted to be vulnerable. She did not feel him taking anything from her; rather, he was giving her everything he had, all his passion and tenderness. Cormac held nothing back as they lay on the ferny earth together.

A sharp rock hidden among the ferns pressed against the small of Lasair's back. She easily could have turned her flesh to mist so the rock caused no pain. But she did not. Instead she gloried in the feeling as she gloried in the thrust and drive of the man above her.

Feeling.

We have avoided such sensations for thousands of years, she thought. We have taken only the perfume of the flower and never experienced the thorns.

Why were we so afraid?

Cormac groaned. The sensations he was experiencing were becoming too intense. I cannot bear it, he thought; I shall be torn apart.

I shall lose myself entirely, thought Lasair as the honeyed sweetness threatened to overcome her.

But at the penultimate moment, neither drew back. With an ecstatic cry they gave of themselves completely, each to the other.

When the flesh between them ceased to be a barrier, Lasair knew the exact instant she might have drawn his life force from him. It was there for the taking. A white light at the core of the man, pulsing.

At the same time, however, she sensed a darkness like a bruise seeping into the light. Her instinct was to flood that darkness with her own radiance, so that he would be whole.

No! screamed her father's desperate voice inside her head.

The tide of passion washed over the pair, lifted them high on its crest, carried them on a journey from which there was no returning. When it finally ebbed they remained locked in one another's arms.

"I love you," said Cormac Casey.

No one had ever said those words to Lasair before. Love was one of the emotions deemed most dangerous and destructive by her people. They used other terms for their affection, but the terms were as superficial as the impulse behind them.

He repeated, "I love you."

"What does that mean?"

Cormac was uncertain how to answer her question. "It means I . . . I just . . . love you!"

She moved just enough to nestle her body more snugly into the angles of his. "But what does love mean?" She was seeking a precise explanation such as Nereth would have given.

But Cormac knew no definition for love other than the feeling itself. The world had just tilted sideways and dropped him off; he could not think clearly. "I suppose it means I care more for you than I do for myself. Much more," he added earnestly.

They lay together quietly for a time, while the trees stood watch. Cormac drifted into sleep but Lasair was wide awake. Indeed, she thought herself more awake than ever before. She was acutely aware of sensations she had never imagined.

When perceived through the glamour of magic the earth was like the landscape of a dream, shifting and amorphous. Now, however, it had become fixed and firm.

The rock dug insistently into her back. Its sharpness provided a defining contrast for the heavy softness in her loins. Held between the two sensations, Lasair lay thinking.

I care for you more than for myself, Cormac had said.

The Sídhe cared for no one but themselves.

Based upon that fact, she should have been able to draw off his vitality without a moment's hesitation to extend her own life. But she had not done so.

Lasair rolled over and propped her upper body on her elbows so she could look down at the sleeping man. Seen thus, he looked very vulnerable and she tensed reflexively, expecting to hear her father's voice booming commands in her ear. But it did not come.

Opening his eyes, Cormac saw a dim shape bending over him. "I was dreaming of you," he said with a smile.

She wanted to tell him the discovery she had just made. "I love you," she whispered.

He reached for her again and drew her to him. "Show me."

She could have slowed time to a crawl so that they would spend years in each other's arms. But when the enchantment finally faded his crisp dark curls would have turned white and his strong muscles would have grown weak, while she would have stayed more or less unchanged. She could not do that to him. Best forego fairy magic, she decided. There was magic enough in the real world, when he was in it.

The real world was waiting for them as they went back along the path from the river, holding hands. A tingle passed from one to the other through their laced fingers.

"I think we should hurry," Lasair said unexpectedly.

"Why? Are you so anxious to be rid of me?" Already he felt confident enough of her to tease her.

"There's going to be a storm, and you are too lightly clad."

"That's nonsense, a bit of rain won't hurt an Irish man. If it did we all would have melted long ago."

She did not reply, merely shook her head and hastened her step, drawing him along with her.

The path ran for some distance in a tunnel of cool shade, before curving up a hill to meet the road from the village. He was glad of her hand guiding him, and almost sorry when they stepped out into brilliant sunlight once more.

At the edge of the village, Fergal met them. He gave Lasair one shocked, white-faced glance, then fixed his eyes firmly on Cormac as if he was afraid to look at the creature by his side. "Me gran sent me to fetch ye, she said there's a bad storm brewing."

Cormac's gaze swept a cloudless sky. "On such a day as this?"

Lasair murmured, "She's right, I told you before. There's a storm just over the horizon, headed this way." She could taste it already—frosty, silvery, furious. Even as she spoke, the wind began to rise and a cloud appeared as if by magic to cloak the sun.

"North wind," commented Fergal, shivering. "Best be inside strong walls when a north wind blows in the summer, that's what me gran always says." He gave Cormac an anxious look. "Are ye coming?"

The man tightened his grip on his companion's hand. "Does that invitation include Miss Leary? I cannot leave her to the mercy of the elements."

Fergal still would not look at her. "Me gran only told me to fetch you," he said with mounting desperation. "Please, sir!"

The wind was growing stronger. On its cold breath were borne the first pellets of sleet. One struck Cormac's cheek just below the eye and drew a tiny drop of blood.

Lasair gasped. "Go inside!" she urged. Tearing her fingers free of his, she gave him a violent shove in the direction of the Hanratty cottage.

"Not without you."

The wind was shrieking like a banshee. Already straw was being torn from the roofs of the less skillfully thatched cabins, and a small flock of hens that had been scratching peacefully in the dust of the road had become airborne, squawking and flapping.

"I'm right behind you!" Lasair shouted to Cormac above the voice of the wind. "Now will you go!"

There was no resisting a storm so sudden, so savage. Cormac ducked his head and ran for the cottage. He could have sworn she was close to his back, using it as a buffer from the wind. He could hear her running footsteps and feel her warmth . . .

At least, he thought he could.

But when he flung himself through the open doorway and turned around, there was no one behind him but Fergal.

"Where is she?" he demanded of the lad.

"Where is who?"

"The woman who was with me."

Fergal swallowed so hard his prominent Adam's apple looked about to leap from his skinny throat. "There was no woman with ye."

Cormac caught the boy by the shirt front. "You're lying! What have you done with her?"

"I haven't done anything with her," Fergal protested. "I've been with ye every step of the way."

A village couple was standing with Mrs. Hanratty on the far side of the room, staring open-mouthed at them as rain began to slash through the doorway. Beside them was a grey-haired priest. "Close that door, Fergal," the widow ordered her grandson. "Can't ye see our neighbors have come in for a wee drop? And here's Father Duggan come to pay us a call. Do ye want them all to catch their deaths?"

Cormac put one hand on the latch. "You can't close the door, she's still out there."

"There's no one out there," argued Fergal, casting a beseeching look in the widow's direction.

The man said, "We came across the road just ahead of you, and there was no one else to be seen."

Even as he spoke the wind roared into the room, then against all logic, reversed its direction and slammed the door shut from the inside. The woman screamed.

The temperature in the cottage was dropping dramatically. Warm breath became visible on cold air. "It's winter," moaned the terrified woman. "How can it be winter in July?"

Father Duggan spoke for the first time, in a voice clotted with phlegm. "Among the fairies the seasons are reversed, so they are. When ice falls in summer, 'tis their doing." He stared straight at Cormac as he spoke. "Have ye brought something evil upon us?"

The village woman fell to her knees, her lips moving in silent prayer. As if in derision the wind howled even louder, buffeting the cottage until Cormac thought the door would give way.

He could not believe any of this was Lasair's doing. The imprint of her body was still on his; the scent of her flesh was in his nostrils. Such beauty could not be evil; he was as sure of that as he was sure of his immortal soul.

Yet she had known about the storm too, long before Fergal found them. How, he wondered, could she have done so, when the day was so warm and the sky so clear?

A chill went through him that had nothing to do with the wind and ice outside.

In the joy of their discovery of one another Cormac had forgotten what Lasair was . . . until now.

The wind screamed and howled, sending its icy fingers through the tiniest chinks in the cottage. The priest began muttering prayers. The neighbour couple clung to one another for warmth and Fergal looked as if he was about to crawl into the fireplace.

"I think we all need a drop o' the crayture," decided the Widow Hanratty, taking down a jug from the shelf.

With a hand that trembled, Cormac reached for the proffered poitín.

Chapter 10

As she hurried toward the fairy fort Lasair tried to think of some way to placate her father. Then she asked herself, why should she? His anger was excessive and unjustified. Cormac Casey had done her no harm. Quite the contrary, he had brought her only pleasure. In those moments when she could hold nothing back from him, he had given instead of taking.

Leary must know this—had he not been spying on them? So how dare he undertake to punish them!

She had always been one of the most amiable of the Sídhe, famed for her pleasant disposition. No one had ever seen Lasair lose her temper. But rage scorched through her now, and she was discovering that the unfamiliar emotion gave her a quite satisfying jolt of courage. Like love, rage could be intoxicating.

The wind had risen to hurricane force, slamming across the countryside and carrying everything before it. The few remaining oaks screamed as they were uprooted. Lakes were whipped to white foam while pellets of ice slashed across the landscape. The terrified inhabitants of Ireland, both human and animal, sought shelter anywhere they could.

Within the great hall of the fairy fort, Leary was waiting for Lasair. He sat alone at the head of the crystal table with his fists clenched in concentration. The others had slipped away, unwilling to observe the scene about to take place. The fairy folk found arguments among themselves distasteful, disturbing their inner harmonies.

Lasair had never stood up to her father before, but now she strode across the room toward him with her pointed chin held high and fire in her eyes. "You exceed your authority," she accused. "I am no child to be bullied, nor am I weak-witted. I can make my own choices and be with whoever I choose, you have no right to interfere."

He met her furious gaze with blank silver eyes. "Interfere? I did not come between you, I did not even try to stop what you were doing with each other."

"You could not have stopped us," she said rashly.

"Ah but I could, my child. Am I not king of this tribe of the Sídhe? My mother came here with Cesair Banba in the First Age of Erin, and I am older than any of you and have been practicing magic longer."

"If you had the power to prevent us, why didn't you?" Lasair demanded to know.

He hesitated, and in that briefest of pauses she understood that his powers were not as great as he wanted her to think.

When Leary spoke again it was in a voice as smooth as cream. "You are my child, I would not employ force against you."

"But you did. A storm of that magnitude is one of the most potent weapons you have, Father. Such a storm only appears in Ireland once in several centuries, yet you turned it on me, on us, today."

"As an object lesson only, to acquaint you with the dangers."

"There is no danger to me except from you. Cormac would never hurt me."

Leary wagged a long, bony finger at his daughter. "You forget that I was able to observe all that happened. Can you deny you opened yourself totally to that human, so he could have done anything he liked with you?"

"I loved him, if that's what you mean. And he loved me. Loves me."

"Love. Ptah!" The old Sídhe spat violently, then wiped his mouth on the back of his wrist. "Love is a condition humans talk themselves into in order to justify doing things animals do without justification. It is a measure of their madness, but that doesn't mean we should embrace the same affliction."

"What are you talking about?"

"Suppose a human man were to say to a woman, I need a female to have sex with, and I also need someone to clean my house and cook my food. In return for these services I'm willing to provide you with the necessities of life. And suppose the woman then said to the man, I need food and shelter and I want to have children. Give them to me and I shall give you what you want in return.

"Is that not simple and straightforward, Lasair? Countless birds make the same arrangements in the hedgerows every spring, and I say they are more honorable than any manipulative human."

She lifted her chin still higher. "Do you think animals can't feel love? What of the swans, who only mate for life? One will grieve to death if the other dies. And wolves and wild geese and . . ."

"Enough!" Leary roared with the voice of the wind. "You are none of those, neither are you a human. You should be eternally grateful to The Source that you are one of the Sídhe, free of human burdens."

"Perhaps I don't want to be!" she flared back at him. "Perhaps I would rather know pain and grief and illness—and tenderness too, and rapture. The very shortness of human life makes emotions even sweeter, don't you see?"

As she spoke, passion fueled the radiance that emanated from Lasair until she burned with a white-hot flame. Leary turned his head aside because he could not bear to look at her. "I would not have thought it possible," he said sadly, "but that wretched man has corrupted you."

The brilliance pulsing from the leannán sídhe illuminated the darkest regions of the mound, until the tiny creatures who spent their lives in its lightless tunnels squeaked and scuttled in alarm. "Cormac did not corrupt me, Father. Perhaps we are the corrupted ones. Were we not once—millennia ago—much like his people? We traded our humanity for sorcery and became what we are, but does that make us any better? I think not.

"We are a small, sad, lonely race, dying out because we fail to reproduce ourselves in sufficient numbers. We mate but we hardly ever conceive any more; perhaps we lack the passion. Other races have vanished from this world and so shall we, Father, through our own foolishness."

There was no denying Lasair had passion, Leary thought. To lose her to a human would be doubly tragic; she might actually be capable of bringing forth a new member of the Sídhe. "Listen to me, my child. I can see I've made you angry. We have misunderstood one another, but the problem is easily mended. Come here to me so I may . . ."

"Embrace me to demonstrate the tenderness you feel for me? But we are not supposed to feel such emotions, remember? No, Father, you cannot have both, the freedom of faerie and the ties of love." As she spoke Lasair was backing away from him. The doorway was behind her, and beyond that, the tunnel leading to the entrance. As she made her way toward them she kept her eyes on Leary, expecting him to come after her or at least make some sort of magical gesture to block her escape.

But he just sat and looked at her.

She could not read the expression on his face because it was one she had never seen there before. Besides, the image of Cormac Casey was stronger. It was to him she spoke as she said, "I have made my choice."

Then she turned and fled.

"The human man will destroy you!" her father's voice thundered after her.

She ran with all the speed her feet possessed, but she used no magic to hasten her journey. When she reached the entrance she flung herself through it and kept running. Only when she reached the top of the Ridge of the Butterflies did Lasair pause long enough to look back.

There was no entrance. The mound was entirely covered by grass.

As she stood atop the ridge the wind began to die. The air was still bitterly cold, however, piercing the gossamer of her gown. Nothing could have been easier than magicking a warm cloak made of the finest fleece for herself, but she resisted the temptation.

If Cormac Casey was cold, he could not magic a warm cloak.

She set her face resolutely in the direction of the village and began to walk. Not drift, not float. Walk. One solid foot after the other, upon the solid earth.

She had no clear plan in mind. She had never needed to make plans before. But as she proceeded she tried to sort through the possibilities.

What if he had another woman? What if he had a wife?

To one of the Sídhe it should not have mattered. The moralities which attempted to limit human behaviour meant nothing to fairy folk, any more than they conformed to the arbitrary laws by which mankind

supposedly governed itself. But Lasair knew enough about the Irish so-
cial order to realise Cormac might not consider himself "free." If that
was the case, he should not want her.

She stopped, frowning. Thinking as she had never thought before.

Wife or not, with Lasair he *had* behaved freely. That much was certain. And he had given every indication of wanting her. Was she not a
leannán sídhe, sweetheart to all of faerie? She had nothing to fear from
any other female of whatever species.

With the abatement of the wind, wildlife was timidly coming out into
the open again. A big red fox emerged from a hole in an earthen bank
and blinked at Lasair.

"I have never been afraid of anything and I'm not going to begin now,"
she told it firmly.

The fox twitched its nose and grinned the knowing grin of its species.

I *am* afraid, thought Lasair. The fox knows. Does he ever fear that
his chosen mate will reject him? And if she did, what would he do?

Lasair was experiencing a veritable tempest of new emotions, infinitely more frightening than the storm Leary had called down. The
closer she got to the village the more excited and nervous and eager and
terrified she became.

There was still time to turn around and go back. Leary would welcome her with open arms, making her safe and secure, free from any
possible hurt.

He would look at her in that superior way of his, with "I told you so,"
in his eyes, and she would be unfree for the rest of her life. Her long,
long life.

At once she wanted desperately to turn around and flee home to the
fairy fort, and longed with equal desperation longed to touch and hold
Cormac Casey again.

At the thought of him her sexual response was stronger and more im-
mediate than ever before, though it was interlaced with strange new feelings which heightened the intensity while leaving her shaken and
confused. No wonder the Sídhe considered love such a dangerous emotion!

Lasair came to an abrupt halt, surprised to discover that the village
lay just ahead. Lost in the maze of her thoughts, she had arrived before
making any plans at all. What would she say to him?

She stood uncertainly for a moment, gazing down at the road as if seeking inspiration. In the muddy ruts left by cartwheels lay rifts of melting sleet.

The ice watched her, as cold and as silvery as her father's eyes.

Chapter 11

A<small>T</small> the height of the storm the fire in the cottage had begun to smoke badly as gusts of wind blew down the chimney. Everyone was coughing. Cormac repeatedly wiped his streaming eyes, but his vision only grew blurrier. At last he could stand it no longer. No matter how bad the storm, he had to go outside for some fresh air.

Father Duggan gave him a hard look as he went toward the door. "Don't be letting anything in here," he warned.

Cormac opened the door just enough to sidle through, so the priest could not claim some devil had crowded past him to invade the cottage and threaten those within.

When he stepped out into the road, he was astonished to find that the storm had blown over. The wind had died as suddenly as it arose, leaving devastation in its wake. Roofs were torn from cabins and the ground was littered with debris. But Cormac was not looking at storm damage, his gaze was fixed on the slender woman who stood in the road facing him.

"You came back," he said. "I thought you had left me."

She replied honestly, "There is no place I had rather be."

They stared at each other across an increasingly painful silence. There were so many things to be said, but neither knew how to say them. At last Cormac managed to ask, "Did the storm have anything to do with you?"

"I didn't cause the wind or the ice." If she said, "It was an effort to intimidate me," would he believe her? Lasair drew a deep breath. "The storm has passed, that's what matters." Then she felt compelled to add, "But it might well come again."

His jaw tightened. "We should seek shelter, then. But I can't take you back there with me." He gestured with a nod toward the Widow Hanratty's. "There's a priest inside."

Lasair drew a second, deeper breath, and tried to keep herself from trembling as she inquired, "Have you a home of your own? Have you . . . a woman in it?"

"I have a home many miles from here, but there's no woman in it, not anymore. My sister used to live there but she died."

Lasair's response was a radiant smile, but when she saw the sudden hurt in his eyes she wiped it from her face. "For your sake I am sorry about your sister, Cormac. You humans suffer so much death, you must find it very painful."

"Don't you? Or is it true that the Sídhe cannot die?"

"We die," she assured him, "but for us it is different. We are more spirit than flesh already, so becoming totally ethereal is but a small step. We also mourn as you mourn your sister, but ours is not grief as you know it. We sing for our dead so that the sound of music will carry them straight back to The Source."

He could not take in what she was saying, although he suspected it was somehow very important. He knew only that every word she spoke confirmed her as one of the Sídhe. Either that, or they were both mad.

Two mad people standing in a muddy road in the middle of the countryside.

Human practicality surfaced. "My home is a good four days from here, Lasair, but I must take you someplace now in case the storm does come back. How far is the next village?"

"You and I have different concepts of distance. If you trust me I can take you to your home very quickly."

If he accepted, and if she could do what she said, then the adventure was real. Magic was real. One giant leap of faith on his part—he who had little faith left—and all would be proven, one way or the other. Against that Cormac must weigh the tangibilities and certainties of life as he knew it.

Meanwhile Lasair was watching him, enchanting him with those huge eyes and the glow in her skin that seemed to come from deep inside.

There was no contest.

"Take me to my home," he said. "Just let me go back inside for a moment and get my things."

Her huge eyes widened further in alarm. "You must not go back in there! They'll try to stop you as my father tried to stop me. Don't you understand? Neither your people nor mine want us to be together!"

At her words a thrill of alarm ran up his spine. "Is there something you're not telling me?"

"We can't discuss this here," Lasair replied. "If you really want to go with me, we should do it now. Later we can talk."

"But all my sketchbooks are inside . . ."

She reached out and caught his hand, clasping it in both of hers. "Are you ready, Cormac?"

He swallowed hard. "I am ready."

"Then close your eyes and look at your home for me."

He closed his eyes as she requested and braced himself, either for the shock of magic or the disappointment of failure.

By the heat of her hands, he could tell how icy his fingers were. He heard Lasair grunt as if she were lifting something heavy and mutter under her breath. When she grunted a second time, warm wind flowed across his face. He had the peculiar sensation that it was not only on the surface of his skin but blowing all the way through him, leaving a faint nausea behind.

"Why are your eyes still closed?" Lasair's soft voice inquired.

Cormac was reluctant to open them. When he did, at first he saw nothing but a grey mist shot through with tiny prickles of multi-colored light. Then the mist cleared to reveal a small stone house with ivy mantling the gable end. The front door was painted bright blue, and blue also were the frames of the windows—to keep out evil spirits. Neglected flowers were dying in the front garden.

The man's knees sagged from shock. "That's the house I was born in!"

She looked at him calmly. "It is the picture you made in your head. I simply followed it to its source."

"How?"

She shrugged. "How do you breathe?"

Cormac stretched out his hand to feel the low wall that enclosed the front garden. The roughly hewn stone was cold to the touch. The paint on the wooden gate was peeling, and when he pushed it open, the rusting hinges creaked.

"Come in," he invited the leannán sídhe.

Lasair hung back, staring at the blue door.

Cormac followed her gaze. "I should have realized . . . I always heard that blue was a barrier to the Good People."

Chuckling, she shook her head. "The stories humans tell! Blue has no effect on the Sídhe, we love all colors. But manmade walls are so rigid and unyielding. I prefer the open air."

"Yet your home is a mound of earth."

"That's different. The fairy fort only appears to be a mound of earth; we shape it to suit ourselves."

"You can do anything you like with this house," he assured her. "I am afraid it has been neglected recently, but . . . Do you not trust me, Lasair? I trusted you enough to let you bring me here. Will you not come a step farther now, with me?"

He reached for her hand as she had reached for his, and with a small sigh, she surrendered to him.

Going back into that house was more difficult than Cormac had expected. The dark loomed just inside the door; dark memories, grief, loss. Had Lasair not been with him he might have turned away. But as soon as she crossed the threshold the hall seemed flooded with light.

She looked around curiously. "You have so many *things*," was her first remark. "Do humans need so many objects, just to live?"

He was taken aback. The house seemed modestly furnished to him. What few valuables it once contained had been sold in the futile effort to keep his sister alive.

"And this is what you call art, I suppose," murmured Lasair, pausing before a framed image of the Crucifixion. She looked at it with pursed lips and frowning brow, then moved on to another, a Holy Family grouping, and a third showing Saint Jerome in prayer.

"They are holy pictures," Cormac explained.

"This is what your religion is about?" She arched an eyebrow. "Is there no place for nature in your faith?"

He let her ramble through the house, content to follow her and admire her grace. He had to follow her. Wherever she went, the light moved with her.

Elsewhere it was dimming fast.

He observed that she touched each surface she passed, exploring its shape and density with tentative fingers. Occasionally she turned to ask him the purpose of one object or another, and she was outrageously amused by the chamber pot under the bed.

The bed itself evoked a different response. Lasair sat down on its very edge and ran her fingers over the quilt, then flung it back. She examined the sheets beneath, well-worn, the hems several times turned, but still possessing most of the delicate embroidery with which his mother had decorated them for her dower chest. "I like these flowers, a bed should always contain flowers." Abruptly she opened her arms. "Come to me," she said.

The room had once belonged to Cormac's parents. Fleetingly, he wondered what his very devout mother would have said if she could see her son with a leannán sídhe in what had been her own marriage bed. But as Lasair's arms folded around him, Cormac ceased to think of anything else.

He did not even hear the thunder that boomed in the distance, gradually coming closer.

Lasair heard it, however, and knew the sound was not natural thunder but the roll of fairy drums.

The trooping of the Sídhe.

Chapter 12

As he lay with her clasped to his heart, Cormac thought he had never felt so complete. Neither the far horizons that had lured him, nor the intricacies of form and line that had intrigued him, had ever been quite enough to satisfy him. But Lasair was enough. In her own self she contained the wonder of the unknown and the perfection of closely observed detail.

Squinting at her in the dim light of the bedroom he observed the faint lines etched in her face, tokens of mortality making her more infinitely dear.

We are more spirit than flesh, Lasair had said, but she felt like solid flesh to him. He was about to immerse himself again in her heat when the thunder sounded so close he could not help hearing it.

At the same moment Lasair tensed beneath him. "They have found us!" she gasped.

"Who?"

"My father. I thought perhaps he might let us be, but I should have known better."

"You had best tell me now," he said grimly. "What does your father have against me? I have always been warned that fairy folk can be dangerous to humans, but what harm could I bring to you?"

Lasair replied, "To love is to be vulnerable. You could do me terrible damage. Just as I could you," she added.

"Do you not love me?"

The huge eyes gazed into his. "I do."

"Then you would not hurt me, any more than I would hurt you."

"Ah, Cormac, if only it were so simple. You mean me no harm, yet you could draw off my magic and I could not prevent you. I donate small amounts gladly to make birds sing and flowers grow, but the demands of a strong human would be a thousand times greater."

He propped himself on one elbow so he could look down at her luminous face. "Was that what happened when you put your hands on my head? The feeling like a bolt of lightning going through my skull—was that your magic?"

"It was. At that moment I felt love for you, the first real love of my life. I could hold nothing back then."

"But it did you no harm, surely."

"Because I ran away at once. I felt terribly weak for a while after, however. Did the magic not have any effect on you?"

He thought back. "When I recovered . . . and found you gone . . . I could see everything so clearly! Then it faded, of course."

"Why should it fade?"

"Because I am losing my eyesight, Lasair." Cormac found it painful to say the words out loud. Ever since the initial diagnosis in Italy he had tried to believe it was a mistake, but by now he knew it was true. Day by day the world was growing dimmer, its outlines more blurred. Taking the commission for illustrations had proved to be a race against time, with the outcome uncertain. He might be able to finish before the blackness closed down forever, but he might not. In recent days the outcome had been growing increasingly certain.

Beyond the house the thunder boomed, insistently.

"Will they take you back?" Cormac asked Lasair.

"They shall try."

"Do you want to go—if loving me is dangerous for you?"

"I don't care how dangerous it is," she burst out. "I want to stay with you."

"If you are weak I can carry you. I should love to carry you."

She bit her tongue to keep from telling him that weakness was not the only danger. If he was going blind, using the full force of her magic might save his eyesight.

But in the expenditure, she would surely die.

Cormac was holding her in his arms and raining kisses on her face. He had not been able to fight successfully for his sister's life but he meant to fight for Lasair, even if that meant pitting himself against the entire army of the Sídhe.

"Stay with me, then," he told the woman in his arms. "I will let no one take you from me, not even the fairy folk. But you must tell me how to fight their magic."

She gave a soft moan. "Don't ask me to betray the secrets of my people!" A horrid suspicion assailed her. What if this was a ploy by the Christian Irish to break down the last defenses of the Sídhe? That's what Leary would say, Leary who had fought so long and so hard to keep what remained of their race intact.

Lasair fixed her most intent gaze on Cormac, trying to look through flesh and bone and determine the quality of the spirit within. But if human frailty was making him blind, love was having the same effect on her. She could see only his face, pleading for her trust.

"There are wards and symbols you can draw to keep the Sídhe from your dwelling," she told him at last, "and by arranging certain materials in alignment with the stars you will be able to overcome any weapon they send against you. I can tell you what to do, but you will have to put everything in place yourself. The design must be the work of human hands."

"I left all my artist's materials at the Widow Hanratty's," Cormac lamented. "I haven't so much as a pencil here."

"A burnt stick from the fireplace will do for drawing the symbols. But you must hurry! We haven't much time."

Cormac set to work at once. She did not need to urge haste upon him, for with every minute that passed his vision was growing poorer. He would have liked to believe it was the darkness preceding the storm but he knew better.

The symbols she described were complicated and must be executed precisely. "Altogether they form one giant pattern," she explained. "If there is the slightest deviation in any one of them, the protection will fail." Blinking, rubbing his eyes, fighting the encroaching darkness, Cormac drew as she dictated. Some designs were for doors and windowsills, others were drawn on surfaces within the house. In his mother's sitting room he was very conscious of the holy pictures watching him from the walls.

Meanwhile Lasair gathered feathers from the ticking mattresses and twigs from the kitchen broom. These were for the arrangements she wanted him to make. The most important items, however, she could not touch.

"If you have iron in the house, bring it now," she instructed. At her bidding he collected the household cutlery and set it out in patterns of diamonds and chevrons inside each doorway and along the front passage. As he worked Lasair stood with her face averted. "I cannot bear the sight of cold iron," she explained. "But neither can my people."

That much of the old legends was true, then, Cormac told himself. By now the interior of the house seemed as dark as night to him, although he had lit all the lamps and candles in the larder. When the time came for him to draw the final set of symbols on the front door, he could see almost nothing.

"I can't do it," he told Lasair.

"You must." She looked beyond him toward the black clouds boiling in the sky. She could hear the hunting horns of faerie drawing nearer, and feel the first cold wind upon her face. "Please, my love, there is so little time left! Leary and the host of the Sídhe will be upon us soon. Without the final sign upon the door completing the pattern, we are powerless against them. They will take me far away, and my father will visit some terrible punishment upon you."

"I can't draw it by touch, Lasair, the design is too intricate. Don't you understand? I can't see!"

Cormac's anguished cry cut through Lasair like a knife. There was only one way she could help him and she was suddenly, agonizingly, afraid.

She was not afraid of Leary, who would not hurt her, though he would surround her with such enchantments that she could never break free and find Cormac again. But he would show her lover no mercy. Leary had an old grudge to settle. No human could match one of the Good People for spite.

Or selfishness.

Magic had freed them of labor. Being able to acquire anything they wanted without having to work for it had made the Sídhe totally selfish. But the help Cormac required would demand a great sacrifice of Lasair. Although dying did not frighten her, she was terrified of leaving the world that contained Cormac Casey.

Meanwhile the sky darkened as the storm grew ever nearer, and behind the thunder she heard her father's voice. "Come back to me, daughter, and I shall forgive you!"

Closer to her ear was Cormac, beseeching her aid without realizing just how much he was asking. "Help me, Lasair! Help me see!"

True love is the rarest of all magic. For those who truly love, there is no choice to be made.

Lifting her two small hands, the leannán sídhe placed one on either side of Cormac's head, folding her fingers over his eyes. At the same moment she whispered, "All that I am or could ever be, I give to you."

Chapter 13

THIS time it was no simple bolt of lightning that lanced through Cormac's head, but a sheet of flame. He had never imagined such agony. A woman would have identified the pain he was suffering as the pangs of birth, except it was taking place within a male skull.

He tore at Lasair's fingers, trying to pull them away from his eyes, but she held on grimly. Her face was frozen in a mask of concentration.

The storm exploded around them. Black clouds closed down, wind howled in inhuman rage. The earth was shaken by the savage assault but Lasair never turned loose of Cormac.

Reading her mind and heart, Leary realized his worst fears were confirmed. There was nothing more he could do. The storm retreated to the hills and in a few moments was gone, as if it had never been.

Sunlight streamed back across the land.

Behind Cormac's eyelids wave after wave of color pulsed, crimson and azure and emerald, amber and violet and sulphur yellow. Each change of color brought an excruciating pain. Bile flooded his mouth, his muscles convulsed, but still Lasair's hands clung to his head.

Then the pain flared to a new intensity. Cormac thought he was slain. He opened his mouth to emit one cry of despair . . .

And the pain was gone. Suddenly. Completely.

His legs collapsed beneath him.

Consciousness returned bit by bit. Initially he was only aware of a solid surface supporting his body. Then he smelled an earthy aroma and realized he was lying on the path in front of his house, with his face pressed into the dirt. He turned his head to one side, expecting more pain.

There was none.

His ears detected distant birdsong and the gentle soughing of a summer breeze. There should be thunder, he thought vaguely.

There was none.

He opened his eyes.

At first he saw nothing but a grey mist shot through with tiny prickles of multi-colored light. Then the mist lifted and he viewed his surroundings with amazement.

Every blade of grass was as sharp and clearly defined as if observed through a magnifying glass. The pebbles on the path near his face displayed such separate and distinct features that each became a world in miniature. And when he raised his eyes and looked farther, he saw . . .

Color! Such color as he had never imagined. Color of blazing intensity and breathtaking luminosity, color such as artists dream about. His eyesight was not only restored, but enhanced a hundredfold. No human had ever been blessed with eyes like those Cormac Casey now possessed.

He had never believed his talent sufficient to allow him to paint with oils like the Old Masters, although he secretly longed to create unforgettable portraits and radiant landscapes. But with his new vision, he could become one of the greatest artists of all time.

And Lasair had done this for him!

He sat up, eager to thank her.

Then he saw her.

With his new-found clarity he not only saw her, but every detail of her figure was engraved upon his horrified heart.

She lay in a boneless heap at his feet, with her small hands flung open like crushed blossoms. There was no color in her face, only the pallor of death. His newly keen eyes detected neither the faintest movement of her bosom nor the tiniest twitch of her nostrils.

"No!" he cried.

Flinging himself upon her body, he cradled it to his chest. He was appalled to discover she was cold; she who had never been cold.

"No," he whispered.

His hands stroked her silken hair. He refused to believe all that life had drained out of her. No. All that life, that magic . . .

. . . Drained out of her. And into him.

Cormac sat very still. Then he turned his head slowly, looking one last time at the Irish countryside beyond his open gate. No human eyes had ever beheld it in such splendor. He could count the individual pinions on birds flying past, he could see rainbows captured within the prisms of distant dewdrops. Light reflected from dust motes in the air was visible to him. If he chose, he could have painted Ireland in such a way that the land itself would be caught on his canvas, held magically outside of time.

He looked down at Lasair's face. The curve of her eyelashes, each perfect and singular. The cobwebbing of lines beside her eyes, deeper than he remembered.

Bending, he pressed his mouth against hers and worked her cold lips open with his tongue. Then with no hesitation and no regret, he began breathing his briefly held magic back into her.

He could feel it going out of him. First there was a trickle of warmth, then a river. Life was going with it. He knew no way to control the flood, nor would he try.

His feet began to grow cold.

Infinitesimally at first, the body in his arms grew warmer. Her chest rose and fell so slightly only someone with perfect eyes could have detected the movement.

But Cormac's eyesight was rapidly reverting to the way it had been before. The brilliant colors were fading . . . he closed his eyes so he would not have to see them go, and went on breathing life into Lasair.

"No!" she gasped, pulling away from him.

She had returned from some far, ethereal place, to find herself encased in flesh. Flesh that she had no power of altering. She was held in the embrace of two strong arms, but even as she recognized them she felt their strength fading as he gave his life to her. In a few more moments she would be fully restored, and he would be dead.

She tore her mouth from his and broke the connection.

A generation later the door of the small stone house was no longer blue, having been through several permutations—red and green and finally simple, polished wood. No arcane symbol was inscribed upon it, for none was needed. The host of the Sídhe had never returned.

Opening to a day of autumn sunshine, the door revealed two people. They stood briefly on the doorstep assessing the weather, which was always uncertain in Ireland. Then they stepped out into the front garden. He carried his sketch pad, she had a basket and some flower shears.

He leaned against the low stone wall and drew her while she worked among the rosebushes. As his charcoal pencil skillfully reproduced her figure in black lines on white paper, he nodded with satisfaction.

Cormac's eyesight was much the same as when he first met Lasair but it had stabilized, deteriorating no further in twenty years, so that he was able to make a living drawing and engraving. He never attempted to paint the radiant Irish countryside, however. The magical spectrum he had briefly glimpsed was gone forever.

His wife was frowning at her roses. "They aren't doing well this year," she remarked over her shoulder. "We may lose this bush."

"I'll buy you another when the new book's published."

"That money is earmarked for Sinead's dowry," she reminded him in a practical tone of voice. "And Lorcan will want to go abroad to study, so we need to be saving all we can. You know how determined your son is to be an artist like his father."

"Better than his father, I hope."

"No one is better than you."

"You are."

She laughed, "I'm no artist."

"You know what I mean," he replied with a smile.

She put down her basket and straightened up to exchange one long, warm look with him. Then she massaged the small of her aching back with her hands, tucked a stray lock of iron-grey hair behind one ear and bent to her flowers once more. She did not look at her husband again but she could feel his love as surely as she felt the sun on her shoulders.

She was smiling too.

Like Cormac's vision, Lasair's flesh had stabilized, leaving her solid and whole and alive. Alive for the same span of time as any other human who did not embody magic.

But perhaps the greatest magic of all was still inside them.

BRIDE PRICE

Roberta Gellis

Chapter 1

THE tall chestnut horse ambled slowly down the road, pausing now and again to snatch a mouthful of grass from the verge. He was beautifully caparisoned, his bridle of silver and the reins studded with shining bronze, and he himself showed signs of past brushing and tender care. Once a sleek creature, a little spoiled, now he was gaunt and dusty with hard travel and glad to snatch at food while the attention of the man who bestrode him was fixed within himself.

Ahead on the road, Findbhair felt the man's coming and drew a deep breath. She had been standing proudly, but suddenly her knees felt weak and she sat down on the stone that marked the distance to Cruachan. She had waited a long time, a very long time, for the man whose eyes she had met once and once only, when she was a child of nine.

While she was a child, every time her mother had laid her will upon her, Findbhair had half expected that Fraoch would come to save her . . . but he had never come. As she grew older, the expectation that Fraoch would come faded, yet she was not less bound to him. Many times over those years men had wooed her, and although her parents were not eager to part with her, some of the men were rich enough and powerful enough that Medb and Ailill would have agreed to a marriage. Some of the suitors were strong, some were wise, some were beautiful, some all three, but even the best of them did not tempt Findbhair and she had refused their offers, bound by that single glance for ten long years.

She had been happy most of the time and fully occupied so that she was able to ignore the faint impulses to "call" Fraoch that swept her now and again. Those impulses had grown steadily stronger, but she had still suppressed them. He should remember too, and a man should come courting a woman. She was not a shameless trull to call a man to her. But it was not only that. Findbhair shivered and drew her cloak closer about her although it was not cold. She had been afraid to "call" him. Because he had not come when she wished for him as a child, she had not believed her need would bring him now.

Findbhair crouched a little lower on the stone. She had managed without him, even though their bonding had brought much grief upon her. But to be banished, driven out of her home . . . But she had not called him even as she fled down the road from Cruachan and onto the forest track that led to Brigid's cottage. Only when she opened the door and realized that Brigid was gone, long gone from the layer of dust on the table, did her misery overcome her and her need burst into summoning.

She had not really expected that call to be answered, even when, faint and far away, she had "heard," "Findbhair? Is that you?" And each day of the week it had taken him to come from Bruigh na Boinne to Cruachan, she had felt him closer and closer but still dared not believe. But now he was here, just beyond the curve of the road. What was she to say to him? Surely he had not come willingly or he would have come sooner. Did she want an unwilling man? And yet if she did not take him, she knew there would be no other man for her. And she wanted love, a soft, steady love, not the torrents of alternating doting, disapproval, affection, rage, and on and on that made up her life with her parents.

When she thought of them, another fear, long coiled within her, lifted its ugly head and stung her. Had the pride that prevented her from summoning Fraoch sooner brought about the disaster that had made her life at home impossible and finally forced her to "call" him? If she did not accept him now that he had come—out of the same pride, out of the need to know he wanted her, was not simply bowing to the force of the bonding—would more ill befall her parents, her country and countrymen? A sob shook her.

"Findbhair?"

She looked up, gasping with surprise. She had been so immersed in her thoughts that she had not heard the horse, walking softly in the dusty road. And then she still sat staring. She had forgotten how beautiful Fraoch was, with hair like coiled gold wires and eyes as bright a gray as sunlit ice, shaded by long lashes, enough darker than his hair to make the eyes as deep as a bottomless pool. His nose was straight, and a thin scar ran from his temple down his cheek to his jaw. The scar was no flaw; it only made his firm chin stronger and added manliness to a mouth that might have been as soft and pretty as a girl's.

"Findbhair? Do you not know me? I know you."

On the words, he came down from his horse, just dropping the rein. The beast, which had been about to amble on, stopped and stood. Findbhair rose from the rock on which she had been seated, but she tore her eyes from his face and dropped her head.

"You mean you recognize me?" she murmured.

He laughed and put out a hand to lift her chin, then shook his head. "No, I do not. I know you only here"—he touched his heart—"and here"—he touched his temple. "I only saw you that once and . . ." He blinked suddenly and shook his head. "You were a little child. How did you grow into a woman so fast?"

"So fast?" Findbhair echoed. "It has been ten years." Resentment pricked her as she remembered how long she had waited. "You were in no hurry to claim me. How much longer might I have waited if I had not 'called' to you?"

To her intense surprise, Fraoch paled. "I do not know," he whispered. Then he drew a long breath, smiled, and added cheerfully, "Thank the Lady Dana that you did. Do you not know that time runs differently for us of the Tuatha de Danaan, slower? We know the seasons but do not count them. To me it was only a few yesterdays since I saw you beside your mother's chair . . ." His voice faded, then came back strongly. "Findbhair, what are you doing here in the road away from Cruachan? And why are there marks of tears on your cheeks?"

"I am banished from the dun," she said.

Fraoch's hand lifted to the hilt of his sword. "For cleaving to our bonding when you were ordered to marry another man? Do you desire that I avenge the insult?"

"No!" Findbhair stepped closer to lay her hand over his. "I never told them," she said.

"Why?" he asked.

Findbhair laughed. "They would not have believed me."

"Are you so often a liar?"

She laughed again and glanced up at him sidelong. "No, not by custom, although I will not tell you that I have never told a lie."

Now it was Fraoch's turn to laugh. "Just as well. I doubt I would have believed that. But why should your father and mother doubt you if you said you were bonded?"

"Do you not know Medb and Ailill?" Findbhair sighed.

"They are ambitious, yes, but—"

"It is not only ambition. Neither is one to accept that a force outside themselves is stronger than they are." Her voice broke on the last few words, and she swallowed before she added, "If I said I was bonded, they would have tried to force a marriage just for spite. Do you think I have had no suitors? Just for being Medb and Ailill's daughter—"

"Not only for that, Findbhair," Fraoch said, his lips curving upward and his eyes slipping down from her face to the soft curves of the body filling the gown exposed by the cloak that had fallen open. "I am aggrieved that you waited so long in your 'calling.' I have sore needed a wife, but each time I thought of taking you, I saw a little fearful maid hiding in the shadow of her mother's chair. What a fool I am!"

"Now I will call you a liar as well as a fool," Findbhair said, her lips thinned with distaste for such blatant flattery and dishonesty. "That you could marry no other woman, I know, but that the women of the Tuatha de Danaan could not assuage your need for a wife . . . I am not such a fool as to believe that."

Fraoch looked down at her, a puzzled crease between his brows. "I never said I did not take pleasure from, and I hope, give pleasure to the women of my dun, but surely you know a wife is more than that. A wife is *with* a man in all things, and he with her. A wife shares joy, and sorrow too, cares enough to think about what her man does and advise him. I hope you and I will lie down and rise up, too, with laughter, but we will not part when we have risen from our bed. I have seen what my liege lord, Angus Óg, has with his wife, Cáer, and I envy that. I desire that, not a light coupling, which will be forgotten in a few hours."

Oddly, despite the tempestuousness, that was true—had been true—of her mother's and father's relationship. Pain closed her throat, but

Findbhair swallowed it down. "If you mean that," she said softly, "I am sorry for misspeaking you." Her heart lurched on the words and she stilled it. If he had had such a need, he had waited ten long years before trying to assuage it.

"Why would I not mean it?" he asked. "Angus's brother, Bodb, is a strong sorcerer. He could have broken the bonding between us if I had wished to be free of it. I did not. I was glad to know I would have a woman who would truly share my life and I hers."

Findbhair simply stared up at him, unable to decide whether he was speaking the truth. She was not at all sure the kind of tie that had bound them could be easily broken. She had not come across any spell for that in her studies with Brigid. To say he could have broken the bond and had not was simply another form of flattery, and the Tuatha de Danaan (the women were as bad as the men) were famous—or perhaps infamous—for their silver-tongued wooing of Milesian folk and their light-hearted abandonment of them too.

"Will you?" he asked.

"Will I what?" Findbhair responded, her thoughts having made her forget his last words.

"Share my life?"

"That I must," she said slowly.

He glanced at her and then away, aware for the first time that she was not as glad as he about their coming together. He knew well that one who loves desires the happiness of the beloved more than his own. His lips parted to ask what was wrong, to say that if she did not want him he would arrange for her to be free of him—but he could not. Although the time of waiting for her had seemed short, he knew why. All that time he had carried within him a warm core, ignited when his eyes met hers, that promised a joy more long-lasting than gold. If he tore that core from within him he would be hollow, empty . . . dead. He might talk and laugh, sing and dance, but like too many of the Danaan who had gone down into the sidhes, there would be no real feeling within him. He needed Findbhair! But if she was not willing? To force her to stay with him was . . . No, not force. He was not lame nor blind nor ugly. Surely bound as she already was, he could win her love. He would woo her.

Fraoch glanced sidelong at her and almost laughed. Findbhair might have been bound to him for ten years, but she did not know him. To

Milesians who heard only twisted tales of those Danaan who had gone down into the sidhes, the Tuatha de Danaan were beautiful monsters who used the common folk and then threw them away. She could not know that Bruigh na Boinne was on the earth, in the sunlight, and that Angus was far different than his kin. Poor Findbhair must be frightened half to death, cast out by her parents and feeling she was completely in the power of a beautiful monster.

"Love," he said softly, "what do you want to do? I will swear to you that I will love you all the days of your life, as Angus swore to Cáer, but why should you believe me?"

"I do not believe you," she said, smiling faintly. "Any woman who believes a man who swears that is a fool. But I must let you try to prove it, must I not?"

"If you will let me try, I have no fear about succeeding," Fraoch said, grinning. "But you have not answered my question. What do you want to do? Shall I go to Cruachan and demand they take you back?"

"No! Oh, Fraoch, I fear I have brought trouble enough upon Connachta to merit being cast out."

He cocked his head and lifted a brow over her outburst, but said only, "Then I will take you back at once to Bruigh na Boinne. You need not marry me immediately or feel that you will be helpless in my hands. Angus and Cáer will protect you, from me as well as from your parents."

A spear of vengeful delight, pain and pleasure together, pierced Findbhair. It would serve her parents right if she disappeared! They would tear themselves and each other apart with grief and guilt. Then she shuddered. Not only themselves. Medb and Ailill were not the kind to suffer alone.

"I cannot do that," she said, and added quickly, "No, not because I do not trust you but because as soon as my mother and father realize I am gone they will ravage the whole country looking for me."

"But we must go either to Cruachan or to Bruigh na Boinne," Fraoch said, half laughing and half annoyed by her silliness. "We cannot stay here on the road forever. Surely if I bring you back and say I have come to offer for you, your mother and father will allow you back into the dun. They cannot really have meant—"

She shivered, then laughed too. "They are not as cruel as I made it seem," she confessed. "In the woods not far from here is a snug cottage. The wisewoman with whom I studied lives there sometimes, and I have her leave to stay there whenever I wish. My father and mother knew I would not be naked in the wild when they bade me go. I just— You do not seem to know what has befallen Connachta. Medb and Ailill are not as they were . . ." She looked at him and shivered again.

Fraoch was thoroughly annoyed. He had expected she would see reason and go back home with him to protect her. He had been sleeping rough for all except the first night because of the urgency he had felt in her call. At the end of his week's hard riding, he had expected the pleasures of a well-maintained bathhouse with a servant to scrub him, a soft guest bed, and a rich dinner. A cottage in the woods was a poor substitute, and he would have been glad to confront Medb and Ailill, whatever their moods, for a guest had guest-right, which no matter how furious, they would not deny.

His lips parted to tell Findbhair that he would bring her to Cruachan, not as Medb's and Ailill's daughter but as his betrothed wife, and as such her father and mother would have to grant her guest-right too. But what had she meant when she said she had brought trouble enough on Connachta to be cast out? He had taken her words to be a girl's silliness, but the level misty green eyes that had met his were sad and afraid, not silly. He put his arms around her.

"Then let us go to this cottage. I see there is something making you very unhappy, but there is no sense talking about it while standing in the road."

Findbhair sighed and leaned against him for a moment. If only he had come of his own free will . . . She freed herself from his embrace, took his hand, and led him up the road toward Cruachan. Fraoch grabbed the reins of his horse as they passed and the beast followed readily without balking. Soon Findbhair turned off into what seemed little more than a game trail. The confidence with which she walked kept Fraoch from asking whether she was sure of her path, and it appeared she was, although it branched repeatedly and many branches were better marked than the trail they followed, for in no long time they came to a small clearing with a thatch-roofed, sod cottage set within it.

"There is no real stable," Findbhair said, "but there is a good shed behind the cottage. If you will take—" She hesitated and looked at Fraoch, who smiled. She was clever to have seen that his horse was no common beast and would have a name of his own.

"His name is Clis."

She smiled back, her lips only a little tremulous with uncertainty, and her voice was steadier, as if she had found some comfort in the thought of the very ordinary chores both would be doing. She said, "If you will take Clis around and unsaddle him, I will bring him some grain."

Suddenly Fraoch felt better too, the warm core inside him blossoming into a rosy tingle that centered in his thighs and loins. So would a wife say and do, and even more wifelike he found her when Clis had been fed and brushed, his furnishings cleaned and draped over a wooden frame, probably used for drying cloth, and he entered the cottage without knocking. Although it was dim inside, the light came from the open door at Fraoch's back and he could see that Findbhair had just lifted the cover of a pot that sent out a most savory odor. His next glance around the room told him he would be denied nothing. A good-sized bed, well furnished with furs and pillows, stood against the wall to his left. In the center of the room a huge cauldron was bubbling over the flames, and a large flat tub, big enough for a man to sit in with his knees bent, was set on the other side of the hearth with two pails of water beside it.

"How did you know how much I wanted a bath?" he asked, smiling at her as she turned from her stew.

Her red-brown brows climbed almost into the wisps of red-brown hair, which had worked free of her braids and curled on her forehead. "I smelled you when you held me," she said. "Bond or no bond, if you did not want a bath when you smelled like that, I would not marry you."

He laughed aloud, filled with warmth, with joy. "That will be no impediment to our joining, I assure you. It is a close race between my wanting that bath and wanting you."

Instead of laughing, too, and beckoning him to come in or holding out her hand to him, Findbhair turned away. A new pang of anxiety went through Fraoch. Had she been serious when she said she would refuse marriage over so small a thing as a bath? Nonsense. She had called him. But only out of harsh need, he reminded himself; she did not really want him, it seemed.

Chapter 2

Fraoch needed to remind himself sternly that he already knew why Findbhair seemed so unwelcoming, but he was not used to rejection for any reason and he hesitated. Findbhair covered the stewpot again, lowered it by the cords around its neck to the pot-shelf in the cauldron, and looked back at him.

"You aren't going to get that bath by standing in the doorway," she said, smiling and reaching for a large ladle that hung from a hook in a roofbeam. "Come around to the tub," she added, following her own instructions, and bent to lift one of the pails.

Fraoch hurried to help her and did so, even though she shook her head at him. When that pail had been emptied, Findbhair began to ladle hot water from the cauldron into the tub while Fraoch unclasped his cloak, loosened his belt and pulled off his inar. When he began to unlace his lena, Findbhair propped the ladle against the tub and came to help him pull it off, then undid the laces on the wrists and neck of his caimsi and pulled that off too. She looked for a moment at his upper body, the swelling muscles under the tanned skin, marred here and there with white scars, one of them half covered by the thick triangle of golden hair on his chest. Her eyes started to drift down, along the narrowing ribbon of hair that ran from the base of his breastbone to his navel, but she jerked them up to his face.

"I forgot to undo your crossgarters," she said, sounding a little breathless and sinking to her knees.

Much soothed by the way Findbhair had looked at him, Fraoch touched her hair and then her ear and felt her hands jerk on the thongs that held his hose. He began to bend toward her, and one hand rose and pushed him upright.

"After your bath," she said. "Right now I would not be sure, if I closed my eyes, whether I was bedding you or Clis."

"I am not so well-endowed as that," he protested, mock anxiety in his voice. "I hope you do not expect it of me."

She gave a little choke of laughter, which sounded less uneasy than her previous remark but her expression was severe when she looked up. "I did not mean that as a compliment."

"You only like little boys?" he asked, widening his eyes into an expression of horror.

"I have no idea what I like," Findbhair snapped. "Milesian women are not so light abed as the women of the Tuatha de Danaan. I have never touched a man, so how should I know—"

He bent and lifted her, kissed her nose and forehead and then her lips. "I am not sorry for it," he murmured, "but I am glad you told me. I will be careful of you, *gràdhaichte*."

She had pushed at him for one moment, before his lips fell on her nose; then she was still, but stiff in his arms. When he finished speaking, she pushed at him again and he let her go.

"What is that—*gràdhaichte?*"

"It means dearling, beloved, in the old tongue."

"Do you speak that language always in Bruigh na Boinne?"

She sounded a little anxious, and Fraoch's heart lifted as he realized she meant to come home with him. If she had not feared she would be a nearly mute outcast in Bruigh na Boinne until she learned the new language, she would not have asked that question. He smiled at her. Touched her cheek.

"No. The old tongue is dying, except for a phrase or a word here and there. In some sidhes they are trying to speak Danaan mainly, but Bruigh na Boinne is not a sidhe, nor will it be while Cáer lives."

Findbhair had dropped to her knees and finished unbinding one cross garter while he spoke. She looked up after untying the other. "Not a sidhe?"

"No. It is not buried in a magic mound but sits like any dun on its hill in the sunshine." He laughed. "When there is sunshine in this land." Then he added, "One way it is a sidhe, I suppose. It is home to us of the Tuatha de Danaan, and it is protected by Angus's presence . . ." He hesitated, then grinned again. "By Cáer's too. Angus would never fight unless the reavers were at the gate and a fight was forced on him, so some grew overbold. But Cáer has not Angus's soft nature. She meets the reavers in the field." He laughed again. "There are many fewer now."

"You are no doubt one of those who goes out with her," Findbhair said.

"Yes, I am." Fraoch, who had been looking inward, reliving the pleasure of those engagements, focused on Findbhair again and saw the thinned line of her lips. "Would you have me hide in the hayloft when the warriors go out to defend our land?"

She sighed. "Almost. I am a little tired of brave warriors standing up for their rights when everyone else's get trampled as a result."

"Cáer is not like that, *gràdhaichte*." Fraoch stroked her hair and her cheek again. "She fights only to protect our own people from raiders on Angus's land. She knows Angus does not seek to—no, cannot—add more to his lios."

Findbhair pulled her head away from his caress, but gently. "We are talking too long, Fraoch. Your bathwater will be cold. Off with those brecc."

He hesitated then grinned. "Are you sure you want to stay? I am not a decent sight for an innocent maiden."

"I have seen men before," she remarked with seeming indifference, but her fingers were a little clumsy in untying the waist string.

"Not like this, I hope," he muttered, uncertain whether to stop her and tell her to go away or let her know by seeing him how desirable he found her.

His uncertainty made any decision too late, and he uttered a little gasp as Findbhair suddenly pulled down the breeches and the cloth rubbed the exposed head of his shaft. As the breeches released it, the member promptly bounded up to a nearly upright position, almost striking Findbhair in the face as it rose. She winced back, lost her balance, and started to topple into the bathtub behind her. Fraoch caught at her and pulled her toward him, inadvertently pressing her face against his shaft. Her lips moved to cry out in surprise, and the shaft hardened further and twitched. Both gasped, and Fraoch stepped back far enough to free her face and pull her upright. There was a moment of silence, while they stared warily at each other.

"In the tub before you do worse," Findbhair said. Her voice was sharp, but one corner of her mouth twitched.

"It is not deep enough to cover me," Fraoch warned, struggling to keep his voice plaintive instead of laughing.

"That is your problem, not mine," she snapped. "If you cannot curb it now, how will it stand to arms later?"

Daring him, was she? Fraoch burst out laughing, rid himself of his breeches and shoes, and stepped into the tub. To his disappointment, when he looked for her, Findbhair had disappeared. Perhaps she had not taken as a jest what he meant as a jest? He thought of going after her, but decided that by the time he had drawn on some clothing, she could be anywhere. He sighed. He had thought the light words that had passed between them marked an easing of her fear.

The water was still warm enough, and he sat down cautiously, not wanting splinters in any delicate portions of his anatomy. The tub was smooth, though, and he shifted back a little so his knees were not so steeply bent. Then he felt around both sides of the tub for a brush or a scrubbing cloth, and when he could not find it, leaned forward to see if either was at the foot.

"Good. Stay just like that," Findbhair said.

"How did you vanish like that and return?" he asked, twisting his head to look at her.

"I am not such a good witch as to be able to vanish," she said, laughing. "I stepped behind the drying rack."

She pointed and he saw that what he had thought was a peculiarly rough inner wall of the cottage was actually a kind of wooden framework, pegged to the floor and fixed to a roof beam, on which were tied bundle after bundle of herbs. Then Findbhair pushed his head forward and began to scrub his back and shoulders with what felt like a coarse woolen cloth but which released a sharp, clean odor and left his skin feeling tingly and fresh as she worked. She did his back and neck, then his arms, then came around the tub and bade him sit upright.

He did so, but deliberately kept his eyes closed and allowed his slightly parted lips to curve up a trifle with pleasure. Fraoch intended to show that he was enjoying Findbhair's ministrations. A woman of the Danaan would have been flattered.

"Here," Findbhair said, thrusting the herb-filled cloth at him, "you can finish washing. I will see to dinner."

His eyes snapped open, and his lips parted farther, but a glance at her expression made him swallow his protest. Thoughtfully, he took the cloth and began scrubbing himself, watching as Findbhair picked up a long toasting fork and fished the cords of the stewpot out of the cauldron. When they were cool enough, she lifted out the pot and, protecting her hands from the heat with the hem of her skirt—which exposed her legs above the knee—removed the lid to stir the contents.

That did not need doing, Fraoch thought, unconsciously murmuring appreciation of both Findbhair's naked legs and the savory odor of the stew. She was making herself busy to keep herself away from him. And that went together with the way she had looked at his body. But she was annoyed when he showed pleasure in her attentions. So she did desire him but did not wish to admit it. Because Milesian women did not offer themselves when they desired a man as the women of the Danaan did? Because she feared that he would take her and then abandon her, as she said was the way of the Danaan?

Fraoch rubbed the herb-filled cloth over his chest, half conscious of enjoying the fresh scent that replaced sour sweat, man's and horse's. Her fear was ridiculous; he could not imagine what had set it into her mind. He was as bound as she and taking her would likely strengthen the bindings, not release them. But if she was frightened and he walking a sword edge because of that, the result would likely be only quarreling. They had been trembling on the brink of that even while jests flew between them. For both of them, the sooner she was bedded and sure of him and of herself, the better off they would be.

Findbhair heard the appreciative noise from the vicinity of the tub and glanced at Fraoch. His eyes were on her exposed legs, but he was also sniffing, and she could not tell whether legs or stew had called forth that hum of approval. And then his eyes lifted and met hers and they danced with mischief the way light dances off wavelets. Abashed, Findbhair looked away, re-covered and returned the stewpot to the cauldron, dropping her skirt. When she next glanced at Fraoch out of the corner of her eye, he had his left foot lifted across his right thigh and was watching himself busily scrub his toes.

Sly as a fox, that one. Findbhair gritted her teeth and went to get a bowl and a double measure of flour to which she added salt and a dollop of lard softened with boiling water from the cauldron, and began to knead. When the dough was ready, she went to fetch the girdle from behind the drying rack. Seeing her go for something, Fraoch called that she had forgotten a drying cloth. It was a good way, he thought, suppressing a grin, to get her to come close to him. She brought it, carrying the girdle in her other hand, but it was the girdle he took from her and set down on the floor.

"There is no sense in making the girdle cakes now," he said, pulling the hand he held to his mouth and kissing it. They're better hot, and . . ." Findbhair jerked at the hand he held, but he did not let go. He stood up, water sheeting off him. "I have a more urgent hunger."

Findbhair jerked harder on her hand and this time he released his hold. "Just like that," she gasped. "Without even asking if my hunger matches yours, or if I am even willing?"

She was angry, but to Fraoch's delight, she did not run away, nor even back away. He took the drying cloth from her arm where it hung forgotten and hastily rubbed off some of the water.

"Findbhair," he said softly, "we are bound and you are my wife. You are afraid of me, afraid of marriage, perhaps. Will words truly ease your fear? You ask if I would take you unwilling. No, of course not. It is my purpose to make you willing, which you said before you would allow me to do."

You did not come, she thought, until I set a summoning on you. How much can you really want me beyond the lust of the moment. "How do I know you will not use me and cast me aside?" Her voice was sour as spoiled mead.

His brows rose. "Why should you fear that? Because I am Danaan? But we are as bound by fate's weavings as the Milesians. Besides, could you leave me? Could you walk out of this cottage with the real intention of never seeing me again?"

Findbhair did not answer, but she could not help envisioning what he said, and as she saw herself walking away, casting a spell of confusion so that he could not follow, a great hand seized her heart and squeezed it. She could feel the blood drain from her face, and she forced herself to breathe, but she would not look up as she said, "No, I could not."

"I have come all the way across Eriu at your call," Fraoch pointed out. "Do you believe I could part from you?"

She knew he could not. The same binding that held her held him, and she shook her head but said bitterly, "That is not enough for me, for you to be bound against your will."

"I have told you more than once that it is not against my will." Findbhair could hear that he was smiling but would not look up, and he went on, "But you will not believe that either until you know how to wield your power over me." He stepped closer, raised her face to his. "Will you not let me teach you that?" And he bent to kiss her lips.

She jerked her head away. "What sort of fool do you think me, to believe you would show me how I could have power over you. Why should you?"

The laughter was gone from his face. "First, because your power over me is the source of the greatest pleasure I can have, and second, because the good of the beloved is more important than one's own good."

His eyes had darkened while he spoke, the gray almost black, and he put an arm around her shoulders. If she could only believe him, Findbhair thought, and then realized it did not matter whether she believed him or not. If she did not accept him, she would never have any man, ever, and her body was ready, very ready, for a man. There was no law that said she must give her heart with her body. If he was like what was said of Danaan men, well then, she could be like Danaan women. So she did not pull away and allowed her head to fall back as his mouth fixed on hers.

His lips were full and soft, dry without harshness, yet it was as if a honeyed potion flooded from them throughout her body. She could feel the tide of warmth flow down her neck and into her breasts, which filled, the nipples hardening so that the cloth of her gown, soft enough until that moment, scratched them, setting off an unbearable tickling that joined that insidious warmth as it ran across her loins and her thighs. The tickling centered in her nether mouth, which filled with moisture and seemed to gape. Without realizing what she was doing, she pressed forward against him, feeling his shaft press into her belly.

It was the wrong place. She rose on her toes, but was still not tall enough. Then a weight that had pulled her back was suddenly gone. When Fraoch's lips released her mouth, she realized that he had removed her cloak pin and the cloak had fallen to the floor. Her eyes, which she had not realized she had closed, opened. His fingers were plucking at the laces of her gown. For an instant a tide of shame as hot as that of her lust flowed over her, but when she looked at him she saw an expression as bemused as she felt.

His eyes were still dark as night and unshed tears glittered in them. "Help me," he whispered, fumbling with her laces with hands that trembled pathetically.

Compared with his distress, her shame seemed nothing. Accustomed as they were, her fingers made short work of ties and fastenings. Gown and undergarments soon lay on the floor with Fraoch's drying cloth. Findbhair had time for a single shiver before she was swept up and under the covers of the bed. Vaguely she remembered some woman telling her she should protest for form's sake, so that if she wished to free herself of the man in the future, she would be able to say that he took her unwilling. But Fraoch's mouth was on hers again, and one hand was playing with her right nipple while the other crept between her thighs and teased the little false tongue in that second mouth.

Without volition her body heaved. Fraoch's fingers slid into her. That felt so good, she clasped her legs around them to hold them, but he slid them free. She heaved again trying to find what she had lost, and was flattened to the bed as Fraoch came atop her. Now she both remembered and felt the hot shaft pressing against her belly and realized what she wanted; she felt for it, tilting herself a little sideways so she could slide her hand between them. He groaned when she seized him, but not with pain, even though she had to push the shaft down to find its sheath.

Positioned, Fraoch thrust gently, causing Findbhair to gasp with the pain of stretching even though the passage was well moistened, but the easy thrust did not seat him. Fraoch groaned again, and then became very busy kissing her throat and ears and mouth, teasing her breasts with one hand, and arching his body so he could seek that little tongue with the other.

Findbhair, assaulted by erotic sensation in every sensitive spot, cried out and heaved, fastening her legs around Fraoch's hips and pressing him down into her as she heaved up against him. He pulled his hand from between them and gasped as he was jammed painfully into the obstruction of Findbhair's maidenhead, but in the next moment the thin membrane tore and he was through. Findbhair gasped too as pain lanced through her loins, but the marvelous sensations in breast and throat and lips drove her to press even closer and writhe against the rod that filled her. That was not enough. She relaxed her legs and as if he knew what she wanted, Fraoch pulled himself a little way out and thrust again.

Moaning with mingled pain and urgent passion, Findbhair urged Fraoch with legs and hips to draw and thrust again, and again, and again. She was beside herself, for though the pain grew less in one way, a different kind of pain that was, strangely enough, all pleasure, grew and grew, until she shrieked aloud again and again in a convulsion of delight that was also agony.

She was not aware when or how that explosion of ecstasy ended and she lay like the dead for a few minutes, so overpowered that she was hardly aware that Fraoch was still moving, though slowly and gently compared with the driven plunging that had brought her to climax. Her eyelashes fluttered; her eyes opened. She saw his face, smiling, above her.

"That is my power over you," he murmured softly. "Now I will give you the key to yours over me." And he whispered to her what would cause him the same joyful torments that he had visited on her.

Findbhair listened and laughed. She had been ignorant of what the sensations she would feel would be like, but she was not really ignorant of the act of love. She had slept all her life in a chamber that was walled off from her mother's only by a thin woven wattle wall. As a child she had slept too soon and too soundly to hear much when her father came, but as she grew older she had learned more than she wanted to know about the intricacies of love play.

"Here?" she whispered, running her hand down Fraoch's spine, between his buttocks, between his legs, scratching ever so gently.

He had shivered when her fingers went down his back, lifted when they touched his buttocks, and thrust so hard he pushed her up in the bed when she touched his privates. Her other hand found other, equally sensitive spots, and he moaned and writhed, gasping, "Wait. Wait." But she only laughed again and tickled his ear with her tongue while one hand stroked his inner thigh and the other caressed the base of his shaft. He plunged even harder, twice, three times, moaning louder and louder until he was crying aloud, arching his body upward to drive himself deeper, and finally collapsing against her, breathing like an overworked bellows.

It had been horrible to hear her parents, Findbhair thought as her eyes closed, but it was not horrible at all to play the game herself. And then sleep overtook her with the suddenness and unexpectedness of falling down a well.

Chapter 3

F INDBHAIR woke as suddenly as she had fallen asleep when she felt Fraoch stir beside her, but without the smallest sense of shock. That was strange, she thought, eyes still closed. She should have been terrified at waking with a man's smell beside her and the ache and stickiness between her thighs that told her she was maiden no longer. But the touch, the smell, was Fraoch—and somehow "right." She had just begun to wonder whether it was "right" for him also, when lips touched her temple.

"Findbhair?" his voice was very soft, tentative.

She opened her eyes. "You are, if not a liar, a menhir of deceit," she said. "You told me you would give me a key to power over you. You said nothing at all about how that key would lock *me* up."

His eyes were sparkling bright again, but wary. "Ah . . . You do not appear *very* angry," he said. "But I was not really deceitful. I knew what your key would do to me, but I could not be sure that my key would turn your lock. There are some women who cannot find joy . . . as you did?"

"Women *you* have made love to?"

Findbhair's brows rose in disbelief. She might not have any personal experience, but she had heard allusions enough to men who satisfied themselves without consideration for their partners. That was not a fault to be attributed to Fraoch. Recalling the explosion of joy/agony that had racked her, she could not decide whether he was joking or teasing her or displaying a false modesty. Thus, her cross-question was all the answer she chose to give to the last three words he had spoken, which were more question than statement.

"Too many among the Danaan," he answered, and she saw a deep sadness in his face. Suddenly he shuddered, and then bent over and kissed her, lightly, but with glowing eyes. "Not you, *gràdhaichte*, you are alive and you make me live also."

Because of his sadness and the way he had shivered, she was shocked by that remark. There were, she knew, creatures that lived by drawing the strength from others. Even as the horrible thought crossed her mind, however, she dismissed it. Danaan he was, but no monster. Victims of the life-leachers were always exhausted by their "pleasure," whereas she was as full of well-being and strength as if she had sucked him dry. Not that she had. Her eyes sought his face, bright and beautiful—and saw that he was distracted, sniffing and turning his head toward the hearth. Instantly, the smell that had been assailing Findbhair's nose developed meaning.

"The stew," she cried, pushing Fraoch aside with such force that he fell over and jumping out of bed. "It will be cooked to glue."

Fraoch lay where he had fallen, laughing. "Ah, well. One must take the bitter with the better. I will settle for stew-glue if you will serve me as you are."

"I am more likely to serve you as you deserve," she cried, quite out of patience with the silliness of men. "Could you not wait until we had eaten before you dragged me into bed?" She ran, naked, only snatching up a garment to shield her hands, to pull the pot out of the caldron.

When that was sitting beside the hearth, she drew on her undergarments, casting a glance at Fraoch, who was still lying in the bed, watching her. She bit her lip as she turned to the dough, which had dried out in places from lying uncovered for so long. He seemed as lazy as any Milesian man and was Danaan, too. Did that mean he would expect her to do everything except fight? Was that why he wanted her? Because the women of the Tuatha de Danaan were too proud to serve him? She glanced back at him, then turned her head aside to grin. Considering the extraordinarily handsome face, the beautiful body, what he had brought to her in bed, no woman would be too proud to serve him.

Fraoch caught not only the sidelong glance but the expression that went with it. He was not accustomed to living without servants, it was true, but not such a fool as to expect any to materialize out of thin air in a one-room cottage. And he knew how to haul water and keep a fire going when hunting or fighting. Since it was clear enough that Findbhair would have to do anything he did not, Fraoch got up and pulled on his brecc and caimsi. As Findbhair worked the dough, he first straightened the furs on the bed and then looked for a task too heavy for her.

First get rid of the bath, he thought, and went to ladle the water out into the empty pail. When he tipped the tub up to get at the last of the water, a soft clang told him that Findbhair had set the girdle on the stones. He turned to look at her and when their eyes met, there was, again, that shock of binding—this time full of the richness of a shared life.

Neither spoke of it. Fraoch stood frozen for a moment, then tipped the remaining water from the tub. Findbhair, through stiff lips, bade him put the bath back behind the drying rack and take out and set up the table that was there before she slapped the rounds of dough onto the girdle. Then Fraoch went out to draw fresh, cool water from the well, from which he first filled two cups from a shelf on the wall and then the cauldron, after which he slid sticks onto the fire under the girdle. He did not touch Findbhair and she stiffened a little when he came close. But when the cakes were baked, the stew in bowls set on the table, and both sitting on stools, Fraoch said, "Why? Findbhair, why did you bind me again? Can you not trust me? I swear I am yours already."

She blinked, but his expression was anxious and a little hurt. And when she put out a questing thought, as Brigid had taught her, there was no yellow-green or reddish purple of deception in him. She shook her head. "I was about to ask you the same question," she said.

"You did not?" he asked.

"No more than I did when I was a child of nine. Why did you choose me?"

"I did not!" A slight flush mounted his cheeks. "I do not think of little maids of nine in that way, Findbhair. That is . . . disgusting!"

"But you were looking at me. I was afraid at first, but then you smiled and—and I belonged to you, and it was right that I should, and I knew you would not hurt me." She dropped her eyes. "But those are the thoughts of a child."

"Still, they are true thoughts. I would not hurt you, child or woman, Findbhair, although I did not bind us—I swear it. I was looking at you because I like children, the Danaan have so few, and I smiled because I thought you were frightened by what Angus asked and how your mother answered and by the coming of the Old Crow. But I have no magic. I could not bind us, then or now."

No magic indeed, she thought. You are magic yourself with your beauty and your soft ways and your silver tongue. But she took a spoonful of the stew and a bite of the girdle-cake before she said thoughtfully, "But if you did not bind us, and I did not—I could not then; I had not yet met Brigid and knew nothing—then why . . ."

"The Morrigan?" he asked uneasily. "She was there. But I could have sworn all her attention was on Angus."

"But she is not here now," Findbhair pointed out. "And though I have heard that she sometimes wears other faces, I have never heard of her going unseen. No, she wants to be seen, to cause the greatest consternation. Besides, I think I would feel her presence."

"Your wisewoman?" Fraoch suggested more cheerfully, spooning up stew and biting into the flatcake himself.

"That is not impossible," Findbhair said slowly. "But if it was Brigid, no ill will come of our binding."

Fraoch smiled broadly. "No. I never thought ill would come of it. Indeed, I am delighted and only wish you were as pleased as I."

All those years, Findbhair thought, and a summoning to bring you to your delight? But the words were less bitter in her mind. She knew how most men set aside thoughts of women when they could think of war or hunting or even breeding cattle. If he was truly delighted now, she would be wise to dismiss her hurtful memories.

"Women of necessity are more cautious than men," she said. "To be left with a full belly and no means of support is all too common for one who yields as readily as I did."

"You expected me to think ill of you?" Fraoch's eyes opened wide and he nearly choked on the mouthful he had taken. "But you are my wife. We are bound and wed and bound again—"

"Wed?" Findbhair echoed. "How? When?"

"By the customs of my people we were wed when I called you wife, when I first saw you by the road. Findbhair! Did you think I lay with you without meaning that? Is that the custom of Milesian men? No wonder you do not trust me. The Danaan are free with their bodies, yes, but only when it is understood on both parts that they are just engaged in play."

She began to laugh. "Bound and wed and bound again."

"Yes, by my custom, the word wife is enough. If I meant other I would have said woman or lemman or some other word that means a pair that bed together. I said wife, and mean it." He hesitated, put down his spoon, and there was eagerness, even avidity, in his eyes. "You said a full belly. Is that likely, Findbhair? Oh, you need not fear any Danaan would abandon a woman with child. I will love you even if you never breed of me, but I will cherish you all the more for bringing me a child."

"From this one coupling, I doubt you will have set seed, but the Milesians seem more fertile than the Danaans. We do not lack for children."

"Well, I will be glad if you breed." He picked up his spoon, took another mouthful, and then said, "And speaking of your getting with child, if it should happen, I do not want my child called 'bastard' by your parents. What little I know of Medb and Ailill tells me it will be needful to be wed by your custom and with witnesses as well as by mine."

She grinned at him. "I would like that. I would like my mother and the other women of the dun to see for what I was waiting. You are *very* beautiful, Fraoch."

He laughed. "I hope I am more than beautiful, for if that was all you were getting, you would be badly cheated. You, too, are beautiful, Findbhair, and you can also cook! Considering what we did to it, this stew is very good. What is more, I doubt your father and mother would be much moved by my appearance. I need to know how to make them willing to give you to me."

Suddenly the laughter died out of her face. "I do not know. You would think that having cast me out, they would be glad to see me taken by a beggar, and perhaps if you were a beggar, they would be angry enough to give me to you. But you are beautiful, and strong, and Danaan, too. Likely just to spite me, they will refuse. They are so angry . . ."

He reached across the table and took her hand. "You said before that you had done enough evil to be cast out. I cannot believe it. You are as sweet and clean as any woman I have ever seen. What did you do, love?"

"Out of pride, I did not call you."

"What? But how could that hurt Connachta?"

"Do you not think it possible that if we were fated to be together and I resisted that fate, that trouble after trouble would be piled upon my parents and Connachta until I swallowed my pride and sent a summoning?"

He sat back, staring at her, and finally said, "I do not think it likely, no. I should think, as in Angus's case, trouble might follow you. That it should fall upon your parents or Connachta is unreasonable—you might never connect the cause and effect."

Findbhair sighed. "Well, maybe you are right about the trouble not happening because I would not summon you, but I still may have caused the disaster that followed the cattle raid of Cuailgne—at least, my mother blames me for it."

"You? Were you on the raid?"

"No, of course not."

"Then how—"

"You know what my mother is?" Findbhair asked.

Fraoch nodded but did not think it safe to reply. She might criticize Medb, but he could not. He continued to eat, and Findbhair, seeming to understand, smiled faintly at him.

"My father loves her," she went on, "and she him, I think, but peace between them is kept only because they are exactly equal in property and thus in power."

"What has property to do with power?"

"That is our law. For a wedded pair, the one who has the most property is head of the household. In many cases it does not matter because the woman does not desire to carry the burdens of defense and justice and law-giving, and gladly yields place to her husband, but with my mother . . ."

"Ah, yes." Fraoch nodded. "I can see that in this case the law might have sharp teeth."

Findbhair nodded briskly. "Each year there is an accounting of all my father's goods and all my mother's. Last year it was discovered that my mother's great stud bull . . . was gone. There were searches and punishments aplenty, but the bull was not found, and so my father was a bull the richer than my mother."

Fraoch shook his head in a kind of disbelief but did not speak, and after swallowing another mouthful, Findbhair continued. "The only bull, the equal of my father's, was the great brown bull of Cuailgne. First my mother tried to buy him and then, when the owner would not sell, to lease him for a few years until the coming bull calves might be judged. Only when neither blandishment nor bribe would move the owner did she send out a raiding party and steal the creature. Those of Cuailgne were too weak to bring war against Connachta, but they appealed to Ulster, and Ulster, holding a long grudge, was eager to take up the challenge."

"I still do not see why your mother should be angry with you," Fraoch said.

"You will in a moment," she said. "Ulster has a great champion called CúChulain and he defeated all the men my mother sent against him except Ferdia, who would not fight because he was of old CúChulain's friend. First my mother tried to force me to promise to wed Ferdia if he would fight—he had asked for me before. I would not do it, and she found other means to drive him to do her will. And then she tried to make me swim the river and seduce CúChulain so he would be weakened by our coupling and more vulnerable in battle. I would not, and CúChulain won. Our army was defeated. For this my mother blames me."

Fraoch put out his hand and took hers. "I am very proud of you, love, for saving yourself, but beset as you were, why did you not summon me or at least tell your mother that you were bonded?"

"Would she have believed me then, when I had never mentioned it before? As a child I kept it secret because that is how children are, and it was *my* secret, mine alone. Later, I was not sure myself what had happened. Five times my father proposed this and that man as a husband, and five times I refused. Some were worthy men, but I found I could not accept. Then I was sure of the bonding, but you did not come to seek me, and out of pride I would not demean myself to call you."

"That was very foolish." However, he was smiling and brushed it aside with a gesture. "But it is done now. So, your mother blamed you for her defeat and—by the by, whatever happened to the brown bull?"

Findbhair's lips tightened over that airy gesture, but what could she say when it was made to excuse her action? "When he was loosed into our meadows, he saw my father's white bull. Before the cowmen could do aught, the two charged at each other and began to fight. Both died, and a dozen men, too, trying to separate them. And my father's mood is now as sour as my mother's."

Fraoch whistled a comprehension of the disaster, but then, irrepressibly light-hearted, he laughed. "It sounds as if your mother and father need better-trained cowherds."

Findbhair drew in an outraged breath, but before she could exclaim at his callousness, the laughter was gone and he was shaking his head.

"No, it is no fault of yours," he said. "But something is at work here, and it is time and more than time that you were well out of it."

"Are you telling me to run away when more trouble is about to fall on my parents?"

"I did not say more trouble was coming. I do not see any reason for that, but your presence in the dun will not help the healing between them. For what were you cast out?"

"My mother bade me cast a spell of withering on a woman who had annoyed her, and I would not. I—"

"Could you?" Fraoch asked a trifly uneasily. "Are you a witch?"

"Perhaps, to the second question, and no, to the first." She held up a hand to stop Fraoch from interrupting and he scraped a last spoonful of stew from his bowl instead. "I am a witch, if knowing how to cast spells makes me a witch, but Brigid, who taught me, put a geis upon me that any spell I cast turn only to good. So, no, I could not cast a spell of withering. Well, I could, but instead of withering her, the spell would probably make the woman rich or ten times as beautiful or five years younger or something of that sort."

"I see," he said, still sounding uneasy, but then he shook his head. "Yes, but it only makes my point. Look, your mother knows your geis, does she not?"

Findbhair nodded. "And I tried to remind her, but she would not hear me. She struck me! She said I was a curse in the dun, and that I was to leave it."

"In other words, she drove you out for nothing." Now Fraoch nodded, as if she had confirmed something he had been thinking. "Yes, you must leave Cruachan, and you need not fear that you are deserting your parents when they are in trouble. Think. Both bulls are dead and thus Ulster will not raid to return the brown bull to Cuailgne. Your mother and father are again exactly equal, although somewhat poorer. But both are angry at the loss and they are punishing each other because, being what they are, they do not know how to comfort one another, which makes them even angrier but eager to find another source for their discomfort—and they have found you."

"Justly, I think," Findbhair said faintly.

"Do not be as silly as they are, please." Fraoch's tone was acerbic. "I am not ignorant of CúChulain, although I had not heard of this particular battle. Do you really think, Findbhair, that your agreement to marry Ferdia or your sleeping with CúChulain would have affected the outcome of the war?"

She shrugged. "No, because Ferdia did fight, and my mother sent another woman, far more seductive than I, I think, and CúChulain refused her."

"It would not have mattered if he had accepted her. CúChulain is a swordsman with such strength and skill as I would not care to meet, nor would Angus. Dallying with a woman, which he has been known to do, has never changed his skill or endurance. But that is aside from the point, which is that your mother knows this as well as I and nonetheless blames you because she must blame someone. Yet knowing the blame to be unjust makes her angrier until she cannot bear to look at you, so she drives you away. Now the fear that ill will come to you will eat even more deeply into her. The only cure for this ill is to have you both out of the dun and *happy*. Then she can put the blame for everying upon you and, knowing you safe and well, let it ease her heart."

"You are not only beautiful, Fraoch," Findbhair breathed, "but you are clever, as clever as you are beautiful, I think."

Fraoch laughed aloud. "When you serve a master like Angus Óg, who sees only the best in everyone and is as innocent and honest as a flower—" he grimaced "—and as simple-minded sometimes, you sharpen your wits to protect him. Thank the Lady Dana, most of that burden is lifted from me now for Cáer is there."

Findbhair cocked her head. "You are not jealous of her for taking your place in Angus's heart?"

He smiled. "Angus's heart is large enough to hold the world. No, I am not jealous of Cáer, but as I told you, I did envy what she and Angus had between them." He breathed deeply, and pushed away his empty stew bowl. "I envy them nothing now. I have what is better for me."

After taking her own last mouthful of stew and chewing the last bit of her girdle cake, Findbhair said slowly, "Yes, you have me if you just wish to take me and leave, but if, as you said, you desire my parents' approval, you may not have me. You may have understood what is driving my mother near demented, but if you think she will part with me readily for all of that, you are mistaken. She is the kind that takes a sour pleasure in biting on a sore tooth."

"If I must, I will simply take you away. The only one who can deny you to me, is yourself." Fraoch smiled and reached across the table to take her hand. "But I have seen what you are, *gràdhaichte*, and if you thought you were leaving misery behind, you would not be happy yourself. So, I must contrive, somehow, to reconcile your parents to our marriage. Now, let us go one step at a time. I do not want them to be able to refuse me out of hand. I must have some hold on you—by their custom—that they must break before they can refuse you to me."

"A hold on me—" Findbhair smiled. "If we lie together for three nights and then come to the dun and say we have done so to bind ourselves in marriage, the only way they could part us is if you did not pay my bride price." Then she frowned. "But they could make that bride price impossible to pay . . ." She hesitated, so obviously thinking that Fraoch remained silent instead of offering reassurances, and at last, she nodded at him. "We must come at dinnertime, when the whole lios is assembled, and you must speak before all. The price will still be high, but it will not be more than a man can pay."

Chapter 4

THE three days and three nights of Fraoch's and Findbhair's hand-fasting were three jewels of peace and contentment both would hold forever in their memories. In the morning, Fraoch hunted for the pot and Findbhair gleaned in the woods and the woodland meadows. He dressed his kill when he returned and Findbhair cooked it, together with her gleanings. In the afternoon, they ate well and then turned to homely tasks in the cottage: Findbhair cleaned it of the dust and spider webs that had accumulated since Brigid had departed, mended the bedding and any damage to their scant clothing; Fraoch repaired a loose board in the floor, plastered a few chinks in the walls, chopped wood, and pegged in two more hooks, which he had carved, for holding clothing. And at night, they made love.

On the fourth morning, after they rose and filled the tub and washed each other, their eyes met and each knew the other was wondering whether they had to break their idyll.

"Another day or two would not hurt," Fraoch said, "would it?"

"No, it would not, but—"

Fraoch sighed. "But it would not be the same. We would both know we were supposed to be elsewhere, doing something else."

"Yes." Findbhair cupped his face in her hands and drew it down so their lips could meet. When she broke the kiss, she said, "They will try to put such strains upon us that will break us apart, my mother to spite me and my father because I am a possession with which he does not wish to part."

"They can kill us, either or both," Fraoch said, with a laugh, "but bound as we are they cannot break us apart. Remember that and the seemings they will put on our actions will disappear."

"I hope so." She sighed. "You are clever, Fraoch, but so are they."

"Then we must plan our first meeting with especial care," he said.

As a result of that planning, Fraoch led Clis onto the barge that ferried guests across the lake to Cruachan just as the petty kings, the barons and liegemen, were taking their places in the great circular mead hall. Beside him, swathed from nosetip to toetip in Fraoch's great cloak, was Findbhair, who Fraoch lifted to ride pillion behind him once they were ashore. Seeing the long blond hair, the bright gray eyes, the richness of horse and horse trappings, the guards on the outer gates hailed him as "guest" and did not delay him.

Within the innermost wall, Fraoch dismounted and lifted Findbhair down. Having given Clis into the keeping of a groom, he walked boldly in at the central of the seven doors to Medb's and Ailill's great circular mead hall and straight up the aisle between the richly decked couches, past the rows of benches—which held fewer men than he remembered when he and Angus had visited Cruachan—and up to the dais, where he stopped and bowed, looking up at Ailill and Medb.

The ard righ's clothing was still magnificent, today a shining white caimsi, its full sleeves with brightly embroidered cuffs showing under the sleeveless but high-collared lena, which was closed with a gold-studded belt. But Ailill looked older, Fraoch thought; although his skin was smooth and healthy-colored, his hair was thinner and there were pouches under his bright, black eyes.

Medb looked older too, although Fraoch could not say why at first. Her hair was just as flaming red, just as abundant, pouring over her shoulders and down her back; her eyes were just as bright—fixed on him now with an avid speculation that was certainly young enough. She was not older in feature or body, he thought, but behind that bright glance was a kind of weariness.

"I bid you welcome to our house," Ailill said, and gestured toward the benches. "To meat and drink, to the warmth of the fire and the shelter of the roof you are also welcome."

Even as he spoke, Medb's hand came out and prodded his upper arm in a kind of warning. But Ailill's expression already showed that he found Fraoch's face familiar, could not place it, and was growing suspicious.

"You may know me," Fraoch said, eager to set Ailill's doubts to rest. "I was here with Angus Óg when he begged your help to win his wife Cáer. My name is Fraoch, and I serve as aire forgaill in Bruigh na Boinne. I thank you for your welcome and I hope you will also welcome my wife." He gestured toward the cloaked and hooded figure beside him.

"You may be sure we do welcome her," Ailill said, his dark face alight with curiosity. The Tuatha de Danaan did not often bring their women with them.

"And will Queen Medb welcome her among her women?" he asked, looking into the queen's brilliant eyes.

She knew it was a trap of some kind, Fraoch saw, and saw also how her eyes flashed around the drinking benches, taking in the expressions of the men there and the women who were grouped to her right. Those were all sullen or sour and the whispers that passed from one to another were closer to growls. Medb curved her lips at Fraoch and nodded her head, doubtless feeling there was more danger from further angering her nobles and liegemen by seeming to violate guest-right than from whatever creature Fraoch was asking her to accept.

"Yes, of course," she said.

Fraoch promptly drew Findbhair forward and lifted the hood from her head, saying, "This is Findbhair a céile Fraoch, to whom I have been bound since last I was in this house—" His voice was swallowed up in Ailill's roar, Medb's shriek, and various shouts of surprise and even approval from the men and women in the hall.

As the noise died down, Ailill shouted, "Bound? Whom by? Who would dare bind my daughter?"

Medb's screech did not quite drown him out, but could be clearly heard. "A céile? My daughter can have no husband without my permission."

"Findbhair is no one's daughter," Fraoch said, his own voice rising clear above all the others. "Did you not cast her out with no more than the clothes she was wearing?" He opened the cloak and turned Findbhair so that all could see what was under it. "In these clothes, Findbhair was driven out of the gate ten days since. No gold, no provision, no well-wishing followed her. She was homeless and no longer had a family, and as such I took her. She called. I came as quickly as my horse could bear me. I put my cloak upon her to clothe her. For three days, I hunted so she could eat, drew water so she could drink, cut wood to keep her warm, and for three nights I lay with her as her husband. Findbhair is my wife by your law of three days living together."

Ailill's face was pale, Medb's red as fire.

"But Findbhair loves you," Fraoch went on, his voice softer in the silence. "She would not leave without telling you what had happened lest you think ill had befallen her and grieve for her. And she loves Cruachan, and wishes to have the right to visit it and you when it is suitable. Moreover, she desires that if she bears my children you will not deny them. Thus, I have brought my wife as a guest to your house. If you wish to acknowledge her again as daughter, I am willing to pay bride price for her and take as dowry what she has prepared for her marriage, her clothing and jewels and chests of linen, her drinking horns and eating platters and cooking pots."

"That is a fair offer," a man's voice called from behind Fraoch.

"That is a fair husband," one of the women cried. "I would take him if he were unwilling to pay as much as a sick goat."

"He is Tuatha de Danaan," came another voice, warning.

"Danaan or not, he took her without any goods and named her wife."

Other voices rose from here and there among the benches but for the most part they were favorable to Fraoch and first one and then more and more of the men and women in the mead hall urged Ailill and Medb to make peace with their daughter. From the tenor of the comments, Fraoch soon understood that many thought Medb or Ailill had discovered Findbhair's attachment to him and that was the cause of the trouble between them.

Apparently Medb's and Ailill's liegemen and their women found it reasonable that they should object to a son-by-marriage from the Danaan, too. Fraoch shrugged that off; Milesians were like that. What was also clear to him was that the shouts had grown somewhat more good-natured and the feeling of sullen tension in the hall eased. If most still thought Medb and Ailill too severe in casting Findbhair out, their cruelty was canceled by Findbhair's disobedient cleverness in summoning her lover and marrying him. Medb and Ailill had been caught in their own trap.

Ailill stood and the crowd quieted, waiting to see what he would say. "Findbhair is beyond price."

"I agree," Fraoch replied promptly. "A good daughter is beyond price to her father and a good wife to her husband, so we are at one on that subject. We are speaking only of a token to seal a marriage already made."

Ailill smiled. "A precious daughter, a precious wife, deserves a precious token as bride price."

Before Fraoch could answer, Findbhair stepped forward. "To you, Ailill-righ, I am not so precious as I once was, for my faith and my heart and my maidenhead are all given." Her voice was clear and firm. "I was put out once for disobedience. I can assure you that I will go again of my own will, forgoing my dowry and trusting my husband to take me as he found me, without home or family, if the 'token' you desire is beyond reason."

"Precious, indeed, is a wife who will defend her husband even against her own kin," Medb snarled from her seat.

"Precious, indeed," Fraoch echoed, laughing as he pulled Findbhair to him and kissed her lightly on the lips.

"Then let the token be only of precious things," Ailill snapped triumphantly. "Let it be fifty silver goblets, fifty golden armbands, and fifty golden Danaan cattle."

A gasp and murmurs of indignation rose from the drinking benches. Such a price was the ransom of great warriors and the purchase of freedom for a lios after a defeat at war, not a price for one girl. But Fraoch laughed aloud again.

"Done!" he cried.

"Fraoch," Findbhair protested softly, putting a hand on his arm. "That was not necessary. I warned you about them."

Her eyes fixed on Findbhair's intimate manner to her husband, Medb leapt to her feet. "Wait," she shouted. Those goods are only the token for sealing our daughter to you. Once you have put down your token, you must prove yourself worthy to carry away your prize. To guarantee the strength of your body, you will swim the lake and bring to Ailill a branch of rowan with ripe berries upon it. To show your cleverness, you

must find a way to lie with Findbhair in her own bed without my saying you nay."

"No!" Findbhair shrieked. "That bride price was not named in good
faith." She seized Fraoch's hand to pull him toward the door.

Effortlessly, Fraoch drew her back to him and put an arm around her.
"To me you are well worth the price of my estate for I can put it into
hands I trust more than my own. I will give over its yield to Angus Óg,
and he will give me the silver cups and golden armlets. The cattle will
come from the lands. Since we will live with Angus and Cáer, my duties as aire forgaill making that necessary in any case, I do not fear that
we will suffer from poverty."

Findbhair stared up at her lover, her husband. A terrible sense of fore-
boding had seized her and it had nothing to do, she was sure, with the
gold or silver or cattle. She had been annoyed with her father for his
greed, and she felt a mixture of pride that Fraoch valued her so highly
and shame that he would yield so tamely to an obviously outrageous demand. But when her mother had said Fraoch must swim the lake and
get into her chamber without her parents' permission—which should
have been funny—she was nearly overpowered with dread. Yet what
could she say? She could not in public warn Fraoch against Medb's demands after he had placed so high a value on her, that would demean
his strength and courage or his wit before the folk of Cruachan.

"It is not a matter of being poor or suffering," Findbhair said, casting an angry glance over Fraoch's shoulder at her parents. "I would follow you barefoot with your goods on my back rather than see you
befooled by my greedy parents."

Fraoch grinned and squeezed her tight. "But I am not befooled by
them. I have the better of the bargain by far. Cattle breed and replace
themselves. The yield of the land will soon buy back silver cups and
golden armlets. And over all the years it may take to restore my estate,
I will have you."

"You can have me without paying a dollop of copper," she cried for
all to hear. "I no longer wish to be a daughter of this house. Let us go
now, with your cloak as my garment, your food and drink in my belly.
Let us seek the shelter of your roof for our living. Leave them my clothing and my linens. I can replace all with a tenth of what you have
promised them."

Fraoch stood looking down at her. She means it now, he thought. She would go with me gladly because she is so angry. But with the thought came the fear that she would not remain glad. In the years to come, he thought, she would begin to doubt that I desired her enough to pay the price her parents set. And what they demand is not out of greed. They are angry and frightened over what they have done and what has come of it. Slowly Fraoch shook his head.

"The cost is not too high for me to pay," he said, smiling again. "And when you are less angry, if you threw away your birthright, you would grieve over your loss."

"Why should I?" she snapped. "I am bitterly ashamed of it now."

"Findbhair," he said gently, still smiling. "There is nothing of which to be ashamed. You know greed is the least part of this price. You are angry now. You will think better of it later."

You fool, her heart cried, I know my mother and father far better than you. They will have it all, the ransom of a rich man's estate as bride price and you dead through their provings! Cannot you sense the danger in my mother's demands? No, she thought, you cannot feel their schemes because it is not really for me—whom you were able to ignore for ten years—that you are paying this price. It is so that all will admire *you*, saying how much you love me, how wealthy you are, how strong and fearless. You are not doing it for me at all, but for yourself.

The thoughts were bitter as gall in her mind and seeped from her thoughts throughout her, leaving her eyes heavy and burning and a foul taste in her mouth so that she almost turned away when Fraoch bent to kiss her. She did yield her lips, but the poison in her head made them as insensitive as stone, and when Medb came down from the dais and put a hand on her shoulder, she turned from Fraoch almost with relief.

"So you are a daughter of this house again," Medb said.

"A *married* daughter," Fraoch put in.

Medb shrugged. "A half-married daughter. Until the bride price is paid you cannot have her in your bed or as companion at your board."

"Now that is the cleverest ploy I have yet come across to get a bride price paid quickly," Fraoch said, his gray eyes sparkling. "Very well, I will leave tomorrow to bring the cattle, silver, and gold. Just as well. It will be warmer when I return and better for swimming a lake. Findbhair—"

His last words sent an icy chill over mind and heart. Fraoch must not swim the lake—must not. But to say it was dangerous would only make him more determined, and she could not say others had not swum it. The swim was often used as a challenge or a dare, but many had *not* survived. Some said there were treacherous currents in the lake, but Findbhair feared it was more than currents that pulled men down to their deaths. No bodies had ever been found . . . ever . . . and—a quick glance at Medb's face deepened Findbhair's chill into freezing terror— her mother knew! Findbhair's eyes filled with tears as she raised them to Fraoch's face.

"Fraoch—" she began, trembling.

"Do not weep, love," he said, leaning toward her, one finger caress- ing her cheek. "We will not be parted long—only for a moon, not more."

Icy fear was melted and boiled away by rage at the conceit displayed in that response. Findbhair nearly strangled. Did every woman he deigned to touch weep if he parted from her for a little while? Oh, he was beautiful, her Fraoch, *and how well he knew it*. But by the time she caught her breath, it was too late to flay him with her tongue; he was already speaking to Medb.

"You may keep her from my bed and my board," he said, looking from Medb, who stood beside her daughter, to Ailill, who had resumed his seat on the dais, "but she is still my wife and only I have a right to scold or chastise her. Whatever she did to displease you, did not displease me, so you cannot punish her in my name. Nor can you afflict her for any injury to yourself. You cast her out for that. When you took her back, it is as if she were newborn, clean and innocent—"

Findbhair's rage washed all away. Fraoch must have thought she was weeping for fear. She touched his hand. Whatever faults Fraoch had, carelessness toward her well-being was not one.

"If she is innocent," Medb interrupted, lips curved in a sly smile, "she is not your wife."

Fraoch flashed a broad smile at Findbhair, then said, "My wife she is—and I have the sheets of our bed to prove that I was first and I was there. Innocent she also is—of any ill will toward you or ill doing toward you from the moment you said she was a daughter of your house *again*. So I will have your oath, yours and that of Ailill-righ, that Findbhair have no more slights put upon her. That she take and hold a married daughter's proper place with no evil words or looks or blows and no duties not befitting a noble wife."

There were murmurs of approval from the men and women on the benches of the High Hall. Medb's full lips thinned, but she was too aware of the evil that had been said and thought about the way she had treated Findbhair since the disastrous cattle raid of Cuailgne. Fraoch had stupidly made her folk believe that it was distaste for a Danaan son-by-marriage that had inspired her last blow at Findbhair, and she was not fool enough to reject that offering—especially as it might rid her of him. Curtly she nodded her head.

Ailill rose to his feet again, smiling broadly. He knew his Medb and was sure that schemes for keeping that rich bride pride, and his daughter too, were brewing in her bright red head. Moreover, he had never been comfortable with the persecution Medb had visited on Findbhair and was delighted to see it ended.

"Done," he said. "And my further oath that even if you feel her price is too high in the end and do not seal the marriage, she will be free of any further punishment."

Chapter 5

FINDBHAIR knew that her father's words, just like her mother's devices, were all designed to create misunderstanding between her and Fraoch. She thought Fraoch knew too, but he made no complaint, his normal light-hearted amusement making his bright gray eyes glisten, whether Medb sent her around the benches to fill cups with mead and ale or seated her beside herself when the tables were set and laden with dinner. Nor did he object when Medb sent her off to her own chamber with the avowed intention of taking Fraoch to a guest house, usually reserved for only the most exalted guests, instead of giving him a bed in the hall.

Findbhair clearly remembered herself saying that her mother and father would use every device that their active minds could seize on to break the marriage. She had warned Fraoch to beware, yet she felt herself falling into the trap when she and Fraoch were not only kept apart but unable to exchange any private words. She found herself wondering why his eyes did not follow her more. She found herself bitterly sure that he was glad to leave, not so he could return more quickly but because he was already tired of her. Worst of all, when she lay in her bed behind the woven wattle wall that divided her from her mother's chamber, she imagined one woman after another slipping through the door of the guest house—and being welcomed.

To think of him abed was a disaster. Her skin got all prickly and her nipples hardened; between her legs her nether lips grew moist; she turned on her face and gritted her teeth. There was no way she could go to him herself, either to sup of him or to expose his lechery. As a child she had discovered there was no escape from her little room. It had no window, and the air spaces under the eaves had been too narrow to let her pass even as a little maid, still flat of breast and bottom. The only way out was through her mother's bedchamber.

If Fraoch was bedding every woman who had cast lascivious eyes upon him that afternoon and evening, she would never speak to him again, she told herself, and then wept because that would punish her more than him. No, she would live with him and watch him so close that he never had a chance to look at another woman. And then she wept again because she did not want a man who had to be watched every moment and knew it was impossible anyway. If Fraoch was aire forgaill to Angus Óg, he would have to travel around the lios to examine the land and give justice.

Findbhair turned and lay on her back, staring up into the thatch of the roof. She had known Fraoch was Danaan and she must accept him as he was and learn to live with Danaan custom or she must tell him not to return with that huge bride price . . . and remain forever an unwed daughter in her parents' house to do their bidding for her bread.

That was no easy decision and it still had not been made the next morning when Findbhair rose early but heavy-eyed from her bed and dressed to go and bid Fraoch a fair going. Was she also to bid him a fair coming? she wondered, and, bemused, almost walked into her mother.

"You have no reason to rise so early," Medb said. "Go back to your bed. A man can mount his horse and ride away without a woman's help." Then she laughed. "Or if he needs help," she added, "I will give it."

A week earlier, Findbhair would have shrunk away and obeyed. Now her hard decision was made easy—anything would be better than living with Medb—and her usually misty green eyes glittered as clear and hard as pale emeralds.

"He is my husband by the law of our land and the law of his," Findbhair said. "I will go to him, to bid him fare well, will you, nill you."

Findbhair did step back as her mother's mighty hand rose. She could not compete physically with Medb, trained warrior as Medb was, but she would not be intimidated any longer. There were other ways to fight.

"If you strike me and force me back," Findbhair said, low but very clear, "I will shame you and bring you down! I will no longer lie as I have always done to shield you from the fruits of your ill will. I will tell the whole lios the real reason why I was cast out; I will show my bruises and cry aloud that you cannot be trusted to keep your oath to any, even to your own daughter and son-by-marriage."

Shock kept Medb from action at first, then calculation, and mixed with the rage over being thwarted was a little spark of pride. Findbhair had always been too gentle for her taste. Because she was so yielding, Medb had always protected her youngest daughter more ferociously than her other children, but she had also used her and been contemptuous of her. Now that she had something for which to fight, apparently Findbhair would fight. But not win! Medb valued a fighter, but not a defeat at that fighter's hands. She was still too sore from her last drubbing. Her lips drew back from her teeth, but she was not smiling.

"Go then," she said, "but remember I tried to spare you pain and shame and you would not obey me."

The words were meaningless to Findbhair at the moment, her whole mind being fixed on her need to reach Fraoch before he left. But after a parting less tender than she had hoped, because her father stood beside her husband and interrupted everything they tried to say to each other, her mother's words came back to her mind. Whatever had Medb expected Fraoch to do in parting that could cause her pain and shame? Turn away from her in scorn? For a moment Findbhair felt sick. Had Medb been welcomed into Fraoch's bed?

She shook her head sharply. She would not believe that, not after he had taken oath of her parents before all in the dun to protect her. Besides, Fraoch had not put any slight upon her, whatever her mother had thought. He had been as warm, as loving and tender, as he could be with her accursed father standing between them and twisting every word they said.

Later in the day as she went about duties that were fitting to her state and station—her father had had words with her mother about some task Medb wanted to lay on Findbhair and Ailill thought unfit—it occurred to Findbhair that her mother might believe all the women who had supped of Fraoch would sneer at her for bestowing so tender a fare well on such a deceiver. But no woman had even looked aside knowingly and one, she who had said she would take him without his paying a sick goat, seemed aggrieved and told Findbhair that there was no need to keep so tight and jealous a hold on her man.

Findbhair had only replied mildly that she had learned well from her father and mother to hold all her possessions with great care, but surely the woman's complaint meant that Fraoch had refused her. Was that because he did not like bold women? No, the women of the Danaan were customarily free with offers of their bodies. So either he did not fancy *that* woman, or he had taken none that night. As the days wore on, Findbhair found more and more reason to believe that Fraoch had slept alone, but by then a new fear was rising in her, that a greater pain and shame than an odd coupling would stain her—Fraoch simply would not return at all.

He had come in one week to her call. That meant a week to ride back, perhaps a day or two to gather the cups and armlets and cattle, and a week to ride again to Cruachan. But twenty days had passed already, and there was no sign of Fraoch, no messenger to say that it was taking longer to gather the value of the bride price than he had expected. That was what her mother had meant, that she should not bless his parting because his coming again was unlikely.

No, it could not be true. They were bound! Yes, and Fraoch had warned her to remember that when doubts rose in her mind, that they were bound to each other and had been since she was a child. But that thought brought no comfort to Findbhair. He had waited ten years, bound or not, before he came to claim her and even then had come only because she called him. If he took another ten years to bring her bride price, she would kill him when he came. And then she remembered that he had told her time ran differently at Bruigh na Boinne, that he had not realized how many years had passed.

Should she call him again? Findbhair wondered. As the thought crossed her mind, she shivered. If she called him, he would come; she knew that. But his coming would be dust and ashes in her mouth and a running sore in her heart, for it would mean what she had half feared all along, that Fraoch was constrained to come to her to claim her as wife, but that he did not truly love her and never would.

That same thought occurred to Fraoch as he rode slowly in advance of his laden packbeasts and herd of kine. The bond held Findbhair, but was she as glad of it as he? She could have summoned him at any time: when her woman's courses had first begun, when the first suitor had applied to have her hand in marriage, whenever she had been troubled or hurt. But she had waited until she was in real extremity, actually driven from her home and family, before she called to him. He had come as fast as ever he could, but she had still been angry. It seemed she had accepted the binding, but did not really welcome it.

Well, not at first, Fraoch thought, smiling as a more pleasant memory—of Findbhair in no garment but her long hair, hanging above him and teasing him with light love touches—displaced that of her anger. Before they went back to Cruachan she had been better pleased, laughing readily with him and helping him plan how to deal with her parents. She had stood beside him against them, too. But she had been angry again when he agreed to their inflated demands and there had been a kind of withdrawal in her. Yet how could he have done otherwise? Could he have haggled over her as if she were a side of beef? Would she not remember that and be far more ashamed of it than of the fact her husband was so eager to have her he would yield too much?

There had been a withdrawal and she had not contested her mother's strictures against lingering in his company, but she had come to bid him fare well. Ailill had said she was still asleep when Medb had left her bedchamber and had not asked to be wakened early and that a man should not show himself to be hanging on a woman's whim. Nonetheless, Fraoch had lingered and Findbhair had come, breathless with hurry and flushed, too, as if she were angry. Angry at whom? Had she come against her will? Had the bond pulled her? Was she bonded against her will, against her liking?

If she was, he had suceeded once in winning her to gladness and could do it again. Had her parents not forced them apart, he could have won her love and her liking too. Now, having separated them, could Medb and Ailill work on her early distaste for the bond and fix her mind on that? When he thought that, he wanted to pick up the pace, to drag the packhorses forward and drive the cattle to run. It seemed to him to be taking forever to cover the ground he had ridden Clis over so swiftly. But to bring fifty skeletons to Cruachan would be stupid, just offering a reason for Medb or Ailill—or even Findbhair herself—to refuse the animals as part of the bride price. Then it would be only to do over again.

He had unconsciously urged Clis into a trot. Fraoch gritted his teeth and reined in his mount. One threat having reminded him of another, his eyes roamed from horizon to horizon, pausing at each outcropping of rock and patch of brush. Another reason not to rush the cattle and packbeasts was that they needed to be strong enough to run at full speed for a time. Such a procession as he led drew raiders as cow dung drew flies and he and Angus's men had fought off several bands already. Better slow and sure. When he arrived, he would be able to explain why he had taken so long.

No explanations were needed, however. When dinner was interrupted by a lookout calling a warning of the advance of a small army of men with a herd of golden cattle, common sense cast out fear and Findbhair burst out laughing. What a fool she had been! She deserved her torment because it had been self-inflicted. How could she have forgotten that Clis had been gaunt and weary from swift running when Fraoch first came in answer to her call? One could not drive cattle at the pace a good horse could make, and especially not if one wanted them to arrive in fit condition to pay a bride price.

Without a word or a glance at Medb or Ailill, Findbhair got to her feet and ran from the hall to welcome her husband. As she went her parents looked at one another. Both were thoroughly angry with her and for the first time in a long time in perfect agreement. After Medb's first attempts to cow her into submission, both father and mother had expended considerable effort to make Findbhair's life a delight. She had been praised and petted by them. They no longer interfered when she was sought out to join in every amusement by men and maidens of her own age. And at Medb's and Ailill's instigation older men and women came to her to warn and tell tales of the Tuatha de Danaan, of the strange, wanton life in the sidhes and the lightmindedness of those people who were beyond all bounds selfish and could fix on no person to love better than their own selves.

Over the weeks that passed, Findbhair had become more silent and heavy-eyed. Medb and Ailill had believed they were succeeding in making her regret her marriage. Both had thought that she was ready to repudiate the bond. They had counted on Fraoch being long delayed in bringing the price they had set and that his slow return would seal Findbhair's resentment against him. Another glance exchanged admitted that they had misjudged their daughter and her almost-husband. Fraoch had returned well within the moon he had set, and Findbhair had run to greet him as if all her doubts and fears had been laid to rest. Medb's green eyes held Ailill's brown, and neither looked away. They rose as one, signing to their nobles and liegemen to continue with their meal, and walked out of the hall.

"He cannot be honest," Medb said. "Where could an honest man gather fifty silver cups, fifty gold armlets, and fifty golden cattle overnight? For he must have done so to arrive as he promised within a moon."

"He came all alone to his wooing," Ailill said, obliquely agreeing that Fraoch, although well dressed and well horsed, could not be a rich man and therefore could not have come by the bride price honestly. "Most men make the greatest show they can when they come to woo a bride. So where does he now come by an army?"

Medb wrinkled her nose. "I do not love him the better for it. If he had tried to come alone or with a few men, likely outlaws would have finished him for us. Then we could have avenged him, which would have soothed Findbhair and made her content to stay with us. And with the bonding to Fraoch gone, she would be willing to accept a husband more useful to us."

"And we would have had the bride price anyway. Likely we could have retaken the cattle and cups and armlets from the outlaws." Ailill sighed over a lost opportunity. "Shall we wait and make him come to us?"

"I think not," Medb replied. "Findbhair will not stand on any cere-mony. She will cross the lake to him—and if we do not stop them, they will be lovers again." She sighed too. "She will forget everything we hoped was weaning her from him. He is enchanting, that Fraoch."

Ailill glanced at her sidelong, a long-stilled warmth rising in him. He had never minded when Medb admired other men or even when she slept with them, any more than he minded when she donned battle dress and fought; in fact, her lust in war or in bed aroused an answering lust in him because she and he were one. But that had been dead since Ul-ster had broken her army and her pride. Medb had rebuilt the army but . . . even her smiles at other men were still without real life or interest. Fraoch had relit a spark in her, but—

"So now?" Ailill said softly. "Make it quick? Some envious cast-off suitor seeking revenge?"

"Not swords." Medb shook her head. "I have seen him fight. Perhaps a long knife in a dark place . . ."

Ailill smiled and took her hand as they went down to take boat across the lake. Fraoch had relit a spark, but she would see him dead without a qualm before she would yield up anything, including her daughter, to one who had taken that possession without permission. What a woman she was!

The idea of long knives in dark places was dropped for good without any more words exchanged when they saw the company that had come with Fraoch. It must be, Medb murmured to Ailill, that what Fraoch had said when he first came into the hall with Findbhair was true, that he had been drawn by her calling too swiftly to gather a company. The whisper tickled Ailill's ear and he brought a hand under his wife's thick hair to stroke her neck. She arched her back like a cat under the caress, but her eyes remained fixed on the troop.

Certainly nothing of strength or splendor was lacking. A score of men there were, each tall and strong and, if not quite as beautiful as Fraoch, easy enough to look upon. All were fair-haired and light-eyed, as was common among the Danaan and so richly dressed as to cast Ailill's and Medb's own finery into the shade.

They all wore red cloaks with four gold pendants to each cloak, and the cloaks were all fastened by silver broaches made in a pattern of four little birds—the symbol of Angus Óg. Their kilts were green and blue with red interweavings and borders or fringes of gold tassels upon them. The kilts were only to their knees, showing greaves with pendants of bronze and shoes with clasps of bronze. Each wore a helmet ornamented with crystal and bronze and a broad golden collar around his neck with a large gem in its clasp and on each arm broad, twisted gold armlets.

Their shields and spears were not so elegant, the shields being battered and the spear points notched with hard use. But the ornaments and bosses of the shields were of red and white bronze with emblems of silver and gold, and the spear shafts had ribs of bronze and collars of silver holding the points at the neck. Every sword hilt looked like worked gold with a large carbuncle atop the pommel.

Medb and Ailill were so absorbed by this display that it took them some time to look for Fraoch and Findbhair. And when they found them, both wished that they had waited still longer. The greeting they had feared would swiftly turn to lovemaking seemed to have gone another way. Apparently their coming had interrupted an argument that might have grown more bitter. It was too late to retreat and their hesitation was a mistake also, for Findbhair rose on her toes and spoke swiftly into Fraoch's ear. He looked surprised, but then nodded and then stepped forward.

In fact, the greeting between Fraoch and Findbhair had been loving enough. Findbhair had not waited for the slow raft, but had taken one of the little coracles drawn up on the shore and paddled herself swiftly across the lake. Seeing her, Fraoch had dismounted and rushed to help her draw up the boat, ending up wet to the knees and having nearly tipped her into the water in his hurry to pull her into his arms. They had kissed with the passionate hunger of their long doubts, and the assuaged fear that she had lost him already, sparked in Findbhair a far sharper terror of losing him anew to her parents' machinations.

"We must go away from here," she breathed as soon as their lips parted.

"Have they hurt you, love?" Fraoch asked.

"No." Findbhair pulled away a little and swallowed. "They have been so kind I have nearly choked on the milk and honey poured over me. But that means that they are trying to make my life in Cruachan so sweet that I will not wish to leave it. And that means that they have not given up their plans to part us. Fraoch—" She hesitated, finding it very hard to force out what she must say.

"Nothing can part us, love. We are bonded and, for me, tighter than ever before. Every night I dreamed you were lying beside me, and every night I reached for you—and woke near weeping when I could not touch you. I thought every day a year on the road back, but I could not drive the cattle faster, and twice, no thrice, we were attacked and had to fight and then collect and rest those damned cows again."

"Attacked?" Findbhair echoed. "You were attacked! Fraoch, did you see any you knew? Could it have been . . ." Her voice failed, but she swallowed hard and continued, "Could it have been my father's or mother's men?" She hunched her shoulders. "They wish you ill, love."

He pulled her tight to him again and held her against his body, silent as he thought back on the bands that had attacked. Finally, he shook his head. "The first attack was outside Connaught, and I knew those raiders. They are from a renegade lios. The others, no, I cannot believe—"

Findbhair pushed him away and interrupted sharply. "You had better believe it, or you will be dead, my parents will be richer by a monstrous bride price, and I will be in their hands again to be traded to Dana-knows-who for some political advantage."

He pulled her even tighter and kissed her before laughing aloud. "You swore by our Lady, Dana!"

"I swore *at* Dana," Findbhair snapped, wresting herself out of his arms again. "You fool, this is nothing to laugh about."

"I was not laughing at your notion that your parents would like me dead nor did I mean I could not believe that. I am sorry to say it, but I *do* believe they would like to see the last of me. What I meant to say was that it was not your father's men or your mother's who attacked us. Actually, attacked is the wrong word. They only wanted to steal the horses and the cattle, not to fight. And those we killed were such scarecrows—not only rags and tatters of clothing but skin and bones of body."

"Well, I am glad of that." Findbhair sighed. "The rags and tatters could be worn apurpose, but no fighting man of Cruachan has been thin of hunger for many years. Dead or maimed in battle, yes, but not starved. And the men of Cruachan would surely have waged battle first and taken the loot over your dead bodies."

"So I thought, which makes Medb and Ailill innocent."

"But not innocent of the desire to be rid of you," she snapped. Having finally stated the shameful idea aloud, she did not want him to forget it.

"Perhaps not of the desire," Fraoch said, grinning at her merrily, "but they will have no opportunity. Angus's men are not here only as cattle herds, but to take you to Bruigh na Boinne if I should die by violence of any kind."

She breathed a long sigh of relief and took his hand. "Then let us go, and go now. Give them their cattle and their cups and armlets and then let us go, even if they say the full price is not paid and will not give me my dowry. I know. I just know that my mother named swimming the lake and getting by her chamber into my room as paths to your death."

Fraoch looked down at her and saw she was in earnest. "Perhaps, but I knew those were traps when I agreed," he said soberly, and then began to grin again. "As for getting through your mother's chamber, I have an idea for that." He laughed aloud. "You may not like it, but I think it will work and it will do Medb and Ailill no harm. And as for the lake—I am a strong swimmer, Findbhair."

"Not strong enough for *that* lake."

He shook his head. "It is not a wide lake, and the water is quiet. I have swum as far in the river near Bruigh na Boinne and there is a strong current there."

Her eyes were wide enough to show whites all around the iris and she gripped his inar in both hands. "There is more than current in that lake I fear—and I fear my mother knows what lives in it."

"Do you say to me that no one has swum that lake and lived? And that no one in the mead hall, not one, would speak a warning?"

Findbhair relaxed her grip a bit and sighed. "I wish I could say it. Then I could have stood up in the hall and claimed the bride price they asked was not fair, to bid you swim was to bid you die. But some have completed the trial. More than have succumbed, but—" her hands tightened again "—but Fraoch, I *know* for you it will be a death trap."

He took her face between his hands and kissed her, but when he released her lips, he was laughing. "Findbhair, that is fear, not reason, speaking. Oh, I am glad of it. I am not complaining that you fear for me. It is sweet, indeed, to know you care, that you are not bound unwilling, but I cannot draw back from the challenge I accepted."

"It is not a fair challenge," she insisted.

He shrugged. "Perhaps not. It is true enough that I do not trust your parents' intentions toward me. Still, it is a challenge others triumphed over. I cannot refuse without better reasons than your fear. I would shame you, myself, and the Danaan—"

"Before whom would you be shamed? None in your lios would know—"

"Findbhair." He put a finger across her lips. "First that is not true. All these men would know. But that is not important, love. *I* would know. And you would know also. And even though it was at your urging that I turned my back on my given word, it would eat at you."

"No it would not! Because I would know that you would be dead if you had not heeded me. Pride! It is all pride! You do not care that I will feel I have been the death of you. You only care for your own feelings. Men! Go to your death then. When you are dead, I will be free!" She saw his face change, and caught at his arm. "No! I did not mean that!"

"It is true, nonetheless," he replied stiffly, all the lighthearted laughter gone from his eyes. "You may not grieve long for me. But what I have sworn, that I will do."

"You idiot!" she cried, and then saw her parents not twenty steps away. "Merciful Dana," she breathed, and rose on tiptoe to whisper in Fraoch's ear. "Meet me in the cottage tonight. I will be there from sunset."

Surprised as he was by the sudden about-face from anger to invitation, Fraoch caught where Findbhair had looked and knew there was no time to question her. He stepped forward to meet Medb and Ailill and, when they were in speaking distance, said, "Fifty golden cattle, as you required. Do you wish to have your cowherds examine them? They are all healthy, but there is no bull among them. Your price was fifty golden cattle."

"Fifty golden cattle, as promised," Ailill said. "Had I expected you to agree—" his lips twisted wryly "—I would have been more careful in my asking. Are they all geldings?"

"No, about half are cows or heifers."

"Fair enough," Medb said grudgingly. "We bid you well come, you and your men."

"There are no witnesses to your acceptance of the cattle," Findbhair said.

Medb cast a sidelong glance at her, but said readily enough. "We will acknowledge them before the lords and liegemen when we look upon the silver cups and golden armlets."

She was true to her word when the whole party, including the packs carrying the remaining part of the physical bride price, were ferried back across the lake and made their way to the mead hall. Then, when Angus's men were seated in places of honor and food and drink set before them, a table was brought so Fraoch could empty the packs.

Fifty silver cups, all of good size and cunningly wrought, stood on the table when he was done, and fifty gold armlets, each twisted of no less than twenty wires, lay beside them. The men and women of Cruachan sat in stunned silence. Since no weight had been specified for cups or armlets, they had expected small thin cups and armlets of one or two wires. What Fraoch had brought was a king's ransom and Medb and Ailill acknowledged they were satisfied with what they saw and with the cattle delivered.

Fraoch nodded his acceptance. "Thus do I value your daughter, King Ailill, Queen Medb," he said. "And thus have I paid for any ill done you by her bonding to a Danaan and my taking her to Bruigh na Boinne."

"You have not paid the full bride price," Medb cried.

Fraoch's eyes flicked to the door through which he and Findbhair had entered the mead hall and where she had parted from him as he and his men carried the packs to the dais, but she was gone from there. Nor did her voice rise in challenge from any other part of the hall. He had wanted her beside him to approve what he was about to say, but he had to answer Medb's accusation at once.

"No. That I admit." Despite his anxiety about Findbhair's silence, Fraoch made himself smile slowly. "But what you said was that I could not have Findbhair in my bed or at my board until I had swum the lake and lain with her in her own bed without your nay-say. If I die during either trial, I will not have Findbhair in my bed or at my board. But the rich bride price is paid—lent me by my lord, Angus Óg—and by Angus's will, Findbhair must have the right to decide where and with whom she wishes to live if she is widowed. These men," he gestured toward the tall, fair Danaans, "are here to see that her choice is freely made, not enforced."

Chapter 6

A DEAD silence greeted Fraoch's statement, and a horrible sinking filled him. He had been so sure that Findbhair would come from wherever she was and say she chose Bruigh na Boinne. His eyes swept the hall, but did not find her.

To say that Medb was furious was to describe the mountains of Uaman as molehills. She fairly glowed with rage and Ailill felt his loins tighten and his heart leap with joy, even as another part of him was almost as angry as she. The fury was all the more intense because of the need to bottle it within. No one could mistake the mood of the nobles and liegemen. All were filled with envy at the prize Fraoch had delivered. All felt it was right that something be given for that price. Any attempt to keep Findbhair against her will would be repudiated, the men of Cruachan standing with the Danaan warriors against their own king and queen.

"What is this talk of dying?" Ailill asked although he was nearly choked between his rage and his excitement. One strong hand rested on Medb's shoulder and her flesh was white under the pressure of his grip.

She showed no sign of the pain she felt but smiled. "Many men have swum that lake," she said. "It is a common test of strength in Cruachan."

There was a murmur of agreement, although not strong, from the benches. Ailill nodded. "Sit," he invited with a smile. "Eat and drink and be welcome, you and yours, to the roof and the fire."

Despite the emptiness in him because Findbhair had withdrawn not only her support but seemingly even her approval, Fraoch smiled at them both and sat down in the space left for him, the guest seat of greatest honor, nearest the dais on the benches now filled with Angus's men. Across the hall came a slender girl with red-brown hair. Fraoch's heart gave one leap before he knew it was not Findbhair and though he still smiled as he accepted the fine gold-adorned drinking horn full of mead and silver platter heaped with bread and succulent roast boar, he was hardly aware of putting the horn to his lips and spearing flesh on his knife.

He had read the roiling rage in his mother- and father-by-marriage. He had thought that Findbhair would understand that he was neither so innocent or so foolhardy as she thought and had moved to protect himself. She had warned him that her parents' purpose in planning to be rid of him was to keep her, and he had neatly cut that possibility away. Then why was she still angry? She had invited him to the cottage, so why had she not supported him and said she would go to Bruigh na Boinne? Why was she hiding? Where was she?

Once the questions formed in contiguity in his mind, Fraoch had to lift his drinking horn hastily to bury his grin. Findbhair had called him an idiot and she was close to right. Why hiding? From her parents, who had certainly seen them together when he arrived and would now doubtless double their efforts to keep them apart. And where else could she be but making her way to the cottage? Clever, clever Findbhair. She had known that Medb and Ailill would be transfixed by the riches emerging from Fraoch's packs. They probably could not believe that she would not be equally fascinated by the payment of her bride price, and so she had taken that time to leave the dun.

Once she was at the cottage, Fraoch believed she would be safe. No one had come near it in the time they had spent there; moreover he had sensed what must be a warding spell each time he approached the place. It had not affected him. Because he was of the Tuatha de Danaan? He pulled his mind from the fascinating but irrelevant question of who the wisewoman Brigid was. What was important was that Findbhair was almost certainly gone from the dun.

Fraoch's legs twitched with the urge to rise and follow her, but he was not that much of a fool. The best he could do for her was to keep her parents interested in him so they would not become aware of her absence. So he raised his drinking horn and then got to his feet to speak.

"I am eager to complete payment," he said. "Will it suit you for me to swim the lake in the morning?"

"That is wholly a matter of your choice," Ailill replied. "We would not hurry you. We would be glad if you would take a day, a week, nay, as long as you like, to rest from your journey."

Fraoch laughed. "I will get little rest until I lie in Findbhair's bed. What is withheld is always too sharply desired to allow restfulness."

He laughed again, to show he was not fully in earnest, reseated himself, and went on to speak of the outlaws who had tried to steal the cattle. He did his best to seem interested in Ailill's exasperated explanations of his attempts to chase down those elusive pests and encouraged Medb to join the talk. He did not hurry his meal or make any excuse to leave the hall. And after the meal was over, he stayed in idle conversation sometimes with his mother- and father-by-marriage, sometimes with the men from Bruigh na Boinne, sometimes with others. But all the time behind his laughing lips and sparkling eyes he seethed with impatience and thought and thought about when it would be safe to go. However no twist allowed him to believe he could disappear until his men had been settled in their bedplaces and he, himself, gone into his guest house.

Medb herself took him there and lingered in the doorway for a few moments. Fraoch did not discourage her and did not hide his admiration for her, letting his eyelids drop just a little over his eyes, and lightly running his tongue across his lower lip. But when she would have stepped inside, he shook his head.

"I have a lake to swim in the morning," he said. "Even to talk to you too long, Queen Medb, might lessen my chance of success."

He raised her hand and kissed it, and used it to turn her away from the door. Her expression was thoughtful and Fraoch had considerable ado not to smile. Perhaps he had flattered her enough so that she was reconsidering the need to have him dead out of spite. Medb was well known for sticking to her plans, sometimes even after those plans were worthless—but, offered sufficient inducements, she had been known to change her plans too. Trying to look regretful, Fraoch stepped out with her, and stood with the door at his back, watching her walk away and then still stood for a while . . . to make sure she would not come back.

She might come later, he knew, and if she did and found him gone she would look for Findbhair and find her gone too. That would set the fat in the fire, to be sure, but Fraoch did not think even Medb would pursue them to Brigid's cottage in the middle of the night. He chuckled. No one would support her in denying him his wife's bed after the bride price he had paid. And he was not about to give up a night in Findbhair's arms after he had been away from her for so long just to appease Medb.

First he had to get out of Cruachan, but that should not be difficult even after dark. The Danaan were known not to mix themselves into Milesian affairs, so he and his men would not be regarded as spies for Ulster—not that there was much chance of Ulster attacking Connaught just now. They had mauled Medb's army, but not Ailill's, and in the battle had been badly mauled themselves. Likely any Danaan would be free to pass, but it would not be wise to let Medb or Ailill hear that *he* had left the dun.

With a short nod to his own thought, Fraoch stepped inside and to the hearth. Snatching a handful of ash from the side, he used it to darken the brilliance of his golden hair to ash brown. A smudging under each cheekbone, another from his mouth to his chin, and a third across his brow made his face older and harder. He stripped off his inar, which was thick with gold embroidery, and drew his cloak over his lena, which was much like that of the other men. Then he walked away from the guest house to the jakes quite openly and without any furtive slinking.

There, having emptied his bladder and exchanged a few words with a man who walked in, he went out in the direction of the mead hall. He never arrived there. Just beyond a storage shed, where a long shadow lay, Fraoch disappeared. A flicker here and there marked his movement to the innermost wall of the dun and along it until he was a few lengths from the gate. He stepped out into the open then and walked up to the guard.

"I am Fraoch's chief herdsman," he said—it was true enough; he was chief of all activities at Bruigh na Boinne, except defense, which was in Cáer's hands. "I need to make sure your cowherds are not having trouble with the cattle."

Fraoch was reasonably sure that neither Medb nor Ailill had given orders to keep his men within. Indeed, he believed they would prefer that the whole group from Bruigh na Boinne disappeared, now that the cattle and gold and silver were at Cruachan. Nor did he think that the guard would fear one man alone intended to spirit away the herd, now that they had been acknowledged. Another fact, of which Fraoch was unaware also played in his favor. The man was accustomed to servants who were nervous over their charges—Medb had that effect on servants—and he opened the side gate for Fraoch without question.

Having been passed out of the first gate, the other guards all assumed he was leaving with permission and let him go. It was their duty, after all, to see that no enemy from without got into Cruachan and did harm, not to keep people from leaving. And, having said he was going to look at the cattle, no one questioned his taking a coracle and paddling himself across the lake. By then the moon was up and the guard saw him making his way toward the cattle pens, at which point he lost the little interest he had had in him.

The moon had not moved much when Fraoch, riding a horse that had been left with the cattle, passed through that moment of discomfort that marked the ward for him, and came into the clearing in front of the cottage. The place looked utterly dark and deserted, and Fraoch pulled up his mount and stared, wondering if he could have misheard Findbhair or if she could have been so cruel as to send him to where he would recall their love most vividly and not come herself.

Findbhair saw him enter the clearing, started to come from behind the tree where she had been watching for him—or for her mother's men—and stopped abruptly. Was that Fraoch? The face was gaunt and lined . . . and then, guessing what he had done, she stifled a chuckle and came forward.

"You are late," she said softly.

"Findbhair!" he exclaimed, sliding off the horse. "You almost made me swallow my heart."

"Clever enough to change your face to get out of Cruachan. Brave enough to swim a lake which has killed so many others. But startled by a woman's voice?"

He was not going to argue with her about the lake, not until after he had gotten her into bed, so all he said was, "In this place, yes. There is a warding. Do you not feel it?"

"No." She felt surprised, then shook her head. "I suppose Brigid set it not to touch me when she told me I was free to come here at any time."

"I suppose so," Fraoch said, then, smiling, returned to defending himself. "Anyway, I thought you would be in the cottage."

Findbhair wondered why he was so willing to talk about nothing. She put her hand on the horse's bridle and led it toward the shed in the back. She could feel him looking at her and, suddenly nervous, began to babble herself.

"Usually no one comes here when Brigid is not in the cottage, but its whereabouts are known. I was afraid if my mother noticed I was gone and was angry enough she might send men to look for me, so I stayed in the wood. I thought—"

"That is why I am late," Fraoch said. "I was also afraid your mother or father would look for you, so I stayed well within their sight. I hoped if they saw me they would not worry about where you might be."

He put his arm around her waist; Findbhair felt the tension in the arm and smiled to herself. Could it be that Fraoch was talking for the same reason she was, that he, too, was uncertain and uneasy. She let her head drop to his shoulder and he drew her closer, his arm no longer tense. Then he dropped his head to kiss her and, both of them blind, walked right into the shed wall.

Both burst out laughing and Fraoch took the rein from Findbhair's hand, tied the horse, and briskly stripped off its gear. When he turned toward her, she flung herself into his arms.

"I love you, Fraoch." She could hear her voice shake but could not tell whether he realized how much she meant what she said. "You have been with me, part of me, nearly all of my life. Even when you are not with me, you *are* with me. If you were gone, half my substance would be gone also. I would be no more than an empty husk. I would be worse than dead. Do you understand?"

"So it is for me, *gràdhaichte*," he murmured soothingly and kissed her.

Findbhair did not think that could be true. She knew he had been a mature man when he first set eyes on her. Ten years in his life could not have the same importance as ten years in hers. She was sure he did not understand, but his lips were so warm, so eager.

All mixed up in her mind were his constant care for her and his apparent indifference to what she would suffer if she lost him, his gentleness and willingness to do anything she desired and his stubborn insistence on fulfilling a stupid point of honor that would destroy her. She almost pulled away to try again to convince him that their bond with each other was worth his betrayal of a promise he did not understand. But she was afraid that nothing she said would move him, that they would both grow angry. Terrified of being denied this last chance at loving him, she pressed herself into his body, clutching at him under his cloak.

"Not here." He pulled his mouth free and chuckled. "There are better places for this than a stable. Come within."

Later, Findbhair thought, when he is weak with joy, I will weep and plead. I will tell him that his death would be far more terrible to me than my own. I will explain that to remove his presence would leave gaping, bleeding holes in me, holes that would never heal. Later, I will explain all that.

The house was fresh and clean, scented with summer herbs because it had been Findbhair's one solace—and greatest pain—to come to the cottage several times a week. For a little while, each time, she was able to pretend that she was making ready for Fraoch's return from his hunting, and she opened the shutters to air the chamber, cleared away what dust had accumulated, brought in fresh flowers and herbs. All too soon the pretense would wear thin and she would feel that he would not return for years, as he had gone when she was a child and not returned. Then she shut the cottage up again and ran back to the dun where feeling her mother's eye on her stiffened her pride and resolve. But this time he had returned as quickly as he could.

From the way he held her, Findbhair was not sure Fraoch would have noticed if the roof had fallen in, but the knowledge that all was ready made her comfortable and assured. Far away, beyond the soothing odors of rose and lavender spiced with rosemary, was terror and horror, but here the scents caressed her, like Fraoch's warm lips and gentle hands.

"Do we need a light or a fire," he whispered, breath tickling her ear.

"I can see you very well," Findbhair sighed, running one hand down his cheek so that her fingers caressed his ear and the other over his buttocks. "And we will warm each other enough in the bed."

When Medb left Fraoch looking after her, she was strangely tempted to wake Findbhair and try to convince her to promise to repudiate her marriage. It was a shame that so tasty a morsel should be devoured by a monster in the lake rather than by Medb herself. The temptation did not outlast her entry into her sleeping house. Findbhair would not agree without the most powerful of reasons, and Medb could provide that only by admitting that she knew how to rouse the monster in the lake. If Findbhair refused and then Fraoch died, Medb was no longer sure her daughter would keep the secret her mother had confided to her. Indeed, Medb suspected that if Fraoch died, Findbhair would take pleasure in betraying her.

Unfortunately, her knowledge did not work the other way: she could rouse the monster but could not prevent it from coming out on its own. If Findbhair agreed and by misfortune the monster woke and pulled Fraoch under . . . Medb shuddered. She had seen a depth to Findbhair since Fraoch had come that she had not previously suspected. If harm came to Fraoch after she had promised his safety, she suspected her daughter's hatred would be deep and eternal and would pursue her until she died in misery.

So Medb went to her bed without going near Findbhair's door and sought pleasanter images. That touch of Fraoch's tongue over his lower lip returned to her mind and she smiled and started to rise, then lay back. If she came when he was still awake, he would refuse her again; but if she slipped into his bed when he was sleeping and roused him sexually, he would pleasure her gladly. She stretched and wriggled herself more comfortable. Or, she thought, smiling, she would fall asleep and the urge would pass.

Medb soon did fall asleep but not deeply, and she woke with the same urge to sup of Fraoch. Then she jerked upright in bed suddenly. Sup of Fraoch! If she did and if Findbhair was made aware of it, likely the foolish child would repudiate Fraoch. Would that mean she and Ailill would have to return the bride price? No, why should they? It would have been his offense that, in lusting after the bride's mother, he had made the bride reject him! Why had she not thought of it sooner? But she shied away from the thought because she knew why. Her mind and body had been dull, half dead, since . . . No. Sup of Fraoch, that was what she must do now.

Stealthily Medb slipped from her bed and and went to the doorway. If Findbhair was still awake, Medb did not want her to realize her

mother had left her chamber. She drew her cloak over her naked body
and then carefully lifted the latching bar. Findbhair must discover what
she had done, but not before she had actually enjoyed that beautiful
piece of man. Standing in the doorway, Medb listened; no sound came
from Findbhair's room. Medb breathed a soft sigh of relief and stepped
out, closing the door behind her.

The moon was well up and she glanced across the small courtyard
toward Ailill's sleeping house. There probably would be a woman with
him . . . Medb hesitated, suddenly more tempted by Ailill's smooth dark
handsomeness and bolder virility than by Fraoch's gentle and elegant
blond beauty. The woman would not matter; she liked Ailill wet with
other juices and Ailill seemed to find her more exciting after blander
meat. Then she shook her head. Ailill would be there tomorrow night,
whereas by then Fraoch would probably be dead and beyond her reach.

She walked quickly and fearlessly past the mead hall toward the row
of guest houses, but when she reached Fraoch's door, she stopped.
Sneaking in on a fighting man was not the wisest thing to do. Medb
frowned. She was not much afraid of being hurt, since she was aware of
how Fraoch might react to stealth, but a violent awakening would not
serve her purpose at all. She bit her lip. Neither would scratching at his
door, since he would be just as wide awake and armored with excuses
by the time he opened to her.

One could but try. Very slowly Medb raised the latch, trying to keep
it from making any noise. When it was up, she pushed against the door,
also slowly. If it were barred . . . But it was not and it opened silently,
making her think that she must try to find out who cared for the guest
houses and reward the servant for keeping the door hinges so well oiled.

Having closed the door equally silently, Medb made her way across
the room to the bed. To touch him without any warning, she was sure
would bring a violent response so she began to hum softly, raising the
pitch of her normally deep voice to a sound closer to that Findbhair
might make. She was a little puzzled when she got no response at all,
no mumble of recognition, not even a shifting in the bed. Frowning but
still cautious she reached out a hand and touched the side of the bed,
ready to jump back or drop to the ground if Fraoch struck at her. Her
hand touched a sleeping fur—a perfectly smooth, unrumpled sleeping
fur.

That was impossible. Even if Fraoch had got in on the other side of the bed, the furs would be pulled up, folded, wrinkled. Her hand flashed out across the bed. Nothing. Smooth. Flat. He had never been in the bed.

Medb jerked upright, lips drawn back into a snarl. A lake to swim? When she found the woman who had tempted him, she would— Nonsense! Why should Fraoch tumble a girl on the hard, damp ground? He would have invited any woman he wished to couple to his comfortable bed in his private guest house. Then where . . .

With a gasp, Medb turned and ran back to her own house, across the bedchamber, to fling open the door to Findbhair's room. It slammed against the wall, but there was no gasp of surprise from the bed. Although she knew it was empty, Medb walked across and felt the bed, which was as smooth, flat, and unused as that in Fraoch's guest house. She almost turned to run out in pursuit. She knew well enough where Fraoch and Findbhair were, but before she had taken a step she remembered other times when she had pursued her daughter to the witch-woman's cottage. She had never found it, and such a loathing of the place had come over her that she had spewed up her guts until she left.

Medb stood a moment longer, breathing hard and cursing her daughter and her son-by-marriage under her breath, but she did not expend much time or effort on that expression of her fury. Turning on her heel, she went out of the room, closing the door quietly behind her, and lit a candle at the hearth. From a clothes chest, she drew out her hunting leathers, stained and mottled with old blood. Then she belted on her sword and made sure of the long dagger in her belt. Disobedient, ungrateful daughter that she was, Findbhair would not have the ease of heart of rejecting Fraoch. She would suffer as she deserved. Fraoch would die!

Calm and cold now, Medb left her sleeping house and walked to the storehouse where the meat was hung. She took from a hook a flayed and gutted carcass of a young pig, wrapped it in a coarse carrying cloth and swung it over her shoulder, grunting only slightly as the weight came on to her. Taking a trussing rope from another hook, she shut the storehouse behind her and walked down to the lake.

She did not need to speak to the guards nor even check her steps when she came to each gate. Seeing her with a limp, wrapped, something on her shoulder, each man in turn averted his face and lowered his eyes, opening the way for her without a sound. If each man wondered who would be missing from the dun in the morning, he also wished he had been blind so that there would not be the smallest chance he would ever breathe a word of what he had seen in his sleep or in his cups. And each prayed that his face had been turned away enough so that she would not know him.

Medb wasted no time thinking about the guards. She knew what they believed and did not care. She turned aside from the dock where the heavy ferry rested, to the nearby beach upon which various small boats were drawn. From them she chose, not the lightest coracle but a somewhat larger vessel into which she heaved the carcass. A good shove slid the boat into the water; she leapt in and began to row vigorously north along the length of the lake to its headwater rather than across it.

Arrived, Medb drove the boat into the shadow cast by the trees, unwrapped the carcass and scored it up and down and back and forth with her knife so that the inner juices began to ooze. Satisfied that the taste and scent of blood would flow through the water, she threaded the rope through the hole made by the hook, let the carcass down into the water, and fastened the rope through the grommet in the bow of the boat.

Taking up the oars, she began to row across the lake and then south toward Cruachan along the cliff on the opposite side, which fell directly to the water. By sighting on the walls of the dun, which showed black against the sky still silvered by the low moon, she found the area where at the top of the cliff grew the rowan tree from which Fraoch must bring a branch to Ailill. There she shipped her oars and cut loose the carcass. That was swiftly done and Medb did not think the guards could have seen or would understand what she had done if they had seen some movement. In any case, it was not important. They would hold their tongues or lose them. Finally she rowed back to where she had taken the boat.

By the time she had beached the boat and returned to her house, Medb was very tired. The candle she had lit was guttering but gave enough light for her to lay aside sword and knife, pull off her clothing, and tuck it back into the chest. The lid fell with a slam. Forgetting, Medb glanced toward Findbhair's door. Her shoulders hunched. Naked, she crouched there, shuddering, unable for the moment to rise.

Ill done, a voice inside her whispered; *that was ill done and you have lost Findbhair more fully, more finally, than by her going to live as the wife of a Danaan.*

She swallowed hard, still shivering, struggled to her feet, and started toward the door, her head turned in the direction of Ailill's sleeping place. With her hand on the latch she stopped and braced her shoulders back. No! She would not! She would not again go to her husband for comfort, like a whipped bitch. What was done was done. She had done it and she would live with it. Ailill had not come to her since he had comforted her and she him after the deaths of the bulls. She would not go to him.

Chapter 7

FINDBHAIR did not perfectly keep her promise to plead with Fraoch when he was weak with joy. For one thing, she did not feel terribly strong herself in the wake of a climax that rendered her nearly senseless. For another, he looked so happy, so utterly content when he drew her back into his arms, cradled her head on his shoulder and closed his eyes that she could not bear to change his mood.

Pleading would have to wait, she thought, too happy, too content herself to believe that any ill could touch them ever again. But it was only the surface of her heart that held joy. Deep within was a black sorrow, and as her heart beat and beat that sorrow was driven out into her veins until it suffused her body. Softly she began to weep.

"Findbhair, what is it?" Fraoch whispered.

"Should I not weep for your dying?" she asked fiercely.

"I hope you will, love," he said, laughing, "because I do not think I will be able to go on living without you. Thus it is best I die first, but not now, not yet."

"Is tomorrow so far away? And what if I feel I cannot live without you—"

"Do you, *gràdhaichte?*"

He began to kiss her hair and eyes, but she struggled free. "I do, and more than that," she said, and went on to tell him how he had become interwoven into her very soul in all the years she had been bound to him and thought about him. That the ten years, which was nothing to him, was more than half of her life and that she did not think, because he was so much a part of her, that she could ever recover from the wounds his death would deal her.

He heard her out, holding her close and stroking her hair. "Findbhair," he said at last, and her heart clenched because she heard the smile in his voice, "I cannot tell you how many years have passed since I was born, but by the reckoning of the Tuatha de Danaan, I am a young man still. And, although you have more than once called me an idiot—and because I love you so much I sometimes do get foolish ideas—the aire forgaill of Angus Óg's lios cannot really be a fool. Nor do I think you a fool, my love. So when you warned me that your mother and father would not willingly let you go even after I had paid their price, I took thought—"

Findbhair drew in a long breath. "You will come away with me! You will not swim that accursed lake!" She should have been light as a feather with relief and joy. Why did she have to force out the words?

"No, love, I took thought to what would make harm to me unprofitable for them. Before all the nobles and liegemen I said that since Angus had lent me the goblets and armlets that he demanded you have free choice of whether you wished to stay in Cruachan or come to him at Bruigh na Boinne if harm befell me."

"They agreed?"

She could feel Fraoch's lips, which rested against her temple, curve into a grin. "With fifty golden armlets and fifty silver cups on the table and fifty golden cattle in their pens? Of course they agreed."

"Fraoch—" She clutched at his shoulder. "Do not trust them. They are sly and clever. They will find a way around any swearing they make."

His lips twitched against her face. "No, love. Not around this promise. There are twenty strong Danaan warriors pledged to protect you from your mother and father and obey only your unconstrained desire. And the nobles and liegemen were so envious of what your parents had received for you that they are determined Medb and Ailill pay in good faith what they owe. Your parents are well aware that their own men will stand against them if they try to hold you. Both understand that you are lost to them whether I live or die—and that if I die, Angus Óg will not be pleased to lose his aire forgaill."

"Are you sure?"

Her voice was faint with hope. For the first time she really had hope that her husband would be able to fulfill the oath he had so unwisely made, and survive.

He chuckled. "Yes, I am sure. Both were so furious I thought they would burst when they understood they could not profit both ways. Still, by the time we were all ready for bed, they were talking to me easily enough and, I think, resigned."

He was about to tell her how Medb had accompanied him to the guest house, but he thought better of it. Best not to put any ideas into Findbhair's head. She did not seem to be aware that his speech had ended more abruptly than usual as he swallowed back that confidence. Her hand had relaxed its tight grip on him, and she had turned her head a little so that her face was not buried against him. He could see the faint sheen of her eyes as she stared up at the roof above. Finally she sighed.

"I still wish you had not agreed to swim that lake. Even if my mother and father are no longer scheming to have you dead—" She hesitated and then laughed softly. "That was *very* clever my love. I am sure they never expected you to make any condition. I made all the objections when you swore to that folly and agreed to every extravagance they named without a thought."

"I did not think anything extravagant to have you in exchange."

She laughed again. "I suppose the Danaan are richer folk than we. No Milesian woman is worth such a bride price."

"But you are Danaan now."

She was silent a moment, then nodded decisively. "Yes. I am Danaan now whether you live or die, but I do not think you will die now. Once my parents understand that I will not be trading goods for them even if I am widowed, they will see it is better to have a good relationship with Lord Angus than to have you dead from their spite and me pouring poison in his ears in Bruigh na Boinne."

"I will not be dead. I am a very strong swimmer, love. Rivers, with their currents, are more of a challenge than a placid lake, and Angus and I and others often contest with each other, swimming upstream. I am not always the victor, but I have never failed to swim the course, which is longer than your lake is wide."

"I wish instead you had never learned to swim and could have said so."

The petulant words pursued the same theme, but her voice was free of the passionate pain that had suffused every word, even every action, even the act of love. Fraoch ran his hand down her cheek, her throat, and on down over her breast. She sighed, but there was no longer the catch of a sob in the sound. Fraoch levered himself up on his elbow enough to bring his head over hers and touch her lips.

The hand that had first clutched his shoulder and then rested on it now slid down his back, over his buttocks, between his legs, scratching and stroking what she found there. Fraoch sighed too, as his shaft filled. It was prisoned against her groin, just where the thigh meets the mount of Venus, and Findbhair twisted her body back and forth, as his fingers played softly with her nipples, so that her pubic hair, tight curled and coarse, rasped against the bared head. He twitched and groaned, but made no attempt to lift himself and plunge into her. He found her nether mouth with the fingers of his other hand, and it was Findbhair's turn to groan, to rub herself against the edge of the hand that passed between her legs.

Their need soon grew too great for such play, and Findbhair pulled him above her, guiding the shaft which throbbed with a life of its own in her hand, into its haven. Fraoch slid home but did not draw and plunge again. He lay quietly within her, moving only slightly and some-how by that restraint driving her pleasure up and up in an expanding spiral that made her whimper and writhe and attempt to push her upper body against his hands so that his gentle touches on her nipples would be harsher. Gently, all the while kissing her, he controlled her at-tempts to hurry to a climax. Even so, it could not be long delayed and when Findbhair's moans and whimpers changed to full-throated cries, Fraoch drew and plunged. Findbhair shrieked as if he had truly impaled her, and shrieked again as his seed sprang forth and his voice mingled with hers.

They slept as if axed, but at the back of Fraoch's mind was the trial he faced and he woke with a start after several hours. The first time his eyes opened, the room was black with no hint of light anywhere. The second time it was still dark but with a faint streak of grayness at each crack in the shutters. He thought of waking Findbhair with a kiss and then changed his mind. She was partly reassured about the swim, but he suspected that as the moment approached she would become more and more fearful and she would doubtless tease him and beg him to abandon the trial. Fraoch frowned. He could not. He was representative of the Tuatha de Danaan to these people who were forgetting what the Danaan were and investing them with all sorts of powers and evil. But Findbhair would not care for that and would probably grow angry. Fraoch did not want to face a trial that might turn deadly with ill words between them.

He slid carefully from the bed and groped his way to the chest by the wall, thankful that this time, instead of flinging their garments away hither and thither, they had made a game of undressing each other, carefully folding each piece and laying it down while the other tickled and kissed the revealed flesh and generally hindered the task.

Laid out in reverse order, the clothing was quickly donned. Fraoch cast a glance at the bed, but the dark hump that was Findbhair had not moved. Hastily now he went to the door, lifted the latch with exquisite care, and slid out. He lowered the latch string tiny bit by tiny bit and was rewarded with the bar slipping silently into place. Outside, he took a deep breath and started for the road, knowing he had plenty of time to walk to where he had left the coracle and intending to leave the horse for Findbhair. However, before he had taken two steps, it occurred to him that if she slept well into the morning and then had to walk to where she had left her coracle, he might have completed his swim before she arrived at the dun. She would be furious, but would forgive him once she saw him safe and sound.

Having led the horse well away from the cottage before he mounted it, Fraoch was so delighted with his escape that he had gone halfway back to the lake before the chill of the morning penetrated his thoughts. It was then that he realized he had left both sword and cloak in Brigid's cottage with Findbhair. He pulled the horse to a stop, but did not turn it. If he returned for the cloak and the sword, he would wake Findbhair. When she saw him dressed and ready to leave, she might weep or be angry. He did not want her to be angry, not if the lake held a real danger. He wanted his last memory of Findbhair to be of her joy in their lovemaking.

Touching the horse with his heel to start it on its way, Fraoch reasoned that he was not really cold, and for what did he need a sword? It would be stupid to add the extra weight for a long swim, and where could he strap the weapon that it would not get in the way? He shook his head sharply. Sword? Ridiculous! He was allowing Findbhair's fears to infect him. Even if there was something in the lake and Medb could call it, he had given her good reason not to do so.

Still, having left the horse where he found it and paddled across the lake again, Fraoch would have liked a private word with his men. Several of them had a touch of the Gift, and he would have liked to ask whether they thought it wise for him to try to carry a sword. Any of the men would have lent him one. He found, however, that a lookout had been kept for him; Medb and Ailill and many others waited his coming ashore in the pink light of true dawn.

Several of Ailill's men grounded his coracle and others reached out hands to help him onto the land. And no sooner had his feet found a balance than Medb was on him. "Alone?" she cried. "Where is my daughter?"

"Safe and still asleep, I hope," Fraoch replied.

"I said that until you had paid the full bride price you could not have Findbhair in your bed or at your board."

"And I did not," Fraoch answered, laughing. "The bed was not mine nor the board, although that does not matter since we did not eat together."

"You have violated the bride price agreement," Medb shouted. "Go and take your men with you—"

Fury rang in her voice and something else also. Ailill's head turned sharply to her. Fraoch noticed that and the odd note in her voice, but he did not have time to consider what he had heard and seen.

"No," Fraoch said. "You can say what you like and order behavior in your own dun, Queen Medb, but I never agreed to yielding my right to my wife elsewhere. All I said was that you had found a clever way to get the bride price paid quickly. And I assure you that loving Findbhair has given me no desire to cheat you. I am ready to swim the lake now."

"Not yet," Ailill put in, his lips smiling but his eyes clouded with worry. Something was wrong with Medb—not the deadness that had come on her after defeat but a kind of sickness under her anger. "It is still too cool," he went on. "Wait, at least, until the sun touches the water. Also I think you should rest a while before you start. You are a strong man, but to paddle across the lake and then swim it twice is more than you agreed to do. Come here within—" he gestured toward a hide shelter back from the boat landing "—and rest."

Fraoch did not want to delay his trial because he wanted to be done with it before Findbhair reached Cruachan. On the other hand, he was aware that what Ailill had said might be true. He was not aware of any weariness, but he had had a lively night and had paddled across the lake. It was all too possible that by the time he started to swim back his arms would be tired. He chuckled and nodded at Ailill. True enough that he wanted the trial finished before Findbhair came, but not finished by his drowning.

As he started to follow Ailill toward the shelter, Medb caught at his arm. "Where is Findbhair?" she insisted.

She sounded more worried than angry and Fraoch thought of the warding of the cottage and shrugged. "In Brigid's cottage," he said. "Asleep."

Findbhair did not sleep as long as Fraoch had hoped, but the chinks in the shutters showed the brightness of a rising sun when she stirred. She reached out for her lover, and her eyes shot open when she realized the bed was empty. For a few moments longer she lay still, sleep-dazed and assuming from her own full bladder that he had gone out to relieve himself. Finally, as she ran her hand in fond reminiscence up and down along the hollow his body had pressed in the mattress, she realized with a shock the bedding was cold. How long could it take for a man to empty himself?

She elbowed herself upright, head turned toward the chest where they had laid their clothing. His was gone. Seeing that, she sprang from the bed toward her own garments, telling herself as she pulled them on that there was nothing strange in dressing to go to the privy. Mornings were chilly. As the thought came, her head turned toward the pegs by the door where Fraoch's cloak still hung beside hers. Then she knew. A man who intends to come back to bed after going to the privy takes his cloak to cover his nakedness.

With a cry of outrage, Findbhair leapt to the door, opened it, and ran outside and around to the back, looking toward the screen of brush that shielded the latrine pit. She had hoped she was wrong, but nothing moved near the privy and a quick turn of her head showed her that the horse was gone too. She hissed with irritation. Idiot! She understood why Fraoch had done it; he had wanted to spare her any renewed fear and worry, but he was an idiot all the same. Likely he was right and common sense would govern her parents' actions, but if by some mischance her mother had discovered they were both missing from their beds, rage and spite might drive Medb to act against her own interests. If I had been with you, Findbhair thought, I could have read my mother far better than you and warned you.

To what purpose? she wondered as she used the privy herself. Knowing that her mother had set some trap for him would not convince Fraoch not to swim the lake. By now Findbhair realized that once Fraoch had given his word, he would perform what he promised despite the cost. She knew little of the Tuatha de Danaan beyond tales of their magic and deceitfulness, but she had seen nothing of that at all in Fraoch. He could be devious, but no twist could be placed on his vow to swim the lake and bring back a branch of rowan with ripe berries on it, so Fraoch would do just that.

If she had the brains of a pea, Findbhair told herself, returning slowly to the front of the cottage, she would get some water, make herself some breakfast, and save herself some hours of terror watching Fraoch cross the lake. If she did not know what he was doing, surely she would not fear so much. After all, she could tell herself when she saw him in her mind's eye being dragged down to the bottom, that he probably was not even in the lake or was at an entirely different place than she had imagined.

She had reentered the cottage and stood staring at a pot in which she could fetch water, not even seeing it, seeing Fraoch surrounded by that terrible swirl of water that always preceded a swimmer being sucked down, when she realized she had been thinking nonsense. Nothing could make her fear less, and she *must* see. With the feeling of necessity came one of revelation. If she could see what was happening, could she cast a spell that would help? Certainly to save a man from death would fall within her geis.

Findbhair whirled back toward the door and her eyes took in the two cloaks hanging side by side on the pegs. For a moment tears blurred her vision because those cloaks looked so right together. Then she drew a breath and pulled her own down and over her shoulders. When she started to lift Fraoch's, however, she discovered that his sword was also hanging from the peg, concealed by the folds of cloth. The moisture dried in Findbhair's mouth.

Defenseless! He would be defenseless! Then she shuddered. A sword was no defense against a whirlpool current. But she knew even as she thought it that the strange whirling of the water in the lake was no current. Something swam in that lake; something no one had ever seen but something that was large enough to draw a man down to his death. Snatching the sword and cloak from the peg, she ran out of the cottage and down the track toward the road to the dun. As she ran she prayed to Dana for strength, for swiftness, and, when she heard hoofbeats, for a strayed horse, for anything that would bring her to the lake on time.

Findbhair got her wish within moments of her making it, but not in the way she wanted. Within one hundred steps of her coming out of the track that led to the cottage onto the main road she saw a lone rider coming toward her. For one instant she thought it was Fraoch coming back; in the next she knew it was not. Nonetheless, she hailed the rider, calling her name, promising reward if he would take her back to Cruachan at once. She was so relieved when she saw the horse slowing that she closed her eyes; she opened them again quickly, but only to look down to make sure Fraoch's sword was wrapped in his cloak and held so that it would not interfere with her riding. She even reached up her free hand, which the rider caught, before she raised her eyes to his face—and saw her mother's most loyal and devoted captain.

Findbhair was so shocked when she recognized Medb's man, that she could not make a sound and did not fight against being lifted to the horse. By the time she had recovered from her fury over her own stupidity, several more men had fallen in behind the captain, coming from hiding places in the wood along the road. Findbhair realized that she could not have escaped them. Even if she had gone through the woods, sooner or later she would have had to come out on the road, and even if she eluded them, she had to cross the lake to reach Fraoch to give him his sword and the coracle would have been seen and stopped.

The knowledge freed her mind from the treadmill of guilt and she began to think of this device and that for escaping, but she never had a chance to use any. As soon as they had crossed the lake—there had been more guards, who came out from hiding places near the dock, and still more guards near the boats on the shore where the dun stood—and had ridden through the three gates, her mother was there.

"I must see Fraoch," Findbhair began.

Medb gave her no time to explain why, however. She pulled Findbhair off the horse, clapped one powerful hand over her daughter's mouth, and dragged her to the sleeping house. There, she cast her into her own room with such violence that Findbhair fell heavily to the ground. By the time she got to her feet, the door was shut and the bar Medb used when her daughter defied her had been dropped into its slots, locking Findbhair firmly within.

For a little while, Findbhair stood staring at the door with unbelieving eyes, wondering what her mother planned to do with her. Hiding her would be useless, even if—she swallowed convulsively and pressed the sword tighter to her—even if Fraoch died. The pressure of the sword hurt; the wrappings had slipped from the hilt, which had bruised her when she had fallen. The awareness that she still held the weapon first added terror to amazement so that she stood paralyzed, her arms pressing the sword into her breast. But Fraoch had to have the sword! He had to have it!

Half mad between the pressure of that knowledge and the knowledge that she could not escape that chamber—she had tried often enough when she was a child—Findbhair tried all the old useless gambits again. She piled stool upon chest and struggled futilely to force herself into the air slits under the eaves. Her arms were scraped and bleeding, her cheeks scratched, her hair torn before she finally gave over her fruitless attempts to rip away the material of the roof or the top of the wall. And she only gave up because the stool tipped under her feet and she nearly fell.

The near disaster frightened her into rationality. For a little while she clung to the wall while her terrified panting slowed. Then she climbed down and stood looking at Fraoch's sword. Tears filled her eyes and rolled down her cheeks. It was too late to bring the sword to him now. He was almost certainly in the lake already. But not dead! Not dead yet! Not so soon. She could still do something—if only she could get out.

Without thinking Findbhair lifted the sheathed sword and pressed it to her breast. The hard metal of the hilt woke the ache in old and new bruises and reminded her that within the bulky sheath was a much thinner but strong shaft. Her brows drew together as she considered whether she could force the sword blade through a crack in the door and somehow lever up the bar that held it shut. Drawing the blade from the sheath made that idea untenable. It was not nearly thin enough to pass easily between the boards of the door and she was sure she was not strong enough to force it between the thick, firmly fastened planks. Besides, with the luck she had been having, she would doubtless break the sword.

Senseless rage seized her again; she dropped the sword, ran to the door, and pounded on it. In her fury she struck wildly—at the door, at the frame that held it, and at the wall, which crackled and sent out a large puff of dust. Momentarily blinded and coughing, Findbhair staggered backward, tripped on the sword, and sat down hard on the floor.

When she had caught her breath and blinked her eyes free of dust-induced tears, she sat staring at the place on the wall her fist had struck. A piece of the mud daub had been knocked free and a network of cracks spread around it. Slowly Findbhair rose to her feet, catching up the sword. She had always known that the wall was nothing more than wattles coated with mud, and that the wall was thin, too, because she could easily hear through it, even what was said at the other end of the room when she was abed. Why had she never thought of getting out that way? she wondered, amazed. Then she could not help smiling. One did not think of walking out through walls, only through doors or possibly windows.

Still smiling, Findbhair lifted the sword, applied the tip to the wall, and pushed. The blade slid through. Carefully, she worked the weapon up and down and from side to side. The dried mud cracked and fell away, showing the twigs that had provided its support. Findbhair twisted the sword; twigs cracked. She drew the weapon out, thrust it against the wall more fiercely, worked it back and forth; more mud cracked away, more twigs broke. Breathing hard, more with hope and excitement than with effort, Findbhair laid down the sword and pushed hard against the twigs. A whole section of twigs broke loose in a shower of dried mud. Although she coughed convulsively, she picked up the sword again.

Chapter 8

As he had been bid, Fraoch rested inside the leather shelter, talking idly with Ailill until a voice called his name from outside. When he replied, his friend Conall entered, carrying a skin of the grease the men of Bruigh na Boinne commonly used to protect themselves when they planned to swim long distances in the river. He thanked Conall, shaking his head over his own carelessness in forgetting, and the older man laughed and replied that Angus had noticed Fraoch's mind was elsewhere and told him to bring the grease. Ailill frowned a little but said nothing even when Conall silently held out a flask from which Fraoch drank. Breathing out as if he had swallowed liquid fire, Fraoch began to remove all his clothing. When he was naked, he twisted a long cloth Conall handed him into a clout to protect his genitals, and the young man helped him to grease his skin.

As Fraoch was rubbing a second coat of grease on his arms and Conall was doing the same on his legs, Medb came in. She stared for a moment at what he was doing and then turned sharply away with an odd expression on her face. Somehow it reminded Fraoch of the tone of voice in which she had complained that he had violated the bride price agreement—rage, yes, that was easy to recognize but under it . . . hope? Hope that he would leave without swimming the lake and now hope that the grease would protect him? But then why was she so angry? He sighed a little and swallowed a laugh. A stupid question; Medb was always angry.

Others had been drifting from the dun to the dock and when Fraoch emerged from the hide shelter there was a respectable audience of witnesses. He nodded at them, took another swallow from the flask Conall extended toward him, then capped it firmly and stuck it next to the long knife he had already tied to his breechclout. Ailill opened his mouth; Fraoch smiled.

"I agreed to swim the lake and bring you a branch with ripe rowan berries on it from the tree on the cliff. You made no other conditions. I will offer on my own not to use a boat or a raft to support myself, but I claim the right to a drink to warm my blood in the cold water."

Ailill shrugged an acceptance, knowing that any protest would make him look small and vindictive, but Fraoch's eyes had flicked to Medb. Surprisingly, she showed no reaction to his desire to carry a "heartlifter." Then she did not expect him to drown owing to chill or exhaustion and likely Findbhair was right; there was something in the lake. He glanced at the sword Conall wore but turned away without speaking. His knife should be enough. The sword would simply be too hard to carry.

Without any further words, Fraoch slipped off the dock into the water. Just as he began the movement, Medb raised a hand and stepped forward. Ailill looked at her, and she shook her head, dropped her hand, and stepped back. Fraoch's attention had been fixed on the water and he had not noticed her, believing that he had all the information she could give. He began to stroke slowly away from the dock to the northwest.

The water was not as cold as he expected, not nearly as cold as the water of the Boinne, which was a pleasant surprise. His arms cut the water with hardly a splash and his legs propelled him forward swiftly without breaking the surface. He was moving so smoothly that the water around him was scarcely disturbed by his passage. To his own surprise his assurances to Findbhair—about it being easier to swim the lake than the river because there was no current tugging at him and pulling him out of his path—were actually true. Of course, sometimes the current was very helpful, when it was going in your direction, and he would lack the help as well as the hindrance. However, from the fading sound of the voices behind him he was making good progress. As he rolled to a stroke, he glanced ahead but as yet saw nothing but water. He had a long way to go.

What he had concentrated on at first, establishing a rhythm, soon became automatic, leaving his mind free. It would do him no good to think about what might be swimming in the lake with him. Anxiety could only tighten his muscles before there was any threat and cause him to tire long before he should. The next most absorbing subject was Findbhair. Was she still lying asleep in the tumbled bed? Was she awake and cursing him furiously as she walked toward the lake. He hoped she would not take a coracle out while he was swimming. Even if she only followed near him, Medb would have the right to complain she was giving assistance. He thought of her in the bed again and felt quite sure he would not need assistance.

That was true enough. Although it took him longer than he had expected to reach the opposite shore—the sun was well up in the sky—he did not feel particularly tired. His breath was still coming evenly and his arms, if heavier than when he started, still lifted easily and plunged in smoothly. His troubles began after he had come quite close to the cliff and dropped his legs to tread water. First, he could see no way to get out of the water below where the rowan tree grew. It was as if someone had taken a knife and cut a smooth line from the top of the hill well below the surface of the water. Although the cliff was not terribly high, about three man heights, he would have to find hand- and toe-holds and hoist himself out, which would be no easy task with the water dragging him down . . . He swam closer to look and did not like what he saw.

The other choice was to swim up lake or down where the hill was not a sheer drop, come out there, and work his way up to the rowan tree on land. Fraoch sighed. It would be easier to get out of the water, but the hillside was thick with underbrush of which he would lay odds a good part was brambles, which would rake his skin to ribbons. Even as he scanned the shoreline for the easiest and closest access, the back of his mind was aware that Findbhair might be appearing at any moment. She was later than he expected already. Perhaps she would not come. If she did, however, she would be on the downlake side and would not see him if he were on the other side of the hill. That decided Fraoch. He swam north along the shore and hauled himself out on a convenient tree that hung over the water.

He was promptly gouged on the shoulder by a broken branch. Cursing, he pulled himself inland more cautiously and squirmed free of the other branches, collecting several more scratches in the process. Nor were the brambles less tangled and barbed than he had feared. By the time he had reached the base of the rowan tree, his body was a tracery of scratches, and blood was oozing slowly from several deeper wounds. At least he did not need to do that again, Fraoch thought. He could dive in from where he stood—no, not dive; he was not sure the water was deep enough. To go in head first would be idiocy. However, if he jumped he would be quite safe. He would make a splash that would probably rise to the sky and look very inelegant, but that was better than hitting his head and drowning.

That decided, Fraoch reached for the nearest branch and drew his knife to cut off a suitable twig with berries. Before the blade had more than nicked the bark, he began to mutter curses under his breath. The berries were green as green, not ripe. For one moment Fraoch was almost consumed in berserker rage, thinking that Ailill and Medb had trapped him for all his cleverness by pledging him to fetch berries that would not ripen for days or weeks. And Findbhair had not warned him! But that anguished thought cooled the rage. If Findbhair had not spoken, there were ripe berries. Fraoch tilted back his head to look, and there they were. He sighed again. Naturally, at the very top of the tree. He would have to climb it.

Sheathing his knife, he worked his way up the trunk and then onto a strong lower branch. With infinite care, he reached up. Not far enough. He found another branch he thought would support his weight. It creaked but held. Fraoch reached up again. His fingertips just touched a branch whose tip held bright, ripe fruit. He strained upward, outward. Not quite. There was no higher limb that would support him, Fraoch thought, and sidled a few inches out along the branch on which he stood. It creaked again as he reached upward a second time. Still, only his fingertips scraped the branch with ripe berries; his target would have been closer had not his support sagged.

Fraoch reached with his left hand for the next limb above him. Steadying himself with that hold, he again stretched for the branch with ripe fruit. He almost gripped it; his nails scraped across the bark as he closed his fingers. Hand still outstretched, Fraoch bent his knees a little and then straightened with a bounce. Two things happened simultaneously: he got a firm hold on the berry-bearing branch, and the one he was standing on cracked.

The thin branch he clutched supported him for just long enough for him to release the hold he had used to steady himself and throw that arm around the trunk of the tree. As he did so, both the cracked branch on which he stood and the berry-bearing branch tore away from the tree. Fraoch uttered a soft cry as the tree bark scraped the skin of the arm he had around the trunk and then a louder one as he slipped downward and the broken stub of the branch tore the flesh of his buttock. Fending himself away with his feet, he dropped the branch with berries and got the other arm around the trunk too, so he could slow his descent. Then slowly, panting between pain and effort, he eased himself down the tree to the ground.

Once safe, Fraoch tore off his clout and pressed the cloth hard against the tear in his buttock with one hand while he uncorked the flask of "heart-lightener" with the other. He took a healthy swallow and then another. When the fire in his mouth and throat had moved down to his belly and was providing a pleasant warmth and a small shield against the pain of tree- and brush-inflicted wounds, he lifted the cloth from his buttock and strained to see. It was impossible, but he did not feel any trickle of running blood so he assumed the pressure had stopped the bleeding. Sighing softly, Fraoch rewound the clout and pushed the flask back into a secure fold. Finally he limped carefully around the tree in search of the branch he had dropped.

Fortunately it was safe, the berries still firmly attached. He drew his knife and cut away all but the main stem from which the berries grew and began to tuck the twig into his clout with his flask. As he started to fold the cloth around it, a berry was crushed. Fraoch stared at the mangled fruit in dismay. If he wrapped the branch as he had intended, his motions in swimming might crush all the berries. Did he dare give Ailill—or Medb, especially Medb—that excuse for saying he had not completed his bride price? Findbhair would surely follow him to Bruigh na Boinne anyway, but . . . Shrugging, Fraoch took a last drink from his flask, gripped the rowan twig firmly in his teeth, and leapt from the cliff, as far out into the lake as he could propel himself.

Although she felt exultant, Findbhair did not imagine her troubles were over when she squeezed herself through the hole she had made in the wall of her chamber and ran out of the sleeping house. She hid the sword under her cloak and pulled the hood over her head. The partial concealment was successful; no one challenged her at the gates. That did not surprise her, really. Medb had not dreamed she would free herself and had not warned the guards to watch for her.

She took the chance of stopping on the second curve of the road to look out at the lake, her throat closing when she could not see Fraoch's head anywhere in the direct line to the rowan tree. Then she realized that the crowd lining the dock and the shore where the boats were drawn up were alertly attentive and all their heads were turned farther north. Following that line, she was just in time to see Fraoch draw himself out of the water onto the trunk of a fallen tree. She very nearly cried out with joy, but she choked back the sound. Everything depended on her avoiding Medb's notice.

While she had worked at breaking through the wall, Findbhair had had plenty of time to decide what she must do, and at the bottom of the road she turned north along the narrow shoreline. Because it was damp and treacherous and nowhere wide enough to beach a boat or for more than one man to come ashore, little effort was made to clear it. Any enemy who tried to land would be easily seen as soon as he climbed onto the flank of the hill that supported Cruachan. But Findbhair was not going to climb the hill. Crouching as low as she could and keeping close to the sharp rise of the hill, she was looking for a fallen tree to which she could cling and whose branches would conceal her.

What she finally settled for was little more than a sapling and not completely fallen, but Findbhair's heart was in her mouth and she imagined every moment that she would see Fraoch in the water again. She could not take forever to chose the ideal instrument. At least something had torn free most of the large roots and toppled the sapling so that it lay in the water held only by a few smaller roots. A strong attack with her knife severed those and digging along the crumbling bank freed the tree completely.

Findbhair placed the scabbarded sword among the sparse branches and fixed it with her cloak, winding the garment around the tree and pinning it firmly with the cloak clasp. She made sure the binding was not too tight, that the weapon would draw easily out of the scabbard, then she pulled off all her clothing except her thigh-length shift, which would not impede her.

She heard a cheer from the dock and turned eagerly, hoping she had been so busy that she had not noticed Fraoch swimming safely back, but she knew it was a false hope; not enough time had passed. And then she saw him, climbing the rowan. Her breath drew in and she bit her lip. It was far across the lake, too far to see details clearly, but surely there was too much red on Fraoch's body. His skin, where it was not tanned by the sun, was fairer than hers. Could he have been burned by the sun to that color? She shook her head, uttering a soft whimper. Blood. That reddish tone on his skin must be blood from the brambles or from falling. Blood! That would surely call the monster.

Shaking with terror, Findbhair waded into the water, pushing the tree with one hand and paddling with the other. She could swim well enough—anyone who spent time in boats even if only to cross and re-cross the lake would be a fool for not learning to swim—but she did not think she could swim across the lake without support and certainly not carrying Fraoch's sword. Her teeth were chattering, whether from fright or from cold, she did not ask herself, only kicked her feet and paddled with her hand, raising her head every moment or two to keep her direction by orienting on the rowan tree.

Fortunately she missed seeing the branch break. A confused noise from the Cruachan shore made her think someone had seen her tree behaving oddly and look over her shoulder, but none were pointing in her direction or looking her way. That told her something had happened on the other shore, but when she let her feet sink and raised her head, she only saw a pale form safe on the ground near the tree. She paddled faster, aware that she was still a long way from the middle of the lake, but she did not seem to move any more quickly. The spreading branches and trailing roots, sunk well into the water were slowing her progress. And she could not try harder; already her arm and legs were tiring.

A huge splash made her fling up her head. Fraoch had jumped into the water. She stopped paddling for a moment and simply clung to the tree, waiting with held breath for his head to come up. As soon as it did, a dark spot breaking the surface of the lake and starting to move, Findbhair oriented on it and began to paddle her tree in that direction. Almost at once, shouts came from the Cruachan shore, as various people noticed the unnatural alteration in direction of the "drifting" tree. Fraoch seemed to hear also. The smooth stroking of his arms stopped and the dark spot that was his head rose higher as he tread water to look around. He shouted something indistinct, and began to swim again, not veering toward her but heading directly toward the Cruachan shore.

The rejection was a shock. Unable to think what else to do, Findbhair continued to paddle toward Fraoch with her eyes fixed on him. As the shock faded, however, her head took in what her eyes saw: she could never catch up; if she continued as she was going, Fraoch would pass far in front of her. She stopped again, simply clinging to the tree and watching him. First she became dimly aware that the tree was drifting downlake; then she realized that if she changed direction and paddled directly downlake, their paths should cross. That was what he had been trying to tell her, she thought. With a much lightened heart, Findbhair stopped straining to see and began to swim with renewed energy.

When she lifted her head again she found she had been too confident and would have to correct her direction. She had moved toward the center of the lake as much as downlake—and she could not see Fraoch. But then a sparkle caught her eye—water falling from his barely lifted arm. He was much closer than she had expected, clearly progressing across the lake faster than she. Findbhair's breath caught. She would miss meeting him at this rate.

Findbhair released the trunk of the tree and grasped its branches, kicking hard to turn it shoreward and down lake. When she had it aimed, she looked for Fraoch again and began to paddle more desperately, weeping with fear. If she did not move faster, she would be behind him in deeper water—from where whatever lived in the lake would come. She had wanted to bring Fraoch his sword, yes, even to die with him if necessary, but not to be pulled down and drowned or torn to bits alone.

Although she did not realize it, Findbhair was herself progressing more rapidly now that she had turned downlake. The slight current in the water, which caught in the trailing roots and branches and drew the tree along—just as the unmoving water had hindered its progress where there was no current—added to her desperate efforts was having an effect. She was afraid to look for Fraoch, afraid to see the distance between them widening; she kept her eyes on the water and so caught the strange disturbance ahead of her just as a jolt on the branches in the water nearly tore the tree from her grip. Terror at last found voice. Findbhair screamed.

The sound smote Fraoch's ears with unexpected force. He had been swimming in a near trance, every sense concentrated on lifting his arm once more, kicking his legs once more, and then once more again. Tired and in pain when he started back across the lake, he had been somewhat revived by the cold water. That strength had taken him about one-third of the way back before he became aware that he was weakening far faster than he should. It must be the blood, he had realized; the water must have washed away the half-formed clots and started his wounds bleeding again. Fraoch was not worried about bleeding to death; none of the wounds were deep or dangerous, but the steady draining might make him faint and cause him to drown. He must get to shore quickly.

He began to stroke faster, his feet rising higher, splashing the water, and then he heard faint cries from the Cruachan shore. The monster? He turned, hand on knife hilt, treading water to look around the lake and saw a small tree turning where there was no current to turn it and determinedly heading toward him. Findbhair! It had to be Findbhair, come to save him from drowning with a tree! A mingling of the wildest love and the greatest fury suffused Fraoch. Indeed he felt more warmth and strength than a whole skin of "heart-lifter" could generate.

He pulled the twig of rowan berries from between his teeth "Go back!" he bellowed. "Go back at once!"

With the words, he doubled over, gripped the twig between his teeth again, and began to swim harder than ever, away from her, directly toward the shore. Fool! Fool of a woman! No, he was the fool for not taking an oath from her that she would not interfere in any way with his attempt to swim the lake. Not that she would have kept the oath if she thought her breaking it would help him. Women!

Now he could not even swim with her to protect her. He dared not go near her, trailing blood in the water as he was. If there was something in the lake, Dana willing, it would be drawn by the blood and come for him, not for her. And then rage overwhelmed fear. He would *murder* her if she were hurt by the monster.

Even love and rage cannot sustain a man forever. All too soon Fraoch felt his arms growing heavier, his legs weakening. He swam on grimly, knowing that he was slowing and the slower he went the more blood he lost but he simply could not increase his stroke. It was growing harder and harder to lift each arm, to kick his feet . . . And then he heard Findbhair scream and scream again.

Energy renewed by terror, Fraoch upended himself in a dive to turn in Findbhair's direction. As he went under, a heavy blow from a smooth, tough-skinned body struck his back, driving him deeper. He twisted away, only to be thrust aside still farther by the branches of a tree, which pushed between him and a dark hollow ringed by little white daggers. The branches caught in the hollow and around it—and that was all Fraoch saw as he rose toward the surface. His head emerged, only to be thwacked by the roots of the tree so that he almost got a mouthful of water. He grabbed the twig of rowan in his hand to gasp for air and saw Findbhair half lifting herself out of the water to push the branches of the tree farther down into the path of the monster.

"I will beat you witless," he choked. "You—"

"Your sword!" Findbhair shrieked. "I have your sword."

Fraoch felt a swirl of water beneath his legs and drew them up, thrusting fiercely downward in the hope of connecting with the body of whatever it was and driving it away. He struck nothing, but in the same instant, the tree roots rotated toward him, catching him on the shoulder and pushing him down into the water and toward the branches. Something brushed against him, so large it almost pulled him away from the tree in its wake.

Instinctively Fraoch grabbed for support, and as his hand slipped along the trunk, it struck the hilt of his sword bound firmly with Findbhair's cloak. He flung his left arm over the trunk of the tree, stuck the rowan twig in among the branches, and drew his sword with his right hand.

"Up on the tree," he yelled at Findbhair, but he did not look at her. His eyes were on the water beyond the roots where something—something so nearly the color of the water that it was hard to see—was coiling or reversing itself. Then it shot forward toward him. He struck down at it with the sword, simultaneously drawing up his legs again to increase the force. It was as mighty a blow as he could launch, but the drag of the water defeated him, slowing the movement of the blade until, though it struck the grey-blue body, it did no more than thrust it down, away from him.

Fool, he thought, knowing the beast was turning and struggling to turn himself to face it. You cannot strike through water as you strike through air. You must use the point, not the blade. But it was too late already. Before he could turn, the creature had struck again and this time fastened its teeth in his already bleeding buttock. Fraoch gasped in with pain, and then shut his mouth as he was dragged underwater.

It was not the first time Fraoch had been hurt in a fight and he did not lose his grip on his sword or his common sense. He forced himself down and around and thrust hard at the soft underbelly of the thing, gripping it with his left arm to provide leverage. The point went in; the violent convulsion of the beast wrenched the blade forward and back, slicing through the flesh, before it broke Fraoch's grip; a cloud of red dyed the water.

Before the creature's blood obscured his sight, a fury with streaming hair ducked under the shadow of the tree trunk, knife flashing in one hand, striking at the head that had its teeth locked in Fraoch's flesh. The knife tore out an eye, scored along the side of the head, plunged into the neck behind the jaw. The teeth released Fraoch, snapped toward the knife, but that was gone. Desperately Fraoch thrust again with his sword, trying to distract the beast. He succeeded; the limber body twisted around to snap at the blade and caught the guts spilling from the gash he had made in its belly.

Fraoch and Findbhair burst upward into the air, gasping and retching. Sick and weak as each was, their minds held but a single thought. Fraoch thrust his sword into its sheath while both shoved at the tree trunk, pushing it shoreward with all the strength left in them. Behind them, the water was erupting, being beaten into reddened froth as the creature died. Fraoch and Findbhair slackened their frantic efforts, turning their heads to watch and make certain they would not be pursued by another of the beasts.

When it was certain they were safe, Findbhair cried, "Are you badly hurt, beloved? Can you raise yourself onto the tree? I will push you to shore."

Fraoch lifted his head and looked toward Cruchan where half his men were in boats paddling toward them and everyone else was shouting or pointing or trying to climb to a higher vantage point to see better. They were closer than he had expected, the battle and their flight had apparently covered some distance. He knew he could still move his leg because he had been doing so while they fled the scene of battle.

"No," he said, and began to look in the branches for his rowan twig.

"I will swim the rest of the way myself. Your parents will have no cause to say I do not hold by my oath when I give it."

"You idiot!" Findbhair screamed as he put the twig between his teeth again and released his hold on the tree.

He had already struck out for shore, swimming more strongly than she had believed possible. There was nothing Findbhair could do but follow as closely as she could without allowing the tree to interfere. And very soon she did not need to worry about him any more. Before he showed any sign of failing, his men were all around, two swam beside him and another came in a boat to take her in. Findbhair told him to take the sword and her cloak and herself struck out for shore. She reached it well ahead of Fraoch, who was swimming slower and slower.

Later, a bard sang of her watching, "Findbhair used afterwards to say of any beautiful thing she saw, that she thought it more beautiful to see Fraoch coming across the dark pool, the white body, the lovely hair, the shapely face, the grey eye, the gentle youth without fault or blemish, his face narrow below, broad above, his body straight and perfect, the branch with the red berries between his throat and his fair face. Findbhair used to say that she had never seen anything half or a third as beautiful as he."

At the moment, however, Findbhair was not looking at Fraoch at all. She was so annoyed with him that she almost wished he would drown. But that did not distract her from the person she knew to be truly at fault. In the clinging wet shift, which hid nothing of her complete womanhood, with the bare knife still in hand, Findbhair confronted her mother and father.

"You bade Fraoch swim that lake and stirred the monster that lives in it," she said, her voice calm, but ringing as clear and loud as ever Medb's had on a battlefield. "If Fraoch dies of his wounds or of ill healing, I will bring down Connaught."

"And Angus Óg and the Tuatha de Danaan will help her," a blue-eyed, grim-lipped Danaan said from behind her shoulder.

Medb and Ailill stared appalled at Findbhair, who had been their softest, gentlest child. She was child no longer. Ailill was not even sure he liked this hard-eyed woman, who turned her back on them and walked down to the shore. That freezing rage—ice instead of Medb's firey fury—chilled his gut. Let Fraoch take her to Bruigh na Boinne, Ailill thought. And good riddance. He looked at Medb and felt better at once. Her face was almost as red as her hair and she was muttering, "Little bitch. I'll make her wish the lake had got him, drowned and eaten."

Chapter 9

FINDBHAIR almost got her angry wish. Fraoch managed to swim to shore alone, but he was swallowing water with every stroke before he crawled out and he had to be supported to Ailill so he could hand him the twig with ripe rowan berries. Then he collapsed. Neither Medb nor Ailill made any protest about the help Fraoch had received, but Findbhair pointed out, loudly and clearly, that the test was to swim the lake, not to fight monsters, so the brief time that he had touched the tree must not count against him.

Then, again, she turned her back on her parents and gestured to the men of the Tuatha de Danaan. Conall and three others lifted Fraoch in a cloak and carried him to the guest house. When he was laid on his stomach on his bed, Findbhair breathed more easily. Although there were teeth marks all around an ugly tear on Fraoch's buttock, the creature had not torn away the flesh. And the water had encouraged bleeding from the bite so likely it was clean. She went to get her healing salves—and to change into dry and more concealing clothing.

Salved and bandaged—the fastening of which had induced some smothered laughter—Fraoch bade his men sharply to leave him in peace. When they were gone, he turned his head to Findbhair and snarled, "What, by all the mischievous sprites in Eriu, did you think you were doing in that lake?"

"Saving the life of an idiot?" Findbhair responded, with an arrogant tilt to her head. "Did I not warn you there was something in that lake?

But did you listen? No. Did you even wake me before you left so I could make sure you had everything you needed with you? No. You left your sword—"

"I know I left my sword," Fraoch said. "How did you think I was going to carry it?"

"In a harness that would hold it on your back! And if you had had it, you could have used it to cut away the brush and not ended up looking as if you were wearing a red open-knit gown. Now will you give over this madness? Lady Dana alone knows what my parents plan to do when you try to pass through my mother's chamber to mine. Let us go away from here—"

"No," Fraoch said, his lips thinning, "and if all you can do is to scold, go away yourself and leave me in peace. I do not need a nurse who only adds to my pain. Begone, and wait until I summon you before you come back."

Findbhair stood with eyes and mouth both agape. Then her jaws shut with an audible snap and her fair skin flushed with rage. She snatched together her healing things, thrust them all anyhow into her basket, turned about and marched out of the guest house, slamming the door behind her. Fraoch sighed softly and his lips twitched. He was very glad she had become angry instead of weeping. Either would serve his purpose, but her anger amused him and her tears would have torn his heart. His eyes closed.

Fraoch was not aware when Medb entered the guest house accompanied by several suspicious Tuatha de Danaan. Conall, who had been seated by the bed, stood up, but Medb only smiled at him. She stood for a little while, looking quietly at Fraoch and finally, when he did not respond, she called his name once. He did not stir even for that, and when two of his men closed in on her she shrugged and left.

Fraoch slept through the rest of the day, rousing barely enough to empty his bladder and to chew and swallow when his men brought him food. He slept through the night, too. When he woke in the morning, he was horribly sore so that relieving himself was torture, but he was also starving and ate like a wolf when food was brought. He knew himself that was a good sign; a man with a fever from festering sores is not hungry. Nonetheless, he fell asleep again as soon as he had swallowed a last mouthful of ale.

When Medb came in, again surrounded by his men, and spoke to him, Froach's eyelids flickered and he let his lips twitch toward a smile. However, he did not open his eyes, although he heard Medb protesting not being allowed to approach and touch him, and eventually turned his head away and drifted deeper into sleep. He really woke when the sleeping furs were pulled away and a hand began to untie the fastening of his bandages.

For one moment he gazed at Findbhair's smiling face, wishing he could draw her down to him and kiss her. Then he said, "I did not summon you." His heart lurched when the light went out of her eyes, but he went on harshly, "I am healing well enough alone. Leave me be."

Fury came to replace hurt on her face. "You are healing because my salves are warding away the evil humors," she snapped. "I already know you are an idiot. You do not need to prove it to me over and over. Let me dress your wounds."

"No," Fraoch said, looking away. This time there would be tears, he thought, his throat tightening, but he must not explain. "I do not want you here. You shamed me, rushing to help me as if I could not have saved myself. Leave your salve with Conall. He will dress my wounds."

Conall was as furious as Findbhair. "You are my lord," he said as soon as she was gone, "and I know you are sick and in pain, but that is no excuse for such churlishness to a gentle and loving lady."

"Hush," Fraoch said. "Lay on the salve and keep your tongue between your teeth. Have you forgotten that I have yet one more trial to pass?"

"You would not have passed the last—no matter what you say—if Findbhair had not come to you. We could see nothing from where we were, and would have been too late when we did see. Your ingratitude is disgusting."

"I know it," Fraoch said, laughing. "If I were not hurt already, she would have tried to split my head for being an ungrateful beast, but she must think ill of me for my ploy to succeed. She must believe Medb has seduced me."

Conall sat staring at him for a moment and then said in a choked voice, "Your wife's mother?"

Fraoch started to shrug, groaned, and desisted. "Oh Medb has tried before and will, I hope, soon try again. She does not care for me, only for making Findbhair so disgusted with me that she will refuse to accompany me to Bruigh na Boinne."

"And so I would advise her myself if you bedded her mother."

"No, I will not go so far as that, but I must somehow get Medb out of her bedchamber so I can pass through it into Findbhair's and lie with Findbhair. Now Medb's purpose is to drive Findbhair and me apart, so she will tell Findbhair what she is doing. I am afraid that if Findbhair knows what I plan she will somehow betray that knowledge and Medb will not come to me."

Conall shook his head. "She has been here twice already, but I thought that only courtesy. Are you sure this is not a fancy of your mind? When she is not raging, Medb has a most caressing manner to any man, but that she wishes to seduce you to anger her daughter . . . I do not believe it."

Fraoch laughed. "How else can she keep her daughter for making the kind of marriage that will benefit Connaught? To kill me is useless because you are all pledged to support Findbhair's decision on where she will go once I am dead. If I were dead, Findbhair would hate Medb and go with you to Angus. Medb must make Findbhair hate me and through me all the Tuatha de Danaan."

"More than she would hate her mother for offering herself to you?"

"Much more." Fraoch grinned. "Findbhair knows Medb of old, but I have sworn I love her and only her and will be faithful. Oh, she will be fit to tear the flesh she has healed from my body for betraying her—with her own mother."

Conall threw up his hands and without further argument applied the salve Findbhair had left. The rest of the day was quiet, but Fraoch slept less and moved about more. On the third day, Fraoch's soreness was beginning to abate, and when Medb came again, this time asking before she entered whether he was awake, he called out himself to say he was. She glanced sidelong at him as she came forward and stood somewhat stiffly by his bed.

"I am come to say that I am sorry you were hurt," she said. "I was angry, but that is past."

Fraoch smiled sweetly as an angel. He was amused by her cleverness in virtually admitting what she had done, without which the apology would have been meaningless. It was a kind of flattery, too, implying he would understand how clever she had been. Fraoch lowered his eyes in acknowledgement, but not so much that he could not see her posture ease. Then he raised his lids again, slowly, making it plain that his eyes were traveling from her rounded hips, over her narrow waist, up to her full, upstanding breasts. His eyes paused there for a moment, and Medb's nipples hardened, thrusting against her gown so that Fraoch could not miss her reaction.

"I am glad of that," he said, not smiling now. "I do not like to think so beautiful a woman could wish me ill."

Medb blinked. This was an easier capitulation than she had expected. Fraoch had rejected her outright once and had been no more than courteous after that. Medb knew she was beautiful, but Danaan women were easily as beautiful and she had been wondering whether she would be able to seduce him. Why was he singing a new tune so suddenly? But even as she asked herself the question, her smile broadened. This was no man of Connaught or Leinster or Ulster. Fraoch was a Danaan and they were known to be as light as dandelion down in flying from woman to woman. Perhaps he blamed Findbhair for his hurt? Perhaps he was only bored with her sweet innocence—Medb knew well how quickly that charm palled. No doubt he wanted a little spice now.

"Oh, I do not wish you ill, not now," she assured him, coming closer.

The two men who had come in with her also came closer. Fraoch glanced at them and they stopped where they were. Then his eyes moved to Medb's and held them.

"Then will you do me the favor," he murmured, "of helping me to while away the time? It is very dull lying here when I can hardly move." He turned his head to Conall. "Let Queen Medb have your seat, and fetch the board and pieces for a game . . . Will fitchneal please you, madam?"

Findbhair was as much bewildered as hurt by Fraoch's second rejection. It seemed impossible that he could truly be angry at her—so angry that he would drive her away—because she had saved his life. She had to seek another answer for his behavior and, unfortunately, she did not need to seek far. She herself had told her mother that Fraoch had driven her away.

It was an incredibly stupid thing to do, but Fraoch's first rejection, coming atop the terror and exhaustion she had endured in the lake and the exhilaration of having survived and confronted her parents, had aroused in her a bursting fury that stripped her of her common sense. She needed to cry aloud of her lover's cruel selfishness, and when Medb came into her bedchamber after her when she had flung herself on her bed and asked, with seeming genuine concern, whether Fraoch was worse, Findbhair spit out her anger and hurt without thinking.

She regretted it the moment after she spoke, but it was too late. Not that Medb taunted her. In fact, she patted her shoulder kindly and shrugged. "It is not your fault," she said mildly. "It is hard to believe—for they have faces like kind gods—that the Tuatha de Danaan are utterly faithless. Not only about women. Likely Fraoch is not angry at all. Likely he is only bored and is using that excuse to be rid of you."

Findbhair cried out in protest and Medb shrugged again and went away, but Findbhair could not help remembering that it had taken Fraoch ten years—and a summoning—to come for her. She turned on her face and wept herself asleep for she was as tired as Fraoch.

She woke in the middle of the afternoon and felt much better. If she were so silly as to burst out with such nonsense—to, of all people, Medb—how could she blame Fraoch for lashing out at the nearest person, and the cause of his pain. She told herself, too, that her mother was known to bend the truth more than a little to suit her purpose. No man who made love to her as Fraoch had in the cottage only the previous night could wish to be rid of his partner. Could he? She shook her head at herself and rose from the bed. It was impossible. They were bound, and wed, and bound again. Medb must be wrong.

That calmed her, and she changed her gown and went to relieve herself and wash before she stopped by the guest house again. Conall came out and said Fraoch had eaten and was once more sleeping like the dead. It did not look as if he would wake before morning. He did not invite her in and said nothing about her returning the next day. A little chill went down Findbhair's spine. Nonetheless, after finding a meal for herself she defiantly spent the rest of the day packing her dower goods. Fraoch would find a way to come to her chamber and lie with her without her mother knowing he was there. He would *want* to lie with her and and he would!

Despite her sleep earlier in the day Findbhair was still tired, and soon gave over packing to fall soundly asleep. In the morning, she shuddered slightly when her eyes fell on the hole she had broken into the wall in her desperation to reach Fraoch. His turning her away seemed a poor reward, but she told herself again it was foolish to be angered by a man exhausted and in pain.

A stop by the guest house lightened her heart. The man on watch informed her that Fraoch had not yet wakened. That was good news because it gave a good reason for no summons to have come to her. Since she was starving, she went off quite cheerfully to break her fast. When she was done, she went to fetch her linens and salves. She very nearly convinced herself he was ashamed over the way he had treated her and that was why he had not sent for her. Like any man, he would not say he was sorry, but he would be relieved to have light hands dress his wounds.

The terrible shock of his cold rejection was all the worse. "Bored . . . rid of you. Bored . . . rid of you," rang in Findbhair's head, and hanging between Fraoch and her, she saw Medb's face with its smug look of satisfaction while she spoke those words. A new suspicion began to work in Findbhair. How did it come about that Medb had seen her run from Fraoch's chamber so she could accost her? Had Medb been there first to poison his mind?

Medb had lost her gamble to be rid of Fraoch, Findbhair thought, and Medb did not like to lose. Surely she would try a new gambit and that, Findbhair's knowledge of her mother told her, would be seduction. But Fraoch knew Medb's ways too. He had denied her before and would again . . . or would he? "Bored . . . rid of you" sounded in her head again. So, although Fraoch's second rejection lay like a fallen horse on her chest, Findbhair found a shadowed space near the guest house and watched.

Sure enough, not much later her mother entered. There was some comfort to be had in the fact that Medb stayed a little longer than Findbhair had, and she emerged looking annoyed, but the short visit did not totally relieve Findbhair's suspicions. She looked about and found a more comfortable place from which to watch Fraoch's door, and the very next day her suspicions were confirmed. When Medb went in on the third day, it was Fraoch's men, even Conall, who came out while Medb remained.

It was all Findbhair could do to keep herself from rushing in and confronting her disgusting mother and her faithless husband. All that held her back was the certain knowledge that the result of such a confrontation could only be complete humiliation: doubtless if she used her tongue, Fraoch would order her out again in Medb's hearing; and if she tried to use force, Medb would pick her up, spank her like a child, and throw her out.

Choking on fury and tears, Findbhair crept around to the back of the guest house to peer in the window. She prayed, alternately and senselessly, for the shutter to be closed so that she could not see what she feared and for it to be open and show Fraoch and Medb locked in an embrace that would end her doubt and all her happiness forever.

The shutter was open, but far from resolving her doubts, what she saw only made her distress more agonizing. Fraoch and her mother were decorously separated by a fitchneal board and not even their hands touched on the pieces. Their low, purring voices, however, were both offering open invitations and what they said, although it seemed to apply to the game they were playing, had double and even triple meanings.

Before she was aware of it, a tiny sound of pain was wrenched from Findbhair. Fraoch seemed too absorbed in both games he was playing—the board game and that with words—to be distracted, but her mother's eyes lifted from the board and flashed to the window—and Medb smiled. If Findbhair had been capable of hurling curses, some dreadful affliction would have taken both her mother and her husband in that moment. Only, because of Brigid's geis, Findbhair had never learned any evil spells. Findbhair turned and fled.

She found herself as dusk was falling in Brigid's cottage. How she had come there, she had no idea but if she had sought the place to find comfort, it had been a terrible mistake. All the time she had spent there with the wisewoman was gone from her memory. Every spot now brought her images of Fraoch and pain and more pain . . . And bitterness and anger rose to meet the pain and twist together with it into a thing so dreadful that Findbhair knew she could not live with that inside her. She could not let those two monsters shame and humiliate her. Some revenge against them she *must* have.

Findbhair stared around blankly, then went like an automaton to draw water, to place kindling in the hearth and find the firemaker. She ground meal, made girdle cakes, smeared them with honey, ate. If the food had a taste, she was unaware of it; her mind was busy with one device after another. First she thought of attacking Fraoch and her mother from the window. Perhaps she could throw a knife . . .

No, that was hopeless. Her mother had seen her looking in and Medb was no stranger to attempts on her life. She would close the window . . . no, she would leave it open because she wanted Findbhair to see Fraoch locked in her arms, faithless. Nonetheless, it was hopeless to think she could hurt them. Medb would keep an eye on the windows or have some kind of shield in place. As she thought, Findbhair cleaned up and banked the fire and eventually lay down on the unmade bed. It was there, where she and Fraoch had lain entwined, that she realized that no physical hurt nor even the death of both could soothe the shame that had been put upon her. They too must live in pain.

Shame for shame . . . Ugliness? Impotence? She knew no spells for those and, no doubt, if she had known them and cast them they would somehow be twisted into good. The shame had to come from outside the spell. What good could be twisted into evil? The answer to that was immediately clear from her own knowledge and experience—pleasure could become as great an evil as a good. She began to weep then and sobbed until she lost awareness between waking and sleeping.

She must have dreamed about the problem the whole night long, Findbhair thought, as she opened her eyes. She was as tired or more tired than she had been when she lay down on the bed, but she had her answers. She could cast a spell for pleasure, for the great good of enjoying a coupling, enjoying it so much and becoming so enamored of one's partner, that no thought, no duty, no danger would induce the partners to part from each other until some outside agency called on them. And when Fraoch and Medb were so coupled, she would call her father, Fraoch's men, and the men of the dun to see them.

Medb would not expect her to do that nor realize she could do it. Her mother had always been contemptuous of her daughter's magic because it could not sicken or maim or kill. Medb would also expect that Findbhair would try to keep the ultimate shame, that her husband had betrayed her with her own mother, a secret, and simply repudiate Fraoch for some crime that would make the bride price Fraoch paid forfeit.

A low chuckle gurgled in Findbhair's throat; the sound made her swallow and shiver. The bride price would be forfeit—yes, it would, but not to Medb and Ailill. For the salving of her pride—because her own mother had violated their kin bond—Findbhair herself would demand her bride price as forfeit . . . fifty golden cattle, fifty golden armlets, fifty silver cups. Findbhair's mouth curved, but all the sweetness was gone from her smile.

She would be well found. With such a dowry, she could have—and rule—any husband she desired. A shudder so violent shook her that she came upright in the bed and, although her stomach was empty, bile rose into her throat. She sat hugging herself, still shivering a little. No, there was no need for her to take any man. She could demand that Medb release women from her army to protect the daughter she had offended. Findbhair got to her feet and took a deep breath. Yes. That would be a fitting punishment for Medb and for Fraoch, and even for Ailill, who smiled with red-lit eyes when his wife played her little games.

Ailill was not smiling at all a week later as he looked down at Fraoch. He had come to Fraoch's chamber in response to a message. One of the Danaan had come softly to his door after all were abed and had whispered to a page that Ailill's son-by-marriage needed urgently to speak to him. Ailill had not been pleased, but he knew such a summons at such an hour was more than an idle invitation and he pushed away the woman beside him and rose from his bed.

The past week had not been pleasant for him. Although the Danaan warriors acted as if what Medb was doing was not important to them, his own men were clearly angry. None had ever liked Medb's free and easy ways, but mostly they had understood why she courted this man and that and why her husband looked on appreciatively. This was different. This time she was fouling her own daughter's nest.

When he protested to Medb, however, she laughed and touched his cheek and said he must be patient for a few days longer. They had gone wrong about trying to get rid of Fraoch, she said. She would arrange that Findbhair would know what her husband intended to do with her own mother; then Findbhair, to keep her pride intact, would reject Fraoch for such reasons as would permit them to keep her bride price.

"Is that not worth," Medb breathed in Ailill's ear, running her hand down his chest and across his belly, "a few sour looks and an act that means no more to me than pissing?"

Yet did it mean so little to her this time? Ailill wondered. There was an odd look about her sometimes and she had not sought his bed as she usually did while she pursued a man. Ailill was more uneasy about the beautiful Danaan than he had ever been with any other. Still, what Medb was doing made sense. They would keep Findbhair's bride price and Findbhair, too. And Findbhair would be far angrier with Fraoch than with her mother, so likely she would be glad to take another husband, just to show her disdain for Fraoch.

Or would she? Findbhair, who was not stupid and had spoken out against her father and mother with high pride and courage to protect her chosen husband, seemed to be refusing to see what was in front of her nose. She made no protest over being excluded from Fraoch's sickbed, so it was not healing spells she sought. Nonetheless, she spent all day, every day, poring over the sticks and strings and herbs and strange signs that she had brought back from Brigid's cottage when the old woman went away. Ailill had told her she would do better to attend herself to what her husband was doing than to cast spells to make him faithful. The eyes she raised to his had been hard as green glass. She needed no spells to make Fraoch faithful, Findbhair had replied, and laughed . . . making Ailill's skin crawl.

Thus, although he was furious with all three—Fraoch, Medb, and Findbhair—when Fraoch's man came, Ailill went with him at once. He felt no better, when Fraoch, sitting up in bed in a chamber lighted by more wax candles than he used in the great hall, greeted him with the sunniest of smiles.

"I thought I had better warn you that if we—you and I—cannot devise some plan to deflect her, Medb is going to be a very, very angry woman very soon."

"Angry?" Ailill echoed, completely at a loss.

Fraoch sighed and then laughed. "Well, I cannot put her off any longer by claiming to be sick and sore so I will have to refuse her outright—"

"Refuse her?" Ailill repeated, and, furious at repeating like an idiot everything Fraoch said, snarled. "Why did you encourage her if you meant all along to refuse her?"

As the words came out Ailill snapped his teeth shut, but Fraoch did not look down his nose and remark—as he well might have done—that that was a strange question for a husband to ask. Instead, a look of the sweetest innocence spread across the Danaan's face and irrepressible laughter made his eyes sparkle like well-polished silver in the light of the candles.

"Because I was sick and sore and I wanted to rest peacefully until my body healed," he said. "I did not want to worry about what might be in my food or drink or what vermin might creep into my chamber or my bed. I did not want my poor Findbhair tormented—"

"You do not think what you have been doing has tormented Findbhair?" Ailill asked.

"I think she is probably more angry than tormented, more especially if her mother has been hinting broadly that I have fallen victim to her seduction. Findbhair will not believe that."

Ailill's eyes widened. That did explain Findbhair's reaction to what he had said to her. Then, suddenly, he was furiously angry for Medb's sake. She was no longer so young, and though to him she was far more exciting than silly girls, she was aware of the passage of time. Moreover, her pride had taken some terrible blows over the cattle raid of Cuailgne. When Fraoch rejected her, she would be devastated.

"How dared you," he snarled. "How dared you lead my poor wife on. Do you care nothing for what she will feel?"

"Indeed, I do," Fraoch said, raising his brows and looking both amused and apprehensive. "That was why my first word to you was that we must make some plan." He cocked his head. "It was not all my doing," he pointed out, chuckling.

"Not all, but enough," Ailill growled.

Fraoch shook his head. "You know it does not really matter whether I responded or not. Medb does not care for me at all. She only wants her way. She said I should not have Findbhair and now she is using this device to break our marriage. You are the only man she really cares about." He frowned. "She wants you. She speaks of you. But something holds her back . . ."

"She came to me in despair and I comforted her," Ailill murmured. "She cannot bear to remember that."

"Oh?" Fraoch sounded brightly interested. "My plan may cure that too."

Ailill twitched when Fraoch spoke. He had been so stricken by a realization of what his own words meant that Fraoch's voice had startled
him. And his heart twisted inside him with hope at a plan to heal the
breach with Medb, but he did not speak, letting Fraoch continue.

"I never lied to Medb. I told her more than once I could not take joy
with her, that Findbhair and I were bound, and wed, and bound again,
but she only laughed."

Sighing, Ailill shrugged. There was, of course, justice in what Fraoch
said. Medb was clear-sighted enough, but when it came to bedding a
man, she could not believe that any would refuse her out of faithful-
ness to another woman. If Fraoch did so, despite what he had said, she
would be bitterly hurt and turn that all to rage.

"So," he asked, "what is this plan?"

Fraoch's eyes grew even brighter. "That you be in my bed instead of
me when she comes to lie with me."

Ailill's mouth dropped open, but it was clear he was not breathing.
Fraoch grinned until his head seemed ready to split.

"She will slay us both," Ailill muttered at last, but his dark eyes were
almost as bright as Fraoch's pale ones and a moment later he burst out
laughing.

"Sit," Fraoch said. And when Ailill had hooked over a stool to the bed-
side, he said, "It must be for tomorrow night. I had much ado to keep
her from coming tonight and had to pretend I did not know why she
wanted to visit me at night when she had already come in the afternoon.
She said then, laughing, that she could not come tomorrow afternoon
and would come at night and hoped I no longer needed a watcher by
my bed while I slept."

"And you replied?"

"To that, nothing, but as I said, I did not lie to her. I actually warned
her that she may not find what she expects to find in my bed."

Fraoch grinned, remembering the conversation. He had said, "You
are a beautiful woman, more beautiful even than the women of the
Tuatha de Danaan, truthfully more beautiful than Findbhair, but it
makes no difference. I am bound to your daughter and only she may I
love."

"I do not care whom you love," Medb had replied, laughing. "I think
if we were abed together and no likelihood that any would know of it,
you would find no difficulty in futtering me, and that is all I seek."

"You may come to my bed if you like," Fraoch had said, smiling slowly, "but I warn you, you will be much surprised at what you will find in it."

"Warned her, did you?" Ailill said, bringing Fraoch back to the present. "Well, that will make her all the angrier with you and the less with me. I know what to say to salve her pride."

"Good enough," Fraoch agreed. "But we need to take care in case she sets a watch—or watches herself—to see if I send out my men. You will take back with you tonight Conall's tunic and cloak. You will wear those, with the cloak hood up so no one will see your dark hair, when you come here after dark tomorrow night. When you get into bed, I will put on Conall's garments and leave. Take what you like of mine to replace Conall's things in the morning."

"If I live until morning," Ailill said, but he was grinning as broadly as Fraoch, and he bundled what Conall offered him under his cloak, warmed even more by the Danaan's courteous smile and nod.

Chapter 10

BECAUSE all of her hints to Findbhair about Fraoch's intended lechery brought no response, Medb decided to use a bludgeon instead of sharp pricks. Once she had Fraoch's agreement, she sought out Findbhair, who was in her chamber looking at the packed baskets that contained her dowry.

"In the past I have sometimes thought well of you, sometimes ill, but never have I felt so much contempt as I feel for you now," Medb said. "Here you sit, waiting for Fraoch to pick you up and use you like an old cloth to wipe away the drippings of his excesses."

There was no sign that Findbhair heard her or even knew she was there, but Medb was determined to win a response. "You are angry with me," she continued. "You wish to blame me for your husband's lechery, but it is nothing to do with me. I do not care for him and he knows it. I offered myself and he grabbed, having supped of you already and desiring a new thing. I did it because I wanted you to see him for what he is, to see what your life will be like when you follow him to Bruigh na Boinne."

"Will it be so different from your life?" Findbhair asked flatly. "Is there not a new woman in Ailill's bed every week?"

Medb laughed. "You know, I know, and every man, woman, and child in Connaught knows that when I beckon, Ailill will cast out whoever is in his bed and come to mine. Try if Fraoch will come as swiftly to you. Go. Ask him."

For a long moment Findbhair did not respond. Then she blinked and cocked her head as if she were listening, and finally she stood up. "Very well," she said. "I will do just that."

She brushed past Medb, walking quickly past Ailill's house, around the hall toward the row of guest houses. She did not pause at the door to ask the man there if Fraoch would see her. She walked in and up to the bed where Fraoch had been lying with his hands behind his head, smiling at the ceiling. He jerked upright when he heard her footsteps, and such a look of joy suffused his face that Findbhair almost did not ask her question. It would not be the first time that Medb had lied to her . . . But the joy had already become mixed with wariness, and Medb did not lie about something so easily disproven.

"My mother says you have invited her to your bed tonight," she said. "Is this true?"

Glee lit Fraoch's eyes. "I would not say I had invited her. She invited herself."

A little tickle formed in Findbhair's throat, a tiny twitch pulled at her lip, an urge to join his glee, to laugh with him. But then her eyes filled with tears. This was no laughing matter. Even among the Danaan, it could not be a jest to couple your wife's mother. Sickness rose in her to replace laughter.

"Did you refuse her?" she asked.

"No."

Fraoch began to laugh, but when he saw Findbhair's expression, he choked. His first thought had been how much she would enjoy his little joke when he explained, but the words froze in his throat. Although he had no magic, he knew somehow that Medb would be aware of what he said. There was no way to warn Findbhair without spoiling every hope for fulfilling the last condition of his bride price, and he saw that Findbhair was not as certain of his love as he had believed and *was* suffering. He was hurt that she had so little faith in him and blazingly angry at Medb for making him hurt her. His laughing lips thinned into a hard line of remarkable cruelty.

"So you intend to lie with her?" Findbhair asked, staring into her husband's altered face.

"You should know the answer to that," he said, "and not need to ask me such a question. "Since you did ask, I will say to you that if you are

wise, you will go to your chamber when it grows dark and wait in your
bed for your answer."

Her eyes widened and her lips parted as if she would speak, but she
clamped them shut and turned away. Fraoch sank back into the bed,
breathing a sigh of relief. That expression of surprise must surely mean
she had understood that he meant to join her in her bed. Then he sat
up again suddenly.

If Medb recognized Ailill despite the dark or if something else made
her suspicious—if she spoke and Ailill did not answer—he needed some
way to keep them in that chamber long enough for him to get to Findbhair and at least mount her. He thought a moment, pursing his lips,
and then nodded. He could block the door which, thanks be to Dana,
opened outward with a stake fixed into the ground and jammed against
it. His lips pursed again; he would have to block the window shutter too.

Fraoch gnawed gently on his lip. It was not so simple. He could not
close the window shutter before Medb entered the house. She knew he
slept with the window open and would think he had closed it to keep
their tryst secret. Since she did not wish to be secret, likely she would
try to open the shutter. If she found it blocked, she would suspect a trap
at once. He sighed. He would have to run around the back and close
the shutter after he had blocked the door.

Having beckoned Conall close, he explained what he would need, too
softly for a listener outside to hear. After a couple of his men brought
in stakes under their cloaks, they set about whittling the ends, one end
sharpened to dig well into the ground if door or shutter thrust against
it, the other flattened at an angle so it would hold without slipping
against the planks of the door. Fraoch was grateful for the employment.
Now that he was so near his goal, time seemed to crawl as if the gods
had decided to halt the sun in the sky.

Time was not crawling for Findbhair; she had been very busy since
she had left Fraoch. His assumption about her understanding had been
no more than wish fulfillment on his part. Findbhair had understood
his words as a final insult and had left the guest house determined to
gather the ingredients and cast the spell she had developed. It was a
complex one for she needed to provide near ecstasy in coupling and a
kind of oblivion with regard to other needs or duties but she did not
want the spell to induce love. That would create terrible havoc in Con-

naught, make Medb and Fraoch indifferent to being caught and held up to ridicule, and give them joy.

By dusk, Findbhair was ready. She had burnt her herbs and her symbols and felt the sparkling tingle of power form. And as it did she had spoken the words in their special rhythm to bind that power into a kind of ball, where it would remain until she spoke the final word, the word of unloosing, which would spread that power over those at whom she aimed it. She felt empty, as if what was Findbhair was gone and when this was over, she would be a new person. She waited patiently for dark, for the moment when her life would be over and she could start anew.

That feeling was so strong that nothing could touch her. She rose and lit the night candle as Medb came to her door and turned to face her as she said, "I am leaving to join Fraoch now. Why do you not come with me so you can watch and be sure how willingly and happily he betrays you."

Findbhair shook her head and replied with utter calm, "You do what you think is best, and I will do the same."

Medb stared at her, furious, but then smiled, sure despite her words, Findbhair would follow. And she was right, of course. Clutching her ball of power, Findbhair hurried to Fraoch's lodging but by a route that would take her around the back of the guest houses. Swiftly as she went, by instinct she also walked softly, keeping to the shadows.

There was not much light; the moon was not yet up and it was a new moon too, but Findbhair had no difficulty recognizing the guest house in which Fraoch was staying. She crept to the side of the window and looked in. At first she was confused because it was very dark within, no night taper lit. Even when her eyes became accustomed, the chamber seemed different. Then she realized that the bed had been shifted so that its length was against the wall rather than protruding out into the room. She felt her heart buck inside her. Had Fraoch guessed she intended to bespell him and tried to make it harder for her to cast her spell?

That was ridiculous. She was not physically throwing the ball of power, although she made the gesture of throwing. It went where her will directed it and moving a bed would not influence that. Surely Fraoch, who lived among the magic-wielding Tuatha de Danaan would know that much. Then why had he moved—

The thought was cut short by the opening of the front door. A paler greyness fell across the floor, but did not reach the bed. She heard the bed straps creak as Fraoch shifted his weight and then an arm came out of the darker shadow and into the greyer light, the hand extended, open, welcoming. A deeper shadow stepped away from the door toward that outstretched hand. The door began to swing closed slowly, but did not shut completely before Medb's outstretched hand met that held out to her.

Findbhair leaned back against the building away from the window, trying to control the fluttering of her heart and her tendency to gasp for breath. She had known what would happen. Medb had told her; Fraoch had told her. She had lived with the knowledge. Why should the sight of that outstretched, welcoming hand hurt so much? The stabbing in her breast and throat was so agonizing that she could not move to cast her spell nor speak the word to unloose it. She heard a soft chuckle, a wordless croon. Then she heard the bed straps groan with her mother's weight. Findbhair began to shake.

Earlier, between dusk and the falling of true dark, Fraoch's men had drawn a small wagon into the courtyard and brought it to the side of the guest house. It was not obtrusive, but a man could crouch behind it and watch the door. When it was dark, Ailill in Connal's cloak—the pale blue one with much gold stitchery on hood, facing, and hem—with the hood up against the chill of the night air, came to the guest house with the nighttime flagon of wine. A few minutes later the cloak emerged again, crossed the small court briskly in the direction of the Hall in which the men slept.

In the black shadow of the wall of the Hall, the cloak momentarily disappeared then came around the end of the building and made for the doorway. A moment later, there was a stirring in the darkest shadow and Fraoch in a plain, dark cloak—its hood also drawn up to hide his bright hair—walked away in the direction of the jakes. Naturally enough, he disappeared behind the wagon and never came out again.

Fortunately he did not have to wait long because his mood was such a terrible mixture of anxiety (in case Medb did not come), merriment (whenever he thought of Medb's reaction when she recognized Ailill), and violent lust (when he thought of lying again with Findbhair and healing all her doubts), that he might well have betrayed himself. However, it was not long before Medb came into the little court, walking slowly and looking back every so often. Did she expect to be followed? Fraoch had to bite his lip hard to restrain a whoop of laughter. If she expected Ailill, she would find him soon enough, and if she expected Findbhair, she would be sadly disappointed.

Nonetheless, when Medb left the door open upon entering the guest house—an invitation to anyone who wanted to see her with a lover, Fraoch's mouth twisted wryly. That woman was the outside of enough and her boldness was making his task harder. But he wasted no time, taking the shorter, thicker stake from the wagon bed and sliding along the side of the house until he could just touch the door and make it begin to swing shut.

He bit his lip with nervousness, afraid Medb would realize the door could not close by itself, until he heard a low chuckle and a sort of crooning welcome. Then he dared push the door shut a little faster, but held it so it would close silently. When no outcry followed the tiny thump of the latch catching, he thrust the pointed end of the stake into the ground with all the strength he had and slanted it downward until the flattened end rested firmly against the door. Then he began to breathe again.

Breathe again he might, but Fraoch was aware he could not afford to waste time on relief; he had not yet made the guest house secure. From the wagon he took the longer stake and walked as swiftly and silently as he could around to the back of the place. Just as he rounded the building, he saw a shadow thrust itself away from the back wall and step toward the window. For just one moment he was paralyzed by doubt and confusion. In that moment the shadow raised its hand in an unmistakable gesture.

Fraoch had no magic himself, but he could not misunderstand a spellcasting. Horrified, believing this was still another trick of Medb's to entrap him but still aware of the need for silence, he dropped the stake and launched himself forward, catching the spellcaster, but not in time. The gesture was complete, a whisper of sound breathed out "*Cuibhrich*"—and the moment their bodies touched, Fraoch knew he held Findbhair. Fury now mingled with fear and he closed one hand on her mouth and gripped her waist with the other, dragging her to the ground.

"What have you done?" Fraoch breathed, shaking her. "Why could you not believe in me and obey me? That is your mother and father within! Findbhair, can we avert whatever spell you cast? I know you meant it for me—"

He stopped abruptly. When he had first brought her to the ground, she had stared at him as if she did not know him, then blinked her eyes and stared again, as if she did not believe what she saw. Then, when he said it was her mother and father within, he felt her body shaking in his hands, and he feared the worst, his heart beating as heavily as if his blood were lead. A moment later horror filled him again as he realized she was laughing, not weeping. Well away from the window he got to his feet, pulled her up, and dragged her farther away to where whispers would not disturb those in the bed.

"Findbhair! Whatever they have done, they are your mother and father! What will happen? Can you stop it?"

She was holding her free arm across her chest under her breasts as if she had laughed so hard she hurt. "I would not dream of doing so," she replied between gasps. "They would not thank me for it."

Fraoch opened his mouth to ask what she meant, but the high cries and deeper groans of delight from within the cottage made it apparent that what she said was literally true. Perhaps the spell she cast had failed or it was only effective if he and Medb were together. In any case, Medb and Ailill were well and truly joined and he had better get himself and Findbhair in the same condition in her bed before they finished and Medb recognized her husband. Dragging Findbhair along behind him, Fraoch rushed around the guest house toward Medb's sleeping quarters.

Before Fraoch reached his goal, the violent delight that had convulsed Medb and Ailill had reached its culmination. When she caught her breath, Medb began to lift her head from her lover's breast. As her cheek slid across the damp curls on his chest, she first froze then jerked upright. Fraoch had virtually no hair on his body. What was more, Medb knew the springy hair she had touched. She knew the hand that had reached out to draw her into the bed. She knew those skilled touches that played her body like a well-known instrument.

"You!"

Hands like steel bands clamped suddenly on her wrists so she could not tear or pummel. But despite her furious expletive, Medb had no de-

sire to strike Ailill; had he not locked her arms in place so that it would
be difficult to bend her elbows, she would have bent forward to rub her
nipples in the crisp curls on his chest.

"Who else?" he asked, laughing. "Did you think I would let that half-
man, that Danaan, have you? If he is what Findbhair wants, so be it.
Let her go to Bruigh na Boinne. I do not care."

"You fool," Medb got out, but she was having difficulty saying the
words. There were better things for which to use one's mouth, she was
thinking, even as she added, "What would he have had of me? Nothing. But we would have had it all, the cattle, the silver cups and golden
armlets, and Findbhair too!"

There was remarkably little conviction in her voice, and Ailill took
the chance of turning his head to kiss one of her arms. "No," he said,
but easily, not as if he were really arguing. "This time you are the fool
Medb—and I, too, because I saw it no better than you did at first. Findbhair was lost to us when she defied us in the Hall before all our people. Did she not tell you she needed no spell to make Fraoch faithful?
Was it not true? Then what do you think she was doing with her sticks
and strings and herbs and symbols? Who knows what you would have
found in this bed—and Fraoch said you would be surprised, did he
not?—if I had not agreed to lie in it."

The words were severe but Ailill's tone was langorous and as he spoke,
his shaft was already swelling, pressing up against Medb's nether lips as
she straddled his body. The sensation was utterly distracting, utterly de-
lightful; she could not resist rubbing herself against him. Ailill sighed
and his shaft got hotter and harder. The grip on her wrists eased enough
for her to bend her arms outward so she could lean forward and press
her nipples into the thick curls on his chest. He thrust upward against
her.

"Besides," he gasped, "it is too late to do anything. Fraoch is surely
doing with Findbhair in her bed exactly what we are doing here."

"I do not like to be bested," Medb muttered, fighting to resist lifting
herself so that his stiffened rod could rise and be positioned.

Ailill's fingers flicked to her breasts, pushing between them and his
chest, squeezing the nipples. Her battle ended and she lifted herself and
then slid down, impaling herself with delight. For a moment Ailill could
not speak at all as his wife wriggled against him, generating a pulse of

such exquisite pleasure that he wondered why he ever bothered with any other woman, but as he held her still lest his joy be too soon over, he found his voice again.

"Have you been bested?" he whispered. "Have you really lost anything, when Fraoch's and Findbhair's doings have let us find each other again? Let them go—and good riddance. We have the bride price and we have each other."

Even those words were unbearably exciting. Medb writhed in Ailill's grip. Never had she found his body so perfect, so stimulating, never. And suddenly she knew that their passion had to be bespelled and she guessed what Findbhair had been contriving, knew how her daughter had planned to punish her for the crime of lying with her precious Danaan. All mixed in with the increasingly wild pleasure she was feeling was a kind of fear mingled with pride connected with Findbhair and the realization that Ailill was right. Findbhair must go—and good riddance.

"Why are we running?" Findbhair gasped as Fraoch pushed her through Medb's bedchamber and into her own.

"Never mind," Fraoch ordered. "Get your clothes off and get into bed."

Compared with the darkness outside, the night candle gave light enough to see. Findbhair blinked at the haste with which Fraoch was tearing off his garments, but his desperate need stirred her own. In a moment she was discarding her own clothing with equal haste. Tired of her, was he? she thought triumphantly, as he seized her and virtually threw her onto the bed. He came atop her, reaching down to draw her legs apart, his rod hot and hard against her belly. Had she been reluctant, his actions would have verged on rape, but in this instance the violence only stimulated her desire. He did not need to pull her legs apart; they opened to him willingly as she reached eagerly to direct his swollen shaft. And her nether mouth swallowed him with such greed that both cried out with relief and, in no long time, cried out again in consummation.

Only this time it was not her name that Fraoch uttered in his joy nor merely a wordless shout. "Done!" he cried. "Done, Mother Dana! Done! Done!"

At the moment his voice rang out, Findbhair was still experiencing the final tremors of her own climax and did not understand. Later, however, when she and Fraoch were lying at rest, her head cradled on his shoulder, she began to find the words ominous. She told herself not to be a fool, not to look for trouble, but she could not sleep and, what was more disturbing, Fraoch had not really relaxed either. His body was tense against her own.

"What did you mean, done?" Findbhair asked.

Fraoch turned his head to her. "I meant that I had paid in full your bride price, that the burden of my vow was lifted from me, and you are mine, all mine, forever."

"You blame me for not listening to you, but you do not listen to me either. How many times did I beg you to forget those stupid, dishonest trials and take me to Bruigh na Boinne? I would have been yours without your being nearly torn apart and nearly breaking my heart."

"No," he said softly. "I had to do it all, every bit, just as I had to swear to whatever unreasonable tasks your parents wished to lay on me because I waited too long to come for you. You forgave me, but you never believed I wanted you and loved you with all my heart. You thought it was the binding that held me, and I would free myself if I could."

"You mean all this lunacy—your driving me away and courting my mother—"

"I never courted your mother," Fraoch protested, grinning. "She did the courting."

Findbhair waved a hand, dismissing his hair-splitting, but she was laughing. "All that nonsense, your willingness to lie with my mother, was all to convince me you loved me?"

"I was never willing to lie with your mother!" Fraoch exclaimed. "I was only willing for her to lay a trap and fall into it herself."

She lay silent a while, and he watched her anxiously until she began to smile again. "I am ashamed to admit it, but I think you have judged rightly. Had you haggled about the bride price and not paid it in full— no matter how unfair—I might have wondered. Now, I do not think I will ever be able to doubt you again—although," she shook her head, "surely I should have been convinced of your desire by your haste to couple with me when my mother was coming to your bed."

He laughed aloud. "I am sorry to abate your pride, but eager as I always am to love you, my haste had little to do with that. Do you not remember that my vow was to lie with you in your chamber on your bed without your mother bidding me nay? I had to be sure to be finished with you before Medb and your father were done and Medb realized how she had been tricked."

Findbhair then began to laugh too. "You need not have feared that," she said between giggles. "You could have taken all night and been done in time."

As she spoke she snuggled closer and was surprised to feel Fraoch stiffen instead of relaxing.

"What is it, love?" she asked.

He lifted himself on an elbow. "That spell," he said, his voice uncertain. "Findbhair, Medb and Aillil sounded well and . . . ah . . . happy when we left the guest house. Did not your spell fail?"

"Oh, no. I am sure it did not."

"You do not care?"

"No, why should I?"

He hesitated then grimaced and said, "Your mother did wish to wrong you, and doubtless you blame your father for allowing her to do so, but to ensorcel them to their ill—"

"I cannot ensorcel anyone to ill. Did I not tell you that Brigid cast a geis upon me that no matter what spell I cast it would turn to good?"

"You mean the spell you cast will not do them any harm? Then why cast it?"

Findbhair chuckled softly. "The spell itself does no harm. It only raises the pleasure of the act of love to so high a pitch that those coupling care nothing for caution or duty or, perhaps, even decency. Moreover, it lends strength and desire to couple again and again, each time with equal or greater pleasure."

"But a man and a woman will die if they cannot stop," Fraoch said harshly.

"Not from this spell. They will sleep when they are tired, and wake to couple again, yes, but only until someone enters the chamber to interrupt them. Then the spell will be broken. I begged several of my fa-

ther's liegemen to call on you early in the morning—" she chuckled
again "—to reason with you on my behalf."

Fraoch frowned. "But I still do not see what you hoped to accomplish
with such a spell."

"Enough." She shrugged. "If my father's men found you in the bed
instead of my father, would not my spell have shown you to all, a foul
beast who would lie with his own bride's mother? Even the most loyal
of your men would not have quarreled with my repudiation of our marriage nor with my assertion that the bride price you paid should be forfeit. Moreover, my mother's offense of futtering her daughter's husband
would have permitted me to demand that the bride price you forfeited
be mine as reparation."

He stared at her, surprised. "There is more of Medb in Findbhair than
I thought. You never seemed to care for the wealth I brought."

"There is, indeed, more Medb in Findbhair than you thought, but it
is not the silver cups and golden armlets that I coveted—although I was
not fool enough to overlook that they would provide me with a living if
I repudiated you and left my parents' dun. No, it was the vengeance my
parents' loss of my bride price would give me that I desired."

"I must remember not to incur your anger," Fraoch said, easing himself down beside her. But the tension was gone from his body and he
drew her close, grinning from ear to ear as he added, "If I do, doubtless
a spell that creates utter delight will result in my hanging myself."

To that Findbhair made no answer, allowing her eyes to close and
melting into his embrace. She had been a fool to doubt him, bound and
wed and bound again as they were. Fraoch was hers, now and forever
. . . but it did no harm that he knew she was no milk-and-water maiden,
that even spells that turned only to good, could be used for many unexpected purposes. It would lend that touch of necessary spice to a long
living together.

Her eyes shot open again, it seemed only moments later, to the sound
of laughter and cheering, but the night had passed. Sunlight poured in
the doorway from her mother's chamber and the room was full of people. Findbhair blinked, clutching the covers to her bare breasts as Fraoch
pulled her to a sitting position beside him.

"And so you can all see," he said, laughing, "that I have lain with Findbhair in her own bed without Queen Medb saying me nay."

A roar of laughter echoed his. "She was too busy," one voice called, and another shouted, "She was having too good a time to worry about you," echoed by many other but similar remarks.

Findbhair's eyes found her mother and father a little to the side at the foot of the bed. The spell had been broken but clearly not too long before. Both were heavy-eyed and full-lipped, but Ailill was laughing and his arm rested on his wife's broad shoulders and Medb was not trying to free herself. She was not laughing, but her expression was of wary consideration rather than rage and she met her daughter's eyes with the steady look she only gave to equals. After a breath-held moment, she shrugged.

"*Fiat,*" she said. "It is finished. The bride price is fully paid."

Glossary

aire forgaill: chief administrative officer, or chancellor
ard righ: high king
beann sídhe or **banshee:** a female spirit who cries out in the night to warn of impending death
Beltane: May Day festival
brecc: breeches
caimsi: shirt worn under the **lena**
céile: spouse
coracle: small boat
cuibhrich: binding
Dana, Our Lady: Celtic goddess
dun: fort
ensorcel: enchant
Eriu: Erin, or Ireland
fitchneal: or fidchell, an ancient Irish board game
geis: spell
girdle-cake: griddle cake
glam dicend: saying
gombeen man: usurer
gràdhaichte: darling
guest-right: the rights and privileges granted to a guest
inar: jacket worn over the **lena**
leannán sídhe: fairy sweetheart
lemman: beloved, paramour

lena: a kind of shirt
lios: a lord's property
menhir: monolith
ogham stones: stones with inscriptions carved in an ancient Irish alphabet
poitín: or poteen—homemade whiskey
rath: a chieftain's fort
Sahmain: or Samhain; feast of All Saints (November 1)
sídhe: Celtic spirits
Tuatha Dé Danann: the Magic People
wisewoman: a woman with occult skills